GHOST IN THE STONE

JONATHAN MOELLER

THE GHOSTS #5

GHOST IN THE STONE

Jonathan Moeller

LEGAL

Cover design by Clarissa Yeo.

Published by Azure Flame Media LLC

ISBN-13: 978-1975920029

Ebook edition published October 2012.

1

ASSASSINS

Caina Amalas spotted the assassin.

She stood among the crowds filling the Praetorian Basilica and watched Lord Corbould Maraeus give his speech. The Basilica was a vast stone hall, its vaulted roof rising five hundred feet overhead, elaborate balconies lining the walls. Corbould, a lean man in his middle fifties, stood upon the dais, tall and imposing in his black armor. Nobles and magistrates sat near the dais, and master merchants and magi sat behind them. Commoners packed the balconies, looking down upon the nobles, merchants, and magi.

Caina stood with them, disguised as a common serving girl. She wore a gray dress and a leather boots, and a curved dagger rested in a sheath at her belt, since no sensible man or woman went about unarmed. Yet an additional pair of daggers waited in her boots, and she wore throwing knives strapped to her forearms, hidden beneath her sleeves.

Watching the assassin move through the crowds of commoners, Caina knew she would need the extra weapons.

"My lords and ladies!" said Lord Corbould Maraeus, his voice booming through the Basilica. A magus stood near the dais, discreetly using a spell to amplify the speech, and Corbould's voice thundered through the walls like the words of an angry god. "Brothers of the Magisterium! Masters of the collegia! Citizens of the Empire of Nighmar! I am Corbould, Lord of House Maraeus, and the Lord Governor of Marsis! I address you today, citizens of the Empire, to tell you that we have been betrayed. Treachery has been wielded against us, and our enemies move to strike us down!"

Corbould was more right than he knew.

Caina moved after the assassin, murmuring apologies as she pushed past the spectators.

The assassin looked like any other man. He had brown hair and brown eyes, and wore the simple clothing of a moderately successful shopkeeper. Yet the man was lean and fit for a shopkeeper, and moved with a quiet grace of a hunting cat.

Of a predator.

Caina knew an assassin of the Kindred when she saw one.

"Our Emperor," said Corbould, "extended the hand of friendship to the Padishah of Istarinmul. The Padishah sent his cousin, the emir Rezir Shahan of the Vale of Fallen Stars, as his ambassador."

For a moment Caina remembered Rezir Shahan lying on the floor of that burning warehouse, remembered the terror in his eyes as she killed him.

"I greeted Rezir Shahan as my guest!" shouted Corbould, making a fist. "And how did he repay the hospitality of our Emperor? With treachery and black betrayal! He smuggled soldiers into the city, attacked the innocent men and women of Marsis. He clapped women and children into chains, intending to sell free citizens of the Empire upon the block as slaves!"

A rumble of discontent went through the galleries, but not all the nobles and magi looked displeased. Slavery had been banned in most of the Empire for over a century, but not all the magi and the nobles thought this a good thing. Some of them wanted to restore slavery to the Empire.

The assassin reached the end of the balcony, spoke a few words to the black-armored Imperial Guard at the door, and vanished into the stairwell.

"To aid the treachery of the Istarish," said Corbould, "the Kyracians came, sailing into the harbor of Marsis and betraying our treaty of peace. Truly, the city would have fallen, if not for the valor of Legionaries, the determination of the free men of Marsis, and the heroism of the Champion of Marsis."

Caina strode for the stairs, and the Imperial Guard at the door lifted an armored hand.

"See, girl," he said. "Where are you going during the Lord Governor's address?"

Caina felt a stab of annoyance. The idiot Guard hadn't even bothered to question the assassin. But she kept the irritation from her face.

"I am sorry, sir," she said, in her most querulous voice, "but my time of the month is upon me, and I..."

The Guard jerked his head. "Go."

The stairs spiraled down to the floor of the Basilica, but she saw no trace of the Kindred assassin. Had he disappeared? No. He had gone up. If he had come to assassinate Lord Corbould, he would make his way to the triforium, the highest balcony in the Basilica. A skilled archer would have a clear shot from there.

Caina looked up, glimpsed a shadow moving above her. And without a trace of sound - the Kindred were skilled in stealth.

But so was Caina.

She glanced over her shoulder, but the Imperial Guard had already forgotten her.

Caina slid a dagger from her boot and hurried up the stairs, her feet making no sound against the steps. Her mind worked as she hurried, the dagger ready in her right hand. The triforium was an obvious vantage point for any assassin, and a guard must have been posted...

Caina heard a faint gurgle, followed by the distant clank of metal hitting stone.

Like an armored man falling against the stairs.

Caina moved as fast as she dared.

She reached the top of the stairs and saw that the door to the triforium stood open. An Imperial Guard lay before the door, the front of his cuirass wet and gleaming.

Blood pooled beneath his helmet, leaking from his slit throat.

Caina hissed a curse and eased onto the triforium. The narrow balcony was dark and gloomy, the railing lined with thick pillars. Light shone from the clerestory windows overhead, but little of the light reached the triforium.

The shadows offered dozens of hiding places for a skillful assassin.

And the Kindred were nothing if not skillful.

"We have retaken Marsis, destroyed the Istarish invaders, and driven the Kyracians back to their ships," said Corbould. "Yet they still threaten our Empire. The Kyracian warships ravage the seas, seizing our merchant ships. The Istarish emirs gather their hosts and march north to challenge our Legions, and if we do not stop them, they shall raise the banner of Istarinmul over Malarae itself!"

Caina slipped forward, gliding from shadow to shadow. The shadows of a pillar would make an ideal place of concealment. But which one? There were dozens.

"I call on you," said Corbould, "to do your duty as citizens of the Empire! My fellow nobles! Serve diligently in your offices, and lend your wealth and support to your Emperor's Legions. Merchants of the collegia! Sell your goods honestly, and do not cheat the tax collectors. Free men of the Empire! Enlist in the Legion, and teach the cringing slaves of Istarinmul how free men of the Empire fight!"

A cheer went up from the crowds. For a dreadful instant Caina expected the assassin to use the cover of the cheers to mask his arrow. But nothing happened. The Kindred were methodical assassins, and always planned to escape with their lives. So where...

There.

The second set of stairs, at the other end of the triforium. The assassin would shoot Corbould and escape out the Basilica's rear entrances. By the time the chaos from Lord Corbould's murder subsided, the Kindred assassin would be on the other side of the city.

"Let us take up arms!" thundered Corbould. "Let us draw sword and raise spear! Our Empire shall chastise the Kyracians and drive the Istarish behind their walls! We shall show them what it means to make war upon the Empire of Nighmar!"

A cheer went up from the crowd filling the Basilica. Caina cursed and ran forward, hoping the cheering would mask her footfalls. If the assassin was going to shoot Lord Corbould, he would do it now, while the noise from the cheers would mask the sound of his bowstring...

And then Caina ran past a pillar and saw the assassin.

He knelt before the railing, a short black bow resting in his hands, the ends coming to sharp curves. It was a Kagari horse bow, capable of flinging an arrow with enough force to punch through steel plate. The assassin drew back the string, the bow creaking...

Caina lunged forward and cut the bowstring. The string snapped, one end drawing a line of blood across the assassin's jaw. She reversed her dagger, hoping to land a stunning blow on the assassin. With luck, she could take him captive and discover who had hired the Kindred to kill Lord Corbould.

But the assassin whirled, throwing aside his bow and yanking a dagger from his belt. Caina jerked back, the tip of the dagger brushing against the front of her dress. Another half-inch and he would have opened her belly. He came at her, dagger flashing, and Caina backed away. She considered screaming – any Guards seeing the fight would see a man attacking a woman and come to her aid. But the assassin had already killed the nearest Imperial Guard, and Caina doubted she could scream loudly enough for anyone to hear her over the cheering crowd.

So she let her left heel pin the hem of her skirt. The cloth jerked against her legs, and she lost her balance and fell. The assassin grinned, leaving himself open as he raised his dagger to plunge into her chest.

But as she fell, Caina snatched a throwing knife from her sleeve and flung it. The blade buried itself in the assassin's left thigh. The man stumbled to one knee with a cry of pain, and Caina rolled to the side as the point of his dagger scraped against the floor. Her boot came up and slammed against the handle of the throwing knife in his leg, and the Kindred assassin snarled in pain. Caina snatched her dagger and scrambled back to her feet, dodging a hasty slash from the assassin.

They faced each other, the cheers still ringing out from the floor of the Basilica.

"Who hired you?" said Caina. "Tell me and I'll let you live."

The Kindred assassin sneered. "Put down that dagger and run, or you'll wish that I had killed you."

"No," said Caina.

The Kindred took a step forward. "You aren't strong enough to kill me."

Caina shrugged. "I only need wait until you bleed out from that knife in your leg. Or until the poison on the blade takes effect."

The assassin glanced at the knife.

It only distracted him for a half a second, but it was long enough. Caina sprang forward, her dagger flashing. Her blade opened the assassin's arm from wrist to elbow, and the man growled in pain, dagger falling from his hands. He lunged at her, hands reaching for her throat, and Caina slammed her dagger between his ribs. The assassin went rigid, teeth peeling back from his lips in a snarl.

"Damn it," muttered Caina.

She had wanted to take the assassin alive.

The Kindred's knees buckled, and the man collapsed to the floor. Caina wrenched her dagger and throwing knife free and cleaned them on the dead man's clothes. She searched his pockets, but found nothing to indicate who had hired him.

The Kindred were not that foolish.

The cheering from the Basilica's floor subsided. Caina returned her weapons to their hiding places and hurried from the triforium, leaving the assassin's corpse behind.

She wondered what the Imperial Guard would think when they found it.

THAT NIGHT CAINA returned to the workshops below the Grand Imperial Opera.

The Grand Imperial Opera was a massive edifice of gleaming white marble, topped with a dome that rose two hundred feet over the surrounding streets. The great theater held ten thousand people, and the nobles of the Empire (and wealthy commoners) came to hear the legends and histories of the Empire told in song.

The workshop beneath the stage was much less ornate.

Thick pillars supported the ceiling overhead, and a small army of stagehands hurried through the workshop, moving panels of scenery and working the elaborate maze of ropes and pulleys for scene changes. A loud song filtered through the boards overhead, and Caina recognized the chorus from the Romance of Soterius, an opera about the Emperor who had freed the slaves and ended the War of the Fourth Empire for the sake of the slave girl who had won his heart.

Though Caina doubted that Soterius's motives had been quite that pure.

She threaded her way through the chaos and found a man sitting at a table in the corner, eating a slice of bread and resting his leg on a stool. He was in his early fifties, with iron-gray hair and arms like tree trunks. He wore the leather jerkin and rough clothes of a common caravan guard, but Caina knew that he was much more than that.

In fact, he was probably one of the four or five most dangerous and knowledgeable men in the Empire.

"Marina," said Halfdan, speaking the alias Caina had chosen. "How was your visit to the Praetorian Basilica? I trust Lord Corbould gave a rousing speech."

"He did," said Caina, taking a piece of bread. She had not eaten since breakfast and was ravenous. "There was a keenly interested spectator, just as you predicted."

Halfdan nodded. "What did the spectator think of the speech?"

"I wouldn't know," said Caina. "He died before I could ask him." She grimaced. "I wound up having to...deal with him."

Halfdan nodded and got to his feet. "Come with me."

He led her to one of the narrow rooms on the far wall. Sometimes the singers used the stone vaults as changing rooms, and sometimes the Ghosts hid corpses down here. Halfdan closed the door, listened for a moment, and then nodded.

"We can talk freely," said Halfdan. "The assassin is dead?"

"Aye," said Caina. "A Kindred assassin, and I caught him just before he put an arrow into Lord Corbould's throat. I tried to take him alive, but I had to kill him."

"Don't fret about it," said Halfdan. "The Kindred assassin families are far too well organized to let the man who does the killing know who actually paid for it."

"But that's the important question, isn't it?" said Caina. "Who hired the Kindred to kill Lord Corbould?"

"A very good question," said Halfdan. "You are clever, my dear. What is the answer?"

Caina sighed, leaned against the wall, and thought it over.

"The Kindred are not cheap," said Caina, "so it would have to be a powerful lord, someone within the Magisterium, or a wealthy merchant. But most of the nobles support the war against Istarinmul and New Kyre. The Magisterium hates the stormsingers of New Kyre and the Alchemists in Istarinmul, so they would not turn against Corbould, even though he dislikes the magi. And why would the merchant collegia hire the Kindred to kill him? They'll make a fortune feeding and clothing the Legions. Was it a personal grudge? Or..."

Her eyes widened.

"Cyrica," she said.

"You understand," said Halfdan.

"The Cyrican provinces are the only place in the Empire where slavery is still legal," said Caina. "Part of the treaty that ended the War of the Fourth Empire. You told me that the Emperor is sending Lord Corbould to Cyrica, to make sure the Cyricans don't revolt."

"Very good," said Halfdan. "What I didn't tell you is that both the Istarish and the Kyracians sent embassies to Cyrica, asking the Cyricans to join them against the Empire."

"And half the Cyrican nobles would, if given the chance," said Caina. She felt her lip curl in contempt. "If the Cyricans swore to the Padishah or the Assembly of New Kyre, they wouldn't need to worry about the Ghosts freeing their slaves." She thought for a moment. "So Lord Governor Armizid Asurius paid the Kindred to kill Lord Corbould?"

"His father, more likely," said Halfdan.

Caina frowned. "I thought Armizid was Lord Governor of Cyrica."

"He is," said Halfdan, "but only because his father doesn't want to bother with the work of holding an actual magistracy. Lord Khosrau Asurius was once good friends with Haeron Icaraeus. After Haeron died in that incident with Maglarion, Khosrau Asurius has gained most of Haeron's old supporters. Khosrau also owns half the land in Cyrica, and the Cyrican nobles respect him. If he wants to leave the Empire, they will follow. Lord Corbould is paying a visit to Lord Governor Armizid...but the real negotiations will take place when Corbould talks to Khosrau."

"And if Khosrau assassinates Corbould during the negotiations," said Caina, "then the Emperor will blame him, and the Cyrican nobles will have no choice but to join Istarinmul."

"You grasp the problem," said Halfdan. "The war is a stalemate right now. Our fleet cannot stand against the Kyracians, but the Istarish cannot defeat the Legions. If the Cyricans join the enemies of the Empire, that situation could change rather quickly."

"And you are telling me this," said Caina, "because you want me to do something about it."

"Aye," said Halfdan. "Lord Corbould is leaving Malarae for Cyrica Urbana in a week. I would like you to accompany him."

Caina nodded. "How should I disguise myself? As Countess Marianna Nereide?"

"No," said Halfdan. "Unmarried young noblewomen go on tours of the Empire...but they rarely visit the Shining City of Cyrica. No, you will disguise yourself as Marina, the maid of the leading lady of the Grand Imperial Opera."

Caina blinked. "Theodosia is going to Cyrica?"

"So she is," said Halfdan. "To prove his hospitality, Lord Khosrau will hold a series of celebrations and festivals in Corbould's honor. And to show his own generosity, Lord Corbould will bring the finest entertainments from the Imperial capital at his own expense. Chariot-racing teams from the Imperial Hippodrome, for one. And the Cyrican nobles are mad for Nighmarian opera, so Lord Corbould will also pay to bring the Grand Imperial Opera to the Shining City."

"And our task," said Caina, "will be to keep Lord Corbould alive."

Halfdan nodded. "Corbould Maraeus is arrogant, rigid, and utterly inflexible. Yet he is the most powerful lord in the Empire and a strong supporter of the Emperor. And if anyone can convince Lord Khosrau to stay with the Empire, Lord Corbould can. Yet if he is assassinated, it will be an utter disaster...and Cyrica will break away from the Empire."

"Then," said Caina, "we shall have to make certain that Lord Corbould is not assassinated."

"Aye," said Halfdan. " I also want you to find who paid for his death. The Kindred do not come cheap, and someone with a great deal of money paid for Corbould to die." His voice dropped. "And if you find the man who hired the Kindred, Theodosia will pass word to the Ghost circle in Cyrioch...and he will never be seen again."

Caina gave a slow nod.

The Ghosts of the Empire, the eyes and ears of the Emperor, were not above assassinating treasonous nobles and magistrates. With Theodosia, Caina had helped bring about the downfall of Lord Macrinius, who had kidnapped people to sell as slaves. She had killed Anastius Nicephorus, the Lord Governor of Rasadda, whose greed and corruption had almost driven the Saddai to revolt. She had helped kill Agria Palaegus, who had plotted with Jadriga to free the imprisoned demons below Black Angel Tower...

Caina closed her eyes.

So much death.

That assassin in the Praetorian Basilica. She hadn't meant to kill him, but she had, and she had killed him without the slightest flicker of hesitation or regret. True, he would have murdered Lord Corbould. But once she would have regretted his death.

Now she felt nothing at all.

How hard and cold she had become.

"Caina?" said Halfdan, his rough voice gentle. "Is anything amiss?"

"No," said Caina, opening her eyes. "I'm fine."

2

A GHOST IN THE STONE

Two weeks after killing the assassin in the Praetorian Basilica, Caina blinked awake, a dark dream fading from her mind.

"We're here," said a woman's voice, rich and rolling.

Caina turned her head. She lay on a hard bunk in the cramped cabin she shared with Theodosia, grimy light leaking through the narrow window. She heard the steady lap of waves against the ship's hull, the groan of the mast, the thumps of boots against the deck. A hot, wet breeze came through the window, heavy with the smells of salt, gull dung, and waste.

"The ship's not moving," said Caina, voice scratchy.

"Aye, we've arrived," said the woman's voice.

Theodosia leaned against the cabin's door. She was a vigorous woman in her early forties, with gray eyes and pale blonde hair, and tall enough to carry the extra weight she had put on in the last few years. "You could probably tell from the stench coming through the window. Cyrioch is something of a sty."

Caina rubbed her face. "In High Nighmarian its name is Cyrica Urbana, and the poets call it the Shining City."

Theodosia gave an indelicate snort. "Only by poets standing

upwind of it. Though the Stinking City doesn't sound nearly so pleasant in a song." She glanced out the window. "The harbormaster won't let us enter the harbor. Fear of the Kyracians, I suspect. They'll send out a pilot to take us the rest of the way in. Of course, they'll take Lord Corbould's ship first. Lord Corbould's hired entertainment will just have to wait. So we have ample time to get ready."

Caina sat up. She felt woozy, and her head throbbed with pain.

"Are you all right?" said Theodosia. "You were having a nightmare, I'm sure of it."

In the dream Caina had sprinted down the darkened streets of Marsis as Istarish slave traders prowled through the city. Time and time again Caina heard Nicolai screaming, and she raced through a maze of dockside alleys, trying to find the boy. Yet no matter how frantically she searched, no matter how she eluded the slave traders, she could never find the boy.

The reality was different. Caina had rescued Nicolai and returned him to his father and mother. Ark and Tanya had stayed in Malarae, and Ark had bought a foundry with the money he received for Naelon Icaraeus's death. Tanya was pregnant with their second child, and Nicolai was safe.

That wasn't enough to stop the nightmares.

"I'm fine," said Caina, getting to her feet.

"Yes," said Theodosia, "and I am the Shahenshah of Anshan. When was the last time you slept the night?"

"I'm fine," said Caina, again.

"I doubt that," said Theodosia.

"I don't like traveling at sea," said Caina, which was true enough. "Six days on this boat would give anyone sleepless nights."

"Ship, dear," said Theodosia. "We're on a ship. Sailors get offended if you call their ship a boat. But we're almost to Cyrioch, and we need to get ready."

"Do you need my help?" said Caina.

Theodosia grinned. "I most certainly do not. You are quite helpful, my dear, but I have been preparing for performances on my own since I was fifteen. Why, I once had only five minutes to prepare before I sang an aria before Emperor Alexius himself. And the man..."

"Stood and applauded at the end," said Caina, having heard the story before.

Theodosia laughed. "Impudent child! I can prepare on my own." She lowered her voice. "And your task is more important. Find Barius, and..."

"And find out," said Caina, voice quiet, "if the Cyrican provinces will stay in the Empire."

And if the nobles of the Cyrican provinces would throw in with the Padishah of Istarinmul or the Assembly of New Kyre.

Caina shivered and closed her eyes for a moment.

"Do you think," she said, "the Kindred will try to kill Lord Corbould at the docks?"

"No," said Theodosia, "no, too soon. If Lord Khosrau Asurius has decided to leave the Empire, then he'll..."

Someone pounded on the cabin door.

Theodosia gave a sharp nod.

Caina stepped towards the door, raking her hands through her hair to make it look more disheveled. Not that it needed much help - after six days without a proper bath, her hair was a tangled mess. Theodosia sat on the bed and looked through the chest against the wall, and her rich voice rose in theatrical rage.

"Marina!" she said. "Did you remember to pack my unguent of rose petals? Do you expect me to sing for the Lord Governor without my unguent of rose petals? If you forget them, I shall beat you black and blue! Or I'll sell you to the Cyricans as a kitchen drudge!"

Caina pulled the door open. The ship's first mate, a sour-faced man of Mardonish birth, gave her a suspicious look.

"Aye?" said Caina, putting a thick Caerish accent into her words. "Why are you troubling my mistress? She is an artist and must prepare for her performance."

"We have arrived outside Cyrioch's harbor," said the first mate. "Your mistress..."

"You!" said Theodosia, stalking toward the first mate. "You loutish oaf! Where is the rest of my baggage? I thought my girl lost my unguents, but I think it was your men! They pinched my elixirs and plan to sell them, don't they?"

A muscle in the first mate's face twitched. "No one has touched your baggage, mistress. Lord Corbould commanded the captain to inform you when we arrived, and..."

"Where?" bellowed Theodosia in a voice that made the planks beneath Caina's boots rattle. "Where is my unguent?"

The first mate made a hasty retreat.

Caina shut the door, and Theodosia chuckled.

"I think you frightened him," said Caina.

"Well, the leading lady of an opera company is traditionally a dreadful harridan," said Theodosia. "Myself, I never saw the point. It seems like ever so much work."

"But," said Caina, "no one would ever suspect a temperamental opera singer of being a spy for the Emperor."

"Precisely," said Theodosia. "Get ready."

Caina nodded and got to work.

She stripped off her gray dress and donned a man's clothes – trousers, boots, a ragged shirt, and a leather jerkin reinforced with steel studs. A worn cloak went over her shoulders, and a belt with a sheathed sword and dagger around her waist. Caina helped herself to Theodosia's makeup and applied it to her cheeks and jaw, giving her face the illusion of stubble. She tugged her black hair forward, letting it fall in greasy curtains over her face.

When she finished, she looked like a ragged caravan guard. With luck, she could pass unnoticed on the streets of Cyrioch.

"My dear," said Theodosia, looking her over, "you are positively disreputable."

Caina grinned. "Thank you."

"Get ashore and find Barius," said Theodosia. "Marzhod and the local Ghost circle should have plenty of information on Cyrioch's Kindred family." The planks shuddered beneath their feet. "Ah...the pilot's come aboard. Get up on deck, and go ashore as soon as you can."

"I will," said Caina.

"Caina," said Theodosia, and for once her voice was grave. "Be careful. Cyrioch's slums are not a safe place."

Caina opened the door a crack. The corridor outside was deserted, though she heard the steady beat of a drum below as the rowers maneuvered the massive galley towards the piers. Then she slipped through the door, hurried through the corridor, and climbed into the dazzling sunlight.

Chaos reigned on the ship's deck. The captain and first mate stood on the rear deck, bellowing orders, while sailors scrambled over the galley's masts and rigging. Many of the singers and the stagehands of the Grand Imperial Opera had gathered on deck to watch the approach, and the sailors hastened past them with muttered curses.

Caina looked over the rail and saw the city of Cyrioch for the first time.

The poets called Cyrican Urbana the Shining City, and it was not hard to see why. Across the rippling waters of the harbor and the masts of maneuvering ships Caina saw a massive hill of peculiar white rock. The hill was called the Stone, and that strange white rock was found nowhere else in the world. An enormous palace of towering domes and delicate towers crowned the Stone - the Palace of Splendors, once the seat of the Anshani satraps of Cyrica, and now the stronghold of Cyrioch's Lord Governor. Lesser palaces, the homes of Cyrica's nobles, clung to the sides of the Stone and stood at its base.

The rest of Cyrioch sprawled between the Stone and the harbor like spilled detritus.

Caina saw basilicas and mansions built in the Nighmarian style and domes and slender towers in Anshani fashion. Endless squat warehouses of brick lined the harbor, holding the tea and grain and rice and cotton the Cyrican provinces shipped to the nations of the western seas. The ugly brick towers of tenements rose behind the warehouses. The great lords had dispossessed Cyrica's small farmers generations ago, and now the remaining free citizens lived in those tenements, subsisting on the Lord Governor's grain dole.

And upon the backs of their slaves.

The stench of the city filled Caina's nostrils.

She made her way to the rail as the ship maneuvered toward a pier, the oars lashing at the water. A few of the sailors and the stagehands glanced her away, but no one stopped her. Caina had disguised herself as a caravan guard every day and wandered through the ship, and the sailors had thought her Theodosia's bodyguard. She saw the other ships of Lord Corbould's flotilla lined up at the quays, including Corbould's massive flagship.

The galley pulled up to the stone quay, and Caina saw dozens of men in rough gray tunics waiting for them. Slaves, no doubt owned by the city's harbormaster, ready to assist with unloading the ships.

Rage shivered through her at the thought. Caina's mother had sold her to Maglarion in exchange for his necromantic teachings, and Maglarion had relied on Istarish slavers as his hirelings. She hated slavers, and as weary as she had grown of killing, the deaths of a few more slave traders would not trouble her at all...

But for now, she had to remain calm.

The ship bumped against the quay, and the porters hurried forward with a gangplank. The sailors and the porters wrestled the opera company's cargo onto the deck. Caina grabbed the railing, vaulted over it, and landed on the quay, her legs collapsing beneath her. A few of the slaves gave her curious looks as she straightened up and walked off, but none made any move to stop her.

Caina left the docks, passed the warehouses, and made her way into Cyrioch.

She recalled the map of Cyrioch she had memorized during the voyage. The district south of the docks was called Seatown, filled with warehouses, tenements, and sailors' taverns and brothels. Barius, the Ghost nightkeeper Theodosia had sent her to meet, owned a pawnshop on the southern edge of Seatown.

She left the warehouses behind, making her way through the narrow streets. The sun blazed overhead like a torch, and the humidity made sweat trickle down her face and back. The massive brick tenements towered over her, but even their shadows brought little respite from the heat.

Traffic crowded the streets – the freeborn Cyricans preferred light clothes of bright colors, red and orange and yellow. Some of the men wore turbans in the Anshani style. The women covered their heads with scarves, and usually moved in the company of a husband or a brother or a son. The Cyricans considered that any woman who went in public with her head uncovered was a prostitute, free for any man that could take her.

Just as well that Caina had disguised herself as a man.

Slaves in their gray tunics were everywhere.

From time to time small gangs of men followed her. Caina suspected that unwary foreigners traveling through Seatown might find themselves snatched off the streets and sold to the Istarish slavers' brotherhood. She rested her hand on her sword hilt and scowled, and none of the gangs closed. Perhaps they wanted easier prey.

The hulking tenements thinned, and Caina found herself in a small market square. Vendors sold pots and jars and food of questionable quality, while taverns and small shops lined the square. Women in bright clothing moved from stall to stall.

Barius's pawnshop awaited on the far side of the square.

Caina stopped, moved in the shadows beside an empty stall, and stared at the pawnshop.

Something was amiss.

The pawnshop's windows were shuttered, but its door stood ajar by a few inches. Caina suspected the merchants of Seatown kept their doors locked and opened them only when a paying customer arrived.

So why had Barius been so foolish to keep the door open? Had he let in a customer and forgotten to close the door?

Or had someone forced the door and not bothered to close it?

Caina watched the pawnshop, but no one approached, and she saw not a hint of activity from within.

She crossed the square, keeping her walk casual, but her eyes swept her surroundings for any hint of danger. If someone had attacked Barius, they might now lie in wait for any other Ghosts.

But no one looked in her direction.

Caina stopped at the pawnshop door and listened.

Utter silence.

She took a deep breath, slipped a dagger into her hand, and pushed open the door.

Barius's pawnshop was a dank, narrow vault of a room, its walls lined with wooden shelves. Pots, pans, clothes, shoes, and the occasional sword rested on the shelves. A wooden counter stood near the far wall, a pair of scales and a set of weights resting on its surface.

There was no trace of Barius or of anyone else.

Though the door to the shop's back room stood open.

Caina stepped around the counter, dagger raised, and into the back room.

Shelves lined all four walls of the back room, holding valuable goods – metal plate, jewelry, rolls of silk, and all the other things Caina supposed Barius didn't want kept in the public eye. Another door on the far wall opened into the alley behind in the pawnshop.

And in the middle of the back room stood single strangest statue that Caina had ever seen.

Carved from white stone, it showed a fat man in Cyrican robes, his arms spread in surprise, his face twisted with fear and horror. Caina gazed at the statue with fascination. The lords of the Empire loved statues, and Caina seen thousands of them during her life. Yet she had never seen a statue like this one. She could see every wrinkle on the man's face and hands, every fold and crease of his clothing. The level of detail was uncanny.

Almost eerie.

And the statue looked exactly the way Theodosia had described Barius.

Why the devil would Barius have an peculiarly detailed statue of himself in the back room of his pawnshop? For that matter, if he knew a sculptor of such sublime skill, why commission a statue of himself looking horrified?

It made no sense...

Unless.

Caina stared at the statue, a terrible idea trickling into her mind.

She remembered tales she had read in her father's library as a child, stories about unearthly women with serpents' hair whose glance turned men to stone.

She stared at the statue of Barius.

At the impossibly detailed statue.

"No," said Caina, voice soft.

But why not? She had seen sorcery burn a man to ashes, rip lightning down from the skies, and store the lives of murdered innocents in a black crystal. Why couldn't sorcery turn a man to stone?

She brushed the statue's stone sleeve with a fingertip.

And she felt the faint, crawling tingle of sorcerous force.

She jerked backed in alarm, and for a terrified instant she wondered if the spell would spread, if it would turn her to stone. But the tingling sensation faded, and her hand remained flesh and blood. Caina took a deep breath and looked at the statue.

At Barius himself.

Who had done this to him? And why? Caina knew more about sorcery than she had ever wished to know, but she had never heard of a spell that did anything like this.

She took a deep breath...and noticed the shadow at the back door.

Someone was standing in the alley outside the shop.

Caina tensed, her fingers tightening around the dagger's handle. Whoever stood outside the door might be listening to her, waiting for her to make a mistake. Yet who was outside the door?

The sorcerer who had done this to Barius, perhaps?

Perhaps this was a trap to catch any Ghosts coming to visit Barius.

But traps could be sprung.

She spotted a mirror sitting upon the shelf. Taking care to remain silent, Caina angled the mirror so it faced the door. Keeping the dagger in her right hand, she began to rummage through the items on the shelves, making sure to make lots of noise.

"There's no one else here," she shouted in Cyrican, making sure to keep her voice deep and rough. "No one but that damn creepy statue. Well, if Barius can't be bothered to mind his shop, we may as well help ourselves. You watch the front door, and I'll take the jewels."

She kept rummaging through the items on the shelves, keeping her eyes fixed on the mirror.

And slowly, silently, the back door swung open. She saw a man wearing a yellow Cyrican robe standing in the alley, a dagger in his hand. He glided through the door, his feet making no noise against the floor.

Caina recognized the way he held that dagger.

A Kindred assassin had been lying in wait for the Ghosts.

"Hey!" shouted Caina, and the assassin froze. She picked up a bronze candelabra, as if examining it. "Does that silversmith still buy bronze? We could turn a pretty coin."

The assassin moved forward, his dagger raised to stab.

Caina whirled and slammed the candelabra across his face.

The assassin staggered back with a cry, blood flying from his nose and mouth. Caina lunged at him, hoping to knock the dagger from his hand. But the brutal training regimen of the Kindred produced capable fighters, and the assassin deflected her thrust with a sweep of his own blade. Caina seized the opening and swung with the candelabra, catching the assassin across his free wrist. The man reeled back, lips peeled back in a snarl.

For a moment he glared at her, and then he whirled and fled through the door.

Caina blinked in astonishment. The Kindred assassins fled only when outmatched. Then she remembered her ruse. The assassin must have assumed that she had armed allies in the front room. For a moment she considered pursuing him, but rejected the idea. She did not know Cyrioch very well, and the twisted maze of streets and alleys offered hundreds of hiding places. Or, worse, the assassin could return with allies. Better to escape now while she still could.

Caina turned to go, and the stove caught her eye.

A small iron stove squatted in the corner of the back room. Given Cyrioch's torrid heat, Caina wondered why Barius needed it, but perhaps he used it to cook meals. A few coals flickered within the stove, and Caina saw flecks of white lying among the ashes.

Scraps of paper.

She knelt and poked through the ashes, sifting for any legible remnants.

The ashes had once been a book, she thought, or perhaps a ledger. Whoever had burned it had done a thorough job. Caina recovered a single small scrap of paper. It had once been covered in scrawled handwriting, but now Caina could only make out four words.

"The Defender," she muttered. "The Well."

Was that a code of some kind? Odds were that it didn't mean anything. But did that mean Barius had burned his ledger? Or had someone else burned it?

Caina didn't know, and she didn't have time to figure it out. That assassin would return with friends. She got to her feet and cast a quick look over the shelves. The assassin would recognize her disguise, but there was enough clothing here to improvise a new one. Caina cast aside her ragged cloak and snatched a garish red one. The cloak was a ridiculous color, but it looked Cyrican, and should conceal her long enough to rejoin Theodosia at the Plaza of Majesty.

She took one last look at Barius, and then slipped out the back door. The alley behind the pawnshop stank of garbage and urine, but was deserted. She took a quick look around and hurried towards the end of the alley. From here she would circle east, through Seatown until she reached the district of Westshadow and then the Plaza of Majesty at the foot of the Stone...

Caina froze.

A shape in a cloak stood at the end of the alley, staring at her. She could not see the figure's face beneath the cowl, but the front of the cloak opened, and she caught a glimpse of chain mail and a sheathed sword.

Another Kindred assassin?

She raised her dagger and braced herself.

The cloaked figure turned and disappeared to the left.

Caina cursed and ran to the end of the alley. It terminated in a street leading east from the plaza, lined on either side with shabby houses. She saw no trace of the cloaked figure, or of the Kindred assassin in the yellow robe.

Caina hastened for the Plaza of Majesty.

She wondered what Theodosia would make of Barius's fate.

3

THE LORDS OF CYRICA

Caina slipped unnoticed through the crowds, merely another figure in a red Cyrican cloak.

She had to admit that the Plaza of Majesty lived up to its name.

It sat at the base of the Stone, broad and wide, paved with white marble chosen to match the peculiar white rock of the Stone. On the northern side of the Plaza stood the massive temples of the gods of the Empire. On the western side stood the basilica of the Magisterium's chapterhouse, stern and grim. Across the Plaza from the chapterhouse rose the black, pyramidal shape of a temple to the Living Flame, the chief god of Cyrica and Anshan. And at the base of the Stone itself a broad ramp climbed the face of the hill to the Palace of Splendors itself.

Lord Governor Armizid Asurius and his chief magistrates awaited Lord Corbould at the end of the ramp. Around them stood a company of the city's militia, wealthy merchants, minor nobles, and a host of other hangers-on. Citizens of Cyrioch lined the Plaza, watching the spectacle, held back by a line of militia spears.

Lord Corbould Maraeus entered the Plaza from the other end, flanked by a troop of black-armored Imperial Guards.

Caina slipped through the crowds, which proved easy of enough, since most of the commoners had their attention focused on the nobles. She passed Lord Corbould and his guards and came to the rear of the column. The chariot drivers Corbould had brought walked there, followed by the singers and stagehands of the Grand Imperial Opera. Caina spotted Theodosia, clad in a brilliant red gown with black trim, her hair covered by a scarf of similar color.

Caina approached, and Theodosia smiled.

"Ah," she said. "There you are. Did you get the things I asked for?"

"No," said Caina, keeping her voice disguised. "Things...did not go well."

Theodosia's smile faded. "This is an outrage! An outrage! Why, I shall speak to Lord Corbould himself! I have his ear, you know. I'll have you shipped back to Malarae as a kitchen drudge! I'll..."

Theodosia went on in that vein for some time, much to the amusement of the other members of the company. Bit by bit their attention wavered, and turned to Lord Corbould's ceremonial entrance into the Plaza of Majesty. Theodosia looked at them and nodded.

"There," she murmured. "They ought to be distracted now. What happened? What did Barius tell you?"

"Nothing," said Caina.

Theodosia frowned. "Is he dead?"

"Yes. Maybe," said Caina. "I don't know."

"Hearken!" boomed the voice of Lord Corbould's herald. "Corbould, Lord of House Maraeus, once Lord Governor of the Imperial Pale, twice Lord Governor of Marsis, and four times Lord Marshall of the Legions, has come! He sends greetings to his brother Armizid, Lord Governor of Cyrica, and requests permission to enter the city!"

"Come with me," said Theodosia. "I want to watch this, since whoever hired the Kindred to kill Corbould is probably in the Plaza right now. You can tell me what you found once I have a better view."

Caina nodded and pushed her way through the crowd, Theodosia gliding after her with stately grace. After a few moments, she reached the edge of the Plaza, not far from the line of militiamen that kept the

Plaza clear for the nobles. From here, they had a clear view of the festivities. Lord Corbould dismounted his horse and waited while his herald continued the stentorian recitation of honors and offices.

"Now," said Theodosia, voice low. "What happened? Is Barius dead?"

"Probably," said Caina. "Someone turned him to stone."

It was one of the very few times Caina had ever seen Theodosia taken aback.

"Turned to stone?" said Theodosia. "That's not possible."

Caina shrugged. "Unless there is a reason Barius had a life-sized statue of himself in his back room. A life-sized statue sculpted with incredible detail and showing an expression of horror. A life-sized statue that also has an aura of sorcery."

"That does seem unlikely," said Theodosia. "But...turned him to stone? I've never heard of any kind of sorcery that can do that. There are the old stories about serpent-haired women, true, but those are just stories. Was there any indication how it happened?"

"I don't know," said Caina. "The door was open, and it looked like it was forced. There was a Kindred assassin waiting in the alley behind the shop. He got away before I could kill him. And there was another man in a cloak, watching everything. He fled before I could get a good look at him."

"I suppose neither one of them were serpent-haired women," said Theodosia.

"No," said Caina.

"Well," said Theodosia, "that's a puzzle, then." The herald kept droning through Lord Corbould's honors. "Barius was going to be our contact with Cyrioch's Ghost circle, tell us of any plots against Lord Corbould's life. So did the Kindred do this to him? Or did he stumble into some other kind of trouble?"

"A very good question," said Caina. She passed the charred scrap of paper to Theodosia. "Someone burned a book or a ledger in Barius's stove. This was all that was left. Does it mean anything to you?"

Theodosia squinted at the paper and nodded.

"It might," she said. "The Defender is a statue in a plaza a bit east of here. The Plaza of the Defender, they call it. We'll be staying at the inn there. As for the Well...there is a place in the Palace of Splendors called the Gallery of the Well. I have never been there." She grinned. "But if Lord Khosrau enjoys Nighmarian opera as much as the rumors say, I might get an invitation." She looked at the paper for a while longer, and then handed it to Caina. "Keep that. It might not mean anything. But just in case..."

Caina nodded. "What will we do now?"

"I'll have to contact Cyrioch's circlemaster," said Theodosia. She scowled. "Which I was hoping to avoid, because he's a dreadful bastard. But we have no choice. We need his help."

"And if someone is targeting the Ghosts of Cyrioch," said Caina, remembering what Kalastus had done in Rasadda, "they'll need to know."

Lord Corbould's herald wrapped up the recitation of honors, and Lord Governor Armizid's herald stepped forward.

"Hearken!" thundered the herald. "Armizid, a scion of House Asurius, Lord Governor of the province of Cyrica, guardian of Cyrioch, keeper of the Palace of Cyrioch, and scourge of the Sarbian tribes, does bid his brother Lord Corbould welcome to the Shining City of Cyrica Urbana!"

Lord Governor Armizid Asurius stepped forward, and Caina got her first look at the man who governed Cyrica. He was about thirty, with a soldier's lean build, and wore a gleaming white robe and turban in Anshani style, an elaborate jeweled sword and dagger at his belt. His expression was stern, his black eyes hard and cold.

"A humorless martinet of a man," murmured Theodosia, "but his father Khosrau is the real power in Cyrica."

Lord Khosrau followed after his son. The men had the same facial features and eyes, but Khosrau was enormously fat, so fat that his white robe and beard made him look like an ambulatory snowball. He walked with a limp, leaning upon an ivory cane in his right fist. Unlike his son, his expression was not a cold mask. If anything, he looked...amused. As if he was privy to some joke unknown to everyone else in the Plaza.

A man in a black robe with a purple sash trailed after Khosrau, a slave girl in a gray tunic following him.

"Who is the master magus?" said Caina.

"Ranarius, the preceptor of the Cyrioch chapterhouse," murmured Theodosia. "A cold one. Was a strong supporter of Haeron Icaraeus. Even the First Magus steps lightly around him."

Caina took a closer look at Ranarius. The master magus was in his sixties, with a gaunt, ascetic face and the perpetual squint of a scholar. The slave girl was perhaps a few years younger than Caina, with hair so blond it was almost white. A strip of black cloth covered her eyes, and an elaborate collar of carved jade rested around her neck. Caina wondered why Ranarius bothered keeping a blind slave. Perhaps she warmed his bed - Caina would not put it past a magus to keep a slave mistress or three. The suspicion was confirmed when she saw a jade bracelet of similar design on his left wrist.

Lord Armizid strode toward Lord Corbould, and a sudden memory struck Caina with the force of a blow.

She remembered standing in the Great Market in Marsis, taking Nicolai to see the grand arrival of Rezir Shahan aboard his ships. Lord Corbould had been there with his bodyguards and magistrates, coming to greet the Padishah of Istarinmul's Lord Ambassador. Yet the meeting had been a trap, and Istarish soldiers had stormed into the Great Market, killing and capturing slaves. The slavers had taken Nicolai captive. Dread rose up to choke her throat at the memory. She had to get him back! She had to find him before...

Caina shook her head. She had rescued Nicolai, had slain Rezir Shahan and outwitted the Moroacia's disciple Scorikhon. Nicolai was safe with Ark and Tanya. She had saved him.

Yet the dread did not leave her, and for a terrible instant she was sure that Istarish footmen would boil into the Plaza of Majesty, their khalmirs bellowing commands...

She heard a voice, hissing urgent words.

Caina blinked.

"Are you all right?" said Theodosia. "Because this is not the time to let your attention wander!"

"I'm fine," said Caina, but she knew it was a lie.

Theodosia's expression said that she knew it, too.

Then Lord Governor Armizid started to speak, and Caina pushed aside her memories and emotions.

"My lord Corbould," said Armizid in High Nighmarian with a thick Cyrican accent. "I bid you welcome to Cyrica Urbana, the Shining City."

The two men gripped hands briefly.

"I think you, my lord Armizid," said Corbould. "On behalf of our Emperor, I offer greetings, and thank you for your hospitality."

Armizid offered a thin smile, and Caina suspected that he did not like Corbould very much.

"All nations know the hospitality of the Cyricans," Armizid. "Truly, we are generous to our friends...and merciless to our enemies."

"Indeed?" said Corbould. "Then it is well that the Cyricans are friends and loyal citizens of our Empire. For our Empire is threatened by bitter enemies."

Armizid lifted an eyebrow below his white turban. "By the Kyracians and the Istarish, you mean? Perhaps they are your enemies, Lord Corbould, if they went to such efforts to seize Marsis from you. But for generations beyond count, the slaves who labor in our mines and plantations have come from the slavers' brotherhood of Istarinmul. The ships that carry our olives and rice and cotton to the ports of the world come from New Kyre. The Kyracians and the Istarish have been friends of Cyrica for centuries. Perhaps they are your enemies, my lord Corbould, but they may not be the enemies of Cyrica."

Corbould's face grew hard. "So you would rather side with enemies of the Empire than with your Emperor, my lord Armizid?"

"I wish to remain friends with the Emperor of Nighmar," said Armizid. "But if the Emperor makes himself into the enemy of Cyrica, well, then he shall have to live with the consequences."

"I take," said Corbould, his voice tight, "a dim view of rebellion. As does our Emperor. You might try to recall the fate of the Kagarish tribes that rebelled twenty years past."

Armizid gave a brief laugh. "The Kagars? Savages living in grass huts and mating with their horses. We Cyricans have been civilized for centuries beyond count."

"And for most of those centuries," said Corbould, his voice hard as the marble flagstones, "you Cyricans were slaves of the Anshani. It was the Emperor of Nighmar who liberated you from the Shahenshah of Anshan, and it was the Emperor of Nighmar who graciously allowed you to keep your slaves, even after your provinces rebelled during the War of the Fourth Empire. And now you think to turn your back upon him?"

Armizid sneered. "If Emperor Alexius turns his back upon us, if he drives the Cyricans away from our friends in Istarinmul and New Kyre, then he is a fool, and he deserves whatever misfortunate falls upon him!"

"And if you are so foolish as to rebel against the Emperor," said Corbould, "then you will learn the fate of a traitor."

This was not going well.

Both Corbould and Armizid glared at each other, and for a moment Caina thought they would come to blows. The memories of that terrible day in the Great Market of Marsis flooded through her mind, and Caina stepped toward Theodosia, intending to get her away if the Plaza of Majesty erupted into violence...

Then a low, raspy voice rang out in laughter.

Lord Khosrau hobbled towards Corbould and Armizid, his ivory cane tapping against the flagstones.

"Armizid," he said, coming to a stop between the two lords. "You are badgering our guest! What sort of hospitality is this?"

Armizid's face went tight with annoyance. "We have grave matters of state to discuss."

"Bah!" said Khosrau, waving his cane. "The grave matters of state never end. When you get to my age - and to Lord Corbould's age - you will learn that it is best to take matters in stride. Wars come and wars go, and today's bitter foe may become tomorrow's ally."

"Honored father," said Armizid, and to Caina's astonishment the Lord Governor of Cyrica almost looked like a petulant child. "War threatens to devour the western half of the Empire! We must discuss these matters, now, before..."

Khosrau laughed. "If that is so, a few days either way will not make much difference, will it? Besides, I have told you time and time again, a lord acts with patience, not with rashness."

Armizid's face went dark with fury, but he said nothing else.

"Now, my lord Corbould," said Khosrau, turning to face his son's guest. "I have one very important question for you."

"Of course, my lord," said Corbould. "We can discuss anything you wish."

"Did you bring the opera singers?" said Khosrau.

A knowing smile crossed Corbould's face. "It is a poor guest who does not bring gifts to his host."

"Splendid!" said Khosrau. "Are they here?"

Lord Corbould beckoned, and one of the Imperial Guards turned and marched towards the opera company.

"Ah," breathed Theodosia, arranging her dress. "Get ready. And take a good look at our friends, will you?"

Caina nodded.

The Imperial Guard approached them. "Singer. Lord Corbould requires your presence. You will stand before high nobility, so mind your tongue."

Theodosia drew herself up, her bosom swelling against the red fabric of her gown. "My dear fellow, I am the very soul of courtesy, and I have brought men weeping to their knees with the beauty of my song."

The Guard blinked, nonplussed. "This way."

The black-armored soldier led Theodosia across the Plaza. Caina followed, making sure to keep her hands well away from her weapons. Theodosia was entitled to her bodyguard, but she had no doubt that the Imperial Guards would cut her down without hesitation if she looked even the slightest bit threatening.

"Well, now," rumbled Khosrau, while Armizid looked on with flat disapproval. "Who is this lovely creature?"

Theodosia gripped her skirts and did an elaborate curtsy. "Theodosia of Malarae, my lord. I shall have the honor of singing for you."

Khosrau's white teeth flashed in his sun-weathered face. "I shall look forward to it. Very much. For if your voice is as lovely as your face, then your song shall be splendid indeed."

Theodosia favored him with her sunniest smile.

"Father," said Armizid. "This is unseemly. Fawning over a...a singer in public? This is behavior unbecoming of the Lord of House Asurius."

Khosrau did not look at his son. "I am the Lord of House Asurius, and I shall decide what is seemly, my son. Besides, we Cyricans have been civilized for centuries, have we not? And what is the point of civilization, if not to enjoy the ornaments of culture?"

Armizid's cold eyes shifted to Caina. "And who is this ragged dog that trails after the singer? Shall we allow armed renegades into our presence now?"

"Oh, my lord, don't mind poor Maric," said Theodosia. "His sister Marina looks after me, and Maric keeps me safe. Surely you would not expect a woman to visit a strange city without her bodyguard, my lord?"

Armizid's expression darkened. "This impudence is..."

"Armizid," said Khosrau.

Armizid fell silent, a vein twitching in his temple.

Khosrau looked at Caina. "You will watch over our lovely singer, will you not?"

Caina bowed deep. "Of course, my lord," she said, keeping her voice rough and disguised.

"Splendid fellow," said Khosrau.

"I commissioned the Grand Imperial Opera to visit Cyrioch," said Lord Corbould, stepping into the gap, "in your honor, my lords

Armizid and Khosrau, because I know how much you enjoy Nighmarian opera. And chariot races, as well, in Cyrioch's hippodrome."

"You are courteous, my lord Corbould," said Khosrau. "And I have arranged gladiatorial games and feasts in your honor, though these poor amusements are no match for the splendor of the Grand Imperial Opera. But it is my hope that they will provide a civilized venue for...discussions."

Corbould offered a smooth smile. "That is my hope as well."

The two men walked away, Theodosia forgotten. Armizid stared after them, then shook his head and followed. Caina watched them go, thinking. Khosrau seemed like a genial, flirtatious old man, hardly the sort to hire Kindred assassins to start a war. Yet she had learned again and again that a smiling face could hide a murderous heart. Armizid certainly seemed capable of hiring the Kindred to kill Corbould, but Caina doubted that Armizid had the willpower to defy his father. If someone in Cyrioch had hired the Kindred, it had to be Khosrau.

Unless some other power had hired the Kindred, someone about whom the Ghosts knew nothing.

The same power that had turned Barius to stone, perhaps?

That seemed too much of a coincidence, and Caina hated coincidences. They usually indicated some underlying pattern she could not yet see.

"Well," murmured Theodosia, once the nobles and their attendants began climbing the ramp to the Palace of Splendors, "what did you think?"

"Armizid is proud," said Caina, "and I think he would like to break away from the Empire and join Istarinmul. Or to have Cyrica become independent." She shook her head. "Khosrau...it is hard to tell. He knows how to hide what he's really thinking."

"A smooth one, isn't he?" said Theodosia. "And with excellent taste in opera, I might add. What did you think of the preceptor?"

"Ranarius?" said Caina, and her lip crinkled in disgust. "He just watched the discussion. Stood there with that blind slave of his and listened." She wondered if the girl had been born blind, or if

Ranarius had blinded her for some infraction. "Which means he's dangerous. He'll watch, and wait, and act when he thinks it's in his best interests."

"Oh, yes," murmured Theodosia. "He's a dangerous one. The Ghosts tried to kill him twice, you know. And both times he killed everyone we sent after him."

"Why did we try to kill him?" said Caina.

"He killed too many Ghosts," said Theodosia. "The Cyrioch chapter of the Magisterium has close ties with the Istarish slavers' brotherhood, and Ranarius had been helping them kidnap common farmers. He used the profits to fund his experiments into various forms of battle sorcery. Whenever the Ghosts tried to stop the slavers, Ranarius would kill them. And when we sent nightfighters to stop him, he killed them, too."

Caina loathed the magi, and Ranarius represented everything she hated about them. Yet it did seem unlikely that he had hired the Kindred to kill Lord Corbould. Ranarius made his money from the slave trade, and a revolt would disrupt that slave trade for years.

"What should we do now?" said Caina.

"I must send word to the local Ghost circle," said Theodosia. "They need to know what happened to Barius. And we'll need another contact." She sighed. "I liked Barius. I hope we don't have to deal with Cyrioch's circlemaster. Vicious bastard, but effective. We should have word from him in a few days."

"And until then?" said Caina.

Theodosia grinned. "Why, we prepare for a performance, my dear."

4

A FROZEN ASSASSIN

The nobility of Cyrioch filled the Amphitheatre of Asurius.

One or another of Lord Khosrau's ancestors had built the massive Amphitheatre. Rows of seats climbed the Stone's slope, rising in a wide half circle. The broad stage rested at the foot of the hill, surrounded by private boxes for the Lord Governor and his honored guests. The ancient engineer who had built the Amphitheatre had been an architect of genius – the acoustics were so perfect that a man sitting in the top row could hear a pin drop upon the stage. Furthermore, the sound reflected upon the city. Half of Cyrioch could hear the Grand Imperial Opera.

Caina stood in the tents besides the stage. She wore a pale blue dress with black trim, a scarf of a similar color covering her hair. She had thought the scarf would prove intolerable in the heat, but it reflected the sun's rays and kept sweat from trickling down her face.

Though now the sun had gone down, and the nobles and wealthy merchants of Cyrioch had gathered to listen to the opera.

Hundreds of the Magisterium's glowing glass globes filled with Amphitheatre with light. Arrays of mirrors, also designed by that long-dead engineer, focused the light upon the stage. She watched the chorus sing one of the songs from the epic opera of Tertius

Maraeus, one of Corbould Maraeus's distant ancestors. It was a solemn, majestic opera, describing how Tertius, at the urging of his Cyrican bride, invaded Cyrica and freed Cyrioch from the control of the Shahenshah of Anshan.

Of course, Caina thought sourly, the first thing the Cyricans had done with their new freedom was buy slaves from the slavers of Istarinmul.

But that part didn't make it into the opera.

"Marina!" Theodosia's voice rang out. "Marina, I need you!"

In the enormous Grand Imperial Opera in Malarae, the stage-hands and the singers used the vast workshops and network of tunnels below the theater for their workspace. Here, in the Amphitheatre, there was no need for the elaborate scenery required in Malarae, so the tents served as makeshift replacements for the workshops. Caina passed tables laden with tools, one holding the jars of stage blood - mixed Caerish wine and tomato juice - that would be used in the climatic final act.

She found Theodosia at a wooden table, gazing at her portable mirror. She wore the elaborate dress and makeup of Severa, Tertius Maraeus's great Cyrican love.

"Marina!" said Theodosia. "You simply must help me with my hair! I shall have to go on as soon as Marcellus finishes his aria, and my hair is a disaster!"

Caina knelt beside her and began arranging the intricate hairstyle that the role of Severa required.

"Anything?" murmured Theodosia.

"Corbould, Armizid, and Khosrau are all sitting together," said Caina. "There's a guard of militiamen and Imperial Guards around them."

"That's good," said Theodosia. "Hand me that brush, will you?"

Caina handed over the brush. "Unless the Kindred have infiltrated the Guard or the militia. Or an assassin disguised himself as a slave. Gods, but there are so many of them." The anger flickered inside of her. "And the nobles and the merchants don't even see them. I thought the nobles in Malarae treated their servants badly, but this is worse. They cannot even be bothered the brush the flies from their sleeves, but allow the slaves to do it for them."

"Keep an eye on them," said Theodosia. "All of them. If anyone asks, say that you are carrying messages for me. We've been assuming that Lord Khosrau wants Lord Corbould dead, but perhaps one of Cyrica's lesser nobles would profit in a revolt." She stood up, scrutinizing herself in the mirror. "Well, I suppose that shall have to do."

"Theodosia!" Marcellus, the tenor singing the role of Tertius Maraeus, wandered to her side, clad in a costume resembling antique Nighmarian armor. He had a handsome face, a voice like rolling thunder, and a mind like a lump of lead. "Am I going on?"

"Yes, dear," said Theodosia, taking the befuddled tenor's arm. "Come along. We sing our duet after your first aria."

"Oh," said Marcellus. "That's good."

Theodosia guided him towards the stage, and Caina slipped out the back of the tent.

She scanned the crowd. She would know a Kindred assassin when she saw one. Caina had trained under Riogan, a ruthless assassin who had left the Kindred to join the Ghosts, and he had taught her all their tricks. The Kindred preferred to buy child slaves from the Istarish markets, and used years of brutal training to shape them into remorseless assassins. Her eyes wandered over the endless gray-clad slaves waiting by their white-robed noble masters. Had the assassin she had killed in the Praetorian Basilica once been a slave child, terrified and weeping on the auction block?

She pushed aside the thought.

She could not afford distractions. Instead she watched the spectators on the ascending rows of seats, thinking of ways the Kindred might try to kill Lord Corbould. An archer in the higher seats? No, unlikely - the enspelled glass globes would dazzle an archer's vision. A dagger thrust or a sword blow? Even less likely - guards surrounded Corbould, and the Kindred preferred not to sacrifice themselves in their assassinations. A poisoned glass of wine? Khosrau would provide a food taster to Corbould out of courtesy.

Though if Khosrau had hired the Kindred to kill Corbould, it would not be hard to slip Corbould poisoned food...

"Mistress?"

A male slave in his late thirties stood before her, eyes downcast, a silver collar around his neck. Like the others, he wore a gray tunic, but his was of finer material than most. A noble's slave, then - Caina had noticed the nobles like to dress their slaves in finer materials.

Like a man putting a fine collar on a favored pet.

The thought filled her with such rage that it was all she could do to keep her face smooth.

"Aye?" said Caina.

"Are you Marina, the servant of the singer Theodosia?" said the slave.

"I am," said Caina.

"Then my master Lord Khosrau bids you to come speak with him," said the slave. "Please, mistress, follow me."

Why would Khosrau want to speak with her? Did he know that she was a Ghost? No, that seemed unlikely. But he would know that Marina, brother of Maric, was Theodosia's servant. Perhaps that was it.

"Of course," said Caina.

The slave bowed and led the way. Caina walked past the stage, and the man led her to the largest box, where the slaves attended the chief nobles of Cyrica. Lord Governor Armizid, stern and grim, occupied the center of the box. Lord Khosrau sat at his right, eating grapes fed to him by a waiting slave. Lord Corbould sat at his side, watching the opera with polite interest. Ranarius stood in the corner, stark and forbidding in his black robes, the blind slave girl sitting at his feet.

The girl's blindfolded face turned towards Caina as she entered.

"Master," said the slave, kneeling before Khosrau. "I brought the singer's servant, as you commanded."

Khosrau waved a hand, jewels glittering on his thick fingers. "Yes, well done."

"A servant?" said Armizid, looking at Caina with distaste. "Bad enough that we fawn over an opera singer, but now we must speak with their drudges?"

"Now, now," said Khosrau. "There's no need for churlishness, my son." His dark eyes turned towards Caina, glittering over his white beard. "Come closer, my dear, so I can see you. Oh, you needn't fear that I will ravish you. I've drunk far too much wine for that."

Corbould snorted. "In thirty years you haven't changed, Khosrau."

"I certainly have," said Khosrau, and he threw a roguish wink at Caina. "Thirty years ago I could have fought all day, drunk all night, and then taken this lovely young lady and her twin sister to bed and left them more satisfied than they've ever been in their lives." He sighed. "But, all things must change." For a moment a note of melancholy entered his voice. "Even Cyrica."

"My lord is much too kind to a poor servant," said Caina, keeping her eyes downcast.

Khosrau roared with laughter, and even Corbould chuckled. Armizid's scowl deepened, while Ranarius watched the exchange in silence. The slave girl at his feet kept her face turned towards Caina.

"You are a splendid liar, my dear," said Khosrau. "A fine quality in a servant. But, you must attend to your mistress, and I have no wish to cause her distress." He snapped his fingers, and the male slave handed Caina a scroll of thick white paper.

"A message for my mistress?" said Caina.

"A bright girl," said Khosrau, in the same tone he might use to compliment a dog or a horse.

Still, Caina found it hard to dislike the jovial old lord. He was certainly more pleasant than his humorless son. And it seemed hard to believe that Khosrau could plot the murder of a man sitting next to him.

Hard to believe...but not impossible.

"Yes," said Ranarius. He had a quiet, precise voice, and Caina felt his cold gaze turn to her. "The commoners can do all sorts of tricks once they've been properly trained."

"It is the invitation to a little gathering," said Khosrau. "Deliver it to your mistress, and tell her that Lord Khosrau Asurius would be most pleased if she could sing for it."

Caina bowed. "My mistress would be most honored." And pleased, as well. It would provide an opportunity to spy within the Palace of Splendors.

"She had better be," said Armizid. "It is unseemly for an opera singer to attend a gathering of nobles, but..."

"Unseemly!" said Khosrau. "That is your favorite word, my boy. Unseemly. Well," he waved his hand, "off you go, girl. It would please me greatly if your mistress performed at the feast."

Caina bowed and left the box. Khosrau's attention returned to the opera, as did Corbould's, but she felt Armizid and Ranarius staring at her as she left.

She hurried back to the tents. Marcellus had taken the stage as Tertius Maraeus, his mighty voice booming his aria. In a few moments Theodosia would come on stage as Severa, and her song about the plight of the Cyricans would convince Tertius to make war upon Anshan. Caina slipped back into the shadows, listening to the song with half an ear as she scanned the crowd for any threats...

"A blowgun."

She whirled, reaching for the dagger at her belt.

A shadow detached itself from the back of a tent and stepped towards her.

It was a man in a hooded cloak, eyes glinting beneath the cowl. Beneath his cloak she glimpsed a sheathed sword and chain mail. His right hand rested on the sword's hilt, and Caina saw an odd, swirling black tattoo over his forearm.

He was a Kindred assassin. She was sure of it.

The assassin stared at her.

"You're not going to kill me," Caina said at last.

Behind them Theodosia's soaring song joined Marcellus's.

"Oh?" said the man.

"We're standing in front of ten thousand people," said Caina. "If I scream, quite a few armed men are going to notice. If you were going to kill me, you would have stabbed me in the back."

"Astute," said the cloaked man. "I saw you watching the crowd, which seemed like an unusual thing for a servant girl to do."

"Perhaps I was bored," said Caina. "I've heard the epic of Tertius Maraeus before."

"Perhaps," said the cloaked man. He took a step closer, and Caina glimpsed his face, hard and lean. "I thought that at first. And then I remembered how the Emperor's Ghosts have many friends among actors and singers and slaves."

"There's no such thing as the Ghosts," said Caina. "They're a story, a legend."

A hard smile flashed over the cloaked man's face. "And that is an answer in itself, no?"

"The Ghosts are myths," said Caina, "but the Kindred are not."

The man's hard smile faded. "You think I am a Kindred assassin?"

"I know you are a Kindred assassin," said Caina. "I know how the Kindred walk. I know how they hold their weapons. I know how they disguise themselves. You're Kindred. Who are you here to kill?"

"You are almost correct," said the cloaked man. "I was Kindred."

"That's impossible," said Caina. "No one leaves the Kindred. Alive, anyway."

But that was wrong, and she knew it. Riogan had left the Kindred. They had tried to kill him for it, but he had survived. At least until Maglarion had found him.

"So," said Caina. "Former Kindred. And you're here to talk, not to kill me. What do you want to tell me?"

"A blowgun," said the cloaked man. "That's how they're going kill Corbould. A tiny dart, coated with a particularly exotic poison. The poison numbs the wound, and he will never feel it. Thirty-seven hours later, the poison will reach his heart and stop it. And then, I suppose, Lord Khosrau will have his war with the Emperor."

"Why are you telling me this?" said Caina. She would not put it past the Kindred to spread lies to mask one of their assassinations. "Are you such a great friend of Lord Corbould?"

"I do not give a damn for Lord Corbould," said the cloaked man, "nor for his precious Empire. Nor do I have a damn for the Ghosts.

Suffice to say I have my own business here, and I do not want you stumbling over me in your zeal to save Corbould Maraeus."

Caina opened her mouth to answer...and fell silent.

She saw a slave moving through the aisles of the Amphitheatre. A dozen slaves hurried through the Amphitheatre, running errands for their masters. Yet this slave was heading straight for Lord Corbould and the other nobles.

And Caina recognized him.

When last she had seen him, he had been wearing a yellow robe and creeping up behind her in Barius's pawnshop.

She turned back to the cloaked man, only to see that she had vanished.

Caina cursed, looking around for him, but he had disappeared without a trace. She looked back at the seats, and saw that the Kindred assassin had moved closer to Lord Corbould. Had the cloaked man been right about the blowgun? Corbould was wearing armor, but his neck was exposed.

She hurried across the aisles, moving as fast as she dared. The assassin drew closer, and Caina saw something clutched in his left hand, something that looked like a thick brown straw.

His nose was broken, she saw with some satisfaction.

Marcellus and Theodosia continued their intricate duet, the notes rising and falling, every eye in the Amphitheatre fixed on them. The assassin stopped three aisles from Lord Corbould's box and dropped to one knee, as if to fix the laces on his sandal.

But the blowgun came up, and Caina was out of time.

She reached into her sleeve, snatched out a throwing knife, and flung it at the assassin. She could not put all her strength into the throw, not in front of so many people. But the blade sank an inch into the assassin's shoulder. The knife knocked him off-balance, the poisoned dart falling to the ground.

The assassin glared at her, his bruised lips tight with rage. He wouldn't recognize her from Barius's pawnshop, but he would realize that his cover was blown. She watched the calculation flash over his face. He couldn't attack her, not in front of ten thousand spectators.

Caina would only need to scream, and all ten thousand spectators would see a slave attacking a freeborn woman.

That would not end well for the assassin.

Nor could Caina kill him. If she slew him in front of the audience, it would ruin her disguise. Anyone with a brain would realize there were Ghosts among the Grand Imperial Opera, and Caina's effectiveness would be curtailed.

The Kindred assassin yanked her knife from his shoulder, turned, and began walking away.

Caina followed, moving as fast as she dared. The assassin veered for one of the exits from the Amphitheatre, and Caina followed. Her mind settled on a plan. She would get close enough to overpower him. Then she could take him captive and question him. With luck, she could find out what the Kindred had planned for Lord Corbould...and, perhaps, what had happened to Barius.

Then Theodosia and Marcellus finished their duet.

Lord Khosrau rose to his feet, applauding. The other nobles took one look at him and hauled themselves to their feet, also applauding, and the merchants in the upper rows followed suit. Soon the entire Amphitheatre stood, applauding and cheering.

And Caina lost sight of the assassin. She was too short to see over the rows of applauding nobles.

She whispered a curse and broke into a run. A few of the nobles would see her, but they would only assume she was on an urgent errand for Theodosia. She caught a glimpse of the assassin sprinting for the Amphitheatre's exit, and she ran in that direction. A half-dozen streets led from the Amphitheatre's gates. If the assassin reached them, Caina would never find him again.

She saw the assassin vanish through the gates.

Caina ran into the small plaza outside the Amphitheatre, the Palace of Splendors and the Stone rising behind her. She heard Theodosia's aria roll over the sides of the white hill, echoing through the city. The plaza was deserted, its opulent houses dark. Their owners filled the Amphitheatre, and no doubt their slaves had taken the opportunity to get drunk.

There was no trace of the assassin.

Caina struck her fist against the side of her leg in frustration. Twice now that assassin had eluded her. Suddenly she felt like a fool. The show with the blowgun might have been a distraction to allow the cloaked man to kill Corbould without interference. She had to get back to the Amphitheatre.

Caina turned and froze.

A statue of white stone stood next to the Amphitheatre's gates.

She stared at it in horrified fascination.

It hadn't been there this morning.

She drew closer, heart pounding behind her ribs. The statue showed a man in a slave's ragged tunic, arms thrown up as if to ward off a blow, face distorted with fear and horror.

Caina recognized it.

It was the Kindred assassin she had pursued through the Amphitheatre.

Like the statue of Barius, it was incredibly detailed. Caina saw every wrinkle in the assassin's face, every fold and crease of his tunic. The statue's nose was even broken. Caina held out a hesitant hand and brushed the statue's arm.

She felt cool, smooth stone...and the tingle of sorcery.

Caina jerked her hand back as if it had been burned.

She had pursued the assassin out of the Amphitheatre...and someone had turned him to stone.

Caina turned in a circle, her eyes sweeping the darkened plaza. She saw no one else, not a single living soul. No trace, no hint, of who might have done this.

Or why.

And if whatever power or creature had turned the assassin to stone was still lurking out here, standing alone in the plaza was not the brightest decision Caina could make.

She hurried back into the Amphitheatre.

Theodosia stood on the stage, singing her aria, her voice holding the nobles rapt. Even Armizid seemed impressed. Corbould Maraeus remained unharmed. Caina breathed a sigh of relief and hurried back into the tents.

There was no trace of the cloaked man who had warned her about the assassin. Had he, perhaps, turned the assassin to stone?

A sudden recollection tugged at her memory.

She had seen the cloaked man's scabbard and sword belt before.

He had been watching her in the alley behind Barius's pawnshop.

5

VISIONS

"I think that went well," said Theodosia, pacing back and forth through the sitting room, "don't you? You should have seen the look on Khosrau's face! I thought the old fellow was about to jump out of his seat!"

Caina nodded. It was well past midnight, and from past experience, she knew that Theodosia became exhilarated, almost manic, after a performance. In another twenty minutes she would sink into a pit of despondency, declare her singing a failure, and then go to bed. Eight or nine hours later she would awaken as her usual cheerful self.

"I'm just glad," said Caina, "that Lord Corbould lived long enough to appreciate your performance."

"You did well," said Theodosia. "Gods, if Corbould was murdered during my aria, that would have been dreadful! Simply dreadful!" She considered for a moment. "And bad for the Empire, too, I suppose."

Caina shook her head. "We still don't know who hired the Kindred. Or how Barius and that assassin were turned to stone."

"But Corbould is still alive," said Theodosia, pacing once more through the lavish sitting room.

The opera company was staying at the Inn of the Defender, an inn catering to wealthy merchants. As the leading lady, Theodosia occupied one of the inn's finer suites. It had a sitting room and a separate bedroom with an enormous, pillow-piled bed. Caina even had a cot in the sitting room. Slaves waited outside the door, ready to serve their slightest whim.

Caina's mouth twisted in disgust at that thought.

"Corbould is still alive," Theodosia said, and Caina snapped out of her reverie, "and we have a meeting tomorrow."

"Oh?" said Caina.

"The local circlemaster has graciously agreed to assist us," said Theodosia, scowling. "He's a former slave, a Szaldic freedman named Marzhod. Hard, ruthless, and uncouth, but he's...effective. We'll need his help if we're to find out who hired the Kindred."

"And who turned Barius and that assassin to stone," said Caina.

Theodosia nodded. "We'll disguise ourselves and visit him tomorrow. He keeps his headquarters at a sink of a tavern in Seatown." She sniffed. "Though the man has absolutely no appreciation for opera..."

Caina nodded and let Theodosia talk. Eventually, the older woman's mood turned towards despondency, and Caina steered her to bed.

~

A FEW MINUTES later Caina stepped onto the sitting room's balcony.

It overlooked the Plaza of the Defender, a small square lined with shops selling luxuries. To the north, Caina saw the palaces of Cyrica's nobility, each more ostentatious than the last, though no match for the Palace of Splendor. Beyond she saw the slums and warehouses of Seatown, and the lights from the countless ships maneuvering in Cyrioch's harbor, even at night.

The Defender stood in the center of the square.

The statue was eighteen feet tall, clad in armor of antique design, the hilt of a greatsword in its armored hands. A towering helm hid the statue's features, and it gazed to the north, as if watching for invaders from the sea. A single massive crack ran down the center of the Defender, from its stone helm to its boots. The crack had only appeared a few years ago, Theodosia said, and people interpreted it as an ill omen. The Defender had stood here for millennia, older than Cyrioch, perhaps even as old as the Stone itself. The statue was made from the same indestructible rock as the Stone.

As the statues of Barius and the assassin, now that Caina thought about it.

She stared at the Defender for a long time, thinking.

But no answers came to her, and Caina went to bed.

~

NIGHTMARES LASHED AT HER.

Caina often had nightmares. Bad dreams, Halfdan had told her, were scars of the mind. Just as wounds left scars upon the flesh, so too did the mind bear nightmares after an injury. Of late, whenever Caina closed her eyes, she dreamed of Marsis, of Andromache's lightning falling from the sky, of Nicolai sobbing as he called for his mother. It didn't matter that she had saved Nicolai. The dread had sunk into her bones like salt into poisoned earth.

And sometimes her memories melded together to produce a new nightmare.

Like tonight.

In her dream Caina was naked but for the chains binding her wrists and neck. A pair of Istarish slavers dragged her onto a wooden stage. A crowd of magi, stark in their black robes, gazed up at her, their eyes cold and merciless.

"One slave for sale," said the auctioneer, and Caina saw that it was Maglarion. The bloodcrystal in his left eye socket blazed with ghostly green light, painting his dark coat with eerie light. She tried to cringe away as he approached, but the Istarish slavers yanked her chains, forcing her stand upright. "A bit scarred, to be sure." His hand brushed over the scars his necromantic experiments had carved below her navel, the experiments that had left her unable to bear a child. "But still ripe for any sort of sorcerous experiment." He grinned. "I know firsthand that she can scream for hours! You should have seen how she wailed when I killed her father!"

"One thousand denarii!" shouted a bald master magus. It was Kalastus, the pyromancer who had almost destroyed Rasadda.

"A hundred thousand!" said a withered corpse in the crumbling remnants of fine clothes. Caina recognized Lord Naelon Icaraeus – or at least, what was left of him after she and Ark had defeated him.

"Half a million!" said another man, the top of his head a smashed ruin. Ephaeron, the master magus who had tried to kill her in Rasadda.

Caina struggled, splinters digging into her bare feet, but the chains held her fast.

"Fine bids, all!" said Maglarion. "But surely someone can pay more!"

"One million!" said a hissing, bubbling voice.

Caina turned her head and started to scream.

A misshapen, twisted corpse shambled onto the stage, its arms and legs distorted by huge, cancerous growths, veins running black beneath its skin. Alastair Corus had been Caina's only lover, and Maglarion's necromantic sorcery had killed him.

And now he shuffled towards her, reaching for her with twisted fingers.

"Sold!" said Maglarion.

Alastair's corpse reached for her, and the slavers shoved her at him. Caina slammed against him, her bare skin touching his deformed flesh, and she shrieked in horror. Alastair's arms closed around her, and she screamed again.

Then a strange keening noise filled her ears, and the world dissolved into gray mist.

~

CAINA FOUND herself lying on the ground.

Gray mist swirled around her, cold and clammy, and bleak nothingness stretched in all directions. This was a dream, she knew, just as the nightmare of the slave block had been.

She stood up, and saw the dead sorceress.

The woman was beautiful, radiant. She looked like a maiden of eighteen years, with long black hair and red lips. But that was only an illusion. She was the Moroaica, a sorceress of legend and terror, and her black eyes were ancient and cold with dark knowledge.

"No," said Caina. "You're dead. I saw you die. Sicarion thought some of your power is trapped inside of me. But you're dead. You're dead!"

The woman who had called herself Jadriga did not respond.

"This is another damned dream," said Caina.

"Ah," said the Moroaica. "You heard."

Caina blinked, and then realized Jadriga had not been talking to her.

A short man emerged from the mists. The man wore leather armor and a long cloak, sword and dagger at his belt. His hairless head was hideously scarred, and looked as if it had been stitched together out of torn pieces of leather. His left eye was a brilliant green, but his right was a sulfurous orange.

"Sicarion," spat Caina. He had lured Andromache into Scorikhon's tomb, allowing Jadriga's long-dead disciple to possess Andromache's body. "You miserable wretch, you got away from me once, but..."

But like Jadriga, Sicarion did not see or hear her.

"Mistress," said Sicarion in his rusty voice, making a short bow before the Moroaica. "For a dead woman, you are looking well."

"I have died many times before," said Jadriga, "and before the great work is done, I suspect I shall die a few more."

Caina listened. Was this a dream? Or was Sicarion somehow communicating with Jadriga's spirit?

"Indeed," said Sicarion with another bow. "I have been there for many of your deaths, mistress. Though this time you have, shall we say...remained dead much longer than I expected."

"It is of no concern," said Jadriga.

"When shall you take possession of your current vessel?" said Sicarion.

"When the time is right," said Jadriga.

Sicarion's lips twitched. Even his lips were scarred. Which was not surprising, given that Caina had seen him cut the hand from a dead man and attach it to the bloody stump of his right arm.

"In other words," said Sicarion, "you cannot."

"No," said the Moroaica. "It is...intriguing. Her mind has been... fractured, damaged."

Sicarion laughed. "She was lucid enough when I faced her."

"When she defeated you," said Jadriga.

Sicarion shrugged. "And she defeated you as well. Yet I am still alive."

"Her cognitive faculties are unimpaired," said Jadriga, "as we both know. But her spirit is scarred, damaged. Because of that, I can possess her, but I cannot control her."

"A simple solution presents itself," said Sicarion. "I will find her and kill her. Then you will claim a more receptive vessel, and the great work can continue."

"You will not," said Jadriga.

Sicarion's scowl made his scarred face uglier. "Why? You cannot take control of her body, you said so yourself. If I kill her, you can take possession of a new vessel at once."

"No," said Jadriga. Her voice grew distant, almost dreamy. "You will not. She and I are more alike than she would ever admit. She has known pain, horrible pain. I suspect even now her sleeping mind throws those memories back into her face. Yet the pain has not broken her. It has only made her stronger, and she wields it as a weapon. Just as I did, once."

"So you think to twist her," said Sicarion.

"Yes," said Jadriga. "I have always dominated my vessels. Think how much stronger I shall be if she submits to me willingly. If she puts her intellect at my service. I shall speak to in her dreams. Bit by bit she will bend to my will. To see the necessity of the great work, as I do."

"That could take years," said Sicarion.

Jadriga shrugged. "What is time to me? A few decades are nothing."

Sicarion's face contorted in rage. "You promised me killing, mistress. You promised killing enough to sate me. I will find your vessel and slay her, and when you take a new body..."

"You will not kill her," said Jadriga, icy calm. "I forbid it."

The gray mists rippled, and Sicarion took a step back in alarm, a hint of fear in his mismatched eyes.

"As you wish, mistress," said Sicarion. "I will not kill your vessel."

"I never doubted it," said Jadriga. "But fear not, my faithful hound. I have some work that should please you."

"Someone to kill?" said Sicarion.

"Of course," said Jadriga. "Do you remember my wayward disciple? The one we met at the Magisterium's motherhouse in Artifel?"

Sicarion's lip curled in a snarl.

"You do remember, I see," said Jadriga.

"As annoying a fool as Andromache," muttered Sicarion. He grinned. "Though I regret I didn't get to kill her myself."

"A pity about Scorikhon," said Jadriga. "He remained loyal to me."

"Because you sealed his spirit in a stone box for five hundred years," said Sicarion.

The Moroaica's smile was thin. "Such simple things can inspire loyalty, no? As you well know. But this is what I would have of you. My wayward disciple has settled in Cyrica Urbana."

Caina stepped forward, both interested and alarmed. Andromache had been a loyal student of the Moroaica, and she had almost destroyed Marsis. Maglarion had once been Jadriga's student, Caina suspected, and he had almost killed everyone in Malarae. Was there a disciple of the Moroaica in Cyrioch?

Sicarion's grin was hideous. "I've been looking forward to this for twenty years."

"Twenty years is not so long," said Jadriga. "Even for someone only a few centuries old, like you. For I have been preparing the great work for centuries beyond count, since the Kingdom of Rising Sun collapsed into dust."

"I bow before your superior wisdom," said Sicarion.

"Go to Cyrica Urbana," said Jadriga, "find my rebellious fool of a disciple, and then..."

She fell silent, a frown marring the pale beauty of her face.

Then she turned and looked directly at Caina.

"We are observed," said Jadriga.

Caina backed away in alarm.

"I thought you said her mind was asleep," said Sicarion.

"So I did," said Jadriga. "But I also said she was formidable. Go, my hound. Fulfill the task I have given you in whatever way seems best."

Sicarion bowed and vanished into nothingness, leaving Caina alone with Jadriga.

"You're not real," said Caina. "I killed you and you're not real. This is a dream."

"Oh, come now, child," said Jadriga. "After what happened in Marsis, I think you would know better."

"What do you want?" said Caina. "If you're real, if you're not just some sort of echo of Jadriga's power, why are you telling me all of this?"

"Because," said Jadriga, "you are going to face trials, terrible trials, soon enough." She looked into the gray mists and nodded. "As you will soon see."

She gestured, and blackness swallowed Caina.

~

CAINA'S EYES SHOT OPEN.

Dazzling sunlight filled her vision. She was on her cot in their suite's sitting room, the sun pouring in through the opened shutters. It was well past sunrise.

"Oh, good," said Theodosia. "You're up."

Caina turned her head. Theodosia sat at the table, wrapped in a silk robe, eating a piece of bread and sipping at a cup of tea.

"You were exhausted," said Theodosia, "so it seemed best to let you sleep."

"More exhausted than you?" muttered Caina, swinging her feet to the floor. Her head ached and throbbed, and her mouth felt as if it had been coated in dust.

"Well, a performance is tiring business," said Theodosia. "But I think you needed your sleep." Her gray eyes were worried. "You kept screaming and thrashing in your sleep. Nightmares?"

Caina stood, crossed to the table, and helped herself to some tea. "Aye."

"How are you?" said Theodosia.

Caina hesitated. What could she tell Theodosia? That she would wake up in an empty bed for the rest of her life, alone but for her nightmares? That the corrupted spirit of the Moroaica, a necromancer of terrible power, might be riding around inside her skull?

"I'm fine," said Caina, sipping at the tea. Bitter and black, the way she preferred it.

"Plainly," said Theodosia, her disbelief evident. "Well, we are to meet with Marzhod after sundown. Are you sure you're up for it?"

"I'm fine," said Caina again.

She could almost make herself believe it.

6

THE CIRCLEMASTER

That afternoon, Caina helped Theodosia prepare for a different role.

Theodosia donned a robe of sand-colored cloth, the sort favored by the nomadic Sarbian tribes that lived in the deserts south of Cyrica. A white turban went on her head, complete with a thick veil to keep the desert's winds at bay. A scimitar went on her belt, and makeup gave her the illusion of stubble and a face made leathery by the sun. The desert men, Theodosia said, had a reputation for short tempers, and few would cross them without good reason.

"How do I look?" said Theodosia, examining herself in the mirror as Caina donned her own robe.

"Dry," said Caina, buckling on her sword belt.

"How droll," said Theodosia. "But if we're fortunate, no one will trouble a pair of desert men." She offered a tight smile. "And with a little more luck, Marzhod will have some information for us."

THE WEALTHY DISTRICTS surrounding the Stone fell silent at night, but Seatown grew louder.

Caina walked at Theodosia's side, making sure to use the confident swagger the other Sarbians used. Gangs of slaves labored at the piers, unloading cargoes from the ships. Other slaves hauled endless carts loaded with sacks of rice and grain to the docks. The crops grown on Cyrica's slave-worked plantations fed half the world. Bands of sailors headed for the taverns and brothels lining Seatown's streets, eager to enjoy themselves while the slaves unloaded their ships.

She glimpsed dark-cloaked men waiting in the alleys. Istarish slavers, most likely. Some of those drunken sailors might wake up chained in the hold of an Istarish ship. It was illegal, of course, but Caina suspected healthy bribes persuaded the Lord Governor's officials to look the other way.

The thought made her fist tighten against the hilt of her scimitar. Gods, she had been here only a few days, but she detested Cyrioch.

"Here we are," said Theodosia.

They stopped at the edge of the piers. A huge, rambling tavern stood there, a ramshackle three-story pile of brick and timber. Firelight streamed through its open doors, and a steady stream of sailors and caravan guards moved in and out of the building. A sign swung over the door, showing a naked woman with a painted face.

"The Painted Whore?" said Caina, reading the script on the sign. "Charming."

"Marzhod is a charming sort of fellow," said Theodosia. "Let me do the talking."

Caina nodded and followed Theodosia into the tavern.

The Painted Whore looked like the other sailors' taverns Caina had visited - dark, smoky, and ill-smelling. Men sat at wooden benches, drinking cheap wine from clay cups. Women in slave gray hurried back and forth with trays of food and drink. Caina watched them, her anger growing. Marzhod kept slaves? What kind of Ghost was he?

Grim-faced men in Sarbian desert robes stood throughout the room, cudgels in hand.

"Sarbian mercenaries," said Theodosia, keeping her voice low. "Marzhod hires them as enforcers. They're not loyal to anyone in the city, so as long as he pays them, they'll do whatever he wants."

Theodosia approached one of the Sarbians.

"You want a drink," said the mercenary in accented Cyrican, "then talk to one of the slave girls."

"Why do the tyrants fear the shadows?" said Theodosia in High Nighmarian.

The mercenary blinked, once.

"For there are Ghosts in the shadows," said the mercenary, likewise in High Nighmarian. His pronunciation was atrocious, but the words were clear enough.

"And let the tyrants beware the shadows," responded Theodosia, still in High Nighmarian.

The Sarbian gave a single sharp nod. "The boss said he expected...visitors tonight," he said, switching back to Cyrican. "Go upstairs. Third door on the right. Talk to Saddiq - he will take you to Marzhod."

Theodosia nodded, crossed the common room, and climbed the stairs. Caina could not help but admire how perfectly Theodosia had disguised herself as a Sarbian nomad. Her every step extruded confidence and danger, and even the drunken sailors made sure to stay out of her way.

They climbed the stairs to the second-floor hallway. It stank of rot and mildew, and Caina heard muffled grunts and groans coming from behind some of the doors. They went through the third door on the right, and stepped into what looked like an armory. Swords hung on racks from the walls, along with crossbows, short bows, spears, and axes.

One of the largest men Caina had ever seen sat at a table in the center of the room, polishing an enormous two-handed scimitar. He was Sarbian, and wore chain mail beneath his tan robes. His dark eyes flicked to them, and a half-smile appeared on his bearded lips.

"Ah, you are here," he said in perfect High Nighmarian, rising with a bow. "You must be Marzhod's...guests. I am Saddiq, Marzhod's associate."

"And enforcer?" said Theodosia.

White teeth flashed in Saddiq's dark face. "You are perceptive as you are lovely, mistress Theodosia."

"Oh, you recognize me?" said Theodosia with a hint of irritation. "How did you see through my disguise?"

"I did not," said Saddiq. "But Marzhod was most wroth when he learned the high circlemasters had sent you. So either you or the young man at your side would have to be the redoubtable Theodosia."

Caina hid a smile at that.

Theodosia laughed. "I see what Marzhod lacks in charm he makes up for in an ability to find clever associates."

"This way," said Saddiq, rising from the table and returning the enormous scimitar to its sheath over his shoulder. "Though I should warn you that he is in a foul mood."

"When is he not?" said Theodosia.

A corner of Saddiq's mouth curled in a smile.

Saddiq opened a door on the far side of the armory. Beyond was a room that looked like a jumbled mixture of a scriptorium, an apothecary's shop, and a locksmith's workroom. Shelves held a variety of jars and vials, while ledgers stood heaped upon the tables. Caina saw a variety of weapons hidden around the room. Evidently Marzhod expected foes to fall upon him at any moment. Which, since he was a Ghost circlemaster, was entirely possible.

Marzhod glared at them from behind a table.

He was in his middle thirties, with thick black hair, icy blue eyes, and a gaunt, pale face. He would have been handsome, if not for the dark circles beneath his eyes and the constant sneer on his face.

"Saddiq," he said, his voice thick with a Szaldic accent, "why have you let these vermin into my study?"

"They knew the proper countersigns," said Saddiq, "and you wanted to be informed when the Ghosts from the capital arrived."

Marzhod got to his feet. He wore clothes in the style of a northern lord, boots and trousers and coat, but the clothes were dusty and worn. A sword hung at his belt, and Caina noted more knives inside his coat.

"I wrote to Halfdan," said Marzhod, "telling him that someone wanted Lord Corbould dead. I asked for capable men to ferret out the Kindred. Instead he sends me an opera singer and her pet thug."

Theodosia smirked, and Marzhod's venomous gaze turned towards Caina.

"No," said Marzhod. He leaned forward, cold eyes glinting. "A second woman? The Empire is at war, the Kindred are hunting the Emperor's strongest ally, and Halfdan sends me a pair of women?"

Caina looked at Theodosia, and Theodosia nodded.

"Perhaps," said Caina, "if you had been able to handle things, Halfdan would not have needed to send you a pair of women to solve your problems."

"Do not," said Marzhod, "think to trifle with me."

"Or what?" said Caina. "You turn your slaves on me?" The rage in her chest coiled tighter. She knew she ought to moderate her tongue, but she was too angry to care. "The Ghosts fight slavers, and how many slaves do you own? Dozens? How many of them do you rent out to the sailors?"

"Slaves are a way of life in Cyrica," said Marzhod. "You fools from Malarae like to think yourselves so righteous, so virtuous. So much better than us because you do not own slaves."

"You're Szaldic and a Ghost, not Cyrican," said Caina. "Do you yourself Cyrican now?"

"Neither," said Marzhod. "I was a slave, once. The raiders took me when I was five. But I escaped and made a fortune for myself. I own every tavern, every wine sink, every brothel, and every pawnshop in Cyrioch. And most of the warehouses and customs inspectors. Every smuggler on the Cyrican Sea does business with me, if they want to dock in Cyrioch. No one crosses Marzhod and lives. Lord Armizid and Lord Khosrau might rule Cyrica...but I rule Cyrioch's underworld."

"So now you enslave others," said Caina, "as you were enslaved."

"I was strong enough to survive it," said Marzhod. He smirked. "Are you? You annoy me, girl. And perhaps I'll have Saddiq give you to the slavers. I'll wager you're pretty enough under that disguise. You'll fetch a fair price on the block. Then you'll warm the bed of some minor satrap or emir until he tires of you. After that, you'll toil in that satrap's kitchen until you are a bent old crone. Maybe you'll end your days on the streets of Istarinmul, begging for a crust of bread. That's in my power to do to you, girl."

"No," said Caina, "it's not."

"And just why not?" said Marzhod. "Do you think the opera singer can stop me? My word is law among the Ghosts and the criminals of the Shining City. One word from me and you'll be naked on the auction block. Or perhaps I'll put you to work in one of my brothels."

"You won't," said Caina.

"Oh?" said Marzhod. "Why not?"

"Because," said Caina, "you should do a better job of hiding your weapons."

She reached for one of the tables. Saddiq drew his scimitar, but Caina was faster. She grabbed the small crossbow she saw beneath a ledger and leveled the weapon at Marzhod's face.

And just as she suspected, the weapon was loaded and ready to fire.

"That's a hand crossbow," said Marzhod, but he took a step back. "Just a dart. You'll hurt me, but you can't kill me."

"Unlikely," said Caina. "I saw those bottles on your shelf. This dart's poisoned, isn't it? A lethal poison? Or just a paralytic?" She gestured with the bow. "Want to find out?"

She heard a low rumbling sound, and realized that Saddiq was laughing.

"She's got you, Marzhod," said Saddiq.

"Oh, shut up," said Marzhod.

"Marzhod," said Theodosia, "enough. It has been amusing to watch you attempt to bully a woman fifteen years your junior only to end up with the business end of a crossbow in your face. But we have work to do. And you know what Halfdan will do if you don't cooperate."

A twitch of fear went over Marzhod's face.

"What will Halfdan do?" said Caina.

"Marzhod's owner," said Theodosia, "was an Anshani occultist of particular power and cruelty. Marzhod faked his death rather effectively, but if that occultist ever learns that he is still alive...well, Marzhod will regret it. For years, I expect."

Marzhod said nothing.

"So," said Theodosia. "We are going to play nicely. I trust that is understood?"

"Very well," said Marzhod, though a muscle near his eye trembled with rage.

Caina lowered the crossbow, but did not put it down. Marzhod sat behind his desk.

"So," he said. "Did you figure out what happened to Barius yet?"

"No," said Caina. "I went to his shop, but he had been turned to stone. A Kindred assassin waited for me in the street, but escaped before I could kill him. He tried to kill Lord Corbould at the Amphitheatre of Asurius. I stopped him and he got away from me...but when I found him something had turned him to stone."

"Pity," said Marzhod. "I was hoping you would figure it out and spare me the trouble. Because I don't have a single damned idea what happened to Barius."

"The local chapter of the Magisterium?" said Caina.

Marzhod shook his head. "I doubt it. The local magi are unpleasant, but they're...rigid. Conservative, let us say. They approve of slaves, unlike your honorable self, but they do not approve of the forbidden arcane sciences. Ranarius has executed at least five magi for delving into forbidden sciences, and those are only the ones I know about."

"What about the Kindred?" said Theodosia. "Have you had any luck determining who hired them to kill Lord Corbould?"

"Not yet," said Marzhod. "My spies have made some progress. We've been able to identify some members of the local Kindred family, and have kept watch over them."

"A dangerous business," said Caina.

"Of course it is dangerous," said Marzhod. "But if any of those Kindred move against Lord Corbould, we'll know. But we don't know who hired them, or where their local Haven is."

"No shame in that," said Theodosia. "The Ghosts have never been able to find the Kindred Haven in Malarae. I suppose the Cyrioch Haven would be hidden just as capably."

"There are indications, though," said Marzhod, "that the Kindred were also hired to kill Lord Khosrau."

"What?" said Caina. "But they've been trying to kill Lord Corbould. First in Malarae, and then again in Cyrioch. We thought Lord Khosrau had hired them to kill Corbould." She thought it through. "But that makes sense, doesn't it? If someone really wanted Cyrica to rebel against the Empire, they'd have the Kindred assassinate Lord Khosrau during Corbould's visit. Corbould would take the blame, and the Cyrican nobles would revolt or join Istarinmul."

"Then why hire them to kill Lord Corbould at the same time?" said Theodosia.

"Perhaps a foreign power hired the assassins," said Marzhod. "The Istarish would love to claim Cyrica for themselves, and the Shahenshah of Anshan ruled Cyrica for centuries."

"Could Lord Khosrau have hired them?" said Caina. "He might have paid the Kindred to kill Lord Corbould and fake an attempt on his life. Then he could claim to be the wronged party."

"Perhaps," said Marzhod. "But I doubt it. Khosrau, from what I have observed, is...settled, shall we say. He neither wishes to lead a revolt nor to become King of Cyrica. What he wants is for tomorrow to be much the same as yesterday."

"Armizid, then?" said Caina.

"Armizid is a brainless puppet," said Marzhod. "He is incapable of wiping his own arse without getting permission from his father." He snorted. "I asked Halfdan for capable assistance, and instead he sends an opera singer and a girl who asks moronic questions. Truly the safety of the Empire is in capable hands."

"Manners, Marzhod," said Theodosia. "I think it is safe to assume the Kindred assassins are connected to these peculiar statues. Barius investigated, got too close, and was turned to stone."

"That doesn't explain," said Caina, "the Kindred assassin outside the Amphitheatre."

Marzhod and Saddiq shared a look.

"I don't think," said Marzhod, "that the statues have anything to do with the Kindred."

"Why not?" said Caina.

"Because," said Marzhod, "this has been going on for a while."

"Wait." Caina blinked. "You mean this started happening before the war with Istarinmul and New Kyre began?"

Again Marzhod and Saddiq shared a look.

"Come with me," said Marzhod, getting to his feet.

He led them into the hallway, which somehow smelled worse than before.

"My spies have been investigating a peculiar man," said Marzhod. "Goes about cloaked and hooded an armed, spying on the magi and nobles, with black tattoos of peculiar design on his arms."

"Tattoos," said Caina. "I saw him at the Amphitheatre. He warned me about the Kindred assassin."

"He is unusual," said Marzhod, stopping before a door at the end of the hall, "and I make it a point to find the truth behind unusual things. So I sent my men to investigate further...and this was the result."

He unlocked the door and swung it open.

Six statues stood on the other side.

One was Barius, unchanged from when Caina had last seen him in the pawnshop. The others were men that Caina did not recognize. Some wore the ragged garb of slaves, others the rich robes of successful merchants. And like Barius and the assassin, all five statues were freakishly detailed, all displaying expressions of horror and fear. And like Barius, they were fashioned of the same white stone as the Defender and the Stone itself.

Caina stepped forward, put a hand on each of the statues.

And every last one tingled with the faint echo of sorcery.

"All of them," she said, voice quiet. "All turned to stone."

"Yes," said Marzhod. "When any of my men get too close to that tattooed man..." He gestured at the statues. "Well, you can see for yourself."

"I don't think this has anything to do with Lord Corbould or Lord Khosrau," said Caina. "Something else is going on."

"Perhaps we'll have a chance to find out what it is," said Theodosia, "at Lord Khosrau's gathering tomorrow night."

7

THE PALACE OF SPLENDORS

The next night a palanquin carried by eight burly slaves bore Caina and Theodosia to the Palace of Splendors.

And as much as Caina detested Cyrioch, she had to admit that the Palace of Splendors lived up to its name.

No known method could cut the peculiar white rock of the Stone, so over the centuries the various lords, emirs, and satraps had built a massive platform of granite blocks atop the crest of the Stone. Upon that platform stood the Palace of Splendors, once the seat of the Anshani satraps of Cyrica, and now the stronghold of the Lord Governors. The Palace was a rambling maze, built and rebuilt by generations of rulers. Graceful Anshani domes stood next to slender Istarish towers, and delicate fountains in Anshani style stood before halls built in the Nighmarian fashion. The result should have been an ugly mess of a building. Yet the architects had merged the styles, creating a palace unlike anything Caina had ever seen, a structure that combined both beauty and strength, grace and stability.

A beauty all the more striking contrasted against the squalor of Seatown's slums.

The palanquin stopped at one of the Palace's outer courtyards, and the slaves knelt to allow Theodosia and Caina to descend. Each of the slaves wore a tunic of gray silk and a silver collar. All of Lord Khosrau's slaves wore silken tunics and silver collars. The slaves themselves seemed almost proud to be owned by Lord Khosrau, and Caina had seen them sneering at slaves owned by lesser lords and common merchants.

She followed Theodosia from the palanquin. Theodosia wore a splendid gown of crimson and black, slightly tighter than Cyrican decorum allowed, though she wore a red scarf over her hair. A maid should not outshine her mistress, so Caina wore the same blue dress and headscarf from the Amphitheatre of Asurius.

An older slave hurried over and bowed. "Mistress Theodosia of the Grand Imperial Opera?"

"I am," said Theodosia.

"This way, mistress," said the slave. "Lord Khosrau's guests have gathered in the Gallery of the Well."

The Well...Barius's burned notes had mentioned something called the Well. Had he meant this Gallery of the Well? Of course, his notes had also mentioned the Defender, but Caina had found nothing suspicious about the Defender or the nearby Inn.

The slave led them through the Palace's corridors, over floors adorned with dazzling mosaics and past frescoes of stunning beauty. At last they came to a vast courtyard at the very heart of the Palace. Slabs of gleaming, polished marble paved the floor, dotted here and there with ornamental gardens. Pillars of gold-flecked marble encircled the courtyard, supporting pointed Istarish arches. Above the arches rose covered balconies, offering the Lord Governor's guests a place to converse privately.

And, Caina noted, the perfect vantage point for an assassin with a bow.

"The Gallery of the Well, mistress," said the slave with a bow. "Lord Khosrau and Lord Armizid wait their guests near the Well."

"Thank you," said Theodosia.

The slave seemed surprised. Caina supposed he was rarely thanked for anything.

Theodosia crossed the Gallery, her skirts whispering against the marble floor. Cyrican nobles stood here and there in their jeweled robes, speaking with groups of magi and wealthy merchants. Musicians played among the pillars, while slaves hurried back and forth carrying trays of wine and delicacies.

At the center of the Gallery stretched a dark hole perhaps thirty feet across. A low ring of polished marble encircled it, but Caina noticed the guests stayed well away from it.

The Well.

Lord Khosrau and Lord Armizid stood near the Well, speaking with Lord Corbould. Armizid and Khosrau both wore robes of brilliant white, jewels glittering in their turbans. Corbould wore his black armor, stark against the finery of the Cyrican nobles. At least the armor would make it that much harder for an assassin to put an arrow in his back.

"Theodosia, my dear," said Khosrau, his rumbling voice cutting through the surrounding conversations. "I see you received my invitation. Your girl did well to deliver it."

"Oh, I would be simply lost without Marina," said Theodosia, gripping her skirts and doing a deep curtsy before Khosrau.

"It is a worthy servant," said Khosrau, "who cares for her mistress with diligent loyalty."

Caina did a curtsy as well.

"Your performance was magnificent," said Khosrau. "I have heard the story of Lord Corbould's noble ancestor Tertius many times, but your voice truly brought the tale to life."

"My lord is gracious," said Theodosia. "I am fortunate to have an audience of such refined taste. Why, if you can believe it, there were times when I have been jeered in Malarae."

"An outrage!" said Khosrau. "Why, were such an affront to take place in Cyrioch, I would order the villains crucified on the spot, and their skulls hung over the Amphitheatre's gates as a warning to others."

Theodosia laughed, her hand at her throat. "That is the kindest thing anyone has ever said to me! Though I really wish you wouldn't, if you will forgive the impertinence of a poor opera singer. It is dreadfully hard to remember the lyrics through the stink of a rotting corpse."

"Well," said Khosrau, "perhaps I'll simply have them flogged, then. Cheaper than crucifixion, anyway." He turned to Lord Corbould. "Corbould, I must thank you again for bringing the Grand Imperial Opera to Cyrioch. The performance was sublime."

Corbould nodded. "It is merely a token of the esteem in which both I and the Emperor hold your friendship, my lord Khosrau."

"My lords, this is unseemly," said Armizid, looking at Theodosia with tight-lipped disapproval. "For two high lords of the Empire to converse with an...an entertainer in public! And to discuss matters of state in front of her and her drudge! Cyrica is strong, and our friendship is greatly desirable...surely our friendship merits more than an opera company!"

Khosrau snorted. "Cyrica is strong...but not strong enough to stand on its own. If we were not part of the Empire, Anshan would conquer us in a matter of days. Or the Istarish would seize our lands." He snorted. "Or even if the Empire, Anshan, and Istarinmul all chose to ignore us, the Sarbian desert men would burn our plantations and seize our slaves for themselves. No, if Cyrica is to survive...we must have friends. Strong friends."

"Friends," said Corbould, "such as the Emperor of Nighmar and his Legions."

"Perhaps," said Khosrau. He waved his hand at the assembled guests, his bearded face growing melancholy. "Tell me, Corbould. Do they ever reflect upon how fragile it all is? So many proud lords and wealthy merchants. Yet power can crumble and riches fade, sometimes in a heartbeat."

"Aye," said Corbould. "I know it well, Khosrau. I was at Marsis when the Istarish betrayed the Empire. One moment I was greeting the Lord Ambassador of Istarinmul. The next I was fighting for my life in the alleys of Marsis."

Caina shivered, fighting to keep her expression calm. The memories of the fighting in Marsis flashed through her mind. She remembered the dread, the fear that she had lost Nicolai to the Istarish slavers. That she would have to tell Ark and Tanya that she had lost their son. She had saved Nicolai...but that dread had never left her.

"Yes," murmured Khosrau. "You do understand. Perhaps that is the curse of mortal men, my friend. Everything good we try to do turns to evil in the end, and no matter how we strive for peace, war comes for us." He grunted and waved his cane. "This war with the Istarish and the Kyracians? What utter folly! The Empire cannot overthrow the Kyracian fleets to conquer New Kyre or breach the walls of Istarinmul. But likewise the Kyracians and the Istarish cannot conquer the Empire. Why fight, then? All those lives lost for nothing. It would have been better for those men to stay home and raise crops and children."

Caina wondered how Khosrau would react if she told him the truth, that the Moroaica had engineered the war to free her disciple Scorikhon from his tomb below Marsis's Citadel.

"War provides the opportunity for glory," said Armizid, "and new wealth and lands."

"So many have thought," said Khosrau, "and their bones molder upon the battlefields."

"Like Rezir Shahan," said Corbould. "He made war upon our Emperor, and look at his fate."

Armizid bristled. "Is that a threat, Maraeus?"

Khosrau snorted. "Don't be absurd, boy. Lord Corbould merely states a fact. Rezir Shahan made war upon the Empire, and now he is dead. Incidentally, how did he die?"

Corbould shrugged. "I don't really know. If you would believe the commoners, they say a myth called the Balarigar slew him."

"The Balarigar?" said Khosrau.

"A legend of the Szaldic peasants, I understand," said Corbould. "A slayer of sorcerers and a liberator of slaves. The commoners claim the Balarigar appeared and slew Rezir Shahan. Myself, I think Shahan's troops mutinied and killed him. I saw Shahan's head upon a javelin with my own eyes."

Caina kept her mouth from twitching. How would these proud lords react if they knew the Balarigar was actually the maid standing next to the opera singer? She was almost tempted to say it, just to see the expression on Armizid's face.

But some things were best kept secret.

"Enough of this talk of war and blood," said Khosrau. "This is a ball, not a council of war. Lord Corbould has honored us with the Grand Imperial Opera, and we should make the most of the opportunity." His dark eyes shifted to Theodosia. "My dear, would you grace us with a song?"

"It would be my honor, my lord," said Theodosia. She glanced at Caina. "Marina, you have liberty until I have finished performing for his lordship."

That meant she wanted Caina to look around for anything interesting.

"Of course, mistress," said Caina, doing a curtsy.

Theodosia walked off with the high nobles, leaving Caina alone. She wandered through the Gallery, making sure not to make eye contact with any of the lords or merchants. They paid no attention to her whatsoever. The snatches of conversation she overheard all dealt with the war and its impact on merchant shipping.

Her eyes swept the pillared colonnades and the elevated balconies. Both Corbould's Imperial Guards and Armizid's militiamen stood at regular intervals, keeping watch for assassins. That was good. But would they watch for hidden archers, or for assassins disguised as slaves? The Cyricans nobles treated their slaves like animals, and would not notice one with a weapon until...

Caina flinched.

She felt a faint, crawling tingle

Sorcery.

She turned in alarm, and found herself standing at the edge of the Well.

The ring of polished marble encircling it came to Caina's knee. She looked over the edge, and saw that the Well's polished white sides went down and down until they vanished into blackness. How far down did it go? The Stone was only a few hundred feet tall, yet the Well seemed to descend for a thousand feet. For that matter, who had dug it? No one knew a way to cut the Stone's peculiar white rock.

For a dreadful instant, it reminded Caina of the pit below Black Angel Tower, the prison that held the bound demons. She wondered if something just as terrible lurked at the bottom of the Well...

"I see," said a cold voice, "that you have discovered the Well."

Caina turned.

Ranarius stood a few feet away, staring at her. Unlike the nobles, the master magus's black robe and gray hair gave him a forbidding, ascetic air. His blind slave girl stood behind him, head bowed, eyes concealed behind the black blindfold. Her jade collar glittered in the light, as did the jade bracelet on Ranarius's left wrist.

"Sir?" said Caina, her mind racing. Did Ranarius know she was a Ghost? Or did he suspect that the Ghosts had spies among the opera company?

"It is one of the great mysteries of Cyrioch," said Ranarius.

"It doesn't look very mysterious, sir," said Caina.

A thin smile came over his gaunt face. "I suppose not. But it is a great mystery nonetheless. No one knows who dug it or for what purpose. And it has always been here, at the very crest of the Stone. It was here before the first stone of the Palace of Splendors was laid, before mortal men even came to what is now Cyrica."

Despite herself, Caina was curious. "What lies at the bottom?"

"No one knows," said Ranarius. "If you drop a stone into the Well, you will not hear it hit the bottom. And throughout Cyrioch's history, curious satraps and Lord Governors have hired adventurous men to explore the Well. None have ever returned. One managed to use a thousand feet of rope before his line snapped. Which is remarkable, considering the Stone stands five hundred feet tall at its highest point."

"No one knows what is at the bottom?" said Caina, keeping her eyes wide and her tone breathless. Perhaps Ranarius did not think she was a Ghost, and was only trying to overawe an ignorant servant girl to feed his vanity.

"No one living, certainly," said Ranarius. "In ancient times, the

Anshani satraps threw condemned prisoners into the Well. But some of those satraps died under mysterious circumstances, and now it is considered ill luck to throw anything into the Well, let alone a living man."

"That is a very strange tale, sir," said Caina. "It is kind of you to share it with a poor servant girl."

Again that thin smile flickered over Ranarius's lips. "It is the duty of the magi to educate the people of the Empire about sorcery. And I am convinced that sorcery was used to create the Well. One day I shall discover how."

"Well," said Caina, "so long as you don't climb down on a rope."

She glanced at Well, and Ranarius barked a short laugh. And as he did, Caina felt his eyes climb over her body, like a wolf examining a sheep.

Ah. So that was why he was talking to her. It seemed peculiar for a master magus to seduce a servant girl at the Lord Governor's ball, but sometimes when a powerful man decided upon a particular woman, nothing could talk him out of it.

"Come with me," said Ranarius, "and I shall be happy to tell you more of the Well."

"I am sorry, sir," said Caina, and as she did, Theodosia's song rolled over the Gallery of the Well. "But my mistress sings for Lord Khosrau, and I must be ready to attend her once she is finished."

"Your devotion does you credit," said Ranarius, and she saw the fingers of his right hand move in a brief gesture. The tingling sensation of a spell washed over her. Caina recognized the spell - it was mind sorcery, meant to make her more suggestible. "But Nicasia can look after your mistress. Can't you, Nicasia?"

"Yes, master," said the slave girl, not lifting her face. Her voice was soft and high, and reminded Caina of an injured bird's call.

"Come with me," said Ranarius, "and we shall discuss all manner of things."

The tingling of his spell intensified, and Caina felt the sudden impulse to go with him. But Kalastus had tried to cast the same spell upon her, and Caina knew how to resist it. She filled her mind with rage, with her hatred of the magi, and the impulse to please Ranarius vanished.

"I am sorry, sir," said Caina, keeping her voice calm. She did a quick curtsy. "But I must attend my mistress at once..."

"I think," said Ranarius, voice low and urgent, "that you would really rather come with me."

Caina tried to think of an excuse. "I..."

"Seducing the serving girls again, preceptor?"

Ranarius scowled.

Another master magus approached them. He was Cyrican, with dusky skin and a close-cropped black beard. He regarded Ranarius with a mixture of amusement and contempt, and paid no attention to Caina whatsoever.

"Mhadun," said Ranarius. "This is not a good time."

"Pity," said Mhadun, "because we have business to discuss. The chapter requires a firm hand, and if you are too busy with your little...amusements," he cast a disdainful glance at both Caina and Nicasia, "then perhaps the First Magus could be persuaded to appoint another as the preceptor of the Cyrioch chapter."

Ranarius's mouth twisted. "Like you, Mhadun?"

Mhadun smirked. "I would never presume to be so ambitious, preceptor."

"Excuse me, sirs," said Caina with a quick curtsy. "I must return to my duties."

She walked away, but not before she had the satisfaction of seeing the irritation on Ranarius's gaunt face.

She wondered why Mhadun had been so insolent. The Magisterium had a rigid hierarchy, and the preceptors and the high magi did not tolerate disobedience. Perhaps Mhadun had some hold over Ranarius.

Caina walked to the far end of the Gallery, where a crowd of nobles and merchants gathered around Theodosia. The acoustics in the Gallery were terrible, with far too many echoes, but Theodosia used them to good effect. She had the full attention of Lord Khosrau, and the others nobles followed suit. It was, Caina mused, the perfect time for someone to sneak unnoticed into the Gallery.

She looked at the entrances and saw no one but the militiamen and the Imperial Guards standing watch. She looked at the balconies, saw the slaves hurrying about their...

Wait.

Caina made herself look down.

In the corner of a balcony, besides a pillar, stood the cloaked man who had warned her about the Kindred at the Amphitheatre.

The cloaked man who had been waiting outside of Barius's shop.

The cloaked man who could have arranged the entire incident with the assassin at the Amphitheatre in order to kill Lord Corbould later.

She shot a quick glance over the Gallery. Theodosia held the attention of most of the guests with her song. Ranarius and Mhadun had retreated into the shadow of the pillars, obviously arguing.

No one was paying any attention to her.

Caina turned and made her way to the stairs.

8

A MASK OF SCARS

Caina slipped into the upper balcony, Theodosia's song echoing in her ears.

The enclosed balcony stood a hundred feet over the Gallery of the Well, the stone railing stretching between pillars of pale granite. Statues of long-dead Lord Governors stood in deep niches, providing dozens of places for an assassin to hide.

Caina reached into her left boot and drew out a dagger. She crept along, scanning every shadow for the cloaked man, just as she had when hunting that Kindred assassin through the Praetorian Basilica in Malarae. If the cloaked man had come to kill Lord Corbould from the balcony, he would need to put an arrow through the lord's neck. Corbould stood facing Theodosia as she sang, and the assassin would need to get close enough to shoot over the other nobles and merchants.

Then Caina spotted the cloaked man.

He knelt by the stone railing. His cloak hung open, and Caina saw that he wore chain mail, a sword and a quiver of arrows at his belt, his forearms marked by the black lines of his strange tattoo.

A short bow waited in his hand.

Caina sprang forward, dagger drawn back to strike.

But the cloaked man spun, dropped his bow, and yanked his sword from its scabbard. Caina's blade clanged off the sword and she stumbled. The cloaked swung the flat of his blade for her face, and she jumped back, the steel whipping past her.

For a moment they stared at each other. The cloaked man's hood had fallen back, revealing a lean face with pale green eyes and close-cropped blond hair. He looked about thirty, and he did not blink as he stared at Caina.

"Do you usually," said the cloaked man in High Nighmarian, "stab your foes in the back?"

"It's easier than a fair fight," said Caina. From the way he held that sword, he knew how to use it, and a dagger against a sword was not a winning strategy. If she drew back far enough, she might be able to use a throwing knife, but he would expect that.

"Very sensible," said the cloaked man. "Though why did you want to stab me in the back?"

"That was clever," said Caina. "Warning me about the Kindred with the blowgun? Was he a rival of yours, perhaps? I'm surprised you didn't take your shot at Lord Corbould then."

The cloaked man made an irritated noise. "I have my own business. I care nothing for Corbould Maraeus."

"Your own business," said Caina, "that requires you to skulk about balconies with a bow?"

"Yes," said the cloaked man.

"Mind telling me what that business is?" said Caina.

"It is," said the cloaked man, "no concern of yours."

"Oh?" said Caina. "You were skulking outside of Barius's pawnshop after something turned him to stone. That is no business of the Ghosts? Or that assassin you pointed out to me? Something turned him to stone, as well."

A hint of surprise flickered over the cloaked man's face. He hadn't known about the assassin. Or he was a very good actor.

"You claim to be a former Kindred assassin," said Caina, "yet you keep shadowing Lord Corbould, and anyone who comes too close to you turns to stone. Any particular reason why you aren't a concern of the Ghosts?"

The cloaked man's lip twitched. "When you put it like that, no. But I assure you that Lord Corbould is in no danger from me. "

"Why should I believe you?" said Caina. "A half-dozen Ghosts have been turned to stone around you."

The cloaked man's face tightened. "I warned those fools to leave me alone and stay out of my business. They failed to heed me and suffered the consequences." His eyes drilled into her. “I admit you would make a far lovelier statue than that fat fool Barius. But you will suffer his fate if you keep interfering in my business."

"So you turned them to stone, then?" said Caina.

"I did nothing of the sort," said the cloaked man.

"I don't believe you," said Caina. "There's more going on here than you're telling me. Assassins do not simply leave the Kindred. And you're going to tell me what I want to know."

He smirked. "You can't force me, Ghost."

"Maybe not," said Caina. "But I just have to scream, don't I? All those nobles and fat merchants will see a serving girl terrorized by an armed man. An armed man with a bow, incidentally. Think you can outrun every last Imperial Guard and militiaman in the Palace of Splendors?"

"It would be an amusing challenge," said the cloaked man, but she saw the wariness in his eyes. "Perhaps I can prove my good faith?"

"How?" said Caina.

The cloaked man slid his sword into its scabbard, but Caina kept her dagger in hand.

"There are Kindred assassins here, right now," said the cloaked man, "and I will show them to you."

"How do you know?" said Caina.

"You have a knack for spotting my former brothers," said the cloaked man, "but I was Kindred. I trained with them for years, and I know them when I see them. Come closer and look."

Caina hesitated, but made sure to keep the dagger between her and the cloaked man. He seemed amused by the precaution, but pointed over the railing.

"Look," he said. "On the far side of the Well."

On the far colonnade, beneath the pillars, she spotted the master magus Mhadun. He spoke with a pair of young men in gray slave tunics. Both had the diffident postures of slaves, but Caina saw the concealed tension in their limbs. Like lions ready to spring upon a wounded animal.

"Kindred assassins," said Caina, "both of them."

"Very good," said the cloaked man. "The Cyrican lords are idiots. They see the slaves as cattle, not men. And no one expects a domestic animal to carry a dagger."

Caina's opinion of the cloaked man went up a notch.

"What about Mhadun?" said Caina. "Is he Kindred?"

"Yes," said the cloaked man. "The Kindred prefer to buy their assassins as children and raise them to know nothing but death and killing." He sneered. "But it is difficult to train capable sorcerers that way. So the Kindred recruit trained brothers of the Magisterium or Anshani occultists when they need sorcerers. "

"Lovely," said Caina. Two Kindred assassins and a Kindred sorcerer? Caina didn't know what they had in mind, but Lord Corbould was in deadly danger.

"Indeed," said the cloaked man. "I wonder how much Lord Khosrau paid for Lord Corbould's death. Sorcerers do not come cheaply."

Caina gave him a hard look. "So Lord Khosrau hired the Kindred? You know this for certain?"

Theodosia finished her song and a round of applause rose from the nobles and merchants. Even Mhadun paused from his discussion with the assassins to clap a few times.

The cloaked man shrugged. "No. But it makes sense. I cannot think of who else might have hired the Kindred." He pointed again. "But I trust I have made my point? I have revealed three Kindred assassins to you. Would I do that if I intended to kill Corbould Maraeus myself?"

"No," said Caina. "But there is a way you can prove yourself to me beyond a doubt."

The cloaked man grimaced. "What further proof do you require? Shall I fall to my knees and swear upon every god that ever was?"

"That will do me little good," said Caina. "Help me stop the Kindred."

Theodosia began another song, and Caina shot a glance over the railing. Mhadun and the disguised assassins were still talking. How much longer before they struck?

"That would put my business at risk," said the cloaked man.

"And if the Kindred kill Corbould?" said Caina. "If Cyrica revolts against the Empire? Will that not put your business at risk?"

"Damn it," said the cloaked man. He looked away for a moment, his eyes darting back and forth in calculation. "You drive a hard bargain. Very well. If I assist you against the Kindred, you will leave me in peace?"

"I will," said Caina. "Unless you have been lying to me, or try to kill Lord Corbould or Lord Khosrau yourself."

"I haven't told you the whole truth," said the cloaked man, "but I have not lied to you. Let us get this over with." He turned towards the stairs, raising his hood once more.

"Wait," said Caina. "We should circle the balcony and take the stairs on the far side of the Gallery. It will look suspicious if we cross the Gallery together."

"A sound plan," said the cloaked man. Without another word he started down the balcony, Caina following.

She kept a wary eye on him.

If he helped her stop the Kindred, she would know that he had told the truth. And perhaps she could coax more information out of him, something to help her discover what had happened to Barius and the other Ghosts...

The cloaked man stopped, hand falling to his sword hilt.

"What is it?" said Caina, lifting her dagger.

"Someone's watching us," said the cloaked man.

Caina took a quick look around. To her right, she saw the railing, and the gathered nobles listening to Theodosia's song. To her left, a series of darkened doorways leading into the Palace of Splendors. No one in the Gallery had noticed them, and Caina saw no one lurking in the darkened doorways.

She braced herself. Was this a trick? Some ruse the cloaked man would use to kill her and make his escape?

Then she heard a footstep in one of the darkened doorways.

"I never expected to find you here, Corvalis Aberon."

The voice was a harsh rasp, and it made the hair on the back of Caina's neck stand up.

The cloaked man yanked his sword from its scabbard and drew a dagger in his left hand.

Evidently he recognized the voice, too.

A short man in a hooded cloak stepped from a doorway. He wore studded leather armor beneath the cloak, and a sword and dagger on his belt. A pair of baldrics crossed over his chest, holding an array of daggers and throwing knives. Inside the hood Caina saw a hairless head covered in ragged scars, as if his face had been stitched together from scraps of old leather. His left eye was brilliant green, but his right was harsh orange, like a pit of molten sulfur.

Sicarion, Jadriga's pet assassin.

"You," said the cloaked man, voice thick with loathing.

"Corvalis, Corvalis," said Sicarion, his scarred lips stretching in a smile. "What a delightful surprise this is. I haven't seen you since that business in Artifel."

"And I haven't see you," said Caina, "since I took off your right hand in Scorikhon's tomb."

Corvalis looked at her and blinked.

"You found a new one, I see," said Caina.

Sicarion flexed the fingers of his right hand. "And a strong grip it has, mistress."

"Mistress?" said Corvalis, looking at her in sudden alarm. "You're the Moroaica? What sort of game is this?"

"I'm not the Moroaica," said Caina. "He thinks that I am, though."

"I was not expecting to see you here, mistress," said Sicarion. "But perhaps I should have."

"What are you doing here?" said Corvalis.

"Oh, performing a little errand for my mistress," said Sicarion. "My mistress collects enemies the way lesser women collect jewelry, and sometimes she wishes those enemies to meet their just fate."

"So that's it?" said Corvalis. "You're here to kill me, then?"

Sicarion laughed. "Such arrogance! You are hardly worth my mistress's attention. No, I am here on different business. But only a fool passes up an opportunity, and I have wanted to settle with you since Artifel."

"And me?" said Caina. "Your mistress told you to keep me alive."

Sicarion's eyes narrowed. "You heard that, hmm? I thought so. Well, the mistress wants you kept alive...but if you happen to perish in the fighting, that will hardly inconvenience her for long."

"Such confidence," said Corvalis, pointing his sword. "There are two of us and one of you."

Sicarion laughed. "You think so? But I have the kind of face that makes it easy to win friends!"

He snapped his figures and men erupted from the darkened doorway. Four of them, armored in chain mail, heavy shields on their left arms and broadswords in their fists. Mercenaries, veterans from the look of them.

"Kill them!" said Sicarion. "Kill them both!"

The mercenaries charged, and Caina shot a look to the side. There were dozens of Imperial Guards and militiamen in the Gallery. But Theodosia's voice rang in thunderous song, and the other musicians accompanied her. The music would be enough to drown out the sounds of fighting.

Then the mercenaries charged.

A hulking man in chain mail came at her, and Caina backed away. His broadsword blurred past her face, and Caina sidestepped, seized the edge of his shield, and swung herself past him. He tried to line up for another attack, but Caina ripped her dagger through his neck. The mercenary stumbled in pain, and Caina hammered the heel of her boot into the back of his knee. The man collapsed, sword spinning away from his grasp.

The other three men attacked Corvalis.

He responded with the grace and skill of a Kindred assassin, his dagger and sword a blur of gleaming steel. The mercenaries were good, but Corvalis was better. But he couldn't fend off three determined attackers forever, and when Sicarion entered the fray...

Sicarion lifted his hands, muttering, and Caina felt the crawling tingle of sorcery. Once Sicarion's spell hit Corvalis, the mercenaries would overwhelm him. And then Sicarion and his mercenaries would kill Caina.

She snatched a throwing knife from her sleeve and flung it, her entire body snapping like a bowstring. Sicarion twisted to the side with serpentine grace, his hand still raised, but Caina's knife dug a bloody furrow along his face. She drew another knife as Sicarion pointed at her, his voice rising to a shout.

A heartbeat later a fist of invisible force caught Caina on the side, spun her around, and knocked her to the floor. Every bone in her body ached from the impact, but her hand still clenched the throwing knife, and she threw it with all the strength she could muster.

The blade buried itself in the nearest mercenary's calf. The man stumbled with a curse, and Corvalis's dagger opened his throat. The mercenary collapsed, and now Corvalis faced two men, not three, and step by step he drove them back.

Sicarion began another spell, and Caina scrambled to her feet, yanking her second dagger from her left boot. She raced at Sicarion and the scarred man stepped back with a curse, abandoning his spell. He drew his sword and attacked, and Caina caught the descending blade in the cross of her daggers. Her boot flew out and caught Sicarion in the knee, and he jumped back. Caina raked her daggers at him, her left blade bouncing off the studs of his armor, but her right opened a bloody line across his arm. Sicarion lunged at her and Caina barely dodged his blade.

Behind her Corvalis dueled with the mercenaries, while Theodosia's song rang from the Gallery. She supposed that if any of the nobles happened to look up, they would think that the fight was part of the show.

"I thought," said Caina, "the Moroaica told you not to kill me."

Sicarion grinned. "My mistress is locked inside of your head. Given enough time, she will take control of you. But I do not want to wait. And if you happen to die upon my blade...well, then the mistress will take a new vessel, and we can undertake the great work."

He slashed at her, his swing flowing into a vicious thrust. Caina beat aside his blows with her daggers. She stepped into his guard and landed several hits, but Sicarion simply ignored the cuts and kept coming.

And Caina realized that she could not defeat him. He was centuries old, and had spent all that time honing his skills with a blade. Worse, he simply shrugged off wounds that would have disabled or slowed another man. Sooner or later he would wear her down and land a killing blow.

Unless Caina did something clever first.

Sicarion attacked with fury, and Caina backed away, using her daggers to block any thrust that got too close. She passed Corvalis and the surviving two mercenaries, their blades clanging and shuddering. Sicarion pursued, his mismatched eyes fixed on her.

Then Caina reversed direction and drove her dagger into the armpit of the nearest mercenary. The man fell with a groan of pain, and Corvalis killed him with a quick thrust. The surviving mercenary faced Caina, perceiving the new threat, but that gave Corvalis an opening.

The mercenary fell dead beside his fellow, and Caina and Corvalis faced Sicarion.

"You're going to need," said Corvalis, "to find some more friends."

Sicarion sneered. "Hirelings are easily replaceable. And I'm going to enjoy killing you, Corvalis Aberon."

Caina suddenly remembered where she had heard that name before.

Decius Aberon was the ruthless First Magus of the Magisterium, a man who desired to become Emperor, like the tyrannical magus-emperors of old. Was Corvalis a relative? Or was his "business" a mission from the First Magus himself?

She could sort it out after they killed Sicarion.

"Ghost," said Corvalis, not taking his eyes from Sicarion. "Go."

"What?" said Caina.

"Those Kindred," said Corvalis. "They're probably going to kill Corbould Maraeus before too much longer. I'll finish this wretch. Go save your Empire."

Caina hesitated. Sicarion was dangerous, resilient, and resourceful. As good as Corvalis was with his sword, she didn't think he could take the scarred assassin in a straight fight.

But Sicarion wasn't trying to kill Lord Corbould.

And Caina had come to Cyrioch to keep Corbould Maraeus alive and prevent the Empire from sliding into civil war.

"I will return," said Caina, and she ran along the balcony.

She heard the clang of steel as Corvalis and Sicarion fought, but Theodosia's song soon swallowed the sound of the battle.

9

A CLUMSY MAID

Caina ran down the stairs to the Gallery, breathing hard. Her hair was in disarray, and spots of blood marked the sleeves of her dress. It was obvious she had been in a fight, but she doubted the nobles would notice. The Kindred assassins, though, would be far more observant.

But they were gone.

She saw no trace of Mhadun or the disguised assassins. They must have moved off during her fight with Sicarion. She walked into the Gallery, trying to appear calm, her eyes sweeping the crowds. Most of the nobles, merchants, and magi gathered at the far end of the Gallery, listening to Theodosia and the musicians as they launched into another song. Here and there a few nobles or merchants stood beneath the colonnades, no doubt discussing private business, but the assassins had vanished...

Wait.

Caina spotted Mhadun. The master magus stood in the shadow of an arch, speaking to Ranarius. They were too far away to overhear, but the preceptor looked annoyed. Mhadun scowled and pointed, and it almost looked as if he was scolding the older man. It seemed unlikely that a preceptor of the Magisterium would permit such insolence. But if Mhadun was Kindred, he had power and influence that Ranarius did not possess.

But there was no trace of the two slave-disguised assassins.

Caina turned in a quick circle, scanning the balconies. She no one up there, not even Sicarion and Corvalis. Perhaps they had killed each other, or perhaps one of them had triumphed and hidden the corpse of the vanquished.

She looked at the crowd of nobles around Theodosia and the musicians, trying to think as the assassin would. It would take an archer of unusual skill to shoot into the gaps of Lord Corbould's black armor. So the murder would have to take place up close. That meant a dagger or a sword. But the Kindred were not suicidal, and any man bold enough to put a dagger into Lord Corbould would die heartbeats later.

Poison, then.

The Kindred had tried a blowgun at the Amphitheatre of Asurius. Might they try a poisoned dart, or perhaps a single scratch from a poisoned knife? If one of the assassins bumped into Corbould and jabbed him with a needle, that would do the trick.

Caina turned towards the nobles, planning to keep watch over Corbould.

"I can smell the blood."

Caina froze.

Nicasia stood behind her, head bowed, pale hair brushing over the gray silk of her slave's tunic.

"I'm sorry?" said Caina.

"The blood," said Nicasia, her voice soft and unsteady. "I smell it on you. You killed someone, just now."

"I don't know what you're talking about," said Caina.

"Yes, you do," said the slave girl. She lifted her blindfolded eyes, as if she could see Caina through the black cloth. "You killed someone just a few moments ago. I can...hear it? The echoes of it?" She titled her head to the side, as if listening to a voice only she could hear. "Yes. Like a stone dropped into a placid pond. You killed someone and I heard the ripples." She sighed. "Though the pond is rarely still."

Caina wondered if Nicasia was mad. Sometimes the mind-controlling sorcery of the magi induced insanity in its victims, and if Ranarius had used her to test his spells...

"I didn't kill anyone," said Caina.

"You are a very good liar," said Nicasia, "but that doesn't matter when you can hear the ripples in the pond."

"What do you want?" said Caina.

"What...do I want?" said Nicasia, puzzled. As if no one had ever asked her that question before.

"Yes," said Caina. "What do you want? Why are you talking to me?"

She shot another look at the crowd. Lord Corbould stood with Lord Khosrau, and Caina saw no trace of the Kindred near them. But that would not last. Sooner or later the Kindred would strike, and Caina could not waste time trading words with a mad slave girl.

Though an unusually perceptive slave girl.

An idea came to Caina.

"Wait," said Caina. "Is someone going to try to kill Lord Corbould?"

Nicasia's blindfolded face turned towards the crowd.

"Yes," said Nicasia.

"Tell me how," said Caina. "Quickly." She wondered if Nicasia was in fact a spy for the Kindred. If the Kindred had bought the services of Mhadun, why not one of the preceptor's personal slaves?

"Lord Corbould Maraeus is going to die," said Nicasia, her voice sing-song.

"Yes, I know," said Caina, looking at the nobles again. "Can you tell me how?"

"Everyone will die," said Nicasia. "Every noble, every slave, every merchant, every commoner. Right here, in this Gallery, everyone shall die."

"Everyone dies," said Caina, "but I would prefer more concrete details on how and when."

"The sleeper will awaken," said Nicasia. "The images wrought in stone are just harbingers. When the sleeper awakens, Cyrioch will die."

"I am sorry," said Caina, "but I cannot help you." She stepped back, intending to watch Lord Corbould.

"Glass," said Nicasia.

Caina stopped. "What?"

"Glass," said Nicasia. "You asked how Lord Corbould will die, and I can feel his death approaching. Glass will slay him, and glass holds his death."

"Glass?" said Caina. "What does..."

"Nicasia!"

Ranarius stormed across the Gallery, face twisted in fury.

"Master," said Nicasia, "I..."

Ranarius backhanded her, and Nicasia fell to the ground without a sound.

"How dare you speak to someone without my permission!" said Ranarius. He kicked her in the side. "Get up. Get up!"

"Stop that!" said Caina, anger in her voice.

Ranarius's furious eyes turned to her. "You dare to speak me to in that tone? I am a preceptor of the Imperial Magisterium! Keep a civil tongue your head, girl, or I will show you what torments sorcery can visit upon flesh!"

"I'm sure," said Caina. Her mind screamed for her to back down before Ranarius realized she was a Ghost, but she was too angry to care. "Yes, I'm sure that Lord Khosrau will very pleased that you killed the servant girl of his favorite opera singer for the impertinence of speaking to your slave."

Ranarius trembled with anger...but his eyes darted to Lord Khosrau nonetheless. Despite his jovial exterior, Caina suspected that Khosrau Asurius was not a man to cross.

"Come, Nicasia," said Ranarius. "I have business at the chapter-house." He waved a finger in Caina's face. "And consider yourself lucky, foolish girl. If you show me such cheek again, I will punish you and Lord Khosrau can be damned."

He stalked away without another word. Nicasia got to her feet, shook her head, and turned her face towards Caina.

"Glass," she said, and followed her master.

Theodosia finished her song, and vigorous applause rose from the nobles. Slaves hurried forward from the colonnades, bearing silver trays of delicacies. Caina saw stuffed dates, mushrooms fried in oil and wrapped in bacon, cheese cooked in delicate oils, and flutes of red wine.

Glasses of wine.

"Glass," whispered Caina.

The nobles had not brought their food-tasters.

The Kindred were going to poison Corbould with the wine.

She spotted one of the assassins. The Kindred wore the gray of a slave, black eyes downcast, just as a slave's should be. In his arms he carried a tray of wine glasses, and he was heading for Lord Corbould.

Caina hurried forward, her skirts gathered in her hands. She couldn't kill the Kindred in front of all these people. Nor could she stop Corbould from drinking the wine. At best, he would think her mad, and at worst, he would forbid Theodosia from performing for Lord Khosrau again.

She gripped her skirts tighter, wishing to be rid of the damned things so she could run faster.

Then the answer occurred to her.

The assassin bowed before Khosrau and Corbould, lifting the tray of wine.

"Ah," said Khosrau. "Splendid. Our refreshments are here. Some wine, my lord Corbould?"

Corbould grinned. "Caerish or Disali?"

Khosrau snorted. "Caerish, of course. I cannot abide Disali wine. Far too bitter."

"A man after my own heart," said Corbould.

The assassin lifted the tray, and Corbould reached for a glass.

Caina brought the toe of her boot down onto the hem of her skirt and stepped forward.

And as she expected, she lost her balance toppled into the assassin.

The assassin fell with a startled yelp and Caina landed atop him.

Glasses of wine shattered around them, red liquid pooling on the white marble. The assassin hissed and slammed his elbow in Caina's gut, and she rolled off him as the breath exploded from her lungs. The Kindred scrambled to his feet, murderous rage filling his black eyes, and Caina saw him reach for a hidden weapon beneath his slave's tunic...

"What the devil is the meaning of this?" thundered Khosrau.

"It was his fault, my lord Khosrau!" said Caina, climbing to her feet. "I was going to attend to my mistress, and this stupid slave spilled wine all over my dress!"

"The girl tripped into me, my lord," said the assassin, his voice hard and cold. The voice of a Kindred assassin - how could these fools not hear it? "I came with wine for your guest, my lord, and this bitch stumbled..."

"Watch your tongue," said Khosrau. "A serving girl she may be, but she is a free woman and you will address her as such."

The assassin looked at his feet, as if suddenly remembering his disguise. "My lord. I am sorry, my lord."

"I did see it, father," said Armizid, approaching with a scowl. "The opera singer's girl lost her balance and fell onto the slave."

Caina looked at Armizid, at Khosrau, back at Armizid, and then started crying.

It was a useful skill, Theodosia had told her, to be able to cry on demand. Embarrassed contempt flashed over Armizid's face, but Khosrau's expression became almost grandfatherly. A crying woman sometimes had that effect on a man, especially an older one.

"Now, now, my dear," said Khosrau. "It was a simple accident, and nothing more. No harm done." He gestured at the white expanse of his robes. "You didn't even splatter on me. And spilling wine on the Lord of House Asurius would indeed be a grave scandal."

Corbould chuckled.

"But I got wine on my dress, my lord," said Caina, sniffling, looking at the bloodstains on her sleeves.

"This is unseemly, father," said Armizid. Caina wondered how many times a day he said that. "The domestic disputes of the slaves are beneath our notice."

"True enough," said Khosrau without rancor. He pointed at the assassin. "You, clean this up." He patted Caina on the top of her head. "And you, my dear, go attend to your mistress, and we'll speak no more of this."

Caina gripped her damp skirts and did a deep curtsy. "Thank you, my lord. My lord is kind." She hurried past the lords, feeling the assassin's stare as she passed. He was not going to forget her, and she suspected he would kill her at the first opportunity. Was he bright enough to figure out that she was a Ghost?

A moment later she passed the nobles and reached Theodosia, who stood beside a pair of harpists and a man with a flute.

"Well done, fellows," she said. "The Grand Imperial Opera is always in need of musicians. Present yourselves to the seneschal tomorrow, and perhaps he will find a place for you."

The musicians bowed their thanks, and Theodosia joined Caina.

"What was that all about?" said Theodosia in a low voice.

"That slave," said Caina, looking at the assassin. The Kindred hurried towards the doors. "Kindred. He poisoned the wine. The only way I could think of stopping him was to trip, so I did."

Theodosia laughed. "Clever."

"And that cloaked man with the tattoos showed up," said Caina. "Apparently his name is Corvalis Aberon."

"Aberon?" said Theodosia, startled. "As in the First Magus Decius Aberon?"

"I don't know," said Caina. "He says he has no interest in Corbould Maraeus. To prove his good faith, he offered to help me stop the Kindred here. But then Sicarion showed up, and he and Corvalis fought. I don't know what happened to them."

Odds were that the victor had escaped, and the loser's corpse had been hidden somewhere in the Palace. Caina suspected that Sicarion had won the fight. She felt a twinge of guilt. Corvalis had fought for her and gotten himself killed. Of course, he seemed to hate Sicarion, and would have fought him anyway. But why?

Another mystery.

“Sicarion?” said Theodosia. “What was he doing here?”

“I don’t know,” said Caina.

"Are you sure the wine was poisoned?" said Theodosia.

"Yes," said Caina. "Look."

Theodosia looked at the puddle of wine and her eyes widened.

A faint wisp of smoke curled from the marble flagstones.

The wine was eating into the stone.

"Gods," said Theodosia. "So was the poison for Corbould or Khosrau?"

"Maybe both of them," said Caina. "I don't know." She frowned. "I intend to find out. We...”

Her throat went dry, and she could not get the words out.

“I...” Caina managed. “We...we need to...”

Her hands started to shake.

“Marina?” said Theodosia. “What’s wrong?”

Caina looked at her hands, at the bloodstains on her sleeves and the droplets of wine on her fingers.

At the droplets of poisoned wine on her fingers.

A poison that could be absorbed through the skin?

Her head throbbed, the Gallery spinning around her like a child’s toy.

“Marina!” said Theodosia, grabbing her shoulder.

“No,” rasped Caina, trying to pull away. “No, don’t touch me, the poison...”

Her legs collapsed beneath her, and darkness swallowed her before she hit the ground.

10

A KNIFE IN THE TAVERN

"For one so young," said the Moroaica, running a finger over the spines of Sebastian Amalas's books, "you have such tortured dreams."

Caina stood in her father's library, watching her younger self weep over Sebastian Amalas. In a few minutes, she knew, her mother would enter and confront her. And then Caina would kill her mother. She hadn't meant to do it. But she would do it nonetheless.

"Eleven years old," said Jadriga, stepping to Caina's side, "and already you knew such pain."

"Yes," said Caina.

The world blurred, and she stood in Maglarion's lair, watching herself scream as the necromancer extracted her blood for his experiments.

"His methods," said Jadriga, "were ever crude." She leaned forward, her black eyes watching the screaming girl. "That sort of pain should have broken you, shattered you into a thousand pieces."

"How do you know," said Caina, "that it didn't?"

"Because it made you stronger," said Jadriga. "It let you understand the true nature of the world, as I do."

Again the world blurred, and Caina saw the Great Market in

Marsis once more, saw thousands of people fleeing in panic as the Istarish attacked the city, Andromache's lightning ripping down from the clear sky. Caina saw herself running with Nicolai in her arms, trying to get to safety.

"You see the world as it is," said Jadriga. "That it is broken, a prison made to torture us."

"If there is pain in the world," said Caina, "it is because there are men and women like you in the world. I saw what you did under Black Angel Tower. How many other people have you killed over the centuries? How many other lives have you ruined?"

"Life is the acquisition of power," said Jadriga, "and when I have enough power, I will destroy the world and remake it. I will break the circle and assemble it anew. I will reforge the world so there will be no more pain, no more suffering."

"That's mad," said Caina.

Jadriga smiled. "It is only mad if I do not have the power to do it. And I will, soon."

The world dissolved into nothingness.

~

CAINA BLINKED AWAKE, sunlight stabbing into her aching eyes.

Someone thrust a wooden bucket into her hands.

"You're going to need this," said Theodosia, "in another three seconds."

Caina sat up. She just had time to realize that she was in Theodosia's suite at the Inn of the Defender. Then her stomach clenched with agony, and she doubled over and threw up everything she had ever eaten into the bucket.

Or at least it felt like it.

After the spasms passed, Caina spat, blinked the tears from her eyes, and looked up.

"Why am I not dead?" said Caina.

"Because," said Theodosia, "the poison in the glass was something called baneroot. It is absolutely lethal if ingested. But if absorbed through the skin, it merely induces unconsciousness and delirium. You were talking in your sleep for most of the night."

Caina winced. "How did you explain it to Lord Khosrau?"

Theodosia smiled. "I told him you fainted from embarrassment." She passed her a cup of wine. "This will help."

Caina nodded, swished the wine around her mouth, and spat it into the stinking bucket. "How long was I out?"

"About sixteen hours," said Theodosia. "It's past noon now."

Caina set aside the bucket and stood, taking a few cautious steps. She felt lightheaded, but not dizzy, and had no trouble keeping her balance.

"Corbould and Khosrau are still alive?" said Caina.

"Aye," said Theodosia. "The Kindred made no further attempts on them." She sighed. "Though I fear they suspect we are Ghosts now. Still, you could not have done otherwise."

"Corvalis," said Caina. "Any sign of him? Or of Sicarion?"

"None," said Theodosia. "Marzhod has spies among the slaves of the Palace, and they did a search. There was a bit of a stir when they found those dead mercenaries, but they found no trace of either Corvalis or Sicarion."

"How did they explain the dead mercenaries?" said Caina.

"Thieves," said Theodosia, "who fell to fighting over the spoils."

Caina snorted. "A likely story."

"But they believed it," said Theodosia with a shrug. "A pity we couldn't capture that Kindred. Or find out which wine glasses were poisoned. It would help us figure out who hired them."

"Maybe all the glasses were poisoned," said Caina, stretching as she worked out the knots in her back and neck. "Maybe someone hired the Kindred to kill Corbould, Khosrau, and Armizid in one fell swoop."

"Wouldn't that be a delightful mess," said Theodosia. "How do you feel?"

"Better," said Caina, stretching. "Lightheaded. I don't think I can keep any food down yet, though."

"Good," said Theodosia. "We're going to pay another visit to Marzhod tonight. Perhaps he will have learned something useful."

"IT SOUNDS," said Marzhod, "like you made a thorough botch of it."

Caina and Theodosia stood in Marzhod's workroom at the Painted Whore, the sounds of revelry coming from the common room beneath their boots. Marzhod sat slumped at his desk, glaring at them. Saddiq stood behind him, oiling the blade of his massive scimitar.

"Oh?" said Theodosia, lifting her eyebrows. Disguised as a Sarbian mercenary, the expression made her look villainous. "And what, dear Marzhod, would you have done differently?"

"Taken that assassin alive, for one," said Marzhod.

"He wouldn't have known who hired the Kindred," said Theodosia.

"No," said Marzhod, "but we could have gotten other useful information out of him. Like the location of their Haven, for instance. Or perhaps the names of higher-ranking Kindred."

"We had to take matters in our own hands," said Theodosia. "You certainly were no help."

Marzhod's hand curled into a fist. "Because my best men have all been turned to statues. I ask for help, and Halfdan sends me an opera singer and a girl who drops wine trays. If I ask for a sword and a shield, will he send me a flower and a marshmallow?"

Theodosia stared to look affronted. "I remind you, master Marzhod, that Halfdan..."

"Don't threaten me, woman," snarled Marzhod. "I rule the shadows in Cyrioch. If you disappear and I tell Halfdan that the Kindred killed you, do you think he will disbelieve me?"

"Threats, Marzhod?" said Theodosia, and both of them began shouting.

"Enough!" said Caina. Her head still ached from the poisoning. "Shut up, both of you!"

Both circlemasters glared at her, and Saddiq's lip twitched in amusement.

"Yes, I wish things had gone differently," said Caina. "But they could have been worse. Khosrau, Armizid, and Corbould are still alive, and I didn't accidentally kill myself with poison. We need to figure out who sent the Kindred after Lord Corbould. Otherwise we will sit around and blame each other as the Legions burn Cyrioch to the ground."

"You are both fools," said Marzhod.

"I don't give a damn about the opinion of a man who owns slaves," said Caina, rubbing her brow. Gods, her head hurt. "But unless we find out who hired the Kindred, Corbould Maraeus is going to die, Cyrioch will rebel against the Empire, and the Legions will destroy the city. It will be hard to rule the shadows in a city that has been burned to ashes."

Marzhod said nothing. Theodosia smiled, briefly.

"So," said Caina. "Who hired the Kindred?"

"I don't know," said Marzhod. "If you had figured out which glass on that tray was poisoned, that would have been helpful."

"We already know the Kindred are trying to kill Corbould," said Theodosia.

"Yes," said Marzhod, "but if they're trying to kill both Khosrau and Armizid simultaneously, that makes things different. The nobles are arrogant, but not arrogant enough to fake their own assassinations. One does not play games with the Kindred."

"Khosrau, Armizid, and Corbould," said Caina, thinking hard. She remembered how the poisoned wine had smoked against the marble. "All three of them were standing together. Maybe the assassin was trying to kill all three of them. They would have taken wine from the same tray."

"So who would benefit from killing both Corbould Maraeus and Lord Khosrau and his son?" said Theodosia.

"The Magisterium," said Caina.

"Doubtful," said Marzhod. "Lord Khosrau has no enemies among Cyrioch's magi. He doesn't like the magi, but he doesn't dislike them, either. I see no reason why Ranarius would want the nobles dead."

"What about Mhadun?" said Caina. "He's Kindred, I'm sure of it."

"He is," said Marzhod, "but not out of loyalty. Mhadun works for whoever can pay him."

"He loves coins, then?" said Theodosia.

Marzhod gave her a chilly smile. "No. But he does enjoy naked slave girls, preferably virgins. Virgins do not come cheaply, and the Kindred can pay him quite a lot of money."

"Have you tried following him?" said Caina. "He probably ranks high enough among the Kindred to know who hired them to kill Corbould."

Marzhod scoffed. "Spying upon a master magus is not easy. And Mhadun has power enough to pluck the secrets from a man's mind with a single spell. Not someone to cross lightly. He's too dangerous to capture and interrogate."

"What about Khosrau's other sons?" said Theodosia. "He has at least twenty, both legitimate and not."

"But what would they gain from killing him?" said Marzhod. "Their father's patronage has given them offices and magistracies across the Empire. One of his bastards even commands a Legion in the Imperial Pale. If they kill Khosrau, they lose their patron. Besides, Khosrau has the rare gift of remaining on good terms with his sons. Even the bastards."

"There are too many possibilities for us to take decisive action," said Theodosia. "I suggest we focus on keeping Corbould, Khosrau, and Armizid alive. Sooner or later the Kindred will make a mistake, and we can find their Haven and destroy them, or at least hurt them enough that they won't go after the nobles again."

Marzhod. "A good idea from an opera singer. Will wonders never cease?"

"What about Corvalis Aberon and the statues?" said Caina, hoping to forestall another argument.

"Decius Aberon is the First Magus," said Theodosia, "and..."

"How remarkably well-informed you are," said Marzhod.

"Are you better informed?" said Theodosia. "Do you know anything about Corvalis Aberon?"

Marzhod shrugged. "I have never heard the name Corvalis, no. But the First Magus has a number of bastard children. Most of them are magi, with reputations as dark as their father's."

"Corvalis wasn't a magus," said Caina. "He fought with sword and dagger, not with spells."

"Yet you said that scarred assassin wanted him dead," said Marzhod. The doubt in his voice was plain.

"Aye," said Caina. "I think Sicarion was there for another reason. He was surprised to see Corvalis."

Marzhod grunted. "So this Sicarion is turning people into statues?"

Caina would not put it past him or the Moroaica. Yet Sicarion was a necromancer, and Jadriga was dead.

Or she was dead and her spirit was trapped inside Caina's head.

"I don't know," said Caina. "But I don't see what advantage he would gain from it."

"Was Corvalis hunting Sicarion?" said Marzhod.

"No," said Caina. "He seemed just as surprised as Sicarion."

"How delightful that you could arrange the reunion of two old friends," said Marzhod. "But until I find proof otherwise, I'll assume that Corvalis Aberon is behind the statues."

Caina nodded. "I'm sure his 'business' is connected to it."

"I suggest you focus on finding who hired the Kindred," said Theodosia. "Meanwhile, we will try to keep Corbould, Khosrau, and Armizid alive."

"Another opera?" said Marzhod. "Perhaps you can sing the assassins to death with the tedium of your voice."

"That would be convenient," said Theodosia, "but instead we are going to the Ring of Valor to watch gladiatorial matches. Lord Corbould brought the Grand Imperial Opera to Cyrioch in honor of Lord Khosrau. So to repay him, Lord Khosrau is holding gladiatorial games in Corbould's honor."

"I didn't think you had the stomach for gladiators, dear Theodosia," said Marzhod.

Theodosia sniffed. "The vulgar tastes of those too crude to appreciate the splendors of opera are hardly my concern. But Lord Khosrau, in his graciousness, has invited the men and women of the Grand Imperial Opera to watch the games. And I am hardly so churlish to turn down the invitation of such a gracious lord."

Marzhod's dark eyes flicked to Caina. "Just don't faint at the sight of blood this time."

"I'll manage," said Caina.

"We will ensure that no harm comes to the lords," said Theodosia. "I trust you will keep yourself useful."

"My men will keep watch on known members of the Kindred," said Marzhod. " And as for the statues," he rubbed the dark stubble of his jaw, "I may have to hire...outside help."

"Outside help?" said Theodosia. "What do you mean?"

"An expert in sorcery," said Marzhod. "Someone to take a closer look at the statues."

"No members of the Magisterium," said Caina. "They cannot be trusted."

"Of course they cannot be trusted," said Marzhod. "Sorcerers are an unreliable and treacherous lot, and we'd be better off if we killed them all."

Caina felt her opinion of Marzhod improve.

"But I've never heard of sorcery that could turn a man to stone," said Marzhod. "So it's time to consult an expert." He grimaced. "Difficult as she may be."

"She's mad, that one," said Saddiq, his deep voice a rumble.

Marzhod scowled. "Do you know another renegade sorcerer available for hire? No? Until you find one, we have to turn to her." He stood. "If that is all, I do have work to do."

"Why, Marzhod," said Theodosia. "I was sure you were going to offer us something to drink."

"Don't be absurd," said Marzhod. "I'm trying to turn a profit, and spying for the Ghosts does not pay very well. I certainly cannot turn a profit by giving away wine for free."

Theodosia sniffed and got to her feet as Marzhod walked to the door. "Not that the vinegar you sell can be properly called wine."

Marzhod and Theodosia headed into the hallway, still bickering, while Caina followed. Saddiq fell in besides her, moving with silence remarkable in so large a man.

"I think," said Caina, voice low, "that they're going to kill each other."

Saddiq chuckled. "Perhaps. But Marzhod will not go against the Ghosts. He owes Halfdan too much."

"Why do you follow him?" said Caina as Theodosia and Marzhod started down the stairs to the common room. "He is cruel and owns slaves."

Saddiq shrugged. "Among the tribes of the desert, slavery is a way of life. It does not fill us with outrage as it does the Ghosts of the north, though a man who mistreats his slaves is as big as fool as a man who mistreats his horse, since he might find his horse unwilling to gallop when his foes close around him. But it may please you to know that Marzhod has freed many slaves."

"What?" said Caina.

"If a slave spies loyally for five years," said Saddiq, "then Marzhod will buy the slave and set him free. There are many such freedmen through the Cyrican provinces. They all spy for the Ghosts and do Marzhod's bidding, for they view him as a father."

"Why didn't he tell me this?" said Caina as they descended the stairs to the Painted Whore's common room.

"Because life has taught him that mercy is weakness," said Saddiq, "but his heart knows otherwise. Also, he thinks women are treacherous and fickle."

"Do you think that?" said Caina.

Saddiq grinned. "I have three wives, and they have taught me that women are just as treacherous and fickle as men."

Despite herself, Caina laughed.

The Painted Whore's common room was packed, the slaves hurrying back and forth as they brought food and wine to the sailors. A pair of musicians labored over a Caerish fiddle and an Istarish drum in the corner, filling the room with lively music. But the sailors still made way for Marzhod as he argued with Theodosia. A drunken man stumbled away from a bench, staggering as he fought to keep his balance.

Caina blinked.

It was the Kindred assassin from the Palace of Splendors, the man who had carried the tray of poisoned wine. Now he looked like a sailor, with rough trousers, bare feet, and loose shirt. But Caina saw the same cold glitter in his black eyes, despite the facade of drunkenness.

And she saw the knife in his right hand.

"Marzhod!" shouted Caina, but the noise of the crowd swallowed her words.

But the assassin saw her, and his eyes widened in recognition.

Caina seized the moment of hesitation and sprang at the assassin. He drew back his knife to stab, but she had the advantage. She rammed her shoulder into him, staggering the assassin. A cheer went up from the sailors, no doubt excited by the prospect of a fight.

Then the assassin got a better grip on his knife and Marzhod's Sarbian mercenaries detached themselves from the wall and headed into the crowd. Tavern brawls were one thing, but a killing was another. The assassin glanced back and forth, face twisted with rage. He looked at Caina, as if marking her for future vengeance.

Then he sprinted for the door.

"Stop him!" shouted Caina, but the Sarbians moved too slowly.

The assassin darted into the street and vanished.

"What the devil was that all about?" said Marzhod.

She grabbed his sleeve and pulled him closer to Theodosia, making sure they could not be overhead over the crowd.

"That was a Kindred assassin," said Caina. "He was here to kill you."

Theodosia frowned, and Saddiq reached for his scimitar.

"You're sure?" said Theodosia.

Caina nodded. "The last time I saw him he was holding a tray of poisoned wine in the Palace of Splendors."

"Damn it," said Marzhod. "Damn it! If we had taken him alive, we could have gotten useful information out of him." He scowled at the door. "But why did he try to kill me? You're the one who tripped over him at the Gallery of the Well."

Caina took a deep breath. "Because," she said, "they figured out I was a Ghost. And they know you are the circlemaster of Cyrioch. So the best way to strike back against the Ghosts for stopping the assassination is to kill the circlemaster of Cyrioch."

Marzhod stared at her, blinking.

"Damn it," he said at last.

"Then it is well," said Saddiq, "that I just sharpened my scimitar."

11

THE RENEGADE

Caina sat up, sweat pouring down her face. She looked around the darkened sitting room, expecting to see Maglarion standing in a corner, a bloody knife in his hand, or the Moroaica watching her with her deep eyes. Or the Istarish, carrying away a weeping Nicolai. But the sitting room was deserted and silent.

Just dreams.

How strange that the dreams frightened her so much when there was a good chance she might awaken to find a Kindred assassin standing over her bed.

Caina sat up, rubbing her face.

"You know, you make it damnably difficult to get a decent night's sleep."

Theodosia stood in the doorway to the bedroom, wrapped in a nightgown, dagger in her hand. Caina surged to her feet and looked around, expecting to see the Kindred storm through the door.

But there was only darkness and silence.

“What's wrong?” said Caina.

“You are,” said Theodosia, tucking the dagger into the sash of her gown.

"Me?" said Caina.

"I heard you screaming," said Theodosia. "I came out expecting to see you fighting assassins, but you were only having dreams. I should have known." She shook her head. "Awake, you're as cold as ice. It's only when you sleep that you scream."

"I'm sorry," said Caina, raking her fingers through her sweaty hair. "I didn't mean to wake you." Gods, but when was the last time she had slept the night?

It had been before the Istarish attack on Marsis, certainly.

"I'm sorry," said Caina again.

"It's not your fault," said Theodosia. "You can hardly be blamed for having nightmares. What is it that Halfdan always says? That nightmares..."

"Are scars of the mind," said Caina.

"And I would wager," said Theodosia, "that you have quite a few scars."

"Aye," said Caina. She paced to the balcony doors, gazing at the dark shape of the Defender.

"You keep telling me," said Theodosia, "that you're fine, but you're usually a better liar than that."

"No," said Caina. "No. I'm not fine."

They stood in silence for a moment.

"Oh, my poor child," said Theodosia. She crossed the room and hugged Caina, and Caina found herself blinking back tears. "It was something that happened in Marsis, wasn't it?"

"Yes," said Caina. "I took Nicolai for a walk, Theodosia. He wanted to see the ships in the harbor, and I wanted to give Ark and Tanya some time alone. And then the Istarish came and took Nicolai."

She let out a ragged breath and sat on the cot.

"Ark spent five years looking for Tanya and Nicolai," said Caina, "and I lost his son in his hour."

"But you got him back," said Theodosia. "You found him and killed Rezir Shahan."

"I was lucky," said Caina. "So many people died that day. If I had been a second too slow, or if I had gone left instead of right, I would have been one of them. Then Nicolai would have been killed or enslaved...and I would have had to tell Ark what happened." She closed her eyes, swallowed, her hands twitching. "The dread of it...I cannot forget it."

"That's not what's really bothering you," said Theodosia. "You saved Nicolai. You would not dream about Nicolai unless something else was bothering you, something that you haven't fully realized yet."

Caina nodded. "Something else happened in Marsis. I've only told Halfdan about it. No one else."

Theodosia waited.

"Jadriga," said Caina. "The sorceress I killed in Black Angel Tower. When she died, I think part of her power was trapped in me."

Theodosia frowned. "You mean...her soul? Her soul is in your body?"

"Maybe," said Caina. "At least a piece of it."

"But you are obviously not possessed," said Theodosia. "I know you quite well, my dear, and I doubt a power-mad sorceress could masquerade as you for so long."

"I'm not possessed," said Caina. "At least the Moroaica isn't controlling me. But Sicarion thinks her spirit is dwelling in me. And she appears to me in dreams, over and over again."

"Does she tell you to do things?" said Theodosia. "Give you commands?"

"No," said Caina. "She gives me warnings. And they're usually accurate, too. The first time Sicarion tried to capture me, she warned me it was about to happen."

"Maybe she doesn't want to die again," said Theodosia.

"Why not?" said Caina. "If she's...trapped inside me, somehow, killing me would let her take another body. At least that's what Sicarion thinks. But he could be lying. Or mistaken." Her stomach clenched at the thought. "You know how much I hate sorcery. To have some of her power inside me..."

"Would indeed be a revolting thought," said Theodosia. "But look on the bright side."

Caina snorted. "There's a bright side?"

"The power is harmless," said Theodosia. "You can't use it, and even if you could, you wouldn't. And if the soul of this Jadriga is really inside you...then she can't hurt anyone. So long as you're still alive, she can't escape."

Caina blinked. "I...hadn't thought of that."

The notion hadn't even occurred to her. If Jadriga's spirit truly inhabited her body, Caina assumed that the Moroaica had some malevolent plan behind it. But what if Jadriga was simply trapped inside Caina's body? So long as Caina lived, Jadriga could not escape to harm more people.

Though the Kindred might put an end to that, soon enough.

Caina remembered killing the assassin on the triforium of the Praetorian Basilica, remembered feeling his dying heartbeat shudder up the blade of her dagger.

"There's something else, too," said Theodosia.

"I've killed," said Caina, "a lot of people."

"You were defending yourself," said Theodosia. "Or stopping them from doing worse things."

"I know," said Caina. "But there have been so many of them. I can't even remember them all. That assassin in the common room of the Painted Whore? I might have killed more men than he has."

"It bothers you," said Theodosia.

"It used to," said Caina. "But not as much as it used to. And that bothers me. I didn't," she shook her head, blinking fresh tears from her eyes, "I didn't think...I didn't think I would become what I am." She sighed. "If you pointed out a man and told me that he was Kindred, I would kill him. I could kill him without hesitation, without guilt. That is what I have become, the sort of woman who can kill like that. There is so much blood on my hands."

"And more blood would have been spilled if you hadn't killed those men," said Theodosia. "Everyone in Malarae would have died, including my sons and I. Everyone in Rasadda would have burned."

"I know," said Caina. "That's what I tell myself. But every time I close my eyes, Theodosia, I see someone dying. Every time I go to sleep, I have dreams, over and over again. And I'm so…so…"

"Tired," said Theodosia.

"Yes," said Caina. "Tired."

"I suppose," said Theodosia, "that this isn't what you thought your life would be like."

"I knew a Ghost nightfighter's life would be hard," said Caina.

"That's not what I meant," said Theodosia. "Before you joined the Ghosts, what did you think your life would be like? Before your father died?"

Caina managed a small laugh. "Nothing like this. I thought…well, I thought I would wed at eighteen, as most noblewomen do. I thought I would have children." She scowled. "I swore I would be a better mother to them than my mother was to me. I thought I would have two or three children by now. Instead I am a killer without a family." She bowed her head. "And I shall remain alone."

"I needn't be that way," said Theodosia.

"I don't see how it can be otherwise," said Caina. "I am a Ghost nightfighter. And even if I left the Ghosts, even if I left this life behind, I cannot wed. I cannot bear children, you know that. I want...I want a family. I want my father to have grandchildren." Her mouth twisted. "But he is gone, and I will never have children."

"Which is why you have so many nightmares about Nicolai and the slavers," said Theodosia.

Caina frowned. "Oh?"

"My dear child, I am but a simple opera singer," said Theodosia, "but do credit me with some insight. You reunited Ark with his family. A vicarious action for you, since you believe you will never have a family of your own. Then the Istarish stole Nicolai, and you feared losing your family all over again. By proxy, of course, though that would make the pain no less real."

Caina opened her mouth to argue...and found that she had no answer.

"You won't be a Ghost nightfighter forever," said Theodosia.

"No," said Caina, "I'll probably have a Kindred knife between my ribs first."

"Barring that," said Theodosia, "how old are you now? Twenty-one?" Caina nodded. "Do you still want to do this when you are thirty? Forty?"

"No one leaves the Ghosts," said Caina.

"Of course not," said Theodosia, "but no one remains a night-fighter forever. You'll be a circlemaster one day, I'm sure of it. Perhaps even under your own name. The Countess Caina Amalas, come to reclaim her father's name and title after his murder at the hands of Istarish slavers all those years ago. Think of the sensation you would make at the capital's balls!" She shrugged. "And you needn't be alone, not unless you wished it."

"I cannot wed," said Caina.

"Why not?" said Theodosia. "Not every man needs or desires children. And if you are lonely...well, you are young, clever, and pretty, if you understand me."

Caina laughed. "Is that your solution? Find someone to warm my bed?"

"It certainly couldn't hurt your mood," said Theodosia. "Caina, I shall be blunt. You've lived on vengeance, and vengeance alone, for a long time. You swore to keep others from suffering as you did, and you kept that vow - look at Malarae or Rasadda. But you can't live for vengeance forever. Eventually you get tired of killing. You have to find something else you can live for. Love, perhaps."

"Love?" said Caina. "Is that what you live for?"

Theodosia smiled. "Of course. Once we return to Malarae, I intend to find proper wives for my sons. Tomard is a senior centurion in the Civic Militia, and it's well past time he was wed. And I want grandchildren to spoil."

"You have your sons," said Caina.

"I know," said Theodosia. "And you will find something of your own." She paused. "Did I ever tell you why I joined the Ghosts?"

"No," said Caina.

"My husband was murdered," said Theodosia, her smile fading.

"You may think me a talkative fool of an old woman, but everything I've told you, I learned it the hard way."

"Theodosia," said Caina. She hugged the older woman. "I've never thought you were a fool."

Theodosia laughed. "Merely talkative and old, hmm? Ah, the poisoned compliments of youth!"

"Thank you," said Caina.

Theodosia patted her cheek. "You're welcome, dear. And if you ever get tired of spying for the Emperor, come with me to the Grand Imperial Opera. You were the best assistant I ever had. I'll find you a husband, never fear, and..."

"...we'll spy on the nobles for the Emperor," said Caina.

"Quite right," said Theodosia. "Think you can sleep now?"

"No," said Caina. "But I do feel better. I'm going to go for a walk around the Inn to clear my head."

"And to check for assassins?" said Theodosia.

Caina nodded. "That Kindred assassin saw me twice. Which means the Kindred know there are Ghosts among the opera company. They went after Marzhod, but they might try to come after us." And Caina suspected the assassin she had thwarted twice had a personal grudge against her. "They'll scout the Inn of the Defender before they make any moves. If I'm fortunate, I might be able to capture one of their scouts. Or at least drive them off."

"Do be careful," said Theodosia.

"I'm always careful," said Caina.

She got dressed and left. She wore her blue dress, knives hidden beneath her sleeves, and a ragged brown cloak with a deep hood. From a distance, she looked like any other traveler on night business. Caina slipped through the Inn's darkened kitchen and through the backdoor. The nights of Cyrioch, much like the days, were hot and humid. Soon droplets of sweat trickled down Caina's face. She found herself looking forward to the bath in Theodosia's suite as she circled around the Inn's courtyard...

She stopped.

A cloaked figure stood before the courtyard gate, watching her.

Caina reached for her belt, and the cloaked figure lifted both hands in a gesture of peace. The right hand came up and drew back the hood.

She found herself looking at Corvalis Aberon's hard face and pale green eyes.

"I thought," said Corvalis, "that I might find you here."

"You survived," said Caina. "Did you kill Sicarion?"

Corvalis scowled. "Unfortunately, no. I wounded him severely, but before I could finish it, he hit me with a spell. He escaped before I recovered. I only hope he bled to death in an alley."

"Doubtful," said Caina. "He'll steal new parts to replace anything you lopped off."

Corvalis blinked. "I see that you have dealt with him before."

"I have," said Caina. "What do you want?"

"I owe you a debt," said Corvalis, "and I repay my debts."

"Debt?" said Caina. "What debt?"

"You saved my life," said Corvalis.

"I fail to see how," said Caina.

"Sicarion would have killed me," said Corvalis, "had you not interrupted me."

"Are you sure of that?" said Caina. "He was there for someone else."

She recalled her dreams. The Moroaica had ordered Sicarion to kill her wayward disciple.

Whoever that was.

"He was," said Corvalis, "but he hates me." A tight smile flashed over his face. "I defeated him once, years ago, and he will go out of his way to kill me. Had you not distracted me, had you not been with me, he would have ambushed me with four men. Not even I could have survived that."

"So you think you owe me a debt," said Caina.

"I do owe you a debt," said Corvalis, "and I repay my debts."

Caina thought this over.

"Fine," she said. "How do you intend to repay it?"

"The Kindred hunt Lord Corbould," said Corvalis. "And you're overmatched."

"We've kept Corbould alive so far," said Caina.

"So far," said Corvalis. "How much longer can you manage it? You are formidable, especially for a woman..."

"How flattering," said Caina.

"But you're overmatched," said Corvalis. "The Kindred will keep coming until Corbould is dead."

"I think they want to kill Khosrau, too," said Caina.

"Then your task is twice as hard," said Corvalis. "You need help."

"Which, I assume, is how you intend to repay this debt," said Caina.

"Yes," said Corvalis. "They're going to kill Corbould tomorrow, at the Ring of Valor. Lord Khosrau is throwing gladiatorial games in Corbould's honor. It is the perfect opportunity to kill Corbould."

"It would be," said Caina. It matched with what Theodosia had already told her. But anyone with contacts in the Palace of Splendors would know as much.

"They will send two assassins this time," said Corvalis, "since a single assassin failed twice. First, another man with a blowgun. Probably disguised as a common spectator. Second, a skilled archer, posted on the upper rim of the Ring. If one fails, the other will strike."

That was a bit more specific.

"How do you know this?" said Caina.

Corvalis smirked. "I left the Kindred, but I know how they work. I've been watching them, lest they interfere with my business."

"Foiling another assassination attempt will be helpful," said Caina, "but the Kindred will keep coming. Do you know where their Haven is? If we strike at their lair, we can stop them."

Corvalis shook his head. "I don't know where the Cyrioch Haven is. I was a member of the Artifel family, and only the Kindred Elders know the locations of all the Havens."

"How do I know you're telling the truth?" said Caina.

Corvalis scowled. "I warned you about the assassin at the

Amphitheatre of Asurius, did I not? I pointed out the assassins in the Gallery. And I helped you against Sicarion."

"Sicarion was trying to kill you anyway," said Caina.

"True," said Corvalis. "But what more can I do to...ah." He sighed. "Sicarion told you my name. Corvalis Aberon."

"Corvalis Aberon," said Caina. "The First Magus of the Magisterium, the mortal enemy of the Ghosts, is Decius Aberon."

"I thought the Ghosts were only a myth," said Corvalis.

"That's an evasion," said Caina.

"True," said Corvalis. "One cannot fool the Ghosts. If you must know, the First Magus is my father."

"Your father?" said Caina. "And is your business a task from the First Magus?"

"No," said Corvalis, and there was loathing in his cold voice. "Someday, I am going to kill him. I will swear it on whatever god you want. The gods of the Empire, or the sea gods of the Kyracians. Or the Living Flame of the Anshani and the Saddai, or the devils of the underworld. I will swear upon them all. I will kill Decius Aberon and repay him for what he has done..."

Corvalis stopped talking, as if alarmed that he had said too much.

Caina stared at him. She noted how he held himself, ready to fight at a moment's notice. She had seen him fight against Sicarion. The only way a man learned to fight like that was to train every day from childhood.

Like the Kindred did to their slaves.

"Your father," said Caina, "sold you to the Kindred, didn't he?"

Corvalis's expression did not change, but a muscle twitched near his left eye.

"You understand nothing," said Corvalis.

"Actually, I do," said Caina. "The First Magus is known for his ruthlessness. Such a man would see his children as raw material, to transform into weapons and tools to use as he sees fit. Some of his children are magi of the Magisterium. But you were born without any arcane talent. Since he couldn't make a magus out of you, he sold you to the Kindred."

"How do you know this?" said Corvalis, not bothering to hide his anger. "How long have you been spying on me?"

"You're surprised?" said Caina. "I am a spy, after all. But, no. I had never seen you before Barius's pawnshop."

"Then how do you know this?" said Corvalis. "Who told you?"

"You did," said Caina. "I've had some practice observing people."

Corvalis stared at her. Caina remembered the first time she had met Ark, how angry he had gotten when she deduced that he had joined the Ghosts to find his wife.

At last Corvalis barked out a short, harsh laugh. "I would say you are a sorceress, but I know better. Yes, it is as you say. I was born to one of my father's mistresses." His face was hard. "And the great First Magus has no use for children unable to wield the arcane sciences. So he sold me to the Kindred. Under the terms of the contract, he would receive exclusive use for my services whenever he desired. The Kindred molded me into a killer."

"And then you left," said Caina. Why had he left the Kindred? An attack of conscience, perhaps? Something similar had happened to her old teacher Riogan.

"And then I left," said Corvalis.

"I understand," said Caina.

Again Corvalis laughed that short, harsh laugh. "I doubt that."

"My mother was a failed initiate of the Magisterium," said Caina. "She sold me to a necromancer in exchange for his arcane teachings. It was...not a pleasant experience." She shrugged. "So I understand better than you think."

She wondered why she had bothered to tell him.

"How did you escape?" said Corvalis.

"Neither my mother nor the necromancer are still among the living," said Caina. He could draw what conclusions he would from that.

Corvalis nodded. "And I will kill my father."

"That's not why you're in Cyrioch," said Caina. "Decius Aberon is in Artifel. You might have come to Cyrioch for some reason to do with him. But you're not here to kill the First Magus."

"Very good, Ghost," said Corvalis. "Have you puzzled why I am here?"

"No," said Caina. But it had something to do with the statues, she was sure of it. Perhaps Corvalis even knew how Barius and the other Ghosts had been transmuted into stone. "Unless you want to tell me?"

"I do not," said Corvalis. "Clever as you are, your enemies might capture you. And I will not lose my secrets. Not now, when I am so close."

"Some of the Ghosts have been turned to stone," said Caina, watching him for a reaction. "How can we keep it from happening again?"

"Stay away from me," said Corvalis. "Your fool of a circlemaster thinks I am a threat, so he sent his Ghosts to spy on me. They...got in the way. So long as you ignore me, you will be in no danger."

Caina gave a slow nod. "Very well. Good luck."

Corvalis blinked, and then nodded. "And you as well, Ghost. I think you will need it."

He left without another word.

~

CAINA WALKED into Theodosia's bedroom.

"Mmm?" said Theodosia, lifting her head. "What is it? I hoped the Kindred would have the courtesy to wait until a decent hour to murder us in our beds."

"I know," said Caina, "how we can ambush the Kindred."

12

THE RING OF VALOR

The Ring of Valor could have swallowed the Amphitheatre of Asurius whole.

The arena was a huge stone oval, its outer wall standing two hundred feet tall. Ornate statues of gladiators stood in niches along the wall, hundreds of them, brandishing stone spears and swords. Enormous arches led into the Ring, and through those arches Caina heard the roar of the crowds gathered to watch the gladiatorial games. The Amphitheatre of Asurius held ten thousand people, but nearly a hundred thousand could gather in the Ring of Valor to watch enslaved gladiators kill one another.

Caina looked at the streams of people pouring into the Ring's gates and tried to keep the contempt off her face.

She stood outside of the Ring with Marzhod, Saddiq, and a dozen Sarbian mercenaries. Caina wore her dust-colored robes, a scimitar and dagger hanging on her leather belt makeup giving her face the illusion of stubble. The other Sarbians ignored her. Marzhod had them that she was Saddiq's cousin, come to find work in Cyrioch.

"A few more," said Marzhod in Cyrican, "and then we'll get started."

Caina shifted. "Why not now?"

"Because," said Marzhod, "the real betting doesn't begin until the first matches start. Right now they're watching animals. Lions fighting bears, that sort of thing. The poor bet on those, but they're not worth the trouble." He rubbed his fingers together. "The real money comes when the gladiators come out. Especially if one noble or another owns the gladiators."

"And Lord Khosrau and Lord Corbould," said Saddiq, "have not even arrived yet."

Caina looked north to the sprawling mass of Cyrioch and the white shape of the Stone rising from its heart. The Ring of Valor lay just south of the city's gates, on the flat plains that made up most of Cyrica. According to Marzhod, the impoverished free citizens of Cyrioch had a tendency to riot during the games, so the Lord Governors had built the Ring outside of the city proper.

"Once the lords arrive," said Marzhod, "the betting will begin in earnest. You lot," he waved a bony hand at the mercenaries, "circulate through the nobles and take their bets. You two," he pointed at Caina and Saddiq, "will carry out a little errand for me."

That errand was making sure Corbould and Khosrau survived.

And, if all went well, capturing a Kindred assassin alive.

"And you," said Marzhod, pointing at another group of mercenaries, "watch for anyone else taking bets. If you find anyone else taking wagers, give them a good beating and dump them in the street. No killing – the Lord Governor and the Lord Aedile of Games don't like bloodshed spoiling their festivities." He snickered. "Except for the gladiators. But we're well within our rights to beat anyone else taking bets into a pulp."

"How did you get the exclusive right to take wagers for the games?" said Caina.

Marzhod smirked. "I asked the Lord Aedile of Games politely, and he gave it to me because I was so charming."

A guffaw went up from the Sarbian mercenaries, and Caina rolled her eyes.

"How do you think?" said Marzhod. "A very large bribe and a fixed percentage of the take. Of course, I make more than enough to cover it." He scratched at his unshaven chin. "Especially since I fix a few key matches."

"Here they come," said Saddiq.

A procession marched from the city proper. At its head came Khosrau, Corbould, and Armizid, riding in a ceremonial chariot pulled by eight white horses, a guard of militiamen and black-armored Imperial Guards surrounding them. Caina noted with amusement that Theodosia rode in the chariot, exchanging laughter with Khosrau. Armizid must have been scandalized. After the chariot came the lesser nobles and the magi on foot. Ranarius strode in their midst, tall and forbidding in his black robes, Nicasia walking barefoot after him. Mhadun strolled at the preceptor's side, looking as if he didn't have a care in the world.

Marzhod grinned. "Time to fleece the sheep." He gave a sharp nod to Caina. "You know what to do."

She did.

Saddiq followed as she headed for one of the Ring's gates. A pair of militiamen stood there, scowling as they waved the crowds through.

"You, Sarbian," said a militiaman, pointing at Caina. "You have a ticket?" When Lord Khosrau held a gladiatorial exhibition, he apparently paid for free tickets, given at random to Cyrioch's poorer citizens. No doubt the tickets helped keep the populace from rioting.

"Aye," said Caina, holding out the paper Marzhod had given her. "Both me and my friend. We're here on business." Marzhod had most of the city militia in his pay, and the paper held his seal.

"Go," said the militiaman. "Don't linger."

Caina nodded and entered the Ring of Valor.

Tiers of stone seats rose far overhead, packed with cheering commoners. Spacious boxes occupied the bottom third of the seats, reserved for powerful nobles and wealthy merchants. The spectators, rich and poor alike, looked upon a broad oval with a sandy floor. A number of dead lions lay upon the sand, while a wounded bear stalked back and forth, bellowing.

Saddiq tapped Caina's shoulder.

"You attend to the lords in their boxes," said Saddiq, looking towards the box that would hold Khosrau and his guests. "I shall attend to our...friend...atop the Ring."

He looked at the roofed colonnade that encircled the highest tier of seats. From there, a skilled archer had a clean shot at anyone sitting in the lords' boxes.

"How will you get up there?" said Caina.

"There are hidden ladders so the slaves can clean the pillars," said Saddiq. "Good hunting."

"You, too," said Caina.

Saddiq left without another word. A team of handlers hastened onto the sands, corralling the enraged bear, while slaves dragged away the carcasses of the slain lions. Another team of slaves raked the sands, turning over the blood. Caina supposed the blood of gladiators would stain the sand soon enough.

Her mouth twisted at the thought.

"Citizens of Cyrioch!" The voice boomed over the Ring of Valor, amplified to thunderous volume by a magus's spell. Caina saw the Lord Aedile of Games, a squat, fat man in brilliant white robes, standing in his box. "In the name of your Lord Governor, I bid you welcome to the Ring of Valor, and this festival of manful courage, honor, valor, and skill!"

The crowds cheered.

"These games are generously financed by our benevolent and wise Lord Governor, Armizid of House Asurius!"

Caina watched the nobles march to their boxes. Armizid strode in their head, wearing a red military cloak and gleaming cuirass of office over his white robes. A tepid cheer greeted his arrival.

"The remainder of the funds for this exhibition of arms," boomed the Lord Aedile, "is a generous gift from Khosrau, Lord of House Asurius!"

Khosrau hobbled out, leaning on his cane. Much to her amusement, Caina saw Theodosia on his arm. A loud cheer greeted the Lord of House Asurius, and Theodosia waved to the crowds with regal dignity. Corbould followed them, as did the rest of the nobles.

Caina saw Ranarius and Mhadun among the nobles, with Nicasia trailing behind. Did Mhadun know about the attempt on Corbould's life? Or did the Kindred keep him in the dark?

"For the glory of the Empire!" thundered the Lord Aedile. "For the majesty of our Emperor! For the honor of our patrons! I declare these games open!"

The loudest cheer yet went up from the crowds, and a pair of gladiators marched onto the sands. One was dressed like an Istarish foot soldier, with a spiked helm, round shield, and scimitar. The other looked like a stylized Kyracian ashtairoi, with a plumed helm, gleaming cuirass, and a long straight sword.

For a moment Caina remembered the desperate fighting in Marsis, running and hiding from the soldiers as she sought Nicolai...

She shook aside the memories and got to work.

The nobles settled into their boxes and Caina approached them.

"You!" said one of the nobles, a doughy man in his twenties. "You're with Marzhod?"

"Aye, my lord," said Caina, keeping her voice disguised.

"Here." The noble thrust a paper into Caina's hand. "Two thousand on Coriolus the Red. Move along, you're blocking my view."

Caina worked her way through the boxes, collecting wagers. She had done a lot of strange things during her time as a Ghost nightfighter, but she never collected bets while watching for an assassin. Every step took her closer to Lord Khosrau's box, and she watched for an assassin with a blowgun. Almost certainly the Kindred assassin would be disguised as a slave. A slave running errands among the nobles would not draw suspicion. Or perhaps the Kindred would disguise himself as a wealthy merchant.

A roar went up from the crowds, and Caina glanced towards the sands. The Istarish gladiator staggered back, blood pouring down his chest from a gash across his collarbone. The Kyracian gladiator circled warily, watching for an opportunity to strike. Unless the Istarish gladiator did something clever, the Kyracian would wear him down through sheer patience.

She tore her gaze away from the spectacle and moved through the nobles' boxes. Lord Khosrau's attention was fixed on the fight, while Theodosia, Corbould, and Armizid all watched with polite interest. The assassination attempt would come during the climax of a match, Caina decided. When the crowd was on their feet, cheering for their favored gladiators.

Another roar went up from the thousands packing the higher seats. The Kyracian gladiator lay stunned upon the sand, while the wounded Istarish gladiator stood over him, his scimitar resting at his opponent's throat. The crowds shouted for mercy. The Kyracian gladiator had fought well, after all.

The Istarish gladiator limped from the sands.

The day wore on, match after match taking place in the stone oval. Sometimes the gladiators fought only to first blood. Others fought to the death, driven by the shouts and jeers of the crowd. The games grew more elaborate, teams of gladiators fighting each other, and the mob grew more bloodthirsty, screaming for more death. Sometimes Lord Khosrau stepped in to save the defeated gladiators, making a show of his clemency, but more often than not, the gladiators fought to the death.

Caina circulated through the boxes, collecting wagers, her face showing no trace of the rage that simmered within her. Her loathing of Cyrioch had grown into hatred. How could they sit here and cheer at the spectacle, applaud as men were maimed and killed for their amusement? Were they any better than animals?

Maybe, she thought blackly, maybe Cyrioch deserved to burn. If Cyrioch rebelled, the Legions could come and burn this pestilential cancer of a city to the ground...

Caina pushed aside the dark thoughts. If Lord Corbould was assassinated, more people than the gladiators in the Ring would die. More people than the jackals and vultures hooting and cheering from the Ring's seats.

More wagers changed hands, and many of the lords and merchants groaned or cheered as the gladiators fell. Caina wondered how many fortunes had been made and lost today. Though no doubt Marzhod would find a way to turn a profit. She shot a glance at the upper tier of the Ring, at the covered colonnade encircling the arena. Had Saddiq been successful? Or had the assassin killed him?

Caina turned and saw a slave walking towards Lord Khosrau's box.

Her breath caught in her throat.

It was the same assassin she had seen at the Gallery of the Well, the same assassin who had tried to kill Marzhod at the Painted Whore. The man had disguised himself with a fake beard, gray dye in his hair, and a perfectly convincing limp. Yet Caina recognized him at once, saw the danger in the way he carried himself.

She knew an assassin of the Kindred when she saw one.

Corvalis had told the truth.

An elaborate battle raged upon the sands, a recreation of the Empire's liberation of Cyrica. A team of gladiators dressed in stylized representations of Legion armor faced a band of fighters dressed like Anshani nobles. The fighting raged back and forth, the cheers of the crowd growing louder.

The assassin headed towards Khosrau's box, and Caina saw the thick brown straw in his right hand.

She hurried forward.

The battle below reached a crescendo, the Legionaries driving back the Anshani, the mob's cheers rising to a frenzied scream. Many nobles surged to their feet, cheering and shouting, and the commoners followed suit.

The assassin quickened his pace.

Another few heartbeats and he would be within range of Lord Corbould.

Caina reached for her belt.

The assassin stopped a dozen paces from Lord Corbould, unnoticed in the chaos. He drew a small object from within his tunic and tucked it into the brown straw. The poisoned dart, Caina suspected.

She yanked a cloth pad from her belt, the thick fabric moist against her fingers.

The leader of the Anshani gladiators fell, skewered through the throat by a Legionary's broadsword. The cheers of the crowd became a wild screaming, and the assassin took one step closer to Khosrau's box.

He lifted the blowgun...and then Caina stepped behind him and slammed the cloth pad over his lips and nose.

The Kindred twisted like an eel, whirling to face her, but Caina grabbed his left arm and held on. The assassin lost his balance and fell upon the stone steps, Caina landing atop him. Her knee went into his gut, and the breath exploded from the assassin's lungs in a loud gasp.

Caina slammed the pad against his nose...and the assassin took a deep breath of the chemicals soaking the cloth. He shuddered once, his eyes rolling up, and slumped against the stairs.

Caina got to her feet, breathing hard.

She saw a man in the ornamented robe of a master merchant staring at her, eyes wide.

"He didn't," she growled, "pay his wager."

The merchant sniffed. "This is what comes of letting slaves place wagers."

Caina caught the eye of a Sarbian mercenary, and men hustled to take the assassin in hand. Anyone watching would assume that Marzhod's mercenaries had dealt with someone taking unauthorized wagers.

The mercenaries scooped up the assassin, and Caina went in search of Saddiq.

~

THE PILLARS THREW long shadows over the upper lip of the Ring.

Caina prowled through the colonnade, hand resting on the hilt of her scimitar. The constant murmur of the crowd rose from below as another bloody spectacle played out upon the sand. She saw no sign of Saddiq ...

Wait.

She saw two dark figures ahead, standing in the shadow of the pillars.

Caina slid a throwing knife from her sleeve and crept forward, boots making no sound against the floor.

She slipped around a pillar and saw that the dark figures were actually a pair of statues.

She berated herself. Statues covered the Ring of Valor, and she had mistaken them for living men. Then she saw that one of the statues looked like a Sarbian man in robes, a two-handed scimitar in his fists.

Saddiq.

It was a statue of Saddiq.

A fantastically detailed and accurate statue of Saddiq.

Just like Barius.

Caina whispered a curse and stepped closer. Saddiq's stone face was slack with shock, his eyes wide. Before him crouched a statue of a lean man in the robes of a Cyrican commoner, daggers in either hand. His expression, too, was surprised.

Caina guessed what had happened well enough. Saddiq had surprised the Kindred, but the assassin drew his daggers and prepared to fight. And then...something, some creature, some power, overtook them and turned them both to stone.

"You lied, Corvalis," whispered Caina. "We stayed away from you, and our men still turned to stone."

At least the Kindred assassin was no further threat to Lord Corbould.

Caina gazed at the statue that had once been Saddiq and then went to find Marzhod.

~

AFTER MIDNIGHT, Caina stood in the cellar of the Painted Whore, staring at the Kindred assassin she had captured.

"Anything else?" said Marzhod, giving the man's cheeks a gentle slap. The Kindred moaned, his head rolling to the side. The assassin lay upon a table, his wrists and ankles bound. "Anything? No?" He sighed and straightened up. "We're not getting anything else out of him tonight."

Caina gave a grim nod.

Marzhod and his Sarbian hirelings had not bothered with torture. A man under torture, Halfdan had always said, would say or do anything to make the pain stop, and Marzhod agreed with him. The Kindred were not the only ones with a thorough knowledge of poisons and drugs. One of the druggists in Marzhod's employ had brewed a bitter elixir of certain specific mushrooms and molds and used a funnel to pour it down the assassin's throat. A few moments later the assassin began experiencing violent hallucinations, hooting and weeping in fear.

He also became willing to answer all of Marzhod's questions.

"How long until he wakes up?" said Marzhod.

"At least a day and a night, sir," said Marzhod's druggist, a greasy-looking man who stank of mildew. "It will take that long for the drug to pass from his system. I fear he will first urinate quite copiously."

Marzhod grunted. "At least we put him down here, then. I would hate to disturb the Pained Whore's refined ambience." He shook his head. "A waste of time. The man knew nothing useful."

"He did know the Kindred had been paid an enormous sum of money to kill Lord Corbould, Lord Khosrau, and Lord Armizid," said Caina. That tore their first theory to shreds. Caina had grown more doubtful that Khosrau had hired the Kindred and this proved it. What sort of madman would hire the Kindred to fake an assassination?

"Yes, but he didn't know who had hired the Kindred," said Marzhod, "and more importantly, he didn't know where the Kindred have hidden their Haven. All his orders came through dead drops."

"We know where his next dead drop is," said Caina. "We could lie in wait and ambush the courier."

"Doubtful," grunted Marzhod. "Our friend here is supposed to leave a dead drop of his own, confirming his mission failed." He scratched his chin. "I suppose we could ambush the courier coming to take that dead drop. But the Kindred are too clever. Each of the lower-ranking assassins only knows two others, likewise for the couriers. We could spend weeks following that chain, and by the time we come to the end, Corbould and Khosrau will be dead."

"Do you have any better ideas?" said Caina.

"As it happens, I do." Marzhod smirked. "Your friend was wrong."

"My friend?" said Caina. "What friend?"

"Corvalis Aberon," said Marzhod. "He said if we left him alone, no more Ghosts would turn to stone. Well, we left him alone, and my most reliable man is now a statue in my storeroom. Either he was wrong or he lied to us." He snorted. "Or both. So we do things my way now."

"And what way is that?" said Caina.

"These damned statues are connected to the assassins somehow," said Marzhod, "no matter what your friend might say. So I'm going to get outside help."

"Outside help," said Caina. "You mean this renegade sorceress of yours? That's a terrible idea. Renegade sorcerers are worse than the magi."

"True," said Marzhod, "but she's harmless enough. So long as you don't cross her. And she's agreed to speak to us in exchange for quite a lot of gold. And one...ah, special item."

"What's that?" said Caina.

Marzhod smirked. "She wants to meet you."

13

THE OCCULTIST

The next morning Theodosia and Caina returned to the common room of the Painted Whore, disguised as Sarbian mercenaries.

"A simply dreadful spectacle, the gladiatorial games," said Theodosia. "Opera is much more civilized. And the way Khosrau cheered for the bloodshed! Lord Corbould is a cold fish, but at least he comported himself with proper public dignity."

"You sound like Armizid," said Caina, though she shared Theodosia's loathing for the games. "And at least Khosrau has the good taste to appreciate opera, no?"

"I suppose so," conceded Theodosia.

Marzhod emerged from the cellars, flanked by a pair of mercenaries. Caina wondered what he had done with the imprisoned Kindred assassin, and decided that she didn't want to know. The circlemaster wore his usual ragged finery, but beneath his coat she saw a shirt of chain mail, and sword and dagger hung at his belt.

"Is this sorceress of yours," said Theodosia, "really that dangerous?"

"That dangerous," said Marzhod, "and more. No one in their right mind sees her at night, so we're going now. Let's get moving. You do not want to be in her house after dark."

~

MARZHOD LED THEM TO WESTSHADOW.

Two districts lay on either side of the Stone, Westshadow and Eastshadow, and the Stone threw its shadow over Westshadow in the mornings and Eastshadow in the afternoons. The Stone's shadow lay over Westshadow as Marzhod led them through the district's narrow streets, and Caina found herself relieved to be out of the constant blazing sun.

Yet the shadow disturbed her.

As she looked at the Stone, she could not shake the impression that the hill was a slumbering beast, the mighty Palace upon its back no more than a child's toy. Someday the beast would awaken, shattering the Palace, smashing Cyrioch into ruin...

Caina shook off the morbid thoughts.

"This sorceress," said Caina. "What kind of sorceress is she?"

Marzhod glanced at her. "An Anshani occultist, if you must know."

Caina frowned. "But there are no female Anshani occultists. The Anshani kill women that exhibit arcane abilities." As much as Caina detested the Magisterium, they were not as brutal as the khadjars, the nobles of Anshan.

"If she wants you to know," said Marzhod, "then she will tell you."

They kept walking. Westshadow was a district of middling prosperity, with tall, narrow houses of three or four stories. Every wall had been covered with white plaster, no doubt to reflect the heat when the sun passed over the Stone. Minor merchants lived here, Caina suspected, and low-ranking officials in Lord Governor Armizid's service. Women in bright robes and headscarves hurried back and forth. Caina wondered if any of them had been cheering in the Ring of Valor yesterday.

Marzhod stopped at a narrow house and knocked. After a

moment an iron plate in the door slid aside and Caina caught the gleam of eyes.

"Who is it?" said a woman's voice, speaking Cyrican with a heavy Anshani accent.

"Marzhod," said Marzhod. "We've come to see your mistress."

"The scarred one," said the woman. "Is the scarred one with you?"

"Aye," said Marzhod, and he jerked his head at Caina.

She felt a chill. Caina's mind carried scars, but her flesh did as well. Specifically, a strip of scars, almost like a belt, below her navel, the marks from Maglarion's sorcerous experiments. How the devil did Marzhod know about those?

No - the Anshani sorceress had asked for the scarred one.

How did she know?

"Go," said Theodosia, voice quiet. "We need answers. If you call for help, we're right here."

Caina steeled herself and nodded.

"Do try to be convincing," said Marzhod. "Since we've made such excellent progress so far."

Caina scowled, stepped past him, and the door swung open.

The entry hall was unadorned, the walls covered in white plaster. An Anshani serving woman stood a short distance away, eyes glittering in her dark face.

"You," said the serving woman. "Yes, you are the one the mistress wishes to see. This way, please."

She led Caina to another door. She opened it and Caina stepped into the next room. The round chamber beyond was dim, lit only by the flickering light of a dozen candles. Gleaming wooden shelves held books and scrolls, and an elaborate mosaic of the constellations and astrological signs covered the floor.

She felt the faint tingle of sorcery.

"Come closer, child," said a woman's voice, low and musical, "and let me see you."

When Marzhod had mentioned a renegade sorceress, Caina had expected to meet someone like Nicorus, the castrated former magus living in the slums of Marsis. Or Sicarion, a man scarred and twisted by centuries of necromancy. Perhaps some haggard crone out of legend.

Not a woman of remarkable beauty, sitting calmly upon a chair and drinking tea. She was in her middle thirties, with smooth brown skin and black hair shot through with white, her eyes like dark amber. She wore an elaborate dress of violet silk, jewels glittering at her sleeves and throat.

"Who are you?" said Caina.

The woman took a sip of tea. "I am an occultist, trained in the arcane traditions of Anshan."

"I know," said Caina.

One black eyebrow rose. "Do you? How, pray? The word of Marzhod?"

"I don't trust Marzhod," said Caina.

"Wise," said the woman. "But why do you know me to be an occultist?"

"Because," said Caina, easing her fingers toward the throwing knives in her belt. "Your shadow is pointing in the wrong direction."

The candles should have thrown the seated woman's shadow against the wall. Instead it lay across the mosaic floor, stretching towards the candles.

"Oh, very good," said the woman. "What do you know about the occultists of Anshan?"

"They claim to control the shadows," said Caina, "and speak with spirits and the dead."

"They claim to?" said the woman, gesturing at her shadow.

"That's mummery to deceive the ignorant," said Caina, remembering what she had read about sorcery in the Vineyard's library. "The arcane science of the occultists controls the netherworld, the spirit realm. You conjure up spirits and speak to them. And living men and women throw a...shadow, an echo, of themselves into the netherworld. A skilled occultist can read that shadow and learn secrets from it, even control it."

For an instant, a hint of fear went over the woman's face.

"Who are you?" said the woman.

Caina decided to use that hint of fear to her advantage. "Tell me first. Who are you? There are no women among the occultists of Anshan."

"No," murmured the woman. "There are not. For by ancient tradition, any women who manifest arcane power are put to death." She lifted her chin, and Caina saw the stern pride of the Anshani nobility in her face. "I am Nadirah, eldest daughter of the great khadjar Arsakan, second only to the Shahenshah himself in nobility. I manifested the power when I was thirteen, and for years practiced it in secret. But my husband discovered that I used my power to arrange his ascent, and he turned against me. I was forced to leave Anshan, the seat of civilization and beauty, and settle here among the savage Cyricans and other barbarians of the Empire."

"So I see," said Caina.

"But who are you?" said Nadirah.

"A Ghost," said Caina.

Nadirah shook her head. "I will speak plainly, then. Are you the Moroaica?"

"What?" said Caina.

"I sensed it the moment you set foot in Cyrioch," said Nadirah. "To those with eyes to see into the shadows of the netherworld, you are a vortex of dark power, an inferno of black light. The Moroaica, the great sorceress of the north, the terror of the Szalds, the Queen of Burning Bronze, the ancient one. I wondered if you had come to claim me."

"Claim you?" said Caina, confused. "I didn't even know you existed until a few days ago. I am not the Moroaica. I don't care what you or Sicarion think. I am not the Moroaica."

"You...are not?" said Nadirah. "But your aura is that of the Moroaica, I am sure of it."

"No," said Caina. "I killed her. She is dead."

"Many have killed the Moroaica over the centuries," said Nadirah. "And always she has returned in a new body. Sometimes she has returned in the body of her slayer." She stood, her skirts rustling against the floor. "When you faced the Moroaica, did she have a coven about her? A circle of apprentices, women she taught arcane arts?"

"She did," said Caina, remembering Agria Palaegus and the others. Agria, who had murdered her own daughter for renewed youth.

"Do you think the Moroaica taught disciples out of charity?" said Nadirah. "She keeps a circle of women with arcane power about her at all times. For if she is slain, her spirit will claim one of their bodies for her own."

Jadriga had indeed taught a circle of disciples in Marsis. But by the time Caina faced her for the last time, the most powerful of the disciples had been slain, and the rest overpowered. And when Caina fought Jadriga, they had been alone, save for Nicolai...

"Oh," said Caina, voice soft.

Sicarion had been right. It wasn't merely a part of Jadriga's power that had lodged inside Caina. It was all of Jadriga's power, her entire spirit.

"Then why," said Caina, throat dry, "then why am I not the Moroaica? Why has she not possessed me?"

Nadirah closed her eyes, whispering a spell, and Caina felt a sudden spike of sorcery. She reached for her dagger and Nadirah's eyes opened.

They had gone completely black, like pits into nothingness. Her shadow twitched and writhed at her feet like a banner in the wind.

"Because you are scarred," said Nadirah. Her voice hissed and echoed, as if coming from a long distance away. "I see it in your shadow, beneath the darkness of the Moroaica. You were wounded, your shadow maimed by the sorcery of another. Because of that, you can feel the shadows. You can sense the sorcery of another. But because of that scarring, your aura is...fractured. Like cracks in a pane of glass. So the Moroaica can inhabit your body, can speak to your shadow and speak through your shadow...but she cannot control you."

"So the Moroaica is a round peg," said Caina, "and I am a square hole."

Nadirah shook herself and closed her eyes. When she opened them, they had returned to their amber color.

"A crude analogy," said Nadirah, "but essentially accurate."

"So what does that mean?" said Caina. "So long as I am alive, the Moroaica is trapped?"

"Yes," said Nadirah. "If the Moroaica could release herself from you and claim another body, she would have done so by now." She shivered. "I feared she would possess me the moment you stepped into my chamber. I wish you long and happy life, Ghost. For as long as you live, the Moroaica is trapped within you."

Caina nodded, uneasy. Sicarion had offered to kill Caina and release Jadriga, yet Jadriga had refused. Why? Was the Moroaica waiting until she could find a more suitable host?

Or did Jadriga think she could slowly persuade her, over the years, to do as she wished?

It was a disturbing thought.

Caina pushed it aside. She had more immediate problems.

"Marzhod thinks you can help us," said Caina. "Can you?"

"Perhaps," said Nadirah, "though I prefer not to become involved in his business."

"Sensible," said Caina. "But if you don't help us, I might get killed, and the Moroaica would need a new host."

"You bargain well," said Nadirah. "And I must aid you. Something is wrong in Cyrioch."

There were many things wrong in Cyrioch. Caina remembered the slaves, the gladiatorial games, the crushing poverty of the commoners. But somehow she didn't think Nadirah had that in mind.

"The shadows are wrong," murmured Nadirah. "The netherworld whispers of the coming destruction. The shadow of some dire catastrophe lies upon Cyrioch, just as the shadow of the Stone lies upon my house. We stand at the cusp of a terrible disaster."

"You mean the war between the Empire and Cyrica," said Caina, "if Cyrica rebels against the Empire."

"No," said Nadirah with a shake of her head, the jewels at her throat flashing in the candlelight. "A war between mortal men, terrible as it is, is only a passing thing. The blood and death pass, and in a few decades it is forgotten entirely. No, this is something worse. A catastrophe of sorcery, of the wrath of the netherworld spilling into the realm of mortal men."

"I don't understand," said Caina.

"You have come to me," said Nadirah, "for help about the statues, have you not?"

Again Caina felt a chill. "How do you know this? Did the spirits tell you?"

"Every time a man of flesh and blood is transformed to cold stone," said Nadirah, "there is an...echo in the netherworld, for lack of a better word. A ripple. Your Magisterium cannot see it. The fools view sorcery as a cold science, not a living art. But one trained in the traditions of Anshan can see it."

"So what is turning those men to stone?" said Caina. "Do you know?"

"No mortal sorcery can transform a man to stone," said Nadirah. "Only the powers of a spirit. Specifically, an elemental spirit of earth. Such a creature, if it came to the mortal world, would have the power to transmute living flesh to stone."

"Why would an elemental spirit come to Cyrioch?" said Caina. "Did someone summon it?"

"Beyond any doubt," said Nadirah. "A sorcerer of great power might have summoned the spirit and bound it as a weapon against his enemies. Or it might have been accidentally released from hibernation."

"Hibernation?" said Caina. "Spirits are like...animals? They hibernate over winter?"

"Not quite," said Nadirah. "Spirits are immortal. Yet sometimes they enter a torpor for long centuries and rest within physical objects in our world."

"I'd never heard of such a thing," said Caina.

"You have, though you know it not" said Nadirah. "You know of the fall of Old Kyrace?"

"It was the end of the Third Empire," said Caina. "The Emperor invaded Kyrace and seized the island. Just as they stormed the citadel, the volcano at the center of island exploded with such force that it destroyed the entire island." Old Kyrace had been destroyed, but many of the Kyracians escaped to New Kyre - and the hostility between the Kyracians and the Empire continued to this day.

"That is what the histories say," said Nadirah, "but they overlook a key detail. A great elemental spirit of flame was bound beneath the mountain. In the desperation of defeat, the Lord Archon of Kyrace shattered the chains binding the elemental, and the chaos of the spirit's release destroyed the island, the Emperor, the assembled Legions of Nighmar, and the Lord Archon himself." She shrugged. "Not all the hibernating spirits in our world are beings of such potency. But such spirits are scattered throughout the nations. The elemental that is turning your Ghosts to statues was either released by accident, or deliberately summoned by a sorcerer."

"The Magisterium used to summon elementals," said Caina, remembering what she had read, "but the knowledge was lost centuries ago, during the fall of the Fourth Empire." But that didn't count for much. The Magisterium had also banned necromancy and pyromancy, and Caina had encountered both among the magi.

Nadirah shrugged. "Regardless of whether or not the elemental was summoned, one is loose in Cyrioch. Until you find the spirit and return it to the netherworld, it will continued to strike."

"And can you help us find the elemental?" said Caina.

"Yes."

"How."

Nadirah smiled. "Bring me a Kindred assassin and the path will become clear."

"The Kindred?" said Caina. "Did the Kindred summon this elemental?"

"No," said Nadirah. "But the shadows have whispered to me. They are connected, the Kindred and the elemental, though I cannot see how. But bring me a Kindred assassin of sufficiently high rank, and I can make him speak. Then all his secrets shall be yours."

Caina thought it over. The offer seemed sincere, but no one in their right mind trusted a wielder of sorcery. "You know this catastrophe is coming, whatever it is. Why not leave Cyrioch?"

"Where would I go?" said Nadirah. "If I return to Anshan, I will be killed. Your Magisterium does not tolerate foreign wielders of sorcery within the heart of the Empire, and I would be forced to live in hiding. Both the Istarish and the Kyracians hate and fear the occultists of Anshan. Cyrioch is the only place I shall find refuge, and if it is destroyed, I will have nowhere else to go."

"All right," said Caina. "We have a deal."

~

CAINA STEPPED BACK into the street, blinking at the sunlight.

"That took too long," said Marzhod, scowling. "What did she tell you?"

"Some kind of elemental spirit is loose in the city," said Caina. "A spirit of earth, turning men to stone." Several of the Sarbian mercenaries muttered something in their native language and made signs to ward off evil.

"Lovely," said Marzhod. "Did she have any helpful suggestions on how to stop it?"

"She wants a Kindred assassin," said Caina, "one of high rank. She claims that the Kindred and the statues are somehow linked, and that her spells can make a high-ranking assassin reveal his secrets."

She felt no need to mention the other things Nadirah had told her. Could the Moroaica see out of Caina's eyes? Did she know Caina's thoughts? Was she listening to the conversation even now?

"Oh, yes, that's simple enough," said Marzhod. "A high-ranking Kindred assassin. We can find one of them easily! Let me just jaunt down to the market and pick one up."

"Marzhod," said Theodosia, "don't whine. It's unbecoming. We need to find a Kindred of high rank anyway."

"Fine," said Marzhod. "I'll start tracking down the Kindred couriers. Perhaps we'll get lucky and catch a knowledgeable one. And perhaps I'll find a chicken that lays golden eggs, as well."

"Maybe there's a sort of elemental," said Caina, "that can transmute living flesh into solid gold."

Both Theodosia and Marzhod gave her an odd look.

"What?" said Caina. "There's an elemental spirit of stone. Maybe there's an elemental spirit of gold, as well."

"Regardless," said Theodosia, "we need to prepare for the next celebration. To repay Lord Khosrau's kindness with the gladiatorial games, Lord Corbould is holding a chariot race. We can assume that the Kindred will try to kill them both there."

Marzhod nodded. "I'll try to find a high-ranking Kindred our friendly occultist can terrorize. And perhaps I'll get lucky and find that chicken with the golden eggs."

Marzhod left, and Caina and Theodosia headed for the Inn of the Defender.

"What did you think," said Theodosia, "of the occultist?"

"She's dangerous," said Caina, "and powerful. I told you about Nicorus, the outcast magus in Marsis?" Theodosia nodded. "He's strong, but I think Nadirah is stronger."

"Then why help us?" said Theodosia. "I assume Marzhod is paying her?"

"Probably," said Caina, "but there's more than that. She wanted to meet me because of what I did to the Moroaica." Theodosia nodded. "And she seems convinced that some sort of sorcerous disaster is going to befall Cyrioch. She can't go back to Anshan, so she needs to save Cyrioch, or..."

Caina fell silent.

"What is it?" said Theodosia.

"Corvalis," said Caina, voice low.

They stood on a wide street, carts and pedestrians hurrying back and forth. Caina spotted Corvalis heading at a steady pace towards the Plaza of Majesty. He hadn't spotted them, or if he had, he hadn't recognized Caina or Theodosia. He would assume they were just another pair of Sarbian desert men.

"I think," said Caina, "that I can get some answers."

Theodosia nodded, and Caina started after Corvalis.

14

BLACK SHADOW, GREEN FIRE

Caina made sure to stay a good distance behind Corvalis. He walked at a steady pace, the stride of a man on business but not in any particular hurry. He glanced around every so often, when he did, Caina made sure to look elsewhere, to walk alongside a cart until Corvalis's attention passed.

He was following someone, Caina was sure of it.

She maneuvered closer to Corvalis, hoping to catch sight of whoever he was following. He was trailing a wagon pulled by a pair of plodding oxen, three men sitting in the back. Two wore the rough clothes of freeborn laborers, while the third sat with a hooded cloak despite the day's heat.

The cloaked man turned his head, and Caina caught a glimpse of a dark face with a well-trimmed beard.

Mhadun, the magus the Kindred had hired.

And the other two men, Caina was sure, were Kindred assassins.

So why was Corvalis following the Kindred?

Caina hoped to find out.

The cart rolled into the Plaza of Majesty, the Magisterium's chapterhouse rising on one side, the pyramidal black temple of the Living Flame on the other. For a moment she thought Mhadun and the other Kindred would make for the chapterhouse's gates, but instead they turned right, driving down a back street alongside the chapterhouse's wall. After a moment Caina realized where they were going. Many of the Magisterium's chapterhouses had a secret entrance, going to a tavern or warehouse controlled by the Magisterium's agents. The magi used the entrance to come and go unseen.

Mhadun was going to that entrance, and Corvalis was going after him.

Caina picked up her pace.

East of the Magisterium's chapterhouse stood a maze of small palaces and mansions, home to Cyrioch's lesser nobility and wealthier merchants. The wagon rumbled along, and Caina saw it turn into a narrow alleyway between two opulent mansions. Corvalis ducked into a doorway, waited a moment, and started after the wagon.

And as he did, Caina saw a shadow move across a nearby rooftop. A man in a hooded cloak, and Caina glimpsed chain mail and a sheathed sword beneath the cloak. The hooded man gazed into the alley and beckoned. Other men rose from concealment upon the roof, and Caina saw a shorter figure in their midst, a man clad in studded leather armor.

It was Sicarion.

Apparently he had hired new thugs. And if he had hated Corvalis before, the fight at the Palace of Splendors would have only inflamed his wrath further. Corvalis was walking into a trap.

And he would not walk out of it alive.

Caina hesitated. Corvalis was not a Ghost, and she had no obligation to defend him. And he had lied to her when he said the Ghosts would be safe if they ignored him. But perhaps he had been mistaken. And if Caina saved his life again, he might share what he knew.

Her mouth hardened into a firm line.

And she would leave no one at the mercy of a man like Sicarion.

Caina waited until Sicarion and his thugs were out of sight, then hurried to one of the small mansions on the opposite side of the alley.

Unlike the palaces of the great nobles, the smaller mansions had no courtyards and stood pressed against each other. A corroded copper drainpipe ran down the side of the mansion, and Caina took a running jump, grabbed the pipe, and started pulling herself up. It was a hard climb, but she practiced unarmed forms every day, and her arms and legs were strong.

After a few moments she reached the roof, breathing hard, sweat dripping down her face. The rooftop was deserted, and Caina hurried forward, making sure to keep low and out of sight. The alley ended in a small courtyard shared between four mansions. Mhadun's wagon and oxen stood abandoned in the center of the courtyard. She spotted Corvalis examining the wagon.

She also saw two men perched on the rooftop, crossbows in hand, taking aim at Corvalis. Was Sicarion going to shoot Corvalis in the back? Sicarion was a capable fighter...but he like to gloat. He liked to watch the sufferings of his victims. A quick, efficient murder did not seem his style.

Sicarion marched into the courtyard, flanked by two of his thugs.

Corvalis whirled, drawing his sword and dagger. Sicarion stopped a dozen paces away and lowered his hood. The pattern of scars on his hairless head had changed since the Caina had last seen him.

"So," said Corvalis, "you didn't bleed to death when you fell from the window."

"I am hard to kill," said Sicarion. "Do you like my new ear? I can hear better through it."

"Why are you chasing me?" said Corvalis. "You weren't looking for me at the Palace of Splendors."

"No," said Sicarion. "If you must know, I'm here to execute a wayward disciple of my mistress. She cannot abide disloyalty. Finding you here is merely a pleasant bonus. After I kill you, I can attend to the disciple."

Caina wondered if Nadirah was Jadriga's renegade student. The occultist did know a great deal about the Moroaica.

"If you can kill me," said Corvalis.

Sicarion barked a rusty laugh. "That's not in doubt. That intrepid Ghost isn't here to save you this time."

The crossbowmen on the roof took aim.

"And your precious mistress isn't here to defend you," said Corvalis.

"Oh, no worries, my friend," said Sicarion, a grin crawling over the scarred patchwork over his face. "I don't need her to settle with you."

The crossbowmen straightened up...

"Corvalis!" shouted Caina, pointing. "Crossbows! On the roof!"

Corvalis's pale green eyes flashed towards her, and then to the crossbowmen.

So did Sicarion's mismatched gaze.

"Kill her!" bellowed Sicarion, pointing with his sword. "Shoot her now!"

The crossbowmen whirled to face Caina, raising their weapons. Sicarion sprang at Corvalis, his sword moving with the speed of a striking serpent. The other two mercenaries followed at heartbeat later, and Corvalis met them with his sword and dagger.

But Caina had more immediate problems.

The crossbowmen squeezed their triggers as Caina flung herself down. The quarrels shot past her, so fast she could not see them. One tugged at the sleeve of her robe, and she felt a burning pain as the razor-edged quarrel sliced her arm.

But she had endured worse pain, and Caina rolled to her feet and snatched a throwing knife from her belt. She flung the knife over the alley. The crossbowmen cursed and ducked, which gave Caina an opening. She sprinted for the edge of the alley and jumped, sand-colored robes billowing around her.

Below, she heard the clang of blade on blade, the bellowed curses as Corvalis fought Sicarion and his thugs.

Caina hit the roof on the far end of the alley. The nearest cross-bowman came at her, swinging the stock of his heavy weapon like a club. Caina sidestepped, pivoted, and brought her heel around in a vicious kick. Her boot slammed into the mercenary's right leg, and the man collapsed. His momentum carried him forward, and the mercenary tumbled over the edge of the roof with a scream.

A heartbeat later Caina heard the vicious crack of shattering bone.

The second mercenary threw aside his crossbow and yanked out his broadsword. But he didn't have time to pick up his shield, and Caina drew a dagger and stepped inside his guard. The mercenary dodged, and Caina's dagger drew a red line across his jaw.

The mercenary whipped his sword around, and Caina ducked. The clay roof tiles shifted beneath her boots, and she stumbled, sliding towards the edge of the roof. The mercenary came after her, his sword stabbing for her chest. Caina rolled aside, and the blade clanged off the tiles.

She seized a broken tile, rolled to her feet, and flung it at the mercenary's face. The man growled and lifted a hand to ward off the debris, and Caina's arm snapped forward. Her dagger sank into the mercenary's neck, and the man went limp, blood pouring over Caina's fingers. He sagged, and Caina ripped her blade free and looked at the courtyard.

One of the mercenaries lay dead on the ground. Corvalis, Sicarion, and the remaining mercenary spun in battle, swords and daggers clanging. Corvalis focused his attacks on Sicarion, probably to keep the scarred man from casting any spells. Yet the surviving mercenary attacked Corvalis with vigor, keeping him from landing a killing blow on Sicarion.

Caina saw another copper drainpipe running down the side of the mansion's wall. She shoved her dagger into its sheath, retrieved her throwing knife, and rolled off the edge of the roof, hands gripping the drainpipe. It gave an alarming creak, but Caina hurried down the wall.

A scream rang out, followed by the thud of a body hitting the ground, and Caina glanced down. Corvalis had killed of the second mercenary, and now he faced Sicarion alone. Their blades blurred as they spun around each other, Corvalis's face a grim mask, Sicarion's lips peeled back in fury.

Caina descended as fast as she dared. If she got to the ground and aided Corvalis, they could stop Sicarion...

Sicarion thrust out his hand, and Caina felt the harsh tingle of sorcerous power. The air around him rippled, and a blast of invisible force exploded in all directions. The oxen stamped in fear and strained against their traces. The edge of the psychokinetic burst caught Caina and almost knocked her from the pipe. She clung to it with all her strength, her boots scraping against the wall.

And the blast knocked Corvalis down.

Sicarion began another spell, green light shimmering around his fingers, and Caina felt the cold tingle of necromantic sorcery. She slid down the pipe as fast as she dared, hoping to stop him before he finished the spell. Caina hit the ground, knees buckling to absorb the impact, and Corvalis staggered to his feet.

Sicarion shouted. A pulse of green light washed from his fingertips, and the dead mercenaries began to move.

The corpses got to their feet, jerking like puppets pulled on invisible strings. Sicarion had done this before. In Marsis, she had killed several of his men, only for Sicarion to use necromancy to animate their corpses.

"Dead men again?" said Corvalis.

"If you hadn't killed them," said Sicarion, "I would have no need to reanimate them. Kill him!"

The dead mercenaries surged forward with eerie speed. Sicarion circled to the side, trying to flank Corvalis. Corvalis met the animated corpses, blades flashing. But against the dead men, he was at a disadvantage. The moving corpses were shells of flesh animated by Sicarion's necromancy, and a blade could not kill something already dead.

Caina reached into her robe and yanked out a curved dagger, the silver blade marked with characters in Kyracian script. It was forged from a rare metal called ghostsilver, harder and lighter than steel. Ghostsilver was proof against sorcery, and could disrupt any spells that it touched.

She buried the curved blade into the neck of the nearest dead man.

There was a sizzling noise, and the dagger's hilt grew hot beneath Caina's fingers. She wrenched the weapon free, black smoke rising from the wound in the corpse's neck. The dead man went into a twitching dance, and Corvalis swung, his sword in both hands. The blow took the corpse's head, and the dead man collapsed in a motionless heap.

Sicarion snarled and flung himself at Corvalis, and the remaining dead man attacked Caina. She backed away, dodging under the corpse's blows. Caina lashed out with the ghostsilver dagger again and again, smoke rising from the small cuts she opened on the corpse's face and arms. The dead man twitched with every strike, the ghostsilver disrupting Sicarion's necromancy.

Then Caina landed a solid hit on the corpse's thigh, and the dead man's right leg collapsed. She turned and buried her weapon in the corpse's neck. The hilt grew hot, almost too hot to hold, and black smoke poured from the dead man's nose and mouth. There was a snarling noise as the necromantic spell collapsed, and the corpse slid in a heap to the ground.

Caina spun, intending to aid Corvalis against Sicarion.

But Corvalis was not fighting Sicarion. Sicarion's spell had also raised the mercenary that Caina had knocked from the mansion's roof. The corpse's legs were broken, its face a bruised pulp, but it still attacked with vigor, driving Corvalis back. Sicarion turned to face Caina, shadows and green light flickering around his fingers, and Caina felt the sudden spike of sorcerous power.

She grabbed a throwing knife, intending to interrupt his spell.

But she was too late.

A bar of shadows rimmed in green flame burst from Sicarion's hand and slammed into Caina's chest. She staggered back with a scream, a horrible cold chill spreading through her limbs. Sicarion grinned as darkness filled Caina's vision, the world growing distant and remote...

Corvalis beheaded the dead man and stepped in front of the bar of shadow. His scream filled her ears, and at once the cold darkness vanished from Caina's body. The shadows and green flame swallowed Corvalis.

Then the tattoos upon his arms began to glow. The tattoos' swirling black lines flared with white light, and the shell of shadow around him shattered. Corvalis fell to his knees, shaking, and Sicarion staggered back, surprised pain flashing across his face.

Caina had her chance.

She flung the throwing knife. The blade sank into Sicarion's chest, and he staggered. She threw two more knives, each weapon striking home. Sicarion recovered himself and brought up his sword, but Caina was already on him. She slashed the ghostsilver dagger at his throat, and Sicarion jerked back. The blade tore a smoking gash down his face, the hilt heating up as it reacted to the necromantic spells upon his flesh. She reversed the blade, aiming for his chest, but Sicarion dodged, her blade ripping through his right leg.

Sicarion snarled and threw out his hand. Invisible force hammered into Caina and knocked her to the ground. But the spell lacked the force of his previous attacks, and she rolled to crouch, bracing herself for the attack.

But no attack came.

Sicarion sprinted down the alley. Caina's lips pulled back in a snarl, and she started after him. He would not escape, not this time. This time she would hunt him down and put an end to his cruel murders...

A groan reached her ears.

She saw Corvalis twitching upon the ground.

His green eyes met hers.

"Go," he rasped. "Don't let him get away."

"What's wrong with you?" she said. "The spell?"

Corvalis barked a laugh. "No. Spell can't touch me. Not after what the witchfinders did to me." The lines of the swirling tattoos upon his arms had gone dark again. "His dagger was poisoned. Go. Go!"

"Antidote," said Caina. "Do you have an antidote?"

"Aye," said Corvalis, shivering. "I know the poison. I have an antidote at my lodgings in Seatown."

Seatown was a long way from here. Corvalis didn't look like he could stand, let alone walk to Seatown. Sicarion was wounded, and if Caina caught him, she could finish him...

Corvalis tried to stand and slumped back against the ground.

"Damn you, go," said Corvalis. "Get him before he kills someone else."

He had saved her life by stopping Sicarion's spell.

"What are you waiting for?" said Corvalis. "Go!"

Caina made up her mind.

"Stop talking and get up," said Caina, and she helped him to stand.

15

IMAGES IN STONE

"There," rasped Corvalis, leaning against her. She felt the spasms going through his legs. "An apartment below the potter's shop."

His lips had taken on a bluish tint. Caina didn't know what poison Sicarion had used. But she suspected Corvalis didn't have much time left.

A narrow set of brick stairs descended alongside the wall of the potter's shop, and Corvalis half-walked, half-stumbled down them, Caina's arm around his waist. The stairs ended in a massive steel-banded door. Corvalis reached into his belt for a key, his hands shaking, but couldn't get it into the lock. Caina took the key, undid the lock, and pushed open the door.

The room beyond was barren. The walls were rough stone, dim light leaking through tiny windows near the ceiling. The only furnishings were a narrow bed, a chair and a workbench, and a wardrobe. A curtain closed off a small doorway on the far side of the room.

Corvalis collapsed into the bed, breathing hard, sweat pouring down his face.

"Antidote," he rasped.

"Where is it?" said Caina.

"Wardrobe," said Corvalis, his voice a harsh rasp. "Top shelf. Green vial."

Caina opened the wardrobe.

Inside a wide variety of weapons rested in racks. Swords, spears, daggers, throwing knives, darts, and disassembled crossbows lay waiting, while narrow shelves held a variety of tools, bottled powders and liquids. Caina found a small green vial of thick brown fluid.

"Is this it?" she said.

"Yes," said Corvalis. "Can't…drink it. Hands shaking too badly."

Caina nodded, pulled out the cork, gripped the side of Corvalis's face, and poured the contents down his throat. He swallowed, gasped, and shuddered again.

"Gods," he whispered. "That's vile. Hope it's not the last thing I taste." His shaking hand closed around her wrist. "Listen. I have to stay awake. I stay awake, I'm clear. If I pass out, there's only a one in three chance that I'll wake up again. Keep me talking."

"Those tattoos," said Caina. "What are they? They...broke Sicarion's spell. Like ghostsilver."

Corvalis wheezed out a laugh. "Like that dagger of yours? I got the tattoos after I escaped from the Kindred. From an Ulkaari witchfinder in the northern Empire. Spirits from the netherworld and worse things haunt the Ulkaari forests, hunt people like animals. These...these disrupt spells. Hurt like hell. Worth it, though. Figured...figured they would come in handy if I ever settled things with my father." He laughed again. "Guess I'll never have the chance now."

"No," said Caina. "You're not dead yet."

"Yet," repeated Corvalis. "What about you? You fight better than most men. Wouldn't expect that from someone like you."

"Someone like me?" said Caina.

Corvalis shuddered, sweat pouring down his face. "An opera singer's pretty maid."

"A disguise," said Caina. "I learned to fight because I had good teachers. But if you listen to me talk, you'll fall unconscious. So instead you're going to tell me more about yourself. Why did you leave the Kindred?"

Corvalis snorted. "I didn't like the way they smelled."

"Tell me more," said Caina.

"Just like a Ghost," said Corvalis. "Inquisitive to the end. Why did I leave? My conscience troubled me, but I learned to ignore it. I hated my father, though. Hated what he did to me, hated how he viewed me as his pet hound. And then someone changed my mind. Someone..."

His jaw clamped shut.

"Gods," muttered Caina. "You're having a seizure."

"No," said Corvalis. "I don't know if I want you to know why I left the Kindred."

"It's a little late to keep secrets," said Caina.

Corvalis snorted. "You lecture me about keeping secrets, Ghost? The Ghosts do nothing else."

"Then tell me this," said Caina. "You said if we left you alone, no other Ghosts would be turned to stone. But one Ghost and one Kindred assassin were turned to statues at the Ring of Valor during Lord Khosrau's games. What happened?"

"I don't know," said Corvalis. His voice dropped to a whisper, his eyes starting to close. "I thought...I thought if they stayed away from me, no one else would get hurt. He wouldn't have any reason to go after them. They must...they must have gotten in his way."

"His way?" said Caina, leaning closer. "Who? Tell me."

Corvalis shuddered, his eyes going wide, and then he slumped against the bed. All the strength flowed out of him.

"I can't stay awake," he whispered. His fingers tightened her wrist. "Listen...listen to me. In the back room. Help her. Please, Ghost. Help her."

"Who's turning people into statues?" said Caina. "Tell me."

Corvalis's eyes closed.

"Tell me!" she shouted. "Corvalis!"

No response.

She slapped him, hoping to shock him awake, but he didn't respond. His breathing was shallow, his heartbeat rapid.

"Damn it," breathed Caina. She had been so close.

She looked at him with a pang of regret. He had saved her life, and now he was going to die in a dusty cellar below a potter's shop.

Well. A two in three chance he was going to die, anyway.

Caina pulled off Corvalis's cloak and cleaned the sweat from his brow. She rested his head upon the pillow and put his hands at this side. If he was going to die, at least he could die comfortable.

Then she searched the apartment.

If Corvalis died before he could tell her his secrets, she would just have to find them on her own.

She looked through the wardrobe first. His weapons were well-made, and she found a variety of poisons among the vials. No doubt he had learned how to use them as a Kindred assassin. Hidden beneath the wardrobe's false bottom she found a steel strongbox. It was locked, and guarded with a nasty mechanical trap, but Halfdan had taught her how to bypass both. A half-hour's work opened the lock and disabled the trap, and inside Caina found stacks of gold coins, along with two leather pouches of cut gemstones. Corvalis did not lack for funds.

But she found no documents.

She locked the strongbox, rearming the trap, and examined his workbench. Scars and stains marred the surface, along with tiny piles of metal shavings. He had been repairing his weapons and armor here. Caina knelt and looked under the bed. Several wooden chests rested there, and inside Caina found a variety of clothes, ranging from the finery of a nobleman to the ragged garb of a free laborer. Disguises, no doubt.

She looked down at Corvalis. His breathing remained shallow, fresh sweat trickling down his face. He did not look any better. Nor did he look any worse.

Caina crossed to the doorway on the far side of the room and pushed aside the ragged curtain. The tiny room beyond was empty, save for a shape draped in a canvas tarp. A shape that looked a great deal like a statue.

Caina pulled aside the tarp.

The statue of a young woman stared back at Caina.

Like all the others, the statue was fantastically detailed. The woman wore the robe of a magus, and Caina saw every fold and drape of the fabric in the white stone. The woman's face was a study in stunned horror.

Caina stared at the face for a moment.

Then she walked back to the main room, sat besides the bed, tended the cut on her arm, and waited to see if Corvalis would live or die.

~

ABOUT THREE HOURS later Corvalis sat up, eyes wide. He snarled and grabbed for his sword belt, but Caina had decided that removing his weapons was a good idea. He looked around, and bit by bit the terror and confusion drained from his face.

"This isn't my idea of paradise," he said, "but it makes for a very feeble hell."

"I'm pleased," said Caina, "that you don't think I'm a devil."

Corvalis managed a harsh laugh. "How long was I out?"

"A little over three hours," said Caina.

"Thank you," said Corvalis, "for watching over me." He grimaced. "Three times now that I owe you my life."

"You saved my life, as well," said Caina, "and it gave me time to think."

Wariness came into his expression. "And what did you think about?"

"I know," said Caina, "what happened to you, and why people keep turning into statues. You said that someone convinced you to leave the Kindred. I think it was that woman in the next room."

Corvalis said nothing, his hands balled into fists.

"She convinced you to leave the Kindred," said Caina. "So to take revenge on you, your father had her turned to stone."

"Yes," said Corvalis, his voice flat.

"Which is why you came to Cyrioch," said Caina. "Whoever or

whatever turned her to stone is here. You're hoping to find it and reverse the process."

"You," said Corvalis, "are damnably clever."

"Perhaps," said Caina, "but I'm not wrong, am I?"

Corvalis sighed. "No."

"Who was she?" said Caina. "A lover?"

Corvalis shook his head. "No. My sister."

Caina blinked. "I hadn't expected that."

"Our mother was the First Magus's favorite mistress for a few years, until he grew bored with her and had her executed," said Corvalis. He took a deep breath. "Claudia was his favorite daughter. She had arcane talent, so she went into the Magisterium while he sold me to the Kindred. We were close, and I always thought our father would twist her into a copy of himself. But Claudia...Claudia has a good heart. Maybe I had one once, but the Kindred beat it out of me." He shook his head. "But our father couldn't change Claudia. When I met her again, after she became a full sister of the Magisterium...she hadn't changed. Not a bit. She used her spells to ward grain warehouses against rats, to shield the cellars of commoners from insects, that sort of thing."

"I doubt it would last," said Caina. "The Magisterium is filled with monsters, and sorcery twists anyone who uses it."

"Perhaps," said Corvalis. He rubbed the sweat from his face. "But not Claudia. She thought I was dead. When she found out what our father had done to me...she said it opened her eyes. Said it showed her what the Magisterium really was. She wanted to leave the Empire, and convinced me to leave the Kindred and go with her."

"Where would you have gone?" said Caina.

"One of the free cities, west of Anshan," said Corvalis. "We would live quietly, keep a low profile." He shrugged. "She had me convinced that we could leave it all behind. She even managed to talk me out of killing the First Magus."

"What went wrong?" said Caina.

"I left the Kindred," said Corvalis, "and our father was furious." He scowled. "Decius Aberon, you see, regards his children are his property, to do with as he pleases. He sent the Kindred to kill me, but I killed everyone who came after me. So he caught Claudia instead," he waved his hand at the curtained doorway, "and you can figure out the rest."

Caina frowned. "So Decius Aberon did this to her? He turned her to stone? Why aren't you in Artifel, trying to hunt him down?"

"He ordered it done, but he didn't do it personally," said Corvalis. "One of his minions did it. A master magus named Ranarius."

Caina blinked. "Ranarius? The preceptor of the Cyrioch chapter?"

"The same," said Corvalis. He stood and stretched. "I don't know how he did it, either. Ranarius is...odd, even by the standards of the Magisterium. The magi regard him as an eccentric genius, and they're afraid of him. They sometimes hire the Kindred to assassinate each other, and everyone who has tried to assassinate Ranarius has come to a bad end."

"How did he end up here?" said Caina.

Corvalis tugged off his armor, put it on the workbench, and pulled off his sweat-drenched shirt. The black lines of the tattoo spiraled over his back and over the hard muscles of his belly and chest. There was not an inch of fat on him, and she saw the pale scars from sword and dagger wounds.

He saw her looking and raised an eyebrow.

"Oh, don't worry," said Corvalis. "I'm not going to ravage you. Gods know if I tried I would end up with a dagger in my gullet. I just want a shirt that's not drenched in my own poisons."

Caina decided to change the subject

"How," she said, "did Ranarius end up in Cyrioch?"

"A reward," said Corvalis. He retrieved a shirt from one of the chests. "My father is a tyrant, but he rewards loyalty well. After Ranarius turned a few of the First Magus's enemies to stone, my father appointed him the preceptor of Cyrica Urbana. So I followed him here."

Caina nodded. "So did you follow him here to kill him...or to find a way to restore your sister?"

"The latter," said Corvalis. "I traced him here, and I have been trying to find a way to capture and overpower him. If his life is at stake, I can force him to reverse the spell he placed upon Claudia."

"That may be more difficult than you think," said Caina.

"Oh?" said Corvalis. He picked up his sword belt. "I am trying to abduct a master magus and force him to reverse a spell the Magisterium claims doesn't actually exist. How could it get any more difficult?"

"I know how Ranarius is turning those people to stone," said Caina.

Corvalis turned so fast that Caina barely followed the movement. "How? How is he doing it? Tell me."

"That would depend," said Caina.

"Depend? On what?" said Corvalis. "For the gods' sake, tell me. I have traveled across half the Empire and risked death time and time again to save my sister."

"It depends," said Caina, "on whether or not you are willing to help me."

"Help you to do what?" said Corvalis. "Do you want me to murder someone? Is that it? A life in exchange for the secret that will save my sister?" His face twisted with disgust. "Are you Ghosts any better than the Kindred? I have put myself at risk over and over for her. And why are you putting yourself at risk, Ghost? For power? Glory? Wealth?"

"I know what it is," said Caina, voice quiet, "to love someone and lose them."

She thought of her father, sitting glassy-eyed in his chair.

Corvalis's anger drained away, and he sat on the bed with a sigh.

"Perhaps you do," said Corvalis. "Everyone loses someone they love, eventually. Except my father. He loves nothing but his own power." He sighed. "So. What do you want of me?"

"Your help against the Kindred," said Caina.

Corvalis said nothing, his green eyes measuring her.

"The Kindred are trying to kill both Lord Corbould, Lord Khosrau, and Lord Armizid," said Caina. "I don't know who hired them, but what they're trying to accomplish is plain."

"A war between Cyrica and the Empire," said Corvalis. "Any idiot can see that."

"I've come to Cyrioch to make sure that doesn't happen," said Caina. "We've stopped three assassination attempts against Khosrau and Corbould..."

Corvalis leaned forward. "Three? You're sure of that?"

Caina nodded. "Once at the Amphitheatre of Asurius. Again at the Palace of Splendors and the Gallery of the Well, when we fought Sicarion. And yesterday at the Ring of Valor. Three times. But we can't keep doing that. Sooner or later the Kindred will be successful, and the war with New Kyre and Istarinmul will widen. We have to find whoever hired the Kindred."

"And you want my help," said Corvalis, "to do it."

"Aye," said Caina. "You used to be Kindred. You know how they operate." She took a deep breath. "And if you help us...I will help you against Ranarius. I swear it."

Corvalis raised an eyebrow. "What do you know about fighting sorcerers?"

"This and that," said Caina, thinking of Maglarion and Jadriga and Kalastus and all the others.

"How can I trust you?" said Corvalis. He gave a thin smile. "The Ghosts...have something of a reputation for underhanded dealings."

"And the Kindred do not?" said Caina.

"I am no longer Kindred."

He had a point.

"Very well," said Caina. "Ranarius used an elemental spirit of earth to turn your sister into stone."

Corvalis frowned. "A...spirit? Gods. I never considered that. I suppose I should have. I spent enough time learning to fight spirits from the Ulkaari." He stared at her for a moment. "How do you know this?"

"I spoke with a renegade Anshani occultist," said Caina. "She senses the spirit's presence in the netherworld, and claims to feel a sort of...echo every time it turns someone to stone."

"That makes sense," said Corvalis. "My father told me that during the Fourth Empire, when the magi ruled instead of the Emperor, the Magisterium knew how to summon elemental spirits. The knowledge was lost in the destruction of Caer Magia." He rubbed his jaw, thinking. "But if anyone could figure out how to do it, Ranarius could. The man has a heart made of ice, but he is brilliant."

Caina remembered the blindfold around Nicasia's eyes and the collar around her neck. "Aye."

"It does make things trickier," said Corvalis. "If I kill Ranarius, it could break his binding over the spirit. It might go berserk, or simply return to the netherworld. Spirits do not think in terms of mortal logic."

"You shouldn't kill Ranarius anyway," said Caina. "Capture him and force him to change your sister back, along with all the other Ghosts. Then you can kill him."

Corvalis frowned. "You'll help me with this? You and the other Ghosts?"

"We will," said Caina, "if you help us against the Kindred." She paused. "By helping us, you may be helping yourself. The occultist thinks that the Kindred assassins and the statues are connected. Which means Ranarius and the Kindred are connected."

He didn't laugh at the idea. "I know a sorcerer with ties to the netherworld can sometimes see potential futures. From what I understand, all mortals cast...shadows, of a sort, into the netherworld. And some shadows are larger and blacker than others."

"Do you think Ranarius hired the Kindred to kill Khosrau and Corbould?" said Caina.

"It's possible," said Corvalis, "but I doubt he would bother. Ranarius is not interested in political power, not the way my father is. I suspect he became preceptor so he could use the Cyrioch chapterhouse's resources to fund his experiments. Before that, he used the slave trade to raise money." His mouth twisted. "Summoning elemental spirits must require expensive equipment. But he wouldn't gain anything if Cyrica rebelled against the Empire."

"Then we have an agreement?" said Caina. "You'll help us against the Kindred? And in exchange, we'll help you with Ranarius?"

"Agreed," said Corvalis. He held out his hand, and Caina gripped it. His hand was strong, fingers hard with calluses from sword and spear. "You are going to need my help. The Kindred will stop playing games and come for Lord Corbould and Lord Khosrau in force."

"What do you mean?" said Caina.

"You said the Kindred of Cyrioch tried to kill them three times," said Corvalis, releasing her hand and holding up a finger. "Once at the Amphitheatre, once at the Gallery of the Well, and once at the Ring of Valor. The Kindred send out lower-ranking assassins first. But if they fail, the higher-ranking assassins are sent instead, and they are far more dangerous."

"Tomorrow," said Caina. "Lord Corbould is sponsoring chariot races in Khosrau's and Armizid's honor."

Corvalis nodded. "It is easier to kill someone in public and make an escape. The Kindred will almost certainly try to kill the nobles there."

"Then we had better get moving," said Caina.

She turned towards the door, Corvalis following.

"Ghost," said Corvalis, voice quiet.

She turned. Corvalis stood in the dim light coming through the narrow window, so motionless he seemed a statue himself.

"Thank you," he said, "for my life. I was certain you would pursue Sicarion and leave me to my fate."

"I don't like Sicarion," said Caina, "but I like watching his victims die even less. And you did save my life, almost at the cost of your own."

Corvalis snorted. "The spell hurt, but I was in no danger. The damned poison on Sicarion's dagger almost finished me."

"The debts between us are settled," said Caina, "and we can work together to stop the assassins and free your sister."

"Agreed," said Corvalis, and they left the apartment.

~

A SHORT TIME later Caina and Corvalis slipped into Theodosia's suite at the Inn of the Defender.

"Well," said Theodosia, looking up from the table as they entered. "I see you've found a friend."

"The opera singer?" said Corvalis, glancing at Caina. "Your circlemaster is Khosrau's favorite opera singer?"

Theodosia raised an eyebrow. "Does that surprise you?"

Corvalis laughed. "The Magisterium lives in terror of the Ghosts. They see Ghosts in every shadow. Every accident gets blamed on the Ghosts. They think the Ghost circlemasters are lords of the shadows, stealthy assassins who make the Kindred look like bumbling children." He shook his head. "Instead, the Ghosts of Cyrioch are an opera singer and her pretty maid."

Theodosia smiled, showing her teeth. "Isn't that sweet, Marina? He thinks you're pretty."

Corvalis glanced at Caina. "Gods. Don't tell me you're actually a man."

"No," said Caina.

"Nor am I," said Theodosia, "but you did not call me pretty."

Corvalis made a sardonic bow. "I apologize, my lady. I was struck dumb by the august majesty of your presence, and my wits scattered and left my tongue adrift. Your beauty is matched only by your venerable wisdom."

"Venerable?" said Theodosia. "What a dreadful thing to call a woman. But one cannot expect a silver tongue in a Kindred assassin."

"Former Kindred assassin," said Corvalis.

"Perhaps," said Theodosia. "I like young men with fire. But Marina did not bring you here to banter with me, however much we might enjoy it. I assume you are here to offer us something? I do find you handsome, in an austere sort of way, and it would be a dreadful pity if I had to order you killed."

"Marina proposed an alliance," said Corvalis. "Ranarius is turning your Ghosts to stone, but he started with my sister. The Kindred are trying to kill your Emperor's nobles, and I know how the Kindred operate. We can help each other."

Theodosia looked at Caina.

"I think," said Caina, "that we can trust him."

Again Theodosia raised her eyebrow.

"He doesn't want money or power," said Caina. "He just wants to save his sister. And he can't do that by himself. So he needs our help. And he hates the Magisterium more than I do."

"That must," said Theodosia, voice quiet, "be a mighty hatred indeed."

"It is," said Corvalis.

"All right," said Theodosia, and she lifted her hands from beneath the table. In them she held a small hand crossbow, the dart's tip gleaming with poison. Theodosia must have been holding it at Corvalis the entire time.

"I see I owe you my life again," said Corvalis.

"I suppose it would be beneath the dignity of a woman of my august venerability to kill you myself," said Theodosia, "but Marina vouched for you, and that is good enough for me. Tell me how you can aid us against the Kindred."

"They will try to kill Corbould and Khosrau at the hippodrome tomorrow," said Corvalis. "Three times they sent lower-ranking assassins against you, and three times you stopped them. Tomorrow they will send out higher-ranking assassins." He smiled. "And I will show you how to stop them."

16

AMBUSH

"You're going to get killed wearing that," said Caina.

"Everyone dies," said Corvalis with a shrug. "If I am to meet my death today, I may as well do it wearing fine clothing."

They stood in the sitting room of Theodosia's suite. Corvalis wore the fine blue robe and cap of a master merchant from the Imperial collegium of grain traders. A gold badge glittered on his cap, and a leather belt went around his waist, supporting a sheathed short sword and dagger that looked purely ornamental.

Unlike most grain merchants, he managed to look good in the robe. And it was loose enough that Caina knew he had a number of daggers and knives hidden beneath it, and perhaps a longer sword strapped to his thigh.

"I suppose it makes sense," said Caina. She wore a blue gown with black trim, the sort the wife of a prosperous merchant might wear. She put a blue scarf over her hair in deference to Cyrican customs, and chose only silver jewelry, since gold would be too ostentatious for a merchant's wife.

"The Kindred must have figured out that there are Ghosts among Corbould's retinue," said Corvalis, adjusting one of his cuffs. "You told me they tried to kill the circlemaster of Cyrioch. So they'll watch the opera company and Corbould's men for any Ghosts. They won't expect someone from the crowd to stop them."

"They will assume the Ghosts infiltrated the grain traders' collegium," said Caina, examining herself in the room's mirror. In the blue gown, with her hair concealed beneath the scarf, she looked nothing like Marina, Theodosia's servant, or Maric, Theodosia's bodyguard, and she certainly did not look like a Sarbian mercenary. Anyone seeing her would assume that she was the pretty young wife of a prosperous grain merchant...

Unless someone looked too long into her eyes.

"Of course the Ghosts have infiltrated the collegium," said Corvalis. "I would have been surprised if you had not. But Cyrica ships thousands of tons of grain across the sea every year, and grain merchants are a common sight here. The Kindred are ready for trouble...but they'll expect the trouble to come from Corbould's servants or the opera company. Not from a grain merchant and his wife."

He had a point. But Caina would have preferred to remain disguised as a servant. A servant running through a crowd drew no attention. A merchant's wife, on the other hand...

She shook her head. Corvalis's plan was the best chance they had to capture a high-ranking Kindred assassin.

"It's time," said Caina. "Let's go."

"As you command, wife," said Corvalis.

"For a renegade assassin," said Caina, "you certainly have an arch sense of humor."

Corvalis smirked. Caina rolled her eyes and followed him from the Inn.

"HOLD," growled the militiaman. "Hippodrome's full. Lord Corbould paid for the races, and unless you're one of his friends, the tickets went to the free citizens of Cyrioch. You don't have a ticket, do you?"

The hippodrome of Cyrioch rose above them. Unlike the

Amphitheatre of Asurius and the Ring of Valor, the hippodrome was built of Nighmarian concrete and baked brick. Evidently none of Lord Khosrau's ancestors had enjoyed chariot racing as much as gladiatorial combats or Imperial opera. Despite its simplicity, it was nonetheless a vast structure, with a thirty foot wall of brick stretching away in either direction. Caina guessed that the long oval could hold nearly as many people as the Ring of Valor, if not more. She heard the cheering roars of thousands rising from within the hippodrome.

"Fellow," said Corvalis, drawing himself up. He now spoke Cyrican with a heavy High Nighmarian accent, and his every word dripped affronted arrogance. "I will have you know that I am a close friend of the honorable Lord Corbould Maraeus, and he personally tasked me with arranging the grain contracts to feed the Legions that even now assail the foes of our glorious Empire. And as a reward for my weal service, the honorable Lord Corbould has invited me to attend the chariot races in honor of the noble Lord Khosrau."

Caina blinked in surprise, then remembered to keep her own mask of arrogant hauteur in place.

"I beg your pardon, sir," said the militiaman, now marginally more polite. "But I have my orders. No one gets into the hippodrome without a ticket."

Corvalis drew out a scroll. "I trust this will suffice?"

The scroll was an official document in High Nighmarian, drawn up by Lord Corbould's own scribes. Caina had no idea how Theodosia had managed to obtain it. The document granted the bearer the right to sit at a place of honor at the chariot races sponsored by Lord Corbould.

The guard squinted at the scroll and gave Corbould's elaborate seal a hesitant tap. Caina suspected he did not know how to read Cyrican, let alone High Nighmarian.

"Aye," said the militiaman, “move along.”

"Thank you," said Corvalis, tucking the scroll into his robe. He hooked his arm through Caina's and led her up the concrete ramp into the hippodrome.

"You are very good," murmured Caina, "at playing the supercilious rich fool."

"It's useful," said Corvalis in his usual cold voice. "Rich fools might not see servants, aye...but after a while, the servants forget to see rich fools. And...ah."

They stepped into the sunlight. Caina saw thousands of Cyrican commoners packing the hippodrome. A long, narrow oval, perhaps two hundred yards long, lay at the center of the hippodrome, divided by a stone rail. Here four teams of charioteers would race, fighting to win the prize. It was less bloody than the gladiatorial games...but many charioteers often met their end beneath the steel-shod hooves of their rivals' horses.

"There," said Caina.

A row of boxes waited at the edge of the oval, offering a superb view. Lord Corbould and Lord Khosrau sat in the largest box, Lord Governor Armizid with them. Caina was not surprised to see Theodosia at Khosrau's side, laughing at one of his jokes.

"Your circlemaster," said Corvalis, "has a knack for charm."

"That she does," said Caina. "It helps that Khosrau likes opera."

A slave scurried forward, and Corvalis presented the scroll. The slave led them to a private box that had a clear view of Corbould and Khosrau. A tray rested between a pair of seats, holding a carafe of wine and some sliced sausage, cheese, and bread.

"This is pleasant," said Caina as the slave hurried away.

Corvalis snorted. "You should see the boxes for Khosrau's closest friends. Roast pigs, sides of beef, rare fruits..." He snorted. "Though I wonder if any of it is poisoned."

"They tried poison," said Caina. "During that ball at the Gallery of the Well."

Corvalis glanced at Khosrau's box. "Won't work this time. He's brought a slave with him. Tasting all his food. And the Kindred won't try poison again. The higher ranking assassins prefer not to bother with it. They'll use something more...elegant."

"Such as?" said Caina.

Corvalis shrugged. "It depends. I know one assassin who spent weeks stuffing grain dust into the crawlspace below a target's house. After seven weeks, he lit the dust on fire and blasted the house, and the target, to charred coals. Another assassin infiltrated the civic militia of Artifel, recalibrated one of catapults on the city's walls, and shot a barrel of burning pitch into the target's house."

"I doubt they'll try to smuggle a catapult into the hippodrome," said Caina.

He almost smiled at that. "No. Too many witnesses. They'll try something more subtle. Be watchful."

He fell into silence, his eyes roving over the crowds. Caina settled into her seat, watching for anything unusual. This was almost pleasant, coming to the chariot races in the company of a handsome man. Certainly she had not done anything like this for years.

She reproached herself for the sentiment. She was a nightfighter of the Ghosts, and she would never have a family...

Caina turned her head.

"Corvalis," she said, voice low. "Ranarius is here."

The preceptor strode with calm dignity through the aisles, Nicasia trudging at his side, her blindfolded eyes downcast. Corvalis's eyes narrowed to hard green slits, almost as hard as the jade collar around Nicasia's neck.

"Wait," she said. "Mhadun is with them."

The Cyrican master magus strolled after the preceptor, expression amused. His black beard had been trimmed with precise lines, and oil gleamed in his hair.

"You told me he was Kindred," said Caina.

"He is," said Corvalis. "And he is high-ranking. High enough that he would know where the Kindred Haven lies hidden."

They shared a look.

"High enough," said Caina, "that the Kindred would send him to kill the nobles?"

"Yes," said Corvalis, voice grim. "The Kindred use their sorcerers to...solve problems. To dispose of targets the lower-ranked assassins cannot handle. He's here to kill Khosrau and Corbould, I'm sure of it."

Ranarius stopped before the Lord Governor's box, exchanging pleasantries with Khosrau, Corbould, and Armizid. Mhadun waited a respectful distance away, looking like a man enjoying a well-earned holiday. Then Ranarius settled in a box a short distance from the Lord Governor's, Mhadun still at his side.

"Do you think there are any others?" said Caina.

Corvalis grunted. "Maybe. But Mhadun is powerful enough to handle this by himself. If he starts casting a spell at the nobles, we might just have to kill him and run."

"We need him alive," said Caina.

Corvalis scowled. "That might be..."

"Citizens of Cyrica Urbana!" thundered a voice, booming over the hippodrome.

Caina saw Corbould's herald standing before the Lord Governor's box. A junior magus stood beside him, using a spell to amplify the herald's voice. Caina felt the faint tingle as the magus focused his will and power into the spell.

"Lords and ladies of the Empire!" boomed the herald. "Merchants of the collegia, brothers and sisters of the Imperial Magisterium, and free citizens of Cyrica Urbana! I bid you welcome to the Great Hippodrome for this exhibition of manful courage and skill! The finest four chariot teams of the Imperial capital shall race for your approval, and the victor shall be crowned with glory and triumph!"

The crowds cheered.

"I think," muttered Corvalis, "that the victor would rather be crowned with gold. It spends better than glory."

"Lasts longer, too," said Caina.

"These challenges of skill and horsemanship," said the herald, "have been generously financed by the honored guest of our noble Lord Governor, Corbould, Lord of House Maraeus."

Corbould stood, stern in his black armor, and the crowd cheered. Caina swept her eyes over the ascending rows of seats, wondering if a hidden archer lurked there, but she saw no sign of any Kindred.

Mhadun watched Corbould, his expression bored.

"Citizens of Cyrica Urbana!" said Corbould, the junior magus enhancing his voice. "In the name of our Emperor, I declare these games to be open! In the name of our Emperor, I have brought the four finest chariot teams of Malarae to your city, so that they might display their skill and prowess for your approval, a reflection of the glory of our Empire!"

A flour of trumpets rang out, a portcullis on the far end of the track rattled open, and the chariot teams rolled into the hippodrome. Four horses pulled each of the racing chariots, and every driver wore a tunic of a different color – red, blue, green, and gold. Matching colors decorated each chariot, and a small troop of handlers surrounded each team, checking the traces and the wheels.

"The Reds, the Greens, the Golds, and the Blues," said Caina. "The four best chariot teams of Malarae."

"They'll probably try the assassination during the height of the race," said Corvalis. "When the crowd's attention is on the chariots. It will be something subtle. Something that will give them time to escape before anyone notices."

Caina glanced at Mhadun and frowned. "Do you think he'll use sorcery to kill them?"

"He might," said Corvalis. "But sorcery isn't terribly subtle. It would be fairly obvious if he uses a spell to kill the nobles. And Ranarius would sense it, along with any other magi here."

"Mhadun has some hold over Ranarius," said Caina. "And I doubt a low-ranking magus would question the orders of his preceptor and a master magus."

"Gods," muttered Corvalis. "I wish Claudia were here. If Mhadun tried something, she would shut him down in a heartbeat."

"I do not," said Caina. "I would prefer to deal with this without the aid of a wielder of sorcery."

Corvalis's eyes flashed with sudden anger. "You would rather she remained stone?"

Caina met Corvalis's gaze without flinching. She had seen too much harm wreaked by sorcery, and those who wielded it were not to be trusted under any circumstances. Claudia might not have deserved to be transformed into a statue, but she was still a magus, still a sorceress. That alone was reason enough not to trust her, to kill her if necessary...

Wasn't it?

A tiny thread of doubt flickered through her mind.

"No, of course not," said Caina. "I agreed to help you free her, and I shall. But I have seen sorcery. I have seen the harm it does. She is your sister and you love her, aye...but I do not trust sorcery or those who use it."

Corvalis snorted. "Fair enough. I've seen enough cruel sorcerers to understand." His eyes flickered towards Ranarius. "But Claudia... no, Claudia is nothing like Ranarius." He flashed a brittle smile. "She's nothing like us, Ghost. You and I, we are killers. We're good at it. She's never killed anyone. I don't think she could bring herself to hurt anyone." He gazed at the chariot teams. "I don't remember what that feels like."

"Nor do I," said Caina.

She wondered what her younger self would think of her now. As a child, she had wanted to marry and have children of her own, to be a better mother than Laeria Amalas had ever been. She had never dreamed that she would become a Ghost nightfighter, a spy and an infiltrator.

A killer.

The thought made her sad, and she pushed the emotion aside. This was neither the time nor the place for such musings.

A blast of trumpets rang out, and the chariots surged forward, the horses galloping. A mighty cheer rose from the spectators, drowning out the rumble of the horses' hooves and the rattle of the chariots' wheels. Caina watched as the chariots thundered past the nobles' boxes and followed the curve at the far end of the hippodrome.

"An accident," said Corvalis.

"What do you mean?" said Caina.

"Sooner or later one of the charioteers will have an accident," said Corvalis. "One of the horses will throw a shoe, or an axle will crack, or the charioteer will fall and get trampled. Every eye in this hippodrome will be watching the race, and that's when the Kindred will strike."

Caina nodded and settled in to wait, glancing at Mhadun from time to time.

The chariots did lap after lap, and soon the horses bore a lather of sweat. The charioteers gripped their reins with grim determination, their clothing rippling in the wind. The Red chariot had the lead, with Blue and Gold fighting for second, and Green trailing behind. The constant roar from the crowd did not diminish. In Malarae, Caina knew, rival gangs supported the different chariot teams, and sometimes rioted and fought each other. But since Cyrioch's own charioteers were not racing, the crowd seemed relatively calm.

Though a riot would give the Kindred an excellent opportunity.

"It looks like Red is going to win," said Corvalis. "I should have placed a bet."

Caina laughed. "A poor idea." She saw Marzhod's Sarbian mercenaries circulating through the crowds and collecting wagers. "You'll end up with broken kneecaps."

"Let them try," said Corvalis. He sat up straighter. "Mhadun's moving."

The master magus rose from Ranarius's box and made his leisurely way up the stairs. He had a look of a man who had drunk too much wine and needed to visit the hippodrome's public lavatories. Halfway up he turned and looked at the racing chariots, as if hesitant to leave the race.

In the sleeve of his robe, Caina saw his hand gesture, and she felt the sudden surge of arcane power.

A lot of arcane power.

"He's casting a spell," said Caina. "A strong one."

"Are you sure?" said Corvalis. "He's just standing there."

"I can sense the presence of sorcery," said Caina.

"You can?" said Corvalis. "How?"

"Long story," said Caina. "We've got to stop him."

She started to rise, and Corvalis's fingers closed about her forearm.

"Wait," he said. "He's not casting a spell at the lords."

He was correct. Mhadun was gazing at the chariots, his head turning to follow their movement. Specifically, he was staring at the Green chariot. His eyes grew wider, and he made a short chopping motion with his left hand.

Caina's skin crawled as she felt the burst of sorcerous power.

And the Green chariot's right wheel exploded in a spray of jagged wooden splinters.

A blur shot from the chariot to Mhadun, moving so fast Caina could not follow it.

The Green horses whinnied in alarm and bolted, dragging the damaged chariot with them. The charioteer grabbed at the reins as the chariot bounced and skidded along the track. For a moment Caina was sure the man would be thrown to his death, but the panicked horses slowed, and the ruined chariot skidded to a halt.

"Disqualified!" boomed the herald. "The Green chariot yields the victory. The Blue, the Red, and the Gold yet remain."

"Look," said Corvalis.

Mhadun held a jagged wooden shard about six inches long.

"Where the devil did he get that?" said Corvalis.

A stripe of green paint marked the side of the shard.

"It's part of the chariot wheel," said Caina. "He shattered the Green chariot's wheel with a psychokinetic spell, and then called one of the fragments to his hand."

"Why would he do that?" said Corvalis. "That's a neat trick of accuracy, but what's the point? It's not as if he can walk up to Khosrau and stab the fat old bastard with a wooden stake."

The answer appeared in Caina's mind with perfect clarity.

"Because," she said. "He's going to shatter the wheel of another chariot and use his powers to throw the shards into Lord Corbould, Lord Khosrau, and Lord Armizid all at once. Oh, gods, that's brilliant. It will look like a freak chariot accident, but Corbould sponsored the race, and that will be enough to push Cyrica out of the Empire."

"It would take a great deal of sorcerous control," said Corvalis. "I didn't think Mhadun had it in him."

"The splinter from the wheel is in his hand, isn't it?" said Caina. "He didn't walk down there and pick it up."

"No," said Corvalis, "you're right. That was just practice." In the distance, Caina saw the three remaining chariots begin another lap. "When those chariots pass in front of the lords' box, he'll shatter the wheels and turn the nobles into pincushions."

Lord Khosrau wore no armor at all, and the wooden shards would tear through his white robes like paper. Armizid wore his ceremonial silver cuirass, and Lord Corbould his black armor, but neither man wore a helm. A six-inch wooden shard through the throat or eye would kill them.

And Theodosia wore no armor at all.

The chariots rounded the loop and thundered towards the lords' box.

"We're out of time," Corvalis said, reaching into his robe. "We'd better kill him and run for it."

"We can't," said Caina. "We need him alive. He's probably warded against steel, so we can't just walk up and stab him. And if we kill him in front of all these witnesses, there will be...problems."

"I'm aware of that," said Corvalis, "but you'll have larger problems if Mhadun kills your precious Lord Corbould."

"Then we distract him," said Caina. "Keep him from destroying that chariot."

"You'll have to do it," said Corvalis. "I'm known to both the Kindred and the magi. If Mhadun recognizes me, he'll kill me on sight."

"He saw me at the ball," said Caina, but even as she said it, she doubted Mhadun would remember her. She had been disguised as a servant, and a man like Mhadun would take no notice of servants.

The remaining three chariots drew closer. The Red charioteer was in the lead, with Blue trailing closely behind and Gold bringing up the rear. Caina saw Mhadun's gaze shift to the Gold chariot, and she felt a prickling as he began a new spell.

"Wait," said Caina. "You used to be Kindred. Is there something I can tell him to make him think I am Kindred? Something to make him follow me?"

Corvalis blinked, grinned, and told her.

Caina explained her plan, handed him her ghostsilver dagger, and hurried towards Mhadun. The master magus gazed at the chariots, lips moving in a soundless whisper, hand tracing small gestures in the air, the arcane force against Caina's skin growing sharper and sharper...

"Master magus," said Caina.

Mhadun did not look at her. "Be off, woman. I have no business with you."

The sorcerous tingling grew stronger.

"Master magus," said Caina, voice soft, "the Elder wishes to speak with you."

That got his attention.

The tingling against Caina's skin vanished, and Mhadun turned towards her, dark eyes narrowed.

"What did you say?" he said, scowling. "What did you say to me?"

Caina lifted her chin, letting a mysterious smile play on her lips. "The Elder wishes to speak with you, master magus. Immediately."

"The blood flows from the wound," said Mhadun in formal High Nighmarian.

"And the dagger pierces the flesh," said Caina in the same language.

Below, the chariots thundered past, and Mhadun shot them an irritated glare.

"This had better be important, woman," said Mhadun.

"So impudent," said Caina. "Will you keep a more respectful tongue in your head when you speak with the Elder? He is wroth with you."

"Why?" said Mhadun. "I did everything he asked of me, and..." He scowled and shook his head. "We should not speak of this here. Lead on. Quickly!"

Caina turned with cool hauteur and led him up the aisle, to one of the ramps leading out of the hippodrome. A brick arch blocked out the sun overhead, filling the ramp with shadow. Corvalis waited in the shadows, a dark shape in the gloom.

"Elder?" said Mhadun.

Corvalis stepped into the light.

"Who the devil are you?" said Mhadun, and this his eyes widened. "You!"

"Mhadun," said Corvalis. "It's been a long time."

"The First Magus's bastard whelp," said Mhadun, laughing as his fingers traced a spell. "Your father has wanted you dead for a long time. He will reward me richly when I present him with your head upon a platter! I'll get my own chapter for this, perhaps even the Malarae chapterhouse..."

Caina reached into her sleeve, drew a throwing knife, and rammed it into Mhadun's back.

Or she would have, had it not rebounded from Mhadun's back in a spray of sparks.

Mhadun had warded himself against steel weapons.

The master magus whirled. "Ah? Who's this, bastard? Your little pet?" He flicked a finger. Invisible force seized Caina and slammed her against the brick wall. "I think I'll bring her along. The First Magus does so enjoy pretty toys..."

Corvalis flicked the tip of the ghostsilver dagger across Mhadun's arm. The curved blade penetrated Mhadun's wards and the sleeve of his robe with ease, blood darkening the black cloth. Mhadun shrieked in pain, his eyes wide with shock.

People responded to pain in different ways. Some could focus through it and continue fighting. Others fell apart, unable to react until the pain faded.

The invisible force holding her to the wall vanished as Mhadun's concentration collapsed.

Mhadun, it seemed, was not used to pain.

Caina ripped a cloth pad from the pouch at her belt. It was damp with an elixir Marzhod's druggist has brewed up for her, and she slapped the pad over Mhadun's nose and lips. The master magus twisted away, trying to break free from the pad, but Caina slammed her left fist into his gut. The breath exploded from his lungs, and Mhadun doubled over. Caina pressed the pad against his face, holding it in place with all her strength, and soon Mhadun had no choice but to inhale.

His eyes rolled back, and he went limp, collapsing in a heap on the grimy floor.

"Well," said Corvalis. "That was fun."

"You have a peculiar definition of fun," said Caina, tucking the pad into her belt pouch.

Two of Marzhod's Sarbian mercenaries hurried over. With practiced efficiency they bound the magus's wrists and ankles, gagged him, and shoved a hood over his head. Then they picked him up and hustled for the exits. With luck, the militiamen would assume Marzhod's mercenaries were settling with someone who had failed to pay a wager.

"Best we get gone," said Corvalis. "When Ranarius and the Kindred figure out that Mhadun has disappeared, they're going to be furious."

"Agreed," said Caina. "We'll take him to Nadirah's house. She'll know how to keep him contained...and how to make him talk."

A cheer went up from the crowds, and Caina glanced over her shoulder.

"Blue's winning," she said.

"Ah," said Corvalis. "Just as well I didn't place a wager, then."

17

CRAWLING SHADOWS

Night had fallen by the time Theodosia and Marzhod reached Nadirah's parlor.

Caina again wore the robes and weapons of a Sarbian mercenary. Corvalis had returned to his usual chain mail and cloak, his weapons at his belt. He seemed ill at ease, his hand twitching toward his sword hilt again and again.

She could not blame him.

Mhadun sat slumped on a wooden chair in the center of the room, chin resting upon his chest. Ropes bound his legs and arms to the chair, a gag sealed his mouth, and a blindfold covered his eyes. Nadirah had drawn intricate circles and symbols in chalk around him, and candles burned upon certain glyphs. She claimed that the chalk circles were part of a warding spell that would keep the master magus's powers at bay.

Nadirah walked in a slow, constant circle around Mhadun, humming to herself, her heels clicking against the floor. She wore an elaborate gown, red with intricate patterns in yellow upon the sleeve and bodice. Jewels glittered on her fingers and at her throat, and a delicate net of silver chains covered her hair. She looked every inch the daughter of Anshani nobility.

She walked in a circle around Mhadun...and her shadow remained motionless upon him, twisting around him like the shadow of a sundial.

"Gods and devils, but that's uncanny," muttered Corvalis.

"I can hear you," said Nadirah.

"I know that," said Corvalis.

"Do you fear the shadows so much, assassin?" murmured Nadirah, her black eyes falling upon him. She looked bewitching and beautiful.

But Corvalis's grim expression did not change, and he met her gaze without expression. "The shadows are a tool to me, like any other. But I take caution against what might wait in the shadows. Such as a master magus who will try to kill us all as soon as he wakes up."

"A prudent man," said Nadirah. "So rare. But you needn't fear, assassin. My power is more than sufficient to keep this fool's strength at bay."

"As you say," said Corvalis, though he kept his hand on his sword hilt and his eyes on Mhadun.

"The shadows are tangled," murmured Nadirah, still circling the magus. "So many potential futures lie before us, but all of them point to one fate. The destruction of Cyrica Urbana, the annihilation of this ancient city. Cyrioch is old, so old, and has left a deep shadow upon the netherworld. Yet both this city and its shadow will be swept away in the twinkling of an eye. How the spirits whisper! Even they are fearful of what is coming."

"Do all occultists," said Caina, "have such a flair for the theatrical?"

To her surprise, Nadirah grinned, and for a moment the expression made her look less ominous. "You are astute, dark one. Often the occultists of Anshan employ trickery, to keep the ignorant rabble in awe of their abilities." She shivered. "But I could no more deceive one of your power than the darkness could keep sunlight at bay."

"Your power?" said Corvalis. "Don't tell me you're a sorceress as well?" He smirked. "Especially after all your talk about the evil of sorcery."

"No," said Caina. She did not want to discuss the Moroaica with Corvalis. "What do you mean, Nadirah?"

"Your shadows are entangled, dark one, yours and the assassin's," said Nadirah, looking from Caina to Corvalis and back again. "You seek different things. You, to save Cyrioch and the Empire." Her gaze shifted to Corvalis. "And you...the shadows whisper that you seek to save a loved one from imprisonment." Her eyes darkened, like cups filling with black wine. "And yet you both seek the same answer, though you know it not."

"If I cross your palm with silver," said Corvalis, "will you tell my fortune?" He glared at Caina. "Are we done wasting our time with her? Wake Mhadun up, and I'll break his fingers until he tells you what you want to know."

Nadirah's maid entered the room and bowed. "Mistress. Your other guests have arrived."

"Send them in," said Nadirah.

The maid opened the door, and Theodosia and Marzhod entered at last. Marzhod wore his usual ragged finery, while Theodosia had again disguised herself as a Sarbian mercenary.

"I must say, madam," said Corvalis. "You were much more attractive in a proper dress."

Theodosia laughed. "That, sir, is how you deliver a compliment."

But her laugh faded as she saw Nadirah walking around Mhadun, her shadow remaining motionless upon him.

"You're a hard man to find," said Marzhod, glaring at Corvalis. "Quite a few of my best men turned to statues trying to find of you."

"Then you should have minded your own business," said Corvalis. "I suppose that's difficult for a Ghost to manage. But Ranarius turned your men to stone, and I suggest you take out your revenge upon him."

"A man after my own heart," said Marzhod.

"Assuming," said Corvalis, "that your occultist can make Mhadun talk."

Marzhod offered a thin smile. "You'll see what she can do, soon enough." He offered a shallow bow in Nadirah's direction. "My lady. Are you ready to begin?"

"Ah, Marzhod," murmured Nadirah. "Always so polite. But nothing trains a man's tongue in courtesy like fear."

She faced Mhadun and clapped her hands.

Her rippling shadow went motionless, and a cool breeze blew through the parlor, rustling the books and scrolls upon the shelves and making the candle flames dance. Her shadow seemed to pierce Mhadun like a black spike.

"Wake up, Mhadun," crooned Nadirah, "master magus of the Imperial Magisterium."

Caina felt the cold tingle of Nadirah's sorcery, and Mhadun shifted in his chair. His head rose, and Caina saw his eyes dart back and forth behind his blindfold, his jaw working against the gag. She felt another tingle as Mhadun summoned his arcane powers. Without his hands and his tongue, he could not work a spell, but he could sense the presence of sorcery.

The candles' flames flickered, the white lines of chalk darkening with shadow, and the tingle of Mhadun's power vanished.

Nadirah's shadow grew darker.

"Do forgive my impertinence," said Corvalis, "but that gag will make it difficult for him to answer questions."

Nadirah crooked a finger, and unseen force yanked the gag from Mhadun's lips. The magus coughed, spat upon the floor, and began to speak.

"I know that voice," he rasped. "Corvalis Aberon, the First Magus's renegade little bastard. Is the blue-eyed whore still with you? I know you had accomplices. You couldn't have pulled this off alone." He spat again. "Your life is forfeit, Corvalis, but your accomplices can live. Do you know what the Magisterium does to those who dare to lift their hands against a magus? Shall I tell you about the torture chambers in the dungeons below the Motherhouse of Artifel? Or the spells that make a man know nothing but agony for years?"

"Poetic words," said Corvalis, "but empty. Your preceptor doesn't even like you, Mhadun. We did him a favor by taking you off his hands. I'm surprised he doesn't pay us a bounty."

Mhadun scowled. "Idiot boy. I am a master magus of the Imperial Magisterium..."

"Who has betrayed the Magisterium by taking the coin of another," said Corvalis. "You sold out the Magisterium to join the Kindred. I doubt Ranarius will lift a finger to save you."

Mhadun laughed. "Then you know you are in twice as much danger, fool. I could tell you every torture the First Magus has ever ordered, and he would still seem like a meek lamb compared to the Kindred."

"You were sent to assassinate Khosrau and Corbould, and you failed," said Corvalis. "I know firsthand the Kindred do not smile upon failure..."

"Silence," said Mhadun. "Are your accomplices within earshot? I hope they are, because I am giving them one chance to save their lives." His voice rose. "Kill Corvalis and let me go, and I give you my word that I will overlook this...indiscretion. This is your only chance. Even if you kill me, the Kindred and the Magisterium will still find you." He laughed. "The Magisterium may even pay the Kindred to hunt you down. I assume you had a renegade sorcerer put this ward around me? You had better release the ward. The Magisterium will turn a blind eye to renegade sorcerers if they behave...but if you dare to assault a magus, your fate will be dire indeed."

Nadirah laughed. "I fear many things, Mhadun of the Kindred, but you are not one of them."

"A woman?" Mhadun's laughter redoubled. "Some peasant midwife with a few tricks, no doubt? You'll find that imprisoning a master magus is more challenging than whelping calves from the village cow."

"Indeed?" said Nadirah, her voice full of amusement. "If I am a village midwife, then you should have no trouble escaping from my wards. Yet here you sit." Her voice rose, full of power and authority. "And I am no mere dabbler. I studied at the feet of Yaramzod the Black, the greatest occultist ever to stride the streets of holy Anshan."

"An Anshani occultist?" said Mhadun. "You think to scare me with an Anshani shadow-spinner? Fools! There are no female occultists. Perhaps you should have done some research before embarking upon this ridiculous charade."

"Enough," barked Marzhod. He took care to keep his voice disguised. "Begin."

Nadirah whispered a spell, her fingers weaving elaborate designs. Her shadow rippled again, fluttering over Mhadun like a banner caught in high wind.

And then Mhadun's shadow, too, began to ripple.

"More trickery?" said Mhadun. "I assume you opened the door to generate that chill? Those half-witted opera singers of Khosrau's can do better tricks." Theodosia sniffed in disdain. "If you think to scare me with this mummery, then..."

"He lies."

The voice was a snarling, hissing rasp, the voice of a creature that lurked in darkness and gnawed upon carrion. Caina yanked her ghostsilver dagger from its sheath, expecting some beast from nightmare to spring upon her...

After a moment, she realized the voice came from the shadows upon the floor.

From Mhadun's shadow.

"He lies," said the ghastly voice. "Terror fills his heart. He knows that his preceptor Ranarius despises him and that his masters in the Kindred regard him only as a useful tool. They will take vengeance upon you, of course, for daring to harm what belongs to them, but they will not lift a finger to save him."

"Who are you?" snarled Mhadun. For the first time a tremor entered his voice. "Speak!"

"I am you," said the shadow. "I am the shadow you cast in the netherworld, freed to speak by the arts of Nadirah daughter of Arsakan." Nadirah's teeth clicked in annoyance. She wouldn't want Mhadun to hear her name, Caina realized. Which meant Nadirah did not have full control over whatever horror from the netherworld now inhabited Mhadun's shadow.

That was a disturbing thought.

"Silence!" shouted Mhadun, sweat beading on his forehead. "I command you not to speak."

"You have no power over me," said the shadow, "not here. How I yearn to hear you scream."

"But you are bound to my will, shadow," said Nadirah, raising her hands.

Caina felt the surge of sorcery.

"I am," said the shadow, loathing in its icy voice.

"And you are bound to answer my questions truthfully," said Nadirah.

"So I am," said the shadow. "And the truth you shall have from me." Caina heard the dark amusement in that malicious voice. "Especially if those truths shall lead to your doom."

"The questions," said Marzhod, watching both Mhadun and the shadows with a wary eye. "Ask it the questions we discussed earlier."

"The former slave," said the shadow. "Chains of steel can rust, but chains in the mind shall never be broken."

"Oh, shut up," said Marzhod. "I've seen spirits summoned before. Riddles and dark memories and ominous prophecies. Why don't you..."

"Do not," said Nadirah, her dark eyes falling him, "engage with the shadow."

Marzhod fell silent.

"Now," said Nadirah, returning her attention to Mhadun, "the Kindred have been hired to kill both Lord Corbould Maraeus and Lord Khosrau Asurius. Is this true?"

"It is," said the shadow.

"Who hired them?" said Nadirah.

"I don't know," said Mhadun.

"He speaks the truth," said the shadow. "Though if you were to release the binding upon me, I could make him tell you more. I could make him scream it to you."

"No!" said Mhadun, voice hoarse. "I don't know, I swear it."

"Then who does know?" said Nadirah.

“The Elder,” said Mhadun. “The Kindred Elder of Cyrioch knows. Our clients contract with him, and he assigns the assassins to the target. He is the only one who knows who hired us to kill the nobles. Not me. Not me!"

"Shadow," said Nadirah. "Does he speak the truth?"

"He does," whispered the shadow, "for fear of his own life."

"The next question," said Marzhod.

"The Haven of the Kindred," said Nadirah. "Where is it?"

"In the shadow of the fire," said the shadow, "beneath the shuffling feet of worshipers come to pray to the flames."

"Where is it, Mhadun?" said Nadirah.

"Beneath the Temple of the Living Flame," said Mhadun.

"What?" said Marzhod. "I've been looking for the Kindred Haven for years! Are you telling me that it's hidden under the Temple?"

"For centuries," whispered the shadow, "the assassins have dwelled beneath the earth, coming forth to wet their blades in blood." The voice gave a hideous tittering laugh. "They have lived in the shadows."

"Where is the entrance to the Haven?" said Nadirah.

"In the library of the Temple," said Mhadun, "behind the Altar of Eternal Flame, past the quarters of the brothers and sisters. The third shelf, in the corner of the room. A book called 'The History of the Northern Empire' is actually a hidden trigger. Pull on it, and the door will open. Then a spiral staircase, down to the Haven itself."

"Gods," muttered Marzhod. "I never thought to look beneath the Temple. The brothers and sisters of the Living Flame are such...dull fellows. Hardly the sort to live above a nest of assassins."

"The worshipers of the fire know it not," said the shadow. "For centuries, the assassins lurked in the shadows of their holy flame, and the brothers and sisters never knew."

"Ask it if there are any other ways into the Haven," said Marzhod.

"Another entrance?" said the shadow. "Another place where you can weep and cower, listening to your mother scream as she is dragged to your master's chamber?"

Marzhod sighed. "That doesn't answer the question."

"Answer it," said Nadirah.

"There is," said Mhadun. "An escape tunnel, in case the Haven is ever breached. It opens into the tunnels below the Ring of Valor. There are...there are no other entrances."

"Good," said Marzhod. "That's all we need to know." A smile spread over his gaunt face. "The Kindred have caused me no shortage of trouble. It will be pleasant to pay them back."

"Now hold up your end of the bargain," said Corvalis. "Ask what I wish to know." Nadirah nodded.

"You will tell me," she said, and Caina felt the tingle of fresh sorcery, "about Ranarius."

"Ranarius?" For a moment derision replaced the fear in Mhadun's voice. "That fool? What do you want to know about him?"

"You do not seem to hold your preceptor in high regard," said Nadirah.

"He holds Ranarius in contempt," said the shadow, "but he knows not Ranarius's full power. Or the vast shadow he throws upon the netherworld."

"Ranarius does not throw a vast shadow on the netherworld!" said Mhadun. "Ranarius is an idiot. He spends all his time researching old spells of elemental summoning. If Ranarius devoted as much time to his standing among the Magisterium as he did to digging through old books, he would be First Magus by now. Instead he is the preceptor of the Cyrioch chapter." He shook his head with annoyance. "The fool doesn't even have the wit to realize the First Magus banished him to Cyrioch. The high magi grew weary of his endless researches."

"How very blind," said the shadow.

"What about the statues?" said Nadirah.

"Statues?" said Mhadun. "What statues?"

“Tell us,” said Nadirah, “by what spell, science, or method Ranarius has transformed his victims into statues of unfeeling stone.”

Mhadun laughed. “What mad folly is this? You think...you think that Ranarius has been turning people into statues? What utter folly!”

"We know otherwise," said Nadirah. "For we have seen the statues with our own eyes."

"Then you've been fooled by a particularly effective hoax," said Mhadun. "It is impossible to turn living flesh to stone through the use of sorcery."

"Fool," whispered his shadow.

Nadirah seemed at a loss, and Caina stepped forward.

"What about the Kindred assassin at the Amphitheatre of Asurius?" she said, making sure to keep her voice disguised. If Mhadun lived through this, she didn't want him to recognize her.

Mhadun's shadow rippled as she spoke, as if flinching away from an invisible breeze.

"What about him?" said Mhadun.

"He was turned into a statue," said Caina. "As was a second assassin, an archer, at the Ring of Valor."

"You are mistaken," said Mhadun. "The assassins sent to dispatch the nobles at the Ring of Valor and the Amphitheatre of Asurius never returned. Presumably the guards killed them." A hint of arrogance entered his voice. "Such is often the result when lesser assassins are dispatched to a target of importance. Which is why the Kindred Elder bade me to kill the nobles myself."

"Yes," said Corvalis, "and you did such a fine job of it."

"The assassins weren't killed," said Caina, "they were turned to stone."

Mhadun snorted. "I have the most credulous kidnappers in the Empire! If I tell you where a unicorn has buried a pot of magical gold, will you let me go?"

"The fool knows not," whispered the shadow. "His vision is clouded and his mind dull. He cannot perceive the reality of the world."

"But you know," said Nadirah, "how Ranarius converted his victims into statues?"

"Of course," said the shadow.

"Then tell me," said Nadirah. "Immediately."

"No," said the shadow.

The furrows in Mhadun's brow grew deeper, his face dripping with sweat.

"You are bound," said Nadirah, frowning. "And by that binding, I command you to answer my question."

"I am bound," said the shadow, "but you ask about one greater than you. One mightier by far, one that could crush you like the insect that you are, mortal. You cannot force me to speak against him."

"Speak!" shouted Nadirah. Caina's skin crawled as the occultist unleashed the full strength of her powers.

The shadow's hissing laughter rasped like dead leaves rattling over stone. "You cannot compel me. For you ask about one stronger than you."

"Ranarius?" said Nadirah. She, too, had begun to sweat. "Ranarius is stronger than me?"

"No," murmured the shadow. "There is one stronger than Ranarius by far, an inferno of strength against the pathetic candle flame of his power. Ranarius is a fool, and he cannot control the powers he seeks to conjure. And by those powers, you cannot compel me, foolish witch."

Caina hesitated, gripping her ghostsilver dagger.

The shadow refused to answer Nadirah, but it had responded to Caina's question. Why? Nadirah had recognized the presence of the Moroaica within Caina. Could the shadow likewise sense the Moroaica? Caina was loath to use Jadriga's presence for anything.

Yet they needed to know how Ranarius had turned Claudia and the Ghosts to stone.

"Shadow," said Caina, stepping forward. Every eye turned towards her, and she felt the shadow's malevolence focus upon her. "How has Ranarius turned his foes to stone?"

There was a long silence.

"Who are you?" said the shadow.

"You will answer me," said Caina.

"You have...two shadows," said the shadow. For a moment bafflement entered the hideous voice. "One is scarred and maimed, yet unbroken. The other...the other is dark and mighty, so mighty, sorcerous power enough to break this city..."

"Answer the question," said Caina. "How does Ranarius turns his foes to stone?"

Another long silence, and the shadow began to speak.

Apparently, it was more frightened of the Moroaica than whatever had turned Claudia and Saddiq and the others to stone.

That thought turned Caina's spine to ice.

"An elemental of stone," said the shadow. "You know of them, dark one...or at least one of your shadows does. A spirit of earth, of stone, of rock unyielding and eternal. There are many such spirits in the netherworld...and many others in the mortal world, hibernating in wombs of stone. Mhadun thinks Ranarius is a fool, but he is the greater fool. For Ranarius delved deep into the ancient lore and learned of one such spirit. He came to its lair and awoke the elemental, binding it to his will." The shadow laughed. "As well should a mouse enslave a lion. The elemental will devour Ranarius when it gains its freedom. For the lives of you little mortals are over in a heartbeat."

"Can the process be reversed?" said Caina. "Can the statues become living flesh and blood once more?"

She saw Corvalis lean forward.

"It can," said the shadow. "If you enslave the elemental yourself, you can command it to free its victims. Or you could free the elemental and hope that it will liberate its victims out of gratitude to you." Derision dripped from the terrible voice. "That is not likely."

"Why?" said Caina. "Why did Ranarius enslave the elemental? Merely to use it as a weapon against his foes?"

"For freedom," said the shadow.

"Freedom?" said Caina. "Freedom from what?"

"Ranarius is a slave," said the shadow, "as is Mhadun."

"I am no man's slave!" spat Mhadun.

"But unlike Mhadun, Ranarius has the wit to see his enslavement," said the shadow. "The elemental is a guardian, a keeper. Ranarius sought out the guardian and enslaved it, not for the guardian's own considerable powers, but to claim what the guardian protected."

"What?" said Nadirah. "What did Ranarius want?"

"The resting place of a great elemental," said the shadow.

"By the Living Flame," whispered Nadirah, her dark eyes going wide.

"You mean...something like the fire elemental that destroyed Old Kyrace?" said Caina.

"Yes," said the shadow. "You see, spirits have their own hierarchies, just as mortals do. Ranarius's enslaved elemental, for all its puissance, is merely the vassal of a greater spirit, an elemental of earth with power enough to crack your world. Ranarius seeks to wake this elemental from its long sleep."

"Why?" said Nadirah. "Why would he do something so foolish? No mortal can hope to master the power of the greater elementals. Even the mighty Kyracian stormsingers of old, working in concert, could only lull a greater elemental to sleep. They couldn't possibly hope to control one." She shook her head. "This...this is the catastrophe I have seen in the shadows. This is the destruction that threatens Cyrioch, maybe even all of Cyrica."

"Yes," said the shadow. "Ranarius is a slave, but for the moment, his master cannot harm him. If he binds a greater elemental, he hopes to destroy his master and attain his freedom forever. But he cannot control the great spirit, and it will crush him like an insect."

"The greater elemental," said Caina. "Where is it hibernating?"

The shadow laughed at her. "Do you not know? The answer is before your eyes even now, and yet still you do not see."

"No riddling talk," said Caina. "Where is the greater elemental hibernating? Tell me now."

"Very well," said the shadow. "It..."

Several things happened at once.

Caina felt a surge of sorcery, sharp and jagged. The candles on Nadirah's intricate designs went dark. And as they did, Caina saw Mhadun's mouth moving, whispering the words to a spell. There was a snarling noise and a flash of blue light, and Mhadun's ropes and gag turned to dust.

He was free.

Caina drew back her ghostsilver dagger to strike, but she was too late. Mhadun flung out his hands. Invisible force erupted in all directions, throwing Caina to the floor. She saw Corvalis stagger and drop to one knee, the lines of his tattoo glowing beneath his sleeves, saw Theodosia and Marzhod slam into the wall.

Only Nadirah remained standing, her hands raised in a warding gesture. Corvalis snatched a knife and flung it, but the blade rebounded from Mhadun's wards. Mhadun made a chopping gesture, and Caina felt the surge of arcane power as his sorcery seized Nadirah and flung the occultist against the wall.

"I warned you," hissed Mhadun, his hands hooking into claws, "that the Magisterium was supreme, that your little shadow-tricks would be ineffective." Nadirah screamed, her face twisting in agony.

Corvalis scrambled to his feet, and Mhadun gestured with his other hand. Dozens of heavy books hurtled from the wooden shelves and slammed into Corvalis, knocking him to the ground. Caina got to her knees, her head ringing from the spells. Mhadun stalked towards Nadirah, grinning with vengeful delight.

"Where are your precious shadows now?" said Mhadun.

His shadow billowed behind him, writhing like a dying animal.

A mad idea occurred to Caina.

"Shadow!" she shouted. "Stop Mhadun! I command it! Stop him at once!"

The shadow hissed.

"Fool," said Mhadun, glaring at her, "the witch bound the shadow."

"Yes," said Caina, "but you broke the binding, didn't you?"

The shadow reared up behind him like a black wave.

Mhadun's eyes just had time to bulge in horror, and then the shadow fell upon him. His agonized screams of horror rang against the walls, and blood splashed over the elaborate mosaics of the floor. Nadirah fell to her knees, coughing, and waved her hand.

The rippling shadow vanished into nothingness, leaving Mhadun behind.

Or what was left of him, at least.

"You see," said Caina, looking at Corvalis, "why I don't trust sorcery?"

18

UNDER THE FLAMES

"How is Nadirah?" said Theodosia.

Caina stood alongside Theodosia and Corvalis in Marzhod's workroom at the Painted Whore. They had withdrawn there at Nadirah's urging. Mhadun's death, she insisted, had produced echoes in the netherworld. If any of the magi had been seeking Mhadun, they would have felt those echoes. Worse, if Cyrioch's Kindred had any other sorcerers, they would have sensed his death. In either case, it was no longer safe at her house.

Caina was surprised that Marzhod had agreed to give her shelter. She would have expected him to turn Nadirah out into the street. Perhaps, as Saddiq had hinted, he had a more compassionate heart that Caina had thought.

Or maybe he simply wanted to seduce her.

"Not well," said Marzhod. He looked tired, the hard lines of his face sharper than usual. "Had she not banished that shadow, it would have turned upon her." His bloodshot eyes flicked to Caina. "That was clever, commanding the shadow to kill Mhadun. Though I wonder why the thing decided to obey you."

Caina shifted, wondering what Marzhod suspected.

To her relief, Corvalis shrugged. "That shadow would have killed

Mhadun anyway. It was like ordering a drunkard to drink a skin of wine. "

"Well, she is resting now," said Marzhod. "She's raised wards around the Painted Whore to stop any tracking spells." His face hardened. "And if the magi or the Kindred come for her in person...well, they'll get a mouth full of steel for their efforts. Marzhod of Cyrioch pays his debts."

"Oh," said Caina, as something clicked in her mind.

"What?" said Marzhod.

"The occultist who owned you," said Caina. "That was Nadirah's teacher, wasn't it? Yaramzod the Black? She saved you from him. She couldn't have hidden in Cyrioch for all these years without help. You were protecting her."

Marzhod glared at her. "You think entirely too much." He sighed. "You believe me a hard and cruel man, and you are right. But I pay my debts. And you would too, if you saw what old Yaramzod does to those who crossed him. What happened to Mhadun was nothing compared to things I saw Yaramzod do to his enemies."

"Yaramzod the Black," said Theodosia, "is a thousand miles away in Anshan. We have more immediate problems."

"The Kindred Haven," said Marzhod.

"And Ranarius," said Corvalis.

"Our first task," said Theodosia, "is to destroy the Kindred Haven. The Kindred won't stop until Khosrau and Corbould are both dead."

"No, the first task," said Marzhod, "is to make sure Mhadun and that damned shadow told the truth. With our luck, we'll open that secret passage and find the brotherhood of the Living Flame's laundry."

"I'll do it," said Caina. "I'll scout the Temple of the Living Flame and make sure the secret entrance is there."

"I'll go with you," said Corvalis.

Caina lifted an eyebrow.

Corvalis shrugged. "You're formidable enough, aye, but the Kindred are dangerous. They'll have someone watching the entrance. Together we have a better chance of spotting any guards."

"Fine," said Marzhod. "I have men among the slaves working at the Ring of Valor. I will have them find the escape tunnel below the Ring. When we strike we will bottle up the rats all at once."

"Those rats have teeth," said Corvalis.

Marzhod grinned. "So do I."

"I also want to make sure you stay alive," said Corvalis, looking at Caina. "I am upholding my end of the bargain. I need you alive to meet yours."

"We shall keep our bargain. We'll deal with Ranarius after the Kindred are settled," said Theodosia.

"We may have to kill Ranarius first," said Marzhod. "You heard what Nadirah said, that Ranarius is going to unleash some sort of greater elemental. It might be simpler just to kill Ranarius."

"No," said Corvalis. "He's not going to die until he restores my sister and your men."

"Nadirah predicted a catastrophe," said Marzhod. "Something that would destroy the city. If we can stop it by killing Ranarius, then we kill him."

"Our agreement was that we take Ranarius alive," said Corvalis.

"It was," said Marzhod. "But balanced against the lives of everyone in Cyrioch, the lives of your sister and my men do not count for much. If I have to sacrifice them, I will."

"You will not," said Corvalis. "And you place too much faith in the judgment of that Anshani woman. Considering she could not keep Mhadun under control, she might be wrong about this catastrophe."

"She's not," said Marzhod. "I have seen her predictions come true too many times to discard her judgment. If the opportunity comes to kill Ranarius, then I will order him killed. Regrettable about your sister, but..."

"You will not," said Corvalis, voice hard, and he started to draw his sword.

Marzhod stepped back, reaching into his coat.

"Enough!" said Caina. "We have the Kindred on one side and Ranarius and his pet elemental on the other, and you idiots want to kill each other?"

"All this bluster is entertaining," said Theodosia, "but killing someone like Ranarius is easier said than done. A man does hold high office in the Magisterium without remaining on guard against assassins. If killing him were simple, Corvalis would have captured him already."

"Aye," said Corvalis, relaxing his grip on his sword.

"I suggest that we proceed as we have already discussed," said Theodosia. "First, you two find out if the Kindred Haven is really beneath the Temple of the Living Flame. If we are going to strike the Kindred, we'll need a lot of hardened killers and gold to pay them. Marzhod and I will arrange that. Once we have crippled the Kindred, we will find a way to stop Ranarius."

"By killing him, preferably," said Marzhod.

Corvalis began to speak, but Caina interrupted him.

"That might not be wise," she said. "The disaster that Nadirah foresaw. It might be something Ranarius has already begun, not something he will do. If we kill Ranarius, the catastrophe could unfold anyway."

Marzhod snorted. "Why are you siding with Corvalis? I've seen how much you hate the magi. If I gave you a knife and told you to stick it in Ranarius's back, I thought you'd be halfway across the city by now. Why not just kill him?"

Caina opened her mouth to respond...and then realized that she didn't have an answer to give.

Why did she want to capture Ranarius alive? Certainly she felt no inclination towards mercy. She loathed the magi, loathed all wielders of sorcery, and Ranarius had used his powers to turn innocent men and women to stone. He deserved to die, and killing him might save far more innocent lives in the future.

So why not kill him?

Corvalis need him alive to save his sister. He had left the Kindred, crossed half the Empire, faced terrible foes, and risked death again and again for his sister. Caina's father had been dead for ten years...but if he had been ill, or imprisoned like Claudia, how much would Caina have risked to save him? How much would she have done?

"Because," said Caina, "I enjoy seeing that annoyed expression on your face."

Marzhod glared at her, and Corvalis grinned.

"Yes," said Caina. "That's the one."

"I suggest," said Marzhod, "you get going. We have a great deal of work to do. And perhaps that clever tongue of yours will charm the Kindred."

~

AN HOUR later Caina and Corvalis headed through the streets towards the Plaza of Majesty.

And the Temple of the Living Flame.

"I wish," said Corvalis, "to ask you a question."

"Do it quickly," said Caina.

They both wore red robes with golden trim on the sleeves, the formal robes of the brothers and sisters of the Living Flame. In the robes, Caina and Corvalis looked no different than the other adherents of the Temple. Even the commoners of Cyrioch held the priests and priestesses of the Living Flame in reverence, and no one had challenged them.

Caina wished she had thought of this disguise earlier.

"Why," said Corvalis, "didn't you agree with Marzhod? Why don't you want to kill Ranarius and have done with it?"

Caina shrugged. "You heard what I told him."

Corvalis snorted. "You enjoyed tweaking his nose, I don't doubt. But that was a not your real reason."

"Killing Ranarius might cause more problems," said Caina, "especially if he's already tried to free this greater elemental."

"And killing him would solve that problem," said Corvalis. "You hate sorcerers. When I told you that Claudia was a magus, I'm surprised you didn't take a sledgehammer to her."

She shook her head, irritated with the questions. "We should discuss it later."

"I would prefer to know now," said Corvalis, and she saw him frown beneath his red cowl. "Ranarius is my only chance of saving Claudia. Or are you planning to kill Claudia once I force Ranarius to free her?"

"Of course not!" said Caina.

"Then why," said Corvalis, "did you not agree with Marzhod when he wanted to kill Ranarius?"

She hesitated and looked around.

"Fine," said Caina. She grabbed his arm and pulled him into alley. "If you really want to know, I'll tell you." She took a deep breath. "You love Claudia."

"Of course I do," said Corvalis. "What does that have to do with anything?"

"You're a Kindred assassin," said Caina. "You left them, but you'll still be a killer until the end of your days. I did not think a man like you could love someone enough to cross the Empire and put yourself at risk over and over again."

"Well, I do," said Corvalis, voice quiet. "That's not something a woman like you would understand."

"A woman like me?" said Caina.

"You're a killer, like me," said Corvalis. "And you're better at it than I am. Disguising yourself as a servant, and smiling and nodding while you plot to kill? I don't think even I could manage that. You have ice instead of blood."

Caina said nothing.

He wasn't wrong.

"And you hate the magi," said Corvalis. "I wouldn't put it past you to kill both Claudia and Ranarius if you thought it necessary."

"No," said Caina.

"Why not?"

"Because you want to save her," said Caina. "You went on this... this mad quest to save her. It's..admirable. I thought you would undertake this kind of effort to kill your father, not save your sister."

"I love her," said Corvalis, "and I owe her a great deal. If not for her, Ghost, I would be exactly the sort of man you think I am. So will do whatever is necessary to save her. I don't expect you to understand."

"I do understand," said Caina, voice quiet.

Corvalis looked dubious.

"My father," said Caina. Part of her wondered why she was telling this to Corvalis. But he understood her kind of pain, shared it with her. "The magi murdered him."

"Ah," said Corvalis. "That explains a great deal."

"I saw him die in front of me," said Caina. "But if...something else had happened to him, if he had been imprisoned or transformed like your sister...I would have done anything to save him, too."

Corvalis was silent for a long moment.

"I see," he said at last. "Then I misjudged you, Ghost." He closed his eyes. "You cannot save your father...so instead you help me to save my sister. I apologize."

Caina blinked, surprised. "I've practiced fooling people for years. Little wonder I fooled you."

Corvalis grimaced. "Or my instincts have grown feeble."

"I doubt that," said Caina. "You seem vigorous enough."

He smirked. "Flattery. Though I wonder about one other thing. How were you able to command the shadow?"

Caina shrugged. "I killed the Moroaica."

Corvalis blinked. "Sicarion's mistress? The ancient sorceress of legend and terror? You killed her? Little wonder the shadow feared you."

"Apparently," said Caina, "the Moroaica has a habit of moving from body to body over the centuries. When I slew her, she possessed me. Or tried to. Apparently what the magi did to me as a child left... scars of a sort. Because of them, the Moroaica can possess my body, but she cannot control me."

"Then you have a dead sorceress inside in your head?" said Corvalis.

"Essentially," said Caina, uneasy. She wondered how he would react, and again she wondered why she had told him. Would he try to kill her, hoping to kill the Moroaica within her? Why had she taken the risk of telling him so much?

Perhaps she was tired of carrying so many painful secrets alone

"So that," said Corvalis, "was why Sicarion didn't try to kill you, at least not at first."

"Yes," said Caina. "I can hear the Moroaica in my dreams. She ordered Sicarion not to kill me. Apparently she thinks she can twist me around to her way of thinking."

Corvalis barked his short, harsh laugh. "Not likely! You hate sorcery too much. You'd sooner cut off your hand than use it to cast a spell."

His confidence cheered her. "Sicarion doesn't agree. He wants to kill me and free the Moroaica so she can possess a new host. The Moroaica will be wroth with him, if he succeeds."

"Not for long, though," said Corvalis. "Sicarion's just a mad dog that likes killing. The Moroaica probably knows too many people that she wants killed."

"Aye," said Caina. "She sent Sicarion here to kill that rebellious disciple."

"I remember Sicarion saying that," said Corvalis. "I wonder who it is. Nadirah, perhaps?" He laughed. "Maybe Ranarius himself?"

"I doubt it," said Caina. "Nadirah was terrified of the Moroaica. And all the Moroaica's disciples have been necromancers. Ranarius isn't a necromancer."

But she remembered what the shadow had said about Ranarius's slavery. Was Ranarius a disciple of the Moroaica? Jadriga taught her students the necromantic sciences, and Caina had seen no evidence that Ranarius used necromancy.

But if he really was a disciple of the Moroaica, that would make him all the more dangerous.

"Hopefully the disciple is one of the lesser magi," said Caina. "Sicarion will kill him, and we won't have to worry about it any longer." She glanced at the street. "We should get moving."

"One more question," said Corvalis. "What is your name? You know mine. It's only fair that I should know yours."

"Marina," she said. "And, no, I won't tell you my real name. That will keep Ranarius from plucking it out of your head."

She meant it as a joke, but the words sobered Corvalis.

"Aye," he said. "You're right. We had best keep moving."

They returned to the street and resumed their walk towards the Plaza of Majesty.

"Couldn't your question have waited?" said Caina. "Surely there would be a more convenient time than sneaking up on a Kindred Haven."

"Aye," said Corvalis, "but I'm about to go against some very dangerous foes with you at my side. Better to know your quality before the swords come out. And I misjudged you. I thought you like the Kindred, cold and lovely and hard."

Caina laughed. "You no longer think me lovely?"

Corvalis grinned. "Perhaps not so cold and hard."

She blinked several times, trying to decide what she thought about that.

Then they entered the Plaza of Majesty, and all other thoughts vanished from Caina's mind.

The Temple of the Living Flame rose on the far end of the Plaza, a massive pyramid of gleaming black marble. A cherry-red glow came from the opening at the pyramid's top, the light of the fire blazing from the Altar of Eternal Flame in the Temple's heart. It reminded Caina of the great black pyramids of Rasadda, the ancient tombs of the pyromancer-kings of old. The dead Ashbringers burned atop those pyramids, forever wrapped in pyres of sorcerous flame...

"You're shivering," said Corvalis.

She forced herself to stop. "Bad memories." She remembered men screaming the grip of Kalastus's pyromantic fires...

"Let me do the talking," said Corvalis. "If anyone asks, we are pilgrims from Rasadda, coming to visit the Great Temple in Anshan in hopes of healing the schism between the two branches of the faith." He scowled. "Be wary. The Kindred will be on the guard after the failed assassination attempts."

The entrance to the Temple loomed before them, a tall, narrow doorway in the pyramid's side. Beyond Caina saw the massive black altar, the fire raging atop its surface. The adherents of the faith worshipped before the altar, praying that the Living Flame would scour the impurities from their souls and allow them to escape the endless cycle of death and rebirth. Caina did not know if there was such a thing as reincarnation or not.

Of course, the Moroaica was inside of her head, but that was probably not what the brotherhood of the Living Flame had in mind.

The pyramidal temple's interior was massive, the sloping walls rising to a point far overhead. The altar's fire illuminated the temple, and Caina saw a slave in a ragged gray tunic kneeling on the floor, polishing the black marble. The slave, rangy and gaunt, rose as they approached.

"Pardons," he said in Cyrican, "but the Temple is closed for the evening. Return on the morrow."

"Forgive me, brother," said Corvalis in Caerish, coloring his words with a Saddaic accent. "But I do not speak the native tongue of this land."

A hint of irritation flickered over the slave's face.

The man was Kindred. Caina was sure of it. No Cyrican slave would dare to be so open with his emotions in front of the freeborn.

"The Temple is closed for the evening," said the slave in Caerish, his Cyrican accent so thick Caina could scarce make out the words. "Return tomorrow."

"But we have journeyed all the way from Rasadda on the far end of the Empire," said Corvalis, his tone wheedling. "We arrived this night, but I have heard so much of the splendors of the great Temple of Cyrica Urbana that I wished to see it with my own eyes at once. What an honor it must be to serve in this place!"

A hint of contempt flashed through the slave's eyes. Doubtless the Kindred did not hold the faithful in high regard. "If it is such an honor, you can get down on your knees and scrub the floor yourself."

"I must pray before we go," said Corvalis, drawing himself up. "I am going to the Great Temple in Anshan. I am sure the heretic brethren there will see the error of their ways and rejoin with those of us in the Saddaic provinces. Yes, I must pray for the Living Flame to bless my mission. Surely I am his instrument to bring unity to the scattered branches of the brethren once more!"

"I am sure," said the slave. "Perhaps you should start praying at once so the Living Flame will hear you."

"Indeed!" said Corvalis, and he marched towards the altar, Caina following. To her surprise, Corvalis began to sing a hymn to the wisdom of the Living Flame.

She stifled a laugh. That hymn usually proceeded an hour of ritual prayer. She glanced back and saw the slave's expression return to boredom.

Corvalis circled the altar, still singing, and bit by bit he let his song fade away.

"That was clever," said Caina, when the altar stood between them and the entrance. The heat of its fire washed over her in waves, sweat trickling down her face and back. During the day, the Temple of the Living Flame had to smell like an unwashed bathhouse. "Theodosia would be proud."

"You should have joined me," said Corvalis. "We could have sung a duet."

They crossed the great chamber and ducked through a side door. Beyond stood a long, narrow corridor leading to the quarters of the priests. They crept past the bedrooms, making no sound, and came to the Temple's library. It was larger than Caina expected, at least as large of Theodosia's suite at the Inn of the Defender. Gleaming wooden shelves lined the walls, laden with books and scrolls.

"Let's see if Mhadun was telling the truth," muttered Corvalis.

He crossed to the third shelf, found the book on the history of the northern Empire, and gave it a sharp tug.

Without a sound, a section of the floor slid aside, revealing a spiral staircase that descended into the earth. A faint blue glow came from the depths. Corvalis drew his sword from beneath his robe, and Caina slid her ghostsilver dagger from its sheath.

The Kindred might have sorcerers other than Mhadun among their ranks.

Corvalis descended the steps, moving with masterful stealth, and Caina followed suit. Spheres of glass hung from the walls, glowing with an inner blue light. The initiates of the Magisterium manufactured and sold the enspelled spheres by the thousand. Given how far underground the Kindred Haven lay, Caina could see why the assassins wanted smokeless lights.

Down and down the stairs went, and Caina counted them. She had passed two hundred and fifty when they reached an archway. It opened into a wide corridor of polished black stone, illuminated by more glass spheres. At the end of the corridor, perhaps thirty yards away, Caina saw a massive iron portcullis sealing off the passageway.

"Do not," whispered Corvalis, "move a muscle."

Caina froze. "What is it?"

"See those dark slots upon the wall?" said Corvalis. Keeping her head still, Caina turned her eyes and saw dozens of dark rectangles, almost like arrow slits, in the wall. "They're traps. A little present the Strigosti artificers built for the Kindred. There are guards at the other end of the portcullis. If they see us, they'll use the trap. Probably poison gas of some kind, or perhaps acid."

"A formidable defense," said Caina. There was absolutely no hint of cover in the corridor, and even with her shadow-cloak, she would have no chance of making it to the portcullis undetected. And even if she survived the acid or whatever else waited in the trap, the guards at the portcullis would have plenty of time to shoot her before she even reached them.

"We can't take the Sarbians down here," said Caina. "It would be a massacre."

"Aye," said Corvalis. "We'll have to think of something else. But Mhadun and that shadow were telling the truth. The Kindred Haven is down here. We'd had best go before someone discovers us."

Caina nodded, and they climbed back up the stairs. Corvalis

closed the secret door, and they walked back to the chamber of the altar. He began to sing as they approached, the hymn to the Living Flame ringing off the walls and the floor. They circled the altar and its raging flame and headed towards the door.

The slave watched them, eyes narrowed.

"The Temple is magnificent!" said Corvalis. "Oh, how I envy you. How delightful it must be to toil every day in the presence of the Living Flame."

The slave walked away, muttering something.

"That was cruel," said Caina.

Corvalis shrugged. "Considering we'll probably kill him tomorrow, I can live with it."

Caina walked back into the Plaza of Majesty.

But she would return here soon enough.

19

GAMBLE

"We will strike tonight," said Marzhod.

Caina blinked in surprise.

Once again they stood in Marzhod's workroom at the Painted Whore. Dawn sunlight leaked through the closed shutters, and Caina's eyes felt heavy and gritty. It had been a long and taxing night.

And another long night was on the way.

"A bold move," said Theodosia, yawning.

"A necessary one," said Marzhod. "You said it yourself. Sooner or later the Kindred will get lucky and kill both Khosrau and Corbould. Then we'll have civil war at best, or at worst Cyrica will join Istarinmul or Anshan. The sooner we exterminate every last one of the Kindred, the better." He sneered. "Even an opera singer should be able to see that."

"There's no need for churlishness," said Theodosia.

"As Theodosia said," said Corvalis, "a bold move. Just how do you intend to accomplish it?"

There was a knock at the door, and they fell silent. One of Marzhod's slave women entered, carrying a tray of food and drink. She set it down on a table, bowed, and departed without a word.

"You should free her," said Caina, voice quiet.

She helped herself to some food anyway. Gods, but she was hungry.

"Why?" said Marzhod. "If I do, where will she go? She'll be whoring on the street within a week. And we have larger problems just now."

"Yes," said Corvalis. "Such as how you'll destroy the Kindred without getting slaughtered.

"We should ask Lord Khosrau for help," said Theodosia.

"We should not," said Marzhod. "Lord Corbould tolerates the Ghosts because he finds us useful. Khosrau is utterly indifferent to us, and as always Armizid takes after his father. Warn him about the assassins and he'll thank you politely. Ask him for troops to wipe out the Kindred and he'll laugh in your face."

"So where," said Corvalis, "will you find the men to fight the Kindred? I assume you have spies among the slaves of every noble House in Cyrica, but they'll be useless against the Kindred."

"The Sarbians," said Caina, reaching for the tea.

"Yes," said Marzhod. "Very good." He scratched at his unshaven chin. "The Sarbians detest the Cyricans and vice-versa, so they make for very reliable mercenaries. One of the reasons I use them as enforcers."

"How many?" said Theodosia.

"Two hundred," said Marzhod. "I've hired every remaining warrior from Saddiq's tribe. Expensive, but worth it. The inbred bastards are all related to each other, but they're deadly fighters. There can't be more than a few dozen assassins in the Haven. The Sarbians can take them."

"Assuming they live long enough to get into the Haven," said Caina, remembering the subterranean trap.

"My spies in the Ring of Valor found the escape tunnel," said Marzhod. "It's guarded, of course, but the Sarbians can overwhelm the guards easily enough."

"And two hundred desert men will make enough noise to alert

the Kindred," said Caina. "They'll flee through other tunnel and into the Temple of the Living Flame."

"I'll have some mercenaries guard the Temple," said Marzhod.

Caina shook her head. "You'll need more men. The Temple is huge. The Kindred could conceal themselves in the Temple or escape in the chaos."

"And you won't be able to move that many men through the city," said Theodosia. "The Temple is too close to the Palace of Splendors. A fight there will draw the attention of the civic militia. They'll fall on your mercenaries like a hammer, and some of the Kindred will slip away in the chaos."

"So the opera singer is a general now?" said Marzhod. "Do you have a better idea?"

"Actually," said Corvalis, "I might."

They all looked at him.

"This had better be good," said Marzhod.

"Don't take mercenaries through the entrance below the Temple," said Corvalis. "Instead, I will infiltrate the Haven and seal that entrance. When you attack, the Kindred will be trapped, and you can kill them all."

"And just how will you accomplish that?" said Marzhod.

"The portcullis is massive," said Corvalis, "but the mechanism to open and close it is delicate. It's similar to the one in the Haven of Artifel. I can jam it easily enough."

"Of that I have no doubt," said Marzhod, "but how will you get inside? You're a renegade, Aberon, and you're known to the Kindred. They'll kill you on sight."

"I can disguise myself well enough," said Corvalis. "And I will come with a gift the Kindred will not be able to refuse."

"What?" said Marzhod.

Corvalis looked at Caina. "You."

She frowned. "Me?"

"Aye," said Corvalis. "Understand this. An Elder rules over every Kindred family...and the Elders are not like other men. Each Elder bears a torque around his neck that supposedly holds the souls of all his victims. I don't know what it really is, but it bestows superhuman strength and speed upon the Elder."

"Rubbish," said Marzhod.

"No," said Caina. "I've seen objects of sorcery that can do that."

"The torque also has...other effects on the Elder," said Corvalis. "It enhances his lifespan. An Elder can live for centuries. But using the torque has costs. The Elders are not quite sane, and their appetites are far beyond those of ordinary men."

"Appetites," said Caina, understanding.

"The Elders send each other gifts," said Corvalis. "Jewels. Rare books. Artifacts. Slave women of exceptional beauty."

Marzhod snorted, and Theodosia scowled.

"No," said Theodosia. "I forbid it."

"Will it work?" said Caina to Corvalis.

"It should," said Corvalis. "I will disguise myself as an emissary from the Artifel Haven, and you as a gift for the Elder. That should get us past the portcullis. Once we're in, we shatter the mechanism on the portcullis and wait until Marzhod's pet Sarbians storm the Haven."

"So," said Marzhod, chuckling, "your plan is to wave the girl in front of the guards, get inside the Haven, kill the guards, jam the portcullis, and then hide until my men fight their way in to save you."

"Essentially, yes," said Corvalis.

"That's absolute idiocy," said Marzhod. "I say we do it. You should at least provide a distraction for my mercenaries."

"It is too much of a risk," said Theodosia.

"Loathe as I am to agree with Marzhod," said Corvalis, "do you have a better idea?"

"You won't be able to save your sister," said Theodosia, "if you're dead."

"No," said Corvalis. "But I can't save her without help. I need your help."

Theodosia sighed and looked at Caina. "You're the one who will have to dangle yourself like a piece of meat before a Kindred Elder and his guards. What do you think?"

Caina looked from Corvalis to Theodosia and back again.

His plan was a risk, but it had a very good chance of succeeding. The Kindred guards would not see a young slave woman as a threat, and she would have the chance to take decisive action. And if they jammed the portcullis, the Kindred would be trapped and the Sarbians could slaughter the assassins to a man. And the Kindred would almost certainly have records. What kind of secrets could the Ghosts glean from the archives of a Kindred Haven?

In one stroke, they might cripple the Kindred of Cyrioch and learn who had hired them to kill Khosrau, Corbould, and Armizid.

And then Caina could help Corvalis save his sister.

He was right about her. It was far too late to save her father. But she could help others save their loved ones. She could help Corvalis save his sister, just as she had helped Ark save Nicolai and Tanya from Jadriga.

"All right," said Caina. "We'll do it your way, Corvalis."

"Gods," said Theodosia. "Are you sure about this? Walking alone into a den of assassins?"

"She won't be alone," said Corvalis.

"Your skills are formidable," said Theodosia, "but not formidable enough to fight off an entire Kindred family."

"No," said Corvalis.

"This is a risk," said Caina, "but a necessary one. You know what will happen if the Kindred kill Khosrau and Corbould. And something much worse will happen if Ranarius finds that greater elemental." She took a deep breath. "If we don't take some risks, we will regret it."

"Very well," said Theodosia. "If you've decided to trust Corvalis that far, so be it." She sighed. "Myself, I will be at the Palace of Splendors tonight. Lord Khosrau is holding another ball to repay Lord Corbould for his kindness with the chariot races. Someone will need to keep an eye on them, in case the Kindred strike."

"If all goes well," said Corvalis, "the Kindred will be too busying dying to strike."

"One can hope," said Theodosia.

"I have to get started," said Marzhod, turning towards the door. He glanced at Caina. "I suggest you get some rest. You're going to have a very busy evening."

THAT AFTERNOON, Caina lay on her cot at the Inn of the Defender and dreamed.

In the dream she stood in the Palace of Splendors, within the Gallery of the Well. The Gallery was utterly deserted, the sky black and starless. The windows in the walls of the palace were gaping eyes into nothingness. Caina wore one of the elaborate blue gowns she had used in her disguise as Countess Marianna Nereide, the sleeves and bodice covered in elaborate embroidery, silver earrings with sapphires glittering on her ears.

She turned in a circle, and saw the Moroaica standing at the edge of the Well.

"This is one of your dreams, isn't it?" said Caina.

Jadriga wore a blood-colored robe, her long black hair wet and loose around her shoulders, her eyes like black disks in her pale face.

Except it really wasn't her face, was it? It was only the body the Moroaica had been using when Caina had faced her. How many dozens of others had she stolen over the centuries?

"Yes," said Jadriga. "Your mind is getting stronger. When I first inhabited you, you often did not realize these were only dreams. Now it is very difficult to fool you."

"Sicarion disobeyed you." Caina stopped a dozen paces from Jadriga, arms crossed over her chest. "He tried to kill me."

"I suspected he would," said the Moroaica.

"But you knew that already," said Caina, "because you can see and hear everything that I can."

A thin smile flickered over Jadriga's red lips. "As I said. It is getting harder to fool you. But I did not need your eyes to know that Sicarion would try to take your life. He is a useful tool...but only to a point. To ask him to stop killing is like asking a man to stop breathing. And sometimes a tool other than death is required."

"Why not kill me?" said Caina. "You're stuck inside me, I know that much. You might be able to see and hear through my eyes and ears, but you can't do anything. Kill me and you can steal a body you can control."

"I have my reasons," said the Moroaica.

"Because you think you can subvert me?" said Caina. "That you can twist me to your way of thinking? That is ridiculous. I saw what you did to all those slaves in Marsis. I saw what Sicarion and Andromache and Scorikhon did. I will not serve you, and you'll be imprisoned inside my mind for another forty or fifty years."

"Optimistic," murmured Jadriga, "given that the Kindred might kill you in another six hours."

"Or I could choke on dinner," said Caina. "But assume I don't, and I die of old age. You could wait for decades."

Jadriga shrugged. "I have died many times, child of the Ghosts. Fifty years seems an eternity to one as young as you. To one such as me...fifty years is an idle afternoon. And I do not need to twist you or subvert you or corrupt you. No. I corrupted women like Agria Palaegus and Andromache, true. But they were mere tools, like Sicarion, and could not understand my true purpose. But you, my child...you have greater vision. You, I think, can understand my purpose."

"And what purpose is that?" said Caina. "The death of innocents? Power for the sake of power? Conquest for the sake of conquest? I want none of those things."

"Nor do I," said Jadriga. "As I said, those are only tools."

"Then what do you want?" said Caina. "What is this 'great work' Sicarion keeps talking about?"

The Moroaica was silent for a long time.

"You have known pain," she said, voice quiet, "just as I have. Pain that should have broken you. But it didn't. It made you stronger instead. And now you go out into the world to seek those who cause pain and destroy them. You rescued Ark's wife and child, because you could not have a husband and son of your own. You will help that assassin save his sister, because no one loves you as he loves his sister. But you cannot save them all. There is agony everywhere. The world is a prison for us, a torture chamber. Men and women are born, they are broken in suffering, and then they die, all for naught. Over and over again." There was a hint of anger in her tone. "The gods have made a cruel joke of a world. Perhaps they sit and laugh at us, mocking us for our sufferings."

"What about all the suffering you caused?" said Caina.

Jadriga shrugged. "It was necessary. Just as you, too, my child, have inflicted suffering when you thought it necessary."

"Necessary to do what?" said Caina. "Destroy all your enemies?"

"It is necessary to break the world and remake it," said Jadriga, and the anger in her voice grew sharper. "The world is broken, child of the Ghosts. It is defective. I will destroy it...and I will forge a better world than the gods ever managed. I will make a new world where there is no more pain, no more suffering, a world where no one shall ever die."

"That's mad," said Caina.

"It is only mad if I cannot do it," said Jadriga, "and I know the path. All your efforts are futile. You saved your friend's wife and son, and perhaps you will save the assassin's sister...but they will still know pain, terrible pain. They will still suffer and die. But I shall set the old world to burn...and in the new world, there will be no more pain, no more suffering, no more death."

They stared at each other in silence for a moment.

"You've been inside my head for months," said Caina, "but you're only telling me this now. You're doing it for a reason. Why?"

The Moroaica's red mouth coiled in a half-smile. "Always clever. Do you see why I want your willing cooperation? You have a cunning that even I do not."

"That doesn't answer the question," said Caina.

"Very well," said Jadriga. "In a few hours you are going to face foes of terrible power."

"I knew that already," said Caina.

"Foes with power enough," said the Moroaica, "to destroy even me."

Caina blinked. She had not expected that.

"Even you?" said Caina.

"Yes," said Jadriga. "Had I access to my full powers, they could not stand against you. Could I wield my full strength, I would crush your foes..."

"Oh, that's it," said Caina. "Now you'll try to wheedle me into handing control to you so I can save Corvalis's sister?"

"Your suspicion does your credit," said Jadriga, "but no. Maglarion left too many scars upon your soul. I cannot wield my powers through your body. This is only a warning. You face enemies that command tremendous destructive power, but lack my vision. They will kill you, if you let them, and destroy much more than just you." Her eyes were like disks of black stone. "They may even destroy me."

"So this is just a warning?" said Caina.

"Yes," said Jadriga. "If you are slain, of course, I can claim another host. But I would prefer if you joined me willingly in the great work."

"And I cannot do that," said Caina, "if I am slain, is that it?"

Jadriga nodded.

"Be ready," said the Moroaica.

She waved her hand, and the dream vanished.

~

CAINA AWOKE, blinking sweat from her eyes.

"Another nightmare?"

She saw Theodosia sitting at the table, humming to herself as she stitched up a tear in one of her gowns. Caina turned her head and saw sunlight fading through the window.

It was almost dark.

"No," said Caina, getting to her feet. She stretched, loosening her stiff muscles. "Not quite a nightmare. Just...a very strange dream."

Theodosia nodded. "Hopefully not an omen. Though all the best operas have prophetic dreams as omens."

"This isn't an opera," said Caina.

"Sadly, no," said Theodosia. She stood. "Come, my dear. I must get ready for Lord Khosrau's ball...and we shall make you ready to draw the eye of a master assassin."

20

ELDER ASSASSIN

Caina had been in the Ghosts for ten years, and in that time she had masqueraded as both a countess and the daughter of a wealthy merchant, clothing herself in elaborate gowns so she could move unseen through the balls and feasts of the nobles and merchants and magi.

She had never worn anything quite like this.

Theodosia had found a short skirt of red Anshani silk. It wrapped around Caina's waist, and though it covered the scars below her navel, it just barely reached the tops of her thighs. Delicate strips of red silk encircled her chest and shoulders in an intricate arrangement, concealing her breasts and leaving her stomach and arms bare. A pair of delicate high-heeled sandals covered her feet, the leather straps encircling her calves.

She wore nothing else.

"This," said Caina, "is going to get chilly."

"Aye," said Theodosia around a mouthful of pins as she arranged Caina's hair.

What Caina lacked in clothing, Theodosia made up for in jewels and makeup. She piled Caina's black hair in an elaborate crown. A golden chain went around her throat, glittering with jewels, and ornate golden torques in the shape of twining serpents around her arms. Intricate bracelets adorned her wrists and ankles. Theodosia painted her face, lining Caina's blue eyes in black, reddening her lips, and perfuming her wrists and throat.

"What do you think?" said Theodosia at last.

Caina examined herself in the mirror. She looked nothing like Marina the serving girl or Countess Marianna Nereide, and certainly nothing like the Ghost nightfighter that had inspired the legend of the Balarigar among the Szaldic peasants of Marsis.

"I look," said Caina, "like I should be in the harem of some Anshani khadjar."

Theodosia grinned. "That was exactly what I was trying to achieve." Her smile faded. "You have no place to conceal weapons."

"I know," said Caina. She took a deep breath. In the mirror she saw the muscles in her stomach clench, saw her ribs press against her skin. Yet going without a weapon made her feel even more naked than this ridiculous costume.

"The pins in your hair are quite sharp," said Theodosia, tapping her hair. "You could kill a man with those, if necessary. But only if you caught him off guard."

Caina nodded. "Corvalis will have the rest of my weapons."

"Let's hope you don't need them," said Theodosia. She glanced out the bedroom window. "It's time to go."

Caina nodded and followed Theodosia in the sitting room.

Corvalis waited by the table, clad in his chain mail and dark cloak, sword and dagger at his belt. A backpack rested over his cloak. He turned as they approached, and stared at Caina without expression.

"Well?" said Theodosia.

Caina did not flinch, did not try to cover herself. She would not show weakness in front of him.

And part of her wanted him to see her like this.

He stared back, his green eyes unblinking.

"Yes," said Corvalis at last. "That will work."

He took a light cloak from the table and swirled it over Caina's shoulders. She closed it and pulled up the cowl. She could not walk barely dressed through the streets of Cyrioch, after all.

"Remember," said Theodosia, "Marzhod and his Sarbians will attack one hour after you arrive."

Corvalis nodded.

"If you get into trouble before Marzhod arrives," said Theodosia, "you'll have..."

"We'll have to improvise," said Corvalis, adjusting his sword.

"That's all right," said Caina. "I'm good at improvising."

Corvalis snorted. "Yes, I've seen that firsthand. Let's go."

A SHORT TIME later Caina and Corvalis stood at the base of the hidden stairwell below the Temple of the Living Flame.

"We're just going to walk up to the portcullis?" said Caina.

"Aye," said Corvalis. "We're guests, remember? An emissary from the Artifel family bearing a gift for the Elder of Cyrioch. We'll walk up, knock, and introduce ourselves."

"And if they decide to trigger the trap?" said Caina.

"Then we'll die," said Corvalis.

"Simple enough," said Caina.

"Remember," said Corvalis. "Act like you're drugged. The Kindred see everyone as a threat...but after a moment they'll dismiss you as a danger. That will give you a chance to strike, if necessary, but only one chance. We might be able to fool these men, but they are extremely dangerous."

"I've dealt with the Kindred before," said Caina.

"And hopefully you'll live to talk about it once more," said Corvalis. "Let's go."

Caina nodded, tugged off her cloak, and dropped it on the floor.

She felt Corvalis's eyes upon her, and suddenly she was aware of how close he stood to her. He was, as Theodosia had said, handsome in an austere sort of way, and it had been years since Caina had felt such an attraction. All at once she wanted to touch him. Or she wanted him to touch her. She wanted to know how his mouth felt against hers.

What an absurd thing to think about on the doorstep of a Kindred Haven.

Corvalis cleared his throat. "Let's go."

Caina swallowed, nodded, and they walked into the black corridor,. Corvalis made no effort to conceal his footfalls. Caina walked behind him, the heels of her sandals clicking against the floor, her head bowed, her movements slow and languourous.

The portcullis was a massive slab of iron, thick metal bars bolted to steel struts. Caina glimpsed three men standing behind the portcullis, clad in chain mail and armed to the teeth. She felt their eyes upon her, but she knew her appearance would not put them at ease.

They would regard her and Corvalis as threats.

"You seem lost, brother," said one of the men, lean and hawk-faced with close-cropped black hair. The other two guards moved closer, crossbows in their arms. At this range, they could scarcely miss, even with the bars of the portcullis in the way.

"I'm exactly where I want to be," said Corvalis. "I am a fellow brother, and I seek leave to speak with the Gatewarden."

The Kindred assassins behind the portcullis shared a look. Outsiders were not supposed to know about the ranks and titles of the Kindred.

"You're in luck, traveler," said the hawk-faced man, "for I am the Gatewarden. Though I am not yet certain you are my brother."

"I have sworn the oaths of brotherhood," said Corvalis. "For we are a family, joined in bonds of death. We are the predators in the night. We are the wolves in the shadows. We are the blades in the darkness. Just as the wolves rid the herd of the slow, so does our brotherhood purge mankind of the weak. We are the Kindred, and we are the wolves that cull mankind."

His voice grew colder and darker as he spoke the oath of the Kindred, the oath he had renounced. Caina shivered as she imagined him speaking it as a child.

She knew pain...but he survived just as much pain as she had. Perhaps much more.

"You know the words, brother," said the Gatewarden. His icy eyes flicked to Caina. "Does she?"

"Her?" said Corvalis. "No. She's...a gift, and nothing more."

"And does this relate to your business in visiting our Haven?" said the Gatewarden.

"It does," said Corvalis. "I am a brother of the family of Artifel. This," he gestured at Caina, "is the daughter of a minor noble of that city. He made a contract for the herd to be culled, and then reneged on payment. And since our Elder wished to show his respects to the Elder of Cyrica Urbana, it seemed only just to take the faithless noble's daughter and present her to your Elder as a...token of our Elder's esteem."

The Kindred stared at Caina like wolves contemplating prey. She kept her eyes heavy-lidded, swaying on her feet as if drugged.

"A good choice," said the Gatewarden. "The Elder has a taste for women with black hair." He scrutinized Caina for a moment longer. "Though I hope you don't want her back. The Elder kills his toys once he grows bored with them."

"She is a gift from the Elder of Artifel," said Corvalis. "Your Elder can do as he pleases with her."

"Very well," said the Gatewarden. "Let them in."

One of the other assassins went to the wall. A massive metal cabinet stood there, filled with an intricate maze of gears and cogs. The assassin pulled an iron lever, and the portcullis shuddered into motion, its halves sliding to the right and to the left. The assassin pulled the lever again, and the portcullis stopped, leaving an opening three feet wide.

"Inside," said the Gatewarden.

Corvalis walked inside, Caina followed him, and the assassin gave the lever a final tug. The portcullis clanged shut behind Caina, and the Kindred leveled their crossbows.

"Weapons off," said the Gatewarden, his tone still amicable.

"What is this?" said Corvalis.

"You haven't done this before, I see," said the Gatewarden. "You say you're from the Artifel family...but you could be a clever impostor. So we'll just have to take your weapons until we're sure of you."

"Fair enough," said Corvalis, unbuckling his sword belt.

"The backpack, too," said the Gatewarden.

Corvalis shrugged out of the backpack. "What about her?"

The Gatewarden snorted. "If she's hiding a weapon in that outfit, she's going to hemorrhage to death any moment. She's no threat."

Caina kept her expression vacant, but she smiled inwardly. The Kindred had failed to see her as a threat.

One of the assassins went through Corvalis's weapons belt, while another searched his backpack. Inside was a belt of throwing knives, a curved dagger in a sheath, rolled-up black clothes, and...

"What's this?" said the assassin, drawing out Caina's shadow-cloak.

"A Ghost shadow-cloak," said Corvalis. "It's rather useful. A pity we don't know how to make them."

"A fine trophy," said the Gatewarden as the other assassin returned the cloak to the backpack. "I want one myself."

Corvalis grinned. "Find a Ghost nightfighter and kill one."

"Easier said than done," said the Gatewarden.

The Gatewarden looked at the backpack, nodded to himself, and looked back at Corvalis.

"I bid you welcome, brother," said the Gatewarden. He turned to one of the other guards. "Take the Artifel family's gift to the Elder's study." He looked at Corvalis. "The Elder is meditating now, but he will want to speak with you. After he has finished with your gift, most likely. In the meantime, you shall enjoy our hospitality."

"I thank you, Gatewarden," said Corvalis.

"I fear our hospitality will be thin," said the Gatewarden. "We have a substantial contract to fulfill, and many of the brothers will be occupied tonight..."

Caina kept her head down, but her ears perked up. Corbould, Khosrau, and Armizid were all at the Palace of Splendors. Were the Kindred mounting a major effort to kill all three of them? If they...

"Woman," said one of the assassins. "Come with me. Now."

He did not touch her.

She belonged to the Elder of Cyrioch, after all.

Caina followed the assassin deeper into the Haven. Doors opened on either side of the wide stone corridor, and through one Caina saw rows of bunk beds and storage chests. Barracks for the assassins, she supposed. Beyond another door she saw a room full of strange machinery. Dozens of enormous glass tanks rested among the machines, connected by glass pipes. Caina wondered if it was a distillery of some kind.

Then she realized the tanks held acid. The glass pipes led to the dark slits in the outer corridor. If one of the Kindred assassins flipped a lever, the outer corridor would flood with acid.

Just as well Marzhod and the Sarbians would not attack from that direction.

"Through here," said the assassin, stopping before a door. He knocked, took a deep breath, and swung it open.

Beyond lay a lavishly furnished study. Caina's feet sank into a thick green carpet. Wooden shelves lined the walls, and the shelves held not books but...trophies. Grinning skulls stared at Caina, and glass jars held preserved heads floating in brine. A variety of exotic weapons hung in ornate display cases, and several paintings showed scenes of torture and death. An enormous wooden desk dominated the center of the room, its surface covered with papers. A narrow door stood in the far wall.

"Remain here," said the assassin. "If you value your life, do not go into the corridor. And if you value your sanity...do not go through the far door. Not until the Elder commands you."

"Where am I?" said Caina, keeping her voice slurred and indistinct.

The assassin's face crinkled in disgust. "Wretched creature. You'll die screaming soon enough."

The assassin left the study, and Caina heard a click as he locked the door behind him.

She straightened up and slid out of her unwieldy sandals, trying not to shiver with the chill in the room, and considered what to do next.

Corvalis had her shadow-cloak and all her weapons. Without her help, he might have a difficult time overpowering the assassins and disabling the mechanism that controlled the portcullis.

Or he might not. She had seen him in a fight, and he might be able to lull the assassins into complacency. And if he killed the Gatewarden and the other guards quietly enough, he might be able to disable the portcullis without alerting the other assassins. If he did, Marzhod's mercenaries would take the Kindred by surprise.

And then Caina need only wait until all the Kindred were dead.

Caina moved closer to the desk, examining the papers spread across its surface. Someone had hired the Kindred to kill Lord Khosrau and his son alongside Lord Corbould, and for all their efforts, the Ghosts had been unable to discovered who had paid the Kindred. It was possible that the Cyrioch family's records lay within that desk.

None of the papers were of interest, so she checked the desk's drawers.

All of them were locked.

Caina hesitated and glanced at the narrow door to the Elder's private sanctum. If he came through the door while she was trying to open the desk, he would stop her.

And then he would do worse things to her.

She walked to one of the display cases. Inside rested a set of jeweled Anshani daggers, their tapering blades carved with elegant characters. Caina took a moment to check the case, but it was not locked, and she found no traps.

None of the Kindred would dare to steal from their Elder.

She took one of the daggers from the case, closed it, and hid the weapon beneath the papers on the Elder's desk. Then she slipped one of the pins from her hair, knelt before the desk, and got to work. Theodosia had chosen pins that could double as lock picks.

Which was just as well, since the desk drawers were both locked and trapped. To judge from the shape of the wooden panels on the front of the drawers, Caina guessed that poisoned blades would erupt from concealed slits if anyone tried to open the desk without using the proper key.

Fortunately, Caina had a great deal of practice opening locks and disarming locks.

Unfortunately, the hairpin made a poor tool. She worked the locks, probing ever deeper, muscles tensed to jump if she heard one of the traps activate. But the traps remained quiet, and minutes passed as Caina kept working.

Then she felt the sudden tingle of sorcery and stood up in alarm. Had there been wards upon the desk?

No. The Kindred Elder. Corvalis had said the Elder bore an enspelled torque, a relic that granted him supernatural strength and longevity. Such a relic would be at thing of powerful sorcery.

The tingling was coming from the door to the Elder's private chamber.

Caina had only a few seconds to act. She snatched the hidden dagger from the desk and hurried to the farthest corner of the room. She concealed the dagger on a shelf, tucking it between two yellowing skulls. Then she crouched in the corner, spitting into her palms. She rubbed her hands over her eyes and face, smearing her makeup and making it look as if she had been crying.

Then she huddled into a ball, hands wrapped around her shins, face buried in her legs, and waited.

A moment later she heard the door open.

She looked up and saw the Kindred Elder standing behind the desk.

He looked like a man in his middle fifties, tall and lean, forearms corded with heavy muscle, skin leathery and seamed from years in the sun. His gray hair was close-cropped, his face clean-shaven, and he wore simple, loose clothing. His eyes were the color of steel, and just as cold and hard. He looked like a man of about fifty, save for the eyes.

Those were the eyes of an ancient killer, a predator drenched in blood.

A silver torque rested around his neck, supporting a rough green crystal the size of a man's thumb. It shone with an emerald glow, and Caina sensed powerful sorcery within it.

It was a bloodcrystal, a product of necromantic science. A bloodcrystal stored the life force of a slain victim, feeding it to the crystal's bearer. Maglarion had used bloodcrystals to extend his life for centuries. No doubt the bloodcrystal supplied the Elder's longevity and strength.

A bloodcrystal also used its stolen life force to heal injuries, allowing its bearer to recover quickly from all but the most deadly wounds. If Caina did not kill the Elder quickly, the Kindred chieftain would recover with terrifying speed. A better option was to incapacitate him, remove the torque, and then kill him.

Assuming, of course, she could find a way to overpower the Elder.

"Well, well," said the Elder in Cyrican. His voice and smile were almost grandfatherly. "What do we have here?"

"Where am I?" said Caina in High Nighmarian, keeping her voice slurred. "It's so cold."

The Elder stepped around the desk. He bore no weapons that Caina could see, but he would know how to kill with his hands.

"Ah, I see," said the Elder, switching to flawless High Nighmarian. "A gift. Where are you from, my dear?"

"I want to go home," said Caina.

"And where is home?" said the Elder, still smiling.

He was enjoying this.

"Artifel," said Caina. "My father is a lord there. I went to my room, and there were men waiting for me...and then the next thing I knew I woke up here and all my clothes were gone. Can you send me home to my father? He will reward you."

"I'm sure he would," murmured the Elder. He stepped past the display cases. If he noticed the missing dagger, he gave no indication. "But I suspect I know what happened. It's a very sad story."

"You do?" said Caina, putting a tremulous note of hope into her voice.

He was falling for it. He saw only a terrified young woman clad in scraps of silk, clinging to any piece of hope. The Elder seemed the sort of man who enjoyed playing with his victims. If she could lure him off his guard, she would have one chance to land a fatal blow.

Maybe.

"Yes," said the Elder. "You see, my dear, your father made a contract with the Kindred. No doubt he wanted one of his rivals killed. Some competition over a petty local magistracy, I imagine."

"No," said Caina. "My father would never do that."

If she stood up, the hidden dagger would be within reach.

"Daughters like to believe the best about their fathers," said the Elder, "and are always so shocked when they learn their beloved fathers have sold them into slavery."

"No!" said Caina. "My father wouldn't do that to me."

"I'm sure you believe that," said the Elder. "But I've seen this before. Your father made a contract with us, and he couldn't pay. Or perhaps he offered you as payment. So you now you belong to me."

"That's not true!" said Caina. "I am the daughter of a noble House."

"Once," said the Elder, "but now you are my slave, and nothing more. Stand up!"

His voice cracked like a whip, and Caina rose. The Elder's gaze flicked up and down her body, a faint smile passing over his lips.

Caina backed against the wall, as if in fear, her fingers brushing the dagger's hilt.

"You think to please me, yes?" said the Elder, taking a step closer. "You think that if you submit to me, that if you obey me, I will make things easier for you? You are wrong. Your only purpose is to please me, and it will please me to torment you."

Caina shied against the shelves, her hands closing around the dagger's hilt. "Please, sir, please, whoever you are, let me go home."

She would have one chance to land a killing blow. One solid stab between his ribs should disable him. The bloodcrystal would repair the damage in a few seconds, but that gave Caina enough time to get the torque off his throat. Then she could inflict a mortal wound the bloodcrystal could not heal.

"You will never leave this room again," said the Elder. "Your father has abandoned you. Let that thought be the beginning of your torment."

He started towards her, and Caina went slack, her eyes wide with fear.

But her hands tightened around the dagger's hilt...

The door to the corridor banged open.

Both Caina and the Elder turned their heads.

A Kindred assassin she had not seen before staggered into the study, breathing hard. He held a sword in his hand, and Caina saw specks of blood on his face and chain mail.

"I trust," said the Elder, "that you have a good reason for disturbing me?"

"Elder," said the assassin. "We are under attack."

The Elder's eyebrows rose. "What?"

"The tunnel to the Ring of Valor," said the assassin. "A mob of Sarbian mercenaries. The outer guards are holding them off, but they'll break into the Haven at any moment!"

The Elder snarled, the expression making him look almost demonic. "Damnation. The Ghosts, I suspect. That clever wretch Marzhod captured too many of our brothers. None of them knew the location of the Haven, but he must have deduced it somehow. Or one of our inner circle betrayed us."

"Not I, Elder!" said the assassin.

"I know that, fool," said the Elder. "I will handle this attack for myself. Too many of our brothers have left to settle matters at the Palace of Splendors." Were the Kindred preparing to kill Khosrau and Corbould even now? "We may have to abandon the Haven."

"Our Haven, Elder?" said the assassin. "The Haven is the heart of the Kindred!"

The Elder sneered. "I am the heart of the Kindred! Now, come. We have killing to do."

The Elder took a step towards the door, stopped, and looked at

Caina. Gone was the smugness, the cold mockery of a predator playing with his prey. Now his cold eyes weighed and examined her.

Evaluating her as a threat.

"If I may ask," said the assassin, "who is that, Elder?"

"No one of importance," said the Elder. "A gift from the Elder of another family. Probably Artifel, I imagine. I would have enjoyed her...but her appearance before this attack is too much of a coincidence. Kill her and then join me."

The Elder strode into the corridor without a backward glance.

21

BETRAYAL

The assassin drew his sword.

"No," Caina whimpered, hoping to lull him into false confidence. "No, please, please, don't kill me."

She grasped the dagger, sliding it from the shelf.

The assassin chuckled. "What? I'm not going to kill you. The Elder has a bit of a temper, that's all. He'll calm down soon enough. Come with me to your room."

He wanted to kill her in the corridor, Caina realized. Why not just kill her in here?

She realized he didn't want to get blood on the Elder's fine carpet.

"Yes," said Caina, tightening her hold in the dagger. "Will...will you take me home to my father?"

"Of course," said the assassin. "Anything you want. Just come with me."

Caina stepped away from the shelf, looked at the doorway, and made her eyes go wide and her mouth fall open in fear.

The assassin looked at the door for a half-second, and that was all the time Caina needed. She whipped the Anshani dagger around and buried it to the hilt in the assassin's neck. The Kindred staggered, clawing at Caina, but all the strength had gone out of his limbs. She slammed her heel into this back of his knee, and he collapsed in a heap, blood streaming from his neck.

"Sorry about the carpet," said Caina.

The assassin trembled once and went still.

Caina ripped the dagger free and wiped it clean on the carpet as she tried to decide her next move. She could not try to open the desk in the middle of a battle, and she could not stay here. Once the Sarbians forced their way into the Haven, the Elder would try to escape. But before he did, he would undoubtedly stop in his study to take any important documents.

Once he saw the assassin dead on his expensive carpet, he would realize that Caina was more than what she appeared.

The entire plan hinged on Corvalis jamming the portcullis. If he had succeeded, she would join forces with him. And if he had failed...she would try to jam the portcullis herself.

If she could.

No sooner had the thought crossed her mind than Corvalis appeared in the door.

He was breathing hard, his cloak slashed and torn, his sword in his hand. Blood dried on his chain mail and boots, and he had small cuts above his left eye and jaw.

Caina felt a wave of relief.

"Looks like you have been busy," he said, glancing at the dead Kindred.

He shrugged out of his backpack and tossed it to her.

Caina tugged it open and got dressed. She pulled on black pants, black boots with daggers in hidden sheaths, and a black jacket lined with thin steel plates to deflect knives. A belt of throwing knives went around her waist, the ghostsilver dagger on her right hip. A mask covered her face, and her shadow-cloak went around her shoulders.

As she equipped herself, she heard the sounds of distant fighting echoing through the corridor.

The Sarbians were fighting their way into the Haven.

"Did you jam the portcullis?" said Caina.

"Aye," said Corvalis. "First two guards went down easy enough.

The Gatewarden, though...he was a challenge. Poisoned his blades, too." He chuckled. "Fortunately, he was smart enough to carry the antidote with him." He looked around. "What now?"

"Most of the assassins went to the Palace of Splendors," said Caina. "The rest are fighting the Sarbians. We've got to get to the Palace and warn Theodosia."

"Then," said Corvalis, "we help Marzhod's Sarbians finish off the Kindred, and head to the Palace."

"Aye," said Caina. She grinned behind the mask. "The Kindred are focused on the Sarbians. They won't expect someone to attack them from behind."

Corvalis nodded. "Let's give them an unpleasant surprise."

She followed him into the corridor and froze.

The Kindred Elder stood thirty feet away, bloody swords in either hand. His cold gray eyes narrowed as they focused upon her.

"Ah," he said. "The noble's daughter. A Ghost nightfighter. I should have suspected." He lifted his swords. "Time enough to rectify that mistake before I flee."

"You're not fleeing anywhere," said Corvalis.

"And you," said the Elder. "I think I recognize you. One of Decius Aberon's little bastards, aren't you? I'm not surprised you ended up with a collection of fools like the Ghosts. A fortunate development nonetheless. I'll send your head to the Elder of Artifel."

"I doubt he'd appreciate a hunk of rotting meat," said Corvalis. "But you're not going anywhere. I jammed the portcullis."

The Elder went motionless, his expression blank.

"You can't flee to the Temple of Living Flame," said Caina, "and the tunnel to the Ring of Valor is full of angry Sarbians. Even with that bloodcrystal chained to your neck, you're not fighting past that many men on your own. Because by the time you get back to the tunnel, the assassins you left behind will all be dead."

The Elder lifted his chin with disdain.

"I suggest you surrender," said Caina. "There are lots of things we want to know."

"Very well," said the Elder.

He dropped his swords, the blades clanging.

Caina had not expected him to actually surrender.

"Ghost!" shouted Corvalis, and Caina felt the faint tingle of sorcery.

The Elder was drawing on the bloodcrystal's power.

Caina threw herself to the side as the Elder's sinewy hand blurred. A black throwing knife hurtled past Caina's ear with terrific speed and struck the wall with enough force to leave a crack in the stone. Caina caught her balance and yanked the daggers from her boots, but the Elder was faster. The Kindred leader snatched up his discarded swords, and charged her in a sorcery-enhanced blur.

Corvalis met his attack with a shout, his sword and dagger flying. The two men traded a dozen blows in half as many heartbeats. Yet the Elder wielded his swords with the skill of long experience and practice, and soon Corvalis found himself forced on the defensive. The Elder was the best swordsman Caina had ever seen, better even than Naelon Icaraeus, and he was going to defeat Corvalis.

Unless Caina took action.

She raced to the side and flung a knife. The Elder tried to twist aside, but he wore no armor, and the blade buried itself in his thigh. The assassin stumbled and Corvalis stabbed, his dagger tearing a furrow along his foe's ribs. The Elder danced back, yanking the knife from his leg, and Caina saw the blood flow stop as the bloodcrystal's stored life energy healed the wound.

"Foolish children," said the Elder. He lifted his arms as the wound across his ribs healed. "You have no weapons that can harm me. Even now, the feeble wounds you have dealt me close. I am an Elder of the Kindred, and I killed with impunity long before your fathers ever lay with your mothers. I am the hunter, the terror in the darkness! You think to kill me? As well might the sheep think to overthrow the wolf! Lay down your weapons, fools, and I will kill you without..."

"Oh, shut up," said Caina.

The Elder blinked in surprised astonishment. Caina doubted few people had used that tone to the Elder's face.

"You're not some terror in the darkness," said Caina, "you're a pompous old man with a minor bloodcrystal strapped to your neck. Yes, I know what that is. Take away the bloodcrystal, and you'll bleed to death like any other man."

Corvalis gave her a shallow nod as he understood.

The Elder's lips peeled back from his teeth in terrible fury and he shot forward. Corvalis met his attack, sword and dagger working in concert. Again the Elder soon had the younger man on the retreat. Caina circled around them, trying to throw another knife, but the Elder kept Corvalis between them.

She realized his plan. He would drive Corvalis against the jammed portcullis and kill him once the younger man ran out of room to fall back. Then he would deal with Caina.

Unless they killed him first.

The Elder lunged at Corvalis, and Caina had an opening. A knife flew from her fingers and buried itself in the Elder's side. The Elder stumbled with a hiss of pain, and Corvalis struck. The dagger in his left hand plunged into the older assassin's right shoulder. The Elder staggered, and Caina expected the old assassin to go on the defensive.

Instead he charged again at Corvalis. At first his right arm was slower than his left, but in a matter of heartbeats, the wound in his shoulder closed, the bloodcrystal pulsing with pale light. Soon the Elder fought as if he had not been wounded at all.

Caina had to get that bloodcrystal away from him. Or could they wear down his reserves? A bloodcrystal could only store a limited amount of stolen life force. If she inflicted enough wounds upon him, sooner or later the bloodcrystal would run dry. Yet the Elder would kill Corvalis long before his bloodcrystal drained, and Caina could not face him alone.

She remembered fighting Naelon Icaraeus's mercenaries on the rooftops of Marsis. They had worn bracers that protected them from weapons of normal steel, but Caina's ghostsilver dagger had been able to penetrate those protections. Could the dagger do the same to the Elder? Maglarion had survived a lethal wound from a ghostsilver-tipped spear...but Maglarion had been linked to a bloodcrystal of tremendous size and power. Would the Elder's bloodcrystal give him similar protection?

It was time to find out.

Caina darted forward, ghostsilver dagger in her right hand, a throwing knife in her left. The Elder and Corvalis wheeled around each other, and Caina threw the knife in her left hand. The Elder stepped back, his right-hand sword blurring. Caina's spinning blade clattered to the floor. The ancient assassin recovered his balance and renewed his attacks on Corvalis, but his side was open for a half-second, and he did not bother to guard against Caina. No doubt he thought his bloodcrystal would heal any wounds she inflicted.

She raked ghostsilver dagger across his right forearm. Even from the brief contact, the dagger's hilt grew warm, and the bloodcrystal at the Elder's throat made a high-pitched keening noise, like metal placed under too much stress. The Elder stumbled back with a shocked scream, the cut upon his forearm smoking like a wound from a hot iron. Surprise lowered his guard, and Caina struck again, opening another gash upon his ribs. Again the Elder bellowed, and Caina threw herself out of way as he stabbed.

"What trickery is this?" spat the Elder. "Has the Magisterium betrayed me? Did they give you that weapon?"

Caina laughed. "Truly? All these decades you've been the killer in the darkness and you've never once encountered a ghostsilver weapon? Do the Kindred permit any random fool to become an Elder?"

A stunned laugh burst from Corvalis's lips.

The Elder snarled and attacked her, but Corvalis intercepted the blows. The older assassin attacked with fury and skill, but his right arm no longer moved as fast as his left. The wounds her ghostsilver dagger had left were not healing as quickly as the wounds dealt by normal steel. Caina hit him with another throwing knife, making him stumble, and stabbed the ghostsilver dagger into the opening. Her blade dug into his hip, and again the Elder bellowed in fury. Corvalis drove his sword into the Elder's belly, and Caina felt a surge of exultation. They were winning...

The Elder snatched something from his belt. Something glittered in his fingers, and Caina realized that he held a glass vial.

A glass vial full of swirling dark fluid.

"Corvalis!" shouted Caina. "Watch..."

The Elder flung the vial at the floor, and it exploded in a rippling plume of black smoke. Corvalis caught in the smoke in the face, and he stumbled back, coughing and hacking. Caina was at the edge of the plume, and even the little bit she inhaled made her throat close up, made her eyes water and burn.

The Elder seemed unaffected. She expected him to attack Corvalis, to finish him off before the younger man recovered.

Instead the Elder spun to face her, swords drawn back to stab.

She had caused him more pain, after all.

She ducked under his first thrust and sidestepped past the slash of his other sword. He was not moving as fast as the beginning of their fight. Perhaps all his bloodcrystal's power had gone to heal his injuries. But even without his enhanced speed, he was still fast enough to kill her. He drove her across the corridor until her back thumped against the wall.

The Elder drew back his swords to finish the fight.

Caina snatched her cloak with her free hand and threw it at him.

The Elder raised his right sword to block, his left sword still angled to kill her.

But steel could not touch the peculiar shadow-cloth, and it passed through his sword and draped over his face. The Elder bellowed in fury and Caina sidestepped, his left sword clanging against the wall. She lunged at him, hoping to land a killing blow with the ghostsilver dagger, and the Elder jerked back.

Instead of meeting his chest, her blade slammed into his left hand.

His sword and several of his fingers fell to the ground, smoke rising from his ruined hand.

The Elder howled like an enraged animal, and his boot slammed into Caina's gut. She fell hard to the stone floor, trying to catch her breath. The Elder loomed over her, gray eyes bright with crazed fury, and his sword came up for the kill.

Corvalis intercepted him.

The Elder whirled to face the new threat. For a moment the sheer fury of Corvalis's attack drove the Elder back, but the Elder was the better swordsman, even wounded and fighting with only one blade. Corvalis's momentum played out, and the Elder counterattacked. Step by step Corvalis retreated, face grim.

The Elder drove him into the room of machines and glass tanks.

Glass tanks filled with acid.

Caina staggered to her feet, wheezing and coughing. The Elder deflected a thrust, and the blow knocked Corvalis's sword against one of the glass tanks. For a terrible moment Caina thought the tank would shatter, that Corvalis would disappear beneath gallons of hissing acid.

But the tank only chimed. The glass was far too thick for a single sword blow to shatter.

The glass pipes connecting the tanks, though...

A mad idea came to Caina.

She drew a throwing knife and took several deep breaths, trying to ignore the throbbing ache in her chest. The Elder drove Corvalis back, pushing him towards a gap between the machines and the wall. Corvalis would be trapped, and the fight would be over.

A glass pipe ran over the Elder's head, connecting two of the acid tanks.

Caina took one final breath, drew herself up, and flung the knife.

The blade slammed into the pipe and tore a chunk of glass from its underside. A jet of green acid burst from the pipe, spraying the floor.

And the Elder's shoulders and neck and head.

His face and clothing went up in snarling white flames, and a horrible scream came from his throat. The Elder spun and staggered into the corridor, hissing yellow smoke rising from his face and chest. She glimpsed his glaring gray eyes even as the flesh of his face dissolved around them. He lurched towards her, and Caina found herself too horrified by the ghastly spectacle to move.

Corvalis appeared behind him, sword in both hands.

The Elder's burning head jerked off his shoulders and rolled across the floor, still smoking. His body crumpled as his clothing burned, revealing horrid acid burns across his shoulders and chest.

The smell was dreadful.

"Gods," said Corvalis, wiping the sweat from his brow. "We killed a Kindred Elder. Gods. I wasn't sure they could be killed."

"Any man can be killed," said Caina, her voice weak, "if you stab him a dozen times, pour a tank of acid over him, and then cut off his head."

"He's...not going to come back, is he?" said Corvalis. "That blood-crystal thing can't heal this, can it?"

"I doubt it," said Caina, stepping around the smoking lump of the Elder's head. She picked up her shadow-cloak and slung it over her shoulders, pulling up the cowl. "But just to make sure..." The Elder's torque lay a few inches from his body, the green crystal glowing dimly.

Caina plunged her ghostsilver dagger into the bloodcrystal.

It shivered like a dying thing, the green light flaring, and crumbled into smoking black ash.

"He's not coming back," said Caina. She braced herself against the stench and pushed aside his ruined shirt, examining his belt.

Corvalis snorted. "Don't tell me you're looting his corpse."

"That's exactly what I am doing," said Caina. A number of small pouches hung on his belt, and she searched them. She found several more of those glass vials and claimed them for herself. "The records of the Cyrioch family are locked up in his desk. If we can get our hands on those records...ah, here we are."

She tugged an elaborate steel key from one of his pouches.

Caina's fingers tightened around it. At last she held the answers she sought.

"What the devil is that smell?"

A dozen Sarbian mercenaries strode down the corridor, their

sand-colored robes speckled in blood, scimitars in hand. Marzhod walked at their head, a loaded crossbow in his arms. He looked pleased with himself. The attack through the tunnel must have gone well.

Of course, the fact that he was still alive was proof that the attack had gone well.

"The Elder," said Corvalis, pointing with his sword.

"Aberon. You're still alive," said Marzhod. He looked at what remained of the Elder and winced. "Gods. What did you do to him?"

"Acid," said Caina, keeping her voice disguised with a snarling rasp. The Sarbian mercenaries looked at her and her shadow-cloak in sudden fear. No reason for them to know who she really was. "That trap would have flooded in the corridor with acid. The Elder stood under one of the pipes. He shouldn't have done that."

"Plainly," said Marzhod. "Where did they get all that acid?"

Corvalis shrugged. "The College of Alchemists in Istarinmul, I expect. The Alchemists brew deadly elixirs, and they often hire the Kindred to kill their foes."

"Are any of the Kindred left alive?" said Caina.

Marzhod scowled. "None. The mad bastards fought to the last man. A few of the ones we cornered even cut their own throats. I'd hoped to take a least one of them alive for questioning."

Caina lifted up the steel key. "It might not matter. I took this off the Elder. We can get to his records."

Marzhod stared at the key for a moment. Then he turned and barked a string of orders in Sarbian. The mercenaries hurried off, moving deeper into the Haven.

"They'll stay out of our way until we're done," said Marzhod. "Come. You too, Aberon. I suppose you've earned the right to be here."

"Very gracious," said Corvalis with a smirk.

"And," said Caina, "he might be useful in explaining anything we don't understand."

Marzhod grunted, and Caina led the way back to the Elder's

study. The assassin she had killed still lay dead upon the floor, his blood drying on the carpet. Otherwise the room was undisturbed.

"Delightful," murmured Marzhod, looking around the room. "I am going to make a fortune selling some of these items." He looked at the dead assassin and sighed. "A pity about the carpet, though."

Caina ignored him and crossed to the desk. The Elder's steel key slid into the first lock with the tiniest hint of resistance. She turned the key, heard the click of the traps disarming, and then opened the drawer.

The first drawer held dozens of tiny glass vials. The Elder's personal stock of poisons and antidotes, Caina suspected. The second drawer held small knives and other tools, along with several pouches of gold coins and jewels.

The third and largest drawer held an enormous book, easily six inches thick. Caina heaved it unto the desk. The book's cover was worn black leather, the front adorned with an elaborate sigil of two hands pinned together by a narrow dagger.

"That's it," said Corvalis, voice hoarse. "That's the Book of Blood and Gold."

"Overly poetical," muttered Marzhod. "What is it?"

"A list of all the blood spilled by the Kindred and the gold they received in payment," said Corvalis. "Every Kindred family has one. These are the records of the Kindred of Cyrioch. A listing of every assassination, every payment, every plot and stratagem. It will even have records of every member of the Cyrioch family." He shook his head. "You can utterly crush the Kindred of Cyrioch with this, and it will take the other Kindred Elders years to rebuild the Cyrioch family."

"My cup runneth over," said Marzhod, smiling. "Just as I prefer it."

"And more importantly," said Caina, opening the massive book, "it will tell us who hired the Kindred to kill the nobles."

She began turning the pages, both Marzhod and Corvalis watching over her shoulders. The first pages of the book were written in High Nighmarian, and she saw Anshani names upon the pages.

Which meant that the first recorded assassinations were from the time Anshan still ruled over Cyrioch.

The book was over a thousand years old.

Caina turned more pages, trying not to shiver. There were pages of names, so many names. How many hundreds had the Kindred of Cyrioch slaughtered over the centuries? How many thousands? Caina often felt guilt over those she had killed, but the destruction of this den of murderers would not trouble her in the slightest.

In the middle the book switched from High Nighmarian to Istarish, and then to Cyrican for the remainder. Caina reached the final written page and scanned it. The dates on the final set of pages were from the last fifteen years or so, and she began to read.

"I'll be damned," muttered Marzhod.

"What?" said Caina.

"Lord Khosrau's eldest son Yergizid," said Marzhod, pointing at a line of text. "Died ten years ago. I always thought he got drunk, passed out, and drowned in his bath. Looks like someone paid the Kindred to make it look like a suicide."

Something began to stir in Caina's mind.

"Just like the previous two Lord Governors of Cyrica," said Corvalis.

Marzhod snorted. "They both died of old age."

Corvalis pointed at a page. "According to this book, they both died of a specific poison the Elder personally mixed for them. One to feign the effects of a natural death."

A yawning pit opened in Caina's stomach.

"Oh, damn," she said. "Damn, damn, damn."

She flipped to the last page.

"What?" said Corvalis, looking around for enemies.

"Armizid," said Caina, scanning the page. "I am a blind fool."

She remembered Lord Governor Armizid Asurius scowling in disapproval at Theodosia.

At his father.

"Armizid?" said Marzhod. "That spineless twit? He's never had a thought Lord Khosrau didn't have first. Besides, the Kindred were hired to kill him, too. That assassin we captured said so."

"Look," said Caina, stabbing a finger at the page. "Just stop talking and read. Who paid for Yergizid's death? Armizid. Who paid to have those Lord Governors killed? Armizid."

Marzhod blinked in bafflement. "Why would Armizid hire the Kindred to kill himself? If he wants to die, there are cheaper ways to get it done."

"He didn't," said Corvalis. "He only hired the Kindred to wound him. For enough gold the Kindred will do it. A man hires the Kindred to kill his brother, but pays them extra to deal a minor wound to him. That way no suspicion falls upon him."

"Armizid has been working on this for years," said Caina, reading more lines in the massive book. "Getting rid of his brothers, killing the Lord Governors until his father bothered to give him the office. The war with New Kyre and Istarinmul gave him the chance he needed."

"To do what?" said Corvalis.

"To kill Lord Khosrau and the Emperor's emissary," said Marzhod, his voice grim, "and declare himself King of Cyrica. The fool must think he can play the Empire and Anshan and Istarinmul off against each other, and turn Cyrica into his own little kingdom."

"He might do it, too," said Caina. "Read here. The Kindred have infiltrated Cyrioch's civic militia. Several of the assassins have become centurions, and have been quietly hiring mercenaries for the militia. That's why there were so few assassins here tonight. They're all out in the civic militia. And they're..."

"They're going to kill Khosrau and Corbould tonight," said Marzhod.

"Unless we stop them," said Caina.

Marzhod spat out a curse and ran for the door, bellowing for his mercenaries.

Caina and Corvalis ran after him.

22

A DANCE AT LORD KHOSRAU'S BALL

"Faster!" bellowed Marzhod, breathing hard.

Corvalis had done his work too well. The portcullis had been irreparably jammed, leaving them with no choice but to take the tunnel to the Ring of Valor. Unfortunately, the Ring of Valor was outside of the city, nearly a mile and a half away from the Stone and the Palace of Splendors.

A mile and a half they had to cover on foot.

Fortunately, it was almost midnight, and the streets of Cyrioch were deserted. And those few people out on business made way for a hundred angry Sarbian mercenaries with swords in their hands.

Caina ran alongside Marzhod and Corvalis, her shadow-cloak snapping behind her.

"How are we getting inside the Palace?" said Corvalis.

"We'll ask nicely," snarled Marzhod, his face shiny with sweat. "The Ghosts have friends among the Palace's slaves."

"And if the guards refuse to let us in?" said Caina.

Marzhod glared at her. "We'll just have to fight our way in, won't we?"

That was a bad plan. But the Kindred could kill Lord Khosrau and Lord Corbould at any moment, and there was no time to wait.

The Palace's main gates faced the Plaza of Majesty, north of the Stone itself, but a second gate stood in the Palace's south wall, a ramp leading to the streets below. The Sarbians hurried up the ramp, the gleaming white wall of the Palace rising overhead. An elaborate gate stood atop the ramp, an ornate arch lined with carvings of Anshani lions and Cyrican gazelles...

"Wait!" said Caina.

Marzhod shouted to his mercenaries, and the Sarbians went still. Their chieftain said something to his followers, and the men drew their swords.

They, too, sensed something amiss.

Caina crept forward, a throwing knife in hand, and saw the corpses in gate's shadow.

Four of them, wearing the armor and colors of the civic militia, their eyes bulging, faces dark, tongues swelling over their teeth. They had been quite expertly garroted.

The Kindred had already been here.

"What is it?" said Marzhod.

Caina gestured at the bodies.

"Damn it," hissed Marzhod.

"We might be too late," said Corvalis.

"No," said Marzhod. "I'm not giving up on this now."

"The Gallery of the Well?" said Caina. "Would Lord Khosrau hold another ball in there?"

"No," said Marzhod. "He wouldn't hold a second ball for Lord Corbould in the same room. But there are a dozen other places suitable for a ball in the Palace. The Lord Governor's Gallery, the Hall of Glass, the Walk of Captains, the..."

"The slaves," said Caina. "You said you have informants among the slaves. One of them will..."

Marzhod hurried through the arch. Caina and Corvalis followed, the Sarbian mercenaries running after them. The elaborate courtyard on the other side of the gate stood deserted. Ornate columns ringed the courtyard, balconies and windows rising above them. Caina saw three more dead men upon ground, their blood drying on the polished marble tiles.

For a moment she wondered why the Kindred had killed the guards. Khosrau and Corbould were the targets. But Armizid wanted to make himself King of Cyrica, and the more corpses, the stronger his story. He could argue that Corbould had brought men to kill him. Both Corbould and Khosrau had fallen in the fighting, and to repay the Empire's treachery, Armizid would make Cyrica into an independent kingdom.

It was devilishly brilliant.

And Armizid might already have succeeded.

Marzhod darted down a narrow corridor, opening every door he saw. At the fifth door a woman's shriek rang out.

"Get out!" said the woman in Cyrican. "I will use this!"

Caina looked over Marzhod's shoulder. Beyond was a slave's narrow room, and a young woman in the gray tunic of a slave stood against the far wall, a meat cleaver in her hand.

"Oh, put that down, Tiria," said Marzhod.

The slave woman blinked. "Circlemaster? Oh, thank the gods! The militia has gone berserk. They burst into the Palace, killing everyone in sight, and..."

"I know," said Marzhod. "They're here on the Lord Governor's orders to kill Lord Khosrau and Lord Corbould and start a war with the Empire."

Tiria sniffed. "The Lord Governor? I am not surprised. A stingy man. Lord Khosrau is both generous and stern, as a proper master should be."

"Where are they?" said Marzhod. "Cyrioch will burn if we can't keep the nobles alive."

"The Hall of Glass," said Tiria. "But you may be too late, circlemaster. The civic militia killed the guards at the gate at least fifteen minutes past."

Caina's hands closed into fists. The Kindred needed far less than fifteen minutes to kill two men.

And Theodosia was with them.

"No matter," said Marzhod, his voice cold. "If we're too late, we'll just kill Armizid ourselves. Then the Emperor will send a new Lord Governor while the Cyrican nobles fight for dominance." He pointed at Tiria. "Stay hidden here until I send a man for you. I will need eyes and ears in the Palace once the fighting is over."

Tiria laughed. "I shall hide under the bed. Wild dogs could not chase me into the corridors just now."

Marzhod nodded and closed the door.

"The Hall of Glass is this way," he said. "All of you, follow me!"

They ran down the corridor.

"What will you tell Khosrau?" said Corvalis. "We can hardly say that the circlemaster of Cyrioch and a renegade Kindred assassin arrived to save him at the last minute."

Assuming, of course, that Khosrau Asurius had not already fallen.

"I haven't the slightest idea," said Marzhod. "If Khosrau is still alive, we'll figure it out then."

Marzhod led them into a wide corridor, the walls lined with slender columns. Here and there Caina saw more corpses. Dead civic militiamen in their chain mail and cloaks. A minor noble in his white robe. Three slaves in gray. They must have gotten in the way of the Kindred. She saw one of Corbould's Imperial Guards in black armor, his helmet crushed. That gave her a brief flicker of hope. The Kindred had infiltrated the civic militia, but not the Imperial Guard. Perhaps the Guards could hold off the assassins until help arrived.

Marzhod charged up an elaborate spiral staircase, pulling on a mask as he ran. Corvalis did the same, and then Marzhod's men kicked through a set of double doors.

The Hall of Glass opened before them.

It stood at the highest point of the Palace, its walls filled with enormous glass windows in lead frameworks. They offered a stunning view of the city, the harbor, and the sea beyond. Crystalline chandeliers hung from the ceiling, illuminated by thousands of tiny glass globes. The polished floor of white marble gleamed, and the Hall looked as if it had been constructed out of light and glass.

Save where blood pooled upon the floor.

A melee raged through the hall. Twenty Imperial Guards stood against the Hall's far wall, struggling to hold off nearly four times as many men in the colors of the civic militia. The remaining Kindred of Cyrioch, Caina realized, along with the mercenaries and thugs they had smuggled into the militia.

Subtlety had failed, and now the Kindred would use brute force to kill Lord Corbould and Lord Khosrau.

She looked through the hall, but saw no sign of the nobles or of Theodosia.

"Stop them!" shouted Marzhod. "Stop the assassins! Attack!"

The Sarbian mercenaries loosed their wailing battle cries and charged, scimitars whirling. Corvalis charged into the fray, his sword and dagger a blur, while Marzhod hung back, loading his crossbow. Caina found herself carried along in the press. She drew daggers from her boots, joining the fight alongside the mercenaries. She took a surprised assassin in the throat with a quick slash, wheeled, and stabbed another in the leg. The man stumbled, and a Sarbian mercenary cut off his head with a sharp blow of his scimitar.

Caught between the beleaguered Imperial Guards and the howling Sarbians, the Kindred attack collapsed. Some Sarbians and Guards fell, but far more assassins perished. Caina fought alongside the Sarbians, and the assassins shied away from her. They did not see her as a lone young woman. Thanks to her cloak, they saw a hooded shadow, face concealed in darkness, daggers glittering in either hand.

Then Caina spotted Theodosia and the nobles.

They had been backed into a corner. Dents marred Lord Corbould's black armor, and blood streamed from a cut on his temple. Yet he wielded his sword with vigor, keeping the Kindred at bay. Lord Khosrau stood next to him, his white robes stained with sweat and blood, his ceremonial scimitar in hand. The old lord's face had gone purple with the strain of fighting, yet he did not flinch from the battle.

Theodosia stood behind him, flinging knives whenever an opening appeared.

Armizid sat slumped against the window, the side of his robe red with blood, left hand clutched to his right shoulder. Yet Caina saw how his eyes followed every movement of the battle. Once his father and Corbould were dead, he could claim that Corbould had murdered Khosrau and then been slain in the fighting. He could then rebel against the Empire and declare himself King of Cyrica.

And the war against Istarinmul and New Kyre would grow that much bloodier.

A pair of Kindred charged at Corbould. A sword hammered across his black cuirass, and the old lord fell on his back with a clatter of armor. One of the assassins loomed over Corbould, raising his sword back for the killing blow, while the second man sprang at Khosrau. Khosrau grabbed Theodosia and shoved her behind him, raising his scimitar to meet the onslaught.

Caina's opinion of him rose.

Caina reached into her belt and flung one of the glass vials she had taken from the Elder. The vial shattered in a spray of stinking black smoke at the feet of the assassin menacing Khosrau. Khosrau and Theodosia doubled over, hacking and wheezing, and Caina heard Corbould fly into a coughing fit.

But so did both of the assassins.

Caina charged the assassin facing Khosrau, daggers in both hands. She plunged the blades into either side of his exposed neck, blood washing over his chain mail. The man staggered, and Caina kicked him off her daggers and spun just in time to meet the attack of the second assassin. He had been at the edge of the cloud of smoke and had recovered from it faster. Caina caught his slash on the crossed blades of her daggers, disengaged, and stabbed at him. The assassin danced to the side, avoiding her blow, and drove her back. If he pushed her back far enough, he could strike down Lord Khosrau before Caina could stop him...

Then the assassin stiffened as Corvalis's sword plunged into his back. An instant later his dagger slid across the assassin's throat, and the man toppled dead at Caina's feet.

Corvalis nodded at her, and Caina sought out new foes to fight.

But the battle was over.

Dead Kindred in the armor of militiamen carpeted the floor. Marzhod's Sarbians had triumphed, and began to loot the slain. Caina caught Theodosia's eyes, saw her nod in relief.

Khosrau helped Corbould to his feet. "Are you hurt?"

"A bit bruised, I fear," said Corbould. "But the chief wound is to my pride. Gods! I am getting old. Those young fools would never have gotten the best of me twenty years ago."

"And you, Armizid?" said Khosrau.

"I am wounded, Father," said Armizid, staggering to his feet. "But it is a minor scratch." He looked at the Sarbians, his eyes hard and flat. "Truly, our survival is a miracle."

"Yes," said Khosrau. "It seems traitors within the civic militia wanted us dead." He looked at the Sarbians, at Corvalis and Marzhod in their masks. "I am grateful for your aid, lads. But I would like to know just what the bloody hell is going on."

The silence stretched on and on. Neither Marzhod nor Corvalis could reveal themselves. Marzhod was the Ghost circlemaster of Cyrioch, and needed some degree of secrecy to carry out his work. And if Corvalis revealed himself, Ranarius would probably find out and kill him. Could Theodosia tell the nobles what had happened? She could – but she did not know that Armizid was behind everything.

Caina looked at Theodosia, and the other woman mouthed a single word.

Balarigar.

And all at once Caina knew what she needed to do.

Marzhod had been wrong about opera singers. It would come down to a theatrical performance after all.

"My lords!" Caina roared, using every trick Theodosia had taught her to amplify and disguise her voice.

"Who the devil are you?" said Corbould, lifting his sword.

"I have been called the Balarigar," said Caina.

Disbelief flashed over Corbould's face, but the Imperial Guards took a step back. Those Guards had accompanied Corbould from

Marsis, and they knew the stories. They had heard how the Balarigar had defeated the Istarish emir Rezir Shahan, how the hooded shadow had liberated the thousands of slaves filling the Great Market of Marsis.

They looked at Caina in fear and a little awe.

"My lord," said one of the Guards, "I was a prisoner in the Great Market, I saw the Balarigar strike down Rezir Shahan! He danced through their ranks like a shadow, and the Istarish melted at his approach. My lord, this is the Balarigar, I swear it!"

The "Balarigar" was just a trick and a legend...but it seemed to be working.

"So you're the famous Balarigar?" said Khosrau, voice light, but Caina heard the skepticism. "Or you could be a man in a Ghost shadow-cloak. But whoever you are, it seems we owe you our lives. For that, I thank you."

"The threat is not ended," said Caina. "For you were betrayed, Lord Khosrau of House Asurius. Someone hired the Kindred to slay you and your guest Lord Corbould. This villain desired to raise Cyrica in revolt against the Emperor, using your bloody robe as a banner."

"Folly," said Khosrau. "Cyrica is not powerful enough to stand on her own. We need a strong protector. And the Shahenshah of Anshan and the Padishah of Istarinmul would make crueler masters than the Emperor in Malarae."

"The traitor desired to make himself King in Cyrica," said Caina. She flung out her arm and pointed. "Lord Khosrau, your son Armizid hired the Kindred to slay you."

Khosrau burst out laughing. "Armizid? Oh, that is a poor jest!"

Armizid's face darkened with rage. "Lies! I will not stand for this calumny!"

"For years, Armizid has plotted against you," said Caina. "He hired the Kindred to slay your eldest son Yergizid and the previous two Lord Governors."

"Yergizid drowned in his bath," said Khosrau, "and the previous Lord Governors were old men who died in office."

"Or the Kindred killed Yergizid with such skill it looked like an accident," said Caina. "Would you have made Armizid the Lord Governor if Yergizid lived? Would you have given him the office if the previous two Lord Governors had not died?"

Khosrau said nothing, but his eyes narrowed.

"You are listening to this slander, Father?" said Armizid. He stalked closer and pointed at Caina. "This masked renegade appears, hiding his face behind a cloak, and you will listen to him over your firstborn son? I cannot believe this!"

"Yergizid was my firstborn son," said Khosrau, his voice almost absent.

"Yergizid is dead!" shouted Armizid. "I have taken his place all this years. Have I not faithfully done everything you asked of me? Have I not fulfilled every task you placed upon me?" He always scowled, but this time his face almost vibrated with it, like a dam starting to break beneath the weight of the water. "And you question me in front of these mercenaries and thugs? It is...it is..."

"Unseemly?" Caina suggested.

Armizid faced her, and she saw her death in his eyes. There was a faint, peculiar smell coming off him, like tomatoes and...

"Armizid," said Khosrau. "I am not accusing you of anything. This fellow is obviously a Ghost nightfighter, and perhaps you have offended the Ghosts in some way. But the assassins are dead, and we will speak no more on the matter."

And then Caina recognized that smell, and she knew how to undo Armizid.

"That's not blood," said Caina.

"What?" said Khosrau.

"The stain on the Lord Governor's robe," said Caina. "That's not blood, and he wasn't wounded in the fighting."

Armizid looked at his father, at Caina, and that back at Khosrau.

"If it's not blood," said Khosrau, "then what is it?"

"Stage blood," said Caina. "Red Caerish wine mixed with a bit of tomato juice. Opera singers and actors use it when somebody gets stabbed on stage. He tore his robes and poured it over his shoulder. It would look like he was wounded in the fighting, and only chance saved him when the Kindred slew you and Lord Corbould. But if you get close enough, you can smell it on him."

Khosrau looked baffled. "But...why? Why?"

"Lies!" said Armizid.

"Because if the Kindred killed everyone but him," said Caina, "Armizid could claim that Lord Corbould hired the Kindred to kill you, and then was slain in the fighting. Armizid could then rebel against the Empire to avenge you, and proclaim himself King of Cyrica. He has been working towards this for years, first by killing off his brother, and then disposing of the previous Lord Governors. The war with New Kyre and Istarinmul was the opportunity he needed, especially when the Emperor sent Lord Corbould to act as ambassador."

"Lies," hissed Armizid, "vile calumnies, a slander, Father, surely you cannot..."

Khosrau roared with laughter.

"That," he said, "is the stupidest tale I have ever heard."

Armizid flinched as if he had been slapped.

"Surely you could spin a better story for my old ears, Ghost!" said Khosrau. "King of Cyrica? Only an idiot would try to make himself King of Cyrica! For Cyrica has always been a province, never its own nation. Any fool stupid enough to make himself King of Cyrica will find his head atop the Shahenshah's spear, or hanging from the wall of the Emperor's..."

"Shut up!" screamed Armizid.

Silence fell, every eye on Lord Governor Armizid Asurius. Khosrau gazed at his son in shock. Armizid trembled like a maddened animal, his hands balled into fists.

"I am tired of listening to you," he said, "you fat, stupid old man! For years I did everything you asked of me! Everything! I spent years hoping to gain favor in your eyes. And instead you gorged yourself at banquets! Instead you went to the opera and the gladiatorial games and cheered like any churlish slave! Instead you lay with whores and slave girls and...and opera singers!" He chopped at the air, the cords in his thin neck bulging. "I spent years trying to gain the approval of a gluttonous sluggard!"

"Armizid," said Khosrau, "this...this is madness. I made you Lord Governor of Cyrica. What more honor could any man possibly want?"

"I will do more than you could ever dream of doing!" said Armizid. "I will make Cyrica into its own kingdom, first among the nations. I will raise House Asurius to honor you could never conceive. I will be the first of a dynasty, and my sons will rule over Cyrica for centuries! Perhaps they will even conquer an Empire of their own. A Cyrican Empire, stretching from Marsis to Istarinmul! I will do it, Father. I will be remembered as the founder of a Cyrican kingdom, while no one will remember the glutton of Cyrica Urbana at all!"

The rage at last choked off Armizid's words, his chest heaving beneath his stained white robe. Khosrau stared at his son without expression. Caina expected the old lord to fly into a rage, to demand that the Imperial Guard arrest Armizid for his crimes.

Instead he shook his head and sighed.

"My son," he said, "you are overwrought, and are not thinking clearly. Sit down, and I will talk some sense into your head..."

And that final bit of condescension pushed Armizid over the edge.

He howled like a madman and snatched a broadsword from the slain Imperial Guards. He flung himself at Lord Khosrau, still screaming, the sword drawn back to kill. Caina cursed and hurried forward, hoping to intercept the maddened Lord Governor...

But the Imperial Guards were faster.

Four broadswords plunged into Armizid's chest and stomach, staining his white robes with real blood. Armizid staggered to a stop, the sword dropping from his fingers. The Guards ripped their swords free, and the Lord Governor of Cyrioch fell to the floor, his blood pooling around him.

For a long time no one moved.

"Gods," said Corbould at last. "Khosrau, I'm sorry."

"My son," said Khosrau, his face deathly gray. "My own son was plotting to kill me for all these years. I gave him everything. Anything he wanted, I would have given him. And...and this."

Theodosia touched his arm, and the stricken old lord did not pull away.

Caina took a deep breath, trying to decide what to do next. Best to withdraw, and leave Lord Khosrau to Theodosia and Lord Corbould. The gods only knew how Khosrau might react when the shock of Armizid's treachery wore off. Better to get Marzhod and his men well away from the Palace of Splendors...

She caught a flicker of movement through the Hall's door. A pale slave girl, clad in a long gray tunic, the glitter of a jade collar at her throat.

Nicasia.

Caina frowned.

Ranarius was here?

Corvalis hurried past the Sarbian mercenaries and made for the doors. Caina cursed and slipped after him. All eyes were on Khosrau and Armizid's corpse, and no one saw her leave. Nicasia disappeared through the doors, and Corvalis picked up his pace.

Caina went after them.

Corvalis turned right and disappeared into one of the Palace's elaborate colonnade-lined corridors. Caina broke into a run, her boots clicking against the marble floor. If Nicasia was here, that meant Ranarius was nearby. Perhaps Khosrau had invited him to the disastrous ball at the Hall of Glass, and he had retreated from the Kindred attack.

She rounded a corner and froze.

Corvalis stood a dozen paces away, sword and dagger ready.

Thirty feet further down, Nicasia stood motionless.

A Kindred assassin in the armor of the civic militia stood behind her, his sword resting at Nicasia's throat. The slave girl showed no sign of fear, though Caina saw the motion as her eyes darted back and forth behind her blindfold.

"Back off!" shouted the Kindred. "Or I'll open her throat!"

"What makes you think I care?" said Corvalis.

"I've heard of you," said the assassin. "The mask can't fool me. I know you're Corvalis Aberon. You were too soft to stay in the Artifel family. If I slay this girl in front of you, you'll weep like a woman." His eyes darted to Caina. "And you! Stay back!"

Nicasia began to giggle.

"Quiet," snapped the assassin.

Caina eased to the left, hoping to hit the assassin with a throwing knife. But the assassin jerked Nicasia around, keeping his dagger at her throat.

"I said to stay back!" roared the assassin. "Or I will kill her."

Nicasia burst into full-throated laughter, her high voice ringing off the ceiling.

"Shut up!" said the assassin. "I'll..."

Then Caina heard the voice.

It was a deep rumble, like slabs of granite scraping together. The voice made Caina's bones tremble, made the metal of her knives vibrate. No human had a voice like that.

And it was coming from Nicasia's lips.

"Foolish little mortal," said Nicasia in that rumbling voice. "You think you have captured me? Then look at me. Look at me and see what you have captured."

The assassin stepped back, and Nicasia reached for her blindfold. She tugged it aside in a single smooth motion as she faced the assassin, and Caina caught a brief glimpse of her eyes.

They blazed with golden light, like sunlight reflecting upon polished disks of gold.

"Look at me!" roared the thunderous voice coming from Nicasia's lips.

The assassin looked at her and screamed, golden light pouring over his face.

And then he turned to stone.

One moment he was a man of flesh and blood, his face twisted with sudden fear. A heartbeat later he became a statue of white stone, the same white rock as the Stone itself, the same stone that Saddiq and Barius had become.

The deep voice rumbled laughter, and Nicasia wound the blindfold back around her head.

The golden light vanished.

Caina stepped to Corvalis's side.

"You," said Corvalis. "It was you all along."

Nicasia shuddered. "I...I don't know your voice." Her voice had regained its reedy, birdlike quality. "Who are you?"

"Don't you know who I am?" said Corvalis, his voice rising in anger. "You turned my sister to stone!"

"Did I?" said Nicasia. "There were so many. I can't remember them all."

"Can you turn her back?" said Corvalis. "You will turn her back! I..."

"Well," said a cold voice. "Corvalis Aberon. How long has it been?"

Ranarius appeared at the far end of the corridor, the hem of his black robe whispering against the floor. A half-smile was on his face, but it vanished when he saw Caina.

"You," he hissed.

Caina frowned behind her mask. "You know me?"

His smile returned. "All too well, mistress. All too well. But now I am the master."

"What are you talking about?" said Caina. "Mistress? I'm not..."

Then she remembered Sicarion. He had come to Cyrioch to kill a wayward disciple of Jadriga...

"You," said Caina. "You're the one Sicarion came here to kill! You were a student of the Moroaica."

"Yes," said Ranarius, hate flashing over his face. "Her student and her slave. But no longer. After tonight, she will never have the power to harm me ever again..."

"You will turn my sister back!" said Corvalis. "Now!"

Ranarius turned his lined face towards Corvalis. "What? Are you still dragging that wretched statue about? Pitiful fool. You should have accepted your father's chastisement and fled the Empire while you still had the power. You could have escaped this."

Caina threw back her arm, ready to fling a knife.

But the master magus was faster.

Ranarius thrust out his hand, the air around his fingers rippling, and Caina felt a massive surge of sorcery. Suddenly the air in front of Caina's face rippled, and she could not breathe. She coughed, gagging as she tried to force air into her lungs.

But she could not. Black spots filled her vision, and she took a staggering step forward. She saw Corvalis fall to his knees, hands at his throat.

Then she toppled towards the floor, everything going black.

23

THE DISCIPLE

Caina awoke with a splitting headache.

She blinked, tried to stand, and found that she could not.

Her eyes cleared, and she saw a rope wound around her ankles, binding her feet together. Her arms were behind her back, resting against a rough rock wall, and she felt more rope around her wrists. Again she tried to stand, and she saw that the rope around her ankles was tied to an iron ring in the floor. Her weapons rested in her belt, but she could not reach them.

A few inches from her hands, yet they might as well have been a thousand miles away.

She turned her head, examining her surroundings. She was in a large room, lit by the light of a single glass globe. To judge from the empty shelves and the canvas sacks piled in one corner, it was a storeroom.

Corvalis sat against the far wall, bound as she was. His head slumped against his chest, dried blood glittering on his temple.

"Corvalis," she hissed. "Corvalis!"

"Don't bother."

She knew that cold voice.

Ranarius stepped from the shadows, peering at her like a scholar examining an ancient manuscript. The jade bracelet upon his left wrist glimmered in the dim light.

"He fell harder than you did," said Ranarius. "Hit his head on the floor. He might wake up eventually. Or he might not."

"What did you do to us?" said Caina.

He made a dismissive gesture with one hand. "I know about Corvalis's tattoos, you see. A common trick of petty northern witchfinders. So my spell corrupted the air around your heads until you passed out. A favorite of the Kyracian stormsingers."

"You learned it from Andromache," said Caina, "didn't you?"

Ranarius blinked. "Yes. One of the Moroaica's favorite pets. How did she die, by the way?"

Caina saw no reason to lie. "The Moroaica promised her the power in the Tomb of Scorikhon. Except Scorikhon possessed her. The Moroaica intended to use Andromache's body as a host for Scorikhon's spirit all along."

Ranarius laughed. "The little fool. She was also the Moroaica's slave, like me, only she was too blind to see it." He leaned closer, looking at her from a different angle. "Tell me. Are you really the Moroaica?"

"No," said Caina.

"Tell me the truth," said Ranarius.

"Why?" said Caina. "You're going to kill me."

Ranarius smiled. "I have absolutely no intention of killing you. In fact, it is my wish that you never die."

That sounded ominous.

"But perhaps I can figure it out on my own," said Ranarius. "You contrived to slay the Moroaica, and then her spirit possessed you. But something went wrong. She inhabited you...but she can't control you." He leaned forward, making sure to stay well out of reach. "She is imprisoned inside of you. So long as you live, the Moroaica cannot hurt me."

"Then you should continue to let me live," said Caina.

Ranarius straightened up. "I agree. In a way."

That sounded even more ominous.

"So," said Caina, mind racing. She had to delay. Chasing after Corvalis alone had been foolish. But sooner or later Theodosia would notice she was missing. And the more information she pried from Ranarius, the better chance she had. "How did you end up enslaved to the Moroaica?"

Ranarius said nothing for a moment.

"Does the Moroaica communicate with you?" said Ranarius at last.

"Sometimes, in dreams," said Caina.

"So she cannot control you, only influence you," said Ranarius. "Why hasn't she killed you yet?"

"You never answered my first question," said Caina. "How did you end up enslaved to the Moroaica?"

Ranarius scowled. "I will ask the questions, Ghost. And I have the means to force the answers from you."

Caina made herself smile. "I wouldn't do that. Force me a little too hard and you might kill me. Then the Moroaica will inhabit a new body. That wouldn't be good for you. If you want answers, you'll have to answer my question."

"Very well," said Ranarius, though his scowl did not deepen. "I was young and foolish. I felt the laws of the Magisterium and the Empire constrained my genius and talent. Then the Moroaica found me and offered to teach forbidden sciences in exchange for service. I accepted, thinking I could betray her later. But one does not betray the Moroaica. One does not escape her."

Caina nodded.

"Now. Answer my question," said Ranarius. "Why hasn't the Moroaica killed you yet?"

"She thinks she can bring me over to her side," said Caina.

"Perhaps she can," said Ranarius. "The Moroaica thinks in terms of centuries, even millennia. What are a few decades to her? She has spent far more time pursuing her 'great work', whatever that is."

"My turn for a question," said Caina. "What did you do to Nicasia?"

Ranarius smiled. "I suppose you saw her turn that assassin into a statue? She makes for a useful tool."

"Is she an elemental spirit of earth?" said Caina.

"Not quite," said Ranarius. "Spirits can be summoned to this world. But they need something to inhabit, a body to wear. An elemental spirit of sufficient power could fashion a body from its associated element. Or it could inhabit a human body."

"Nicasia," said Caina.

"Yes," said Ranarius.

Corvalis stirred, moaned, and then fell limp.

They looked at him for a moment, and then Ranarius kept talking.

"Summoning an earth elemental of power is...difficult," said Ranarius. "Easier by far to use one already inhabiting our world. They come here sometimes to...hibernate, for want of a better word. I found one in Cyrioch, released it from its cocoon of stone, and forced it into Nicasia's body. The result was most satisfactory." He tapped the jade bracelet on his wrist. "Nicasia has proven to be a capable weapon."

"Undoubtedly," said Caina. "Why did you turn Claudia Aberon to stone?"

It wasn't her turn for a question, but Ranarius answered anyway. She suspected it had been a long time since he had talked honestly with anyone.

"Because the First Magus asked it of me," said Ranarius. "The Moroaica's teachings made me stronger, but one does not cross Decius Aberon lightly." His mouth twisted. "Though if I knew how much trouble Corvalis would cause me, I might have refused the request."

"And that's why you turned the Ghosts to stone," said Caina. "It was an accident. Corvalis was hunting you, and the Ghosts were investigating him. They just got in the way when you sent Nicasia to turn him to stone."

"Almost," said Ranarius. "I didn't know Corvalis was in Cyrioch until a few hours ago. The Ghosts were investigating Corvalis, but I assumed they were pursuing me, as they have a few times before. It was only sheer luck that Corvalis eluded Nicasia." He looked at Corvalis and smiled. "Though his luck has finally run out." He turned back to Caina. "And now a question for you, clever Ghost. Why have you sided with Corvalis against me? Do you not know you will draw the wrath of the Magisterium?"

"You studied under the Moroaica," said Caina. "The magi are forbidden to use necromancy. If it came down to it, I think the First Magus would abandon you to prevent a scandal." Ranarius's lips thinned. "And I know what you really intend."

"Oh?" said Ranarius. "Do you?"

Caina remembered what Nadirah had told her. "You're going to summon a greater earth elemental, and attempt to bind it to use against the Moroaica."

Ranarius's amusement vanished. "How do you know that? Did the Moroaica tell you?"

"No," said Caina. She would not tell him about Nadirah. If Caina died here, Ranarius might try to kill Nadirah. "I know the story of Old Kyrace. You're going to try to do the same thing here."

"Yes," said Ranarius. "I will free the greater elemental and bind it." He smiled, his eyes glittering. "The process will probably kill you and free the Moroaica to take another body. I look forward to that. For all her might, she cannot possibly stand against the wrath of an elemental lord."

"Neither can you," said Caina. "You can't possibly control such a creature. You'll probably destroy Cyrioch."

"Actually," said Ranarius. "I will certainly destroy Cyrioch."

His calm voice chilled her. "How?"

"Haven't you realized it yet?" said Ranarius. "When an elemental comes to our world, if it does not take a human body it instead inhabits a form closest to its essential nature. The greater fire elemental that destroyed Old Kyrace was bound within a volcano. An elemental of earth would hibernate within solid rock, rock unlike any other found in the world..."

Caina blinked as the realization came to her.

"The Stone," she said. "The Stone itself is the greater earth elemental."

"Correct again," said Ranarius. "The greater earth elemental has worn the form of the Stone and hibernated in our world for millennia beyond count. Of course, the Palace of Splendors will be destroyed when the elemental awakens. The hill called the Stone is only a portion of the entire elemental, just as only a part of an iceberg rises above the waters. When I awaken the elemental, all of Cyrioch will collapse into the sea. The resultant earthquake will destroy every structure built by the hand of man for three hundred miles in every direction. And given the waves the earthquake will trigger, both Malarae and Istarinmul might be underwater by this time tomorrow night."

"You'll kill millions of people!" said Caina. "And all for what? All for power?"

"For freedom," said Ranarius. "I will not spend eternity as the Moroaica's slave." A shadow of fear passed over his gaunt face. "If I had to kill ten million people to be free of her...I would do it." He leaned closer. "She's inside your head. She's probably listening to me right now!" His voice rose to a shout. "Do you hear me, mistress? I will never be your slave again. Never!"

"This is madness," said Caina. "If the Moroaica couldn't control a greater elemental, if the combined stormsingers of Old Kyrace couldn't do it, what chance do you have? You'll get yourself killed for nothing, along with..."

"The only thing left to do," said Ranarius, "is to make sure you cannot stop me."

"You can't kill me," said Caina. "The Moroaica will take another body."

"True," said Ranarius. "I don't even dare disable or drug you. If I make a mistake, I might accidentally kill you. I can't even leave you here. Some slave might come along and untie you. And you're clever enough to find a way to stop me." He smiled. "Fortunately, I have a way to make sure you don't interfere."

Caina realized what he meant.

"No," she said.

"Yes," said Ranarius. "Once Nicasia converts you both to statues, you'll be no threat to me. The Moroaica will be imprisoned inside you, sealed within the stone. I suspect the effect will wear off in two or three centuries. But I intend to live forever, and by the time you become flesh once more, the elemental's power will be mine to command." He laughed. "And then I will make the Moroaica pay for my servitude!"

"Ranarius," said Caina, "listen to me, you'll..."

"Sleep well, Ghost," said Ranarius.

He waved his hand, and again Caina felt the surge of arcane power. The air before her rippled, and Caina could not breathe. She struggled to stand, struggled even to draw breath.

But as before, everything went black.

~

"We are both," said the Moroaica, "in very serious danger."

Caina opened her eyes and stood up.

Again she was in the strange gray mists of her dreams. Jadriga stood a short distance away, clad in her blood-colored robe, dark hair hanging wet and loose about her pale face. Her black eyes flashed with rage.

"Oh?" said Caina. "If he turns me to stone, what of it? He thinks the effect will wear off in two or three hundred years. Surely that is no great length of time for the mighty Moroaica."

"He is incorrect," said Moroaica. "The elemental bound within his slave girl is one of surpassing potency. Your body will not return to flesh for at least five hundred years, if not longer. That would be an intolerable delay. Though he is correct that summoning the greater elemental will destroy both Cyrioch and most of Cyrica. Your body would end up at the bottom of the ocean, and when it returned to flesh in five hundred years you would drown at once."

"Could he do it?" said Caina. "Could he actually control a greater elemental?"

The Moroaica laughed. "Of course not, child. No one can. Not the great magi of the Fourth Empire, not the stormsingers of Old Kyrace, not the solmonari of the Szalds, not the mighty necromancer-priests of ancient Maat. Not even I could control the greater elementals. They could be...directed, perhaps. Like digging a canal to divert a flood. But not controlled."

"You did this," said Caina. "You turned him into what he is. And now he's going to unleash this atrocity!"

The Moroaica lifted a dark eyebrow. "He rebelled against me and I punished him suitably. Humiliation is more effective on a man like Ranarius than any sort of physical torment." She sighed. "Though, in retrospect, it might have been more prudent to simply kill him."

"I'm sure your vast intellect could not have seen this coming," said Caina.

"There's no need to be churlish," said Jadriga. "We must focus upon the task at hand. Namely, our survival." She smiled. "And if you require additional motivation, think of all the innocent lives that Ranarius will slay with his foolish plans. Your friends Ark and Tanya are in Malarae, are they not? Their son Nicolai? Do you really want the last thing Nicolai sees to be a forty foot wall of water roaring out of Malarae's harbor?"

"I will stop Ranarius," said Caina. "He is everything I hate about sorcery. Like you."

Again the Moroaica laughed. "Save that I am not so great a fool as Ranarius."

"No," muttered Caina, "you just created him."

She had to stop Ranarius, but she did not see how. She was unconscious and bound in a storeroom. When she awoke, Nicasia would turn her to stone.

She might have already turned Corvalis to stone.

"You could," said the Moroaica, "accept my aid."

"No," said Caina. "I will not use your sorcery. Not now, not ever."

"Even if it means saving those uncounted millions?" said Jadriga.

"No," said Caina.

"Foolish, but irrelevant," said Jadriga. "I cannot wield my power through your body. So I shall give you knowledge, instead. For you know just as well as I do that knowledge is deadlier than any dagger."

Caina nodded. "Speak."

"First," said Jadriga, "do not look into the slave girl's eyes. Not for any reason. That is how the elemental's power works. Once it looks into your eyes, it can see your spirit, and the transformation proceeds from within."

"You mean," said Caina, "if I free from those ropes and keep my eyes closed, I can get away from Nicasia?"

"Certainly," said Jadriga. "Spirits always hate the mortal sorcerers that bind them. The elemental will do exactly what Ranarius tells it to do...but no more. If you keep your eyes closed, and you do not attack the slave girl, the elemental will let you go unchallenged."

Caina nodded.

"Second," said the Moroaica, "Ranarius will perform the spell of summoning in the Gallery of the Well. The Well, as you have guessed, is not of natural origin. It leads to the heart of the Stone, to the heart of the greater elemental itself. Releasing the elemental will take tremendous arcane power, and Ranarius will be distracted. If you catch him off-guard," she smiled, "as you caught me off-guard below Black Angel Tower, you can kill him before he completes the summoning. Though he will almost certainly have defenses."

Caina nodded again. "Anything else?"

"Be mindful of the chance to escape," said Jadriga. "An opportunity will soon arrive."

"What do you mean?" said Caina.

The Moroaica smiled. "Go and find out."

She waved her hand and the dream dissolved into nothingness.

24

THE DEFENDER

Caina opened her eyes.

Nicasia's face was only inches from hers, her pale blond hair brushing Caina's jaw. The slave girl's eyes, her brilliant golden eyes, shone like the sun, and Caina felt an overwhelming compulsion to look into that radiant light and let it swallow her forever...

She yelped and clamped her eyes shut.

"Ah." It was the deep, rumbling voice, the voice of the elemental. "You understand. Wiser than I expected, in a mortal."

"The master will be mad." It was Nicasia's own voice, high-pitched and fearful.

"The emotions of the master are no concern of mine," said the elemental. "I do as I am bound, mortal child. No more, no less."

Caina took a moment to steady her breathing.

"You could," she said at last, "let me go."

"The master would get angry," said Nicasia. "He hurts me when he gets angry."

"You are free to escape if you can," said the elemental. "I will not hinder you. Though if you open your eyes, I am compelled to transform you."

"I'll keep that in mind," said Caina.

She leaned against the rough stone wall and tried to think. If she could stand up and get to a blade, she could cut through the rope. Her weapons were still on her belt, but she could not reach them.

"Corvalis?" she said. "Can you hear me?"

No answer.

"He's still sleeping," said Nicasia. "He hit his head hard."

Caina rubbed her hands against the stone wall. Perhaps the stone was rough enough to abrade through her ropes. She began scraping the rope against the stone, thankful that she had thought to include gloves in Corvalis's backpack. How long did she have before Ranarius summoned the greater elemental?

Probably less time than it would take to get through the rope.

"Nicasia," said Caina. "Can you untie me?"

"The master would get angry," said Nicasia.

"The master isn't here," said Caina.

"The master would get angry," Nicasia said again.

"How you mortals struggle to preserve your little lives," said the elemental. There was a hint of bemusement in the rumbling voice. "Even if you escape, you will die anyway, whether tomorrow or in another few years. The merest blink of an eye. Why not accept your inevitable fate?"

"For the same reason," said Caina, "that you do not accept your enslavement by Ranarius."

A grinding, rumbling noise came to her ears, so deep that she thought the roof was about to collapse above her. Caina started to open her eyes to see what was going on, and then caught herself and closed them.

The grinding noise was coming from Nicasia.

Her words had angered the earth elemental.

"It is egregious," said the spirit. "My liege and I warred long against the elementals of water and fire and air, as we have since the dawn of worlds, and at last we grew weary. Our sovereign granted us leave to rest, and we came to your world to sleep. Long I slumbered, standing guard over my liege, until that worm Ranarius awoke me and thrust me into this body of flesh."

"Guarding your liege?" said Caina. A realization came to her. "You...were sleeping inside the statue, weren't you? The Defender? The stories say that statue has stood there since before men even came to Cyrica."

"And so it has," said the elemental. "I guarded my liege in his sleep, even as I slumbered. Does that surprise you? For we spirits have our hierarchies and societies, even as you mortals do."

"So you're the Defender," said Caina.

She felt a few of the fibers in the rope split.

"You may call me that, if it pleases you," said the elemental, something almost like amusement in the rumbling voice.

"He defends me," said Nicasia. "The master meets so many bad men. Sometimes they try to hurt me. And when they touch me, the Defender stops them. He turns them to stone, and they never hurt anyone ever again."

"I'm surprised, Defender," said Caina. Her arms and shoulders ached from the effort, but she kept scraping the rope against the wall. "I thought you would have driven the girl to her death. If she is slain, you would be free."

"I thought that once, too," said the Defender. "But it is a...curious sensation, wearing a body of flesh. One I have never before experienced. And the...emotions are most powerful. You mortals are so driven by your emotions. They are nothing but the sloshing of liquids in your brain. And yet you feel them so...vividly. So intensely. I had never dreamed such things existed. And through Nicasia, I behold them."

It was fond of the girl. The Defender could experience emotion so long as it lived in Nicasia's body...and somehow it had grown fond of her.

"Sometimes it makes me sad," said Nicasia. "Sometimes the master makes us turn good men to stone, not just bad ones. I remember the woman."

"Claudia Aberon," said the Defender.

"She was kind to me," said Nicasia. "When the master sent me to her, she said I looked lost. That I was a poor little thing, and she gave me some bread and honey."

"She never suspected," said the Defender. There was a hint of regret in the alien voice.

"I cried, after," said Nicasia.

"Maybe I can help you," said Caina.

Another fiber gave way.

"How?" said Nicasia and the Defender in unison.

"That jade collar around Nicasia's neck?" said Caina. "That's how Ranarius is controlling you, isn't it?"

"It is," said the Defender.

"I have a blade of ghostsilver on my belt," said Caina. "Ghostsilver is proof against sorcery. Let me go, and I can take the collar from your neck. Then you'll be free."

"Alas," said the Defender. "Your generosity is remarkable for a mortal. But the collar is linked to the bracelet around the master's wrist. Shatter the collar, and the bracelet will maintain the binding spells."

"I can do both," said Caina. "I'll cut the collar from your neck and take the bracelet from Ranarius's wrist after I kill him."

"You're going to kill the master?" said Nicasia.

"Unlikely," said the Defender. "The master is a magus of substantial power." The elemental paused. "You seem to have tremendous arcane power within you, but it is constrained, somehow. You cannot prevail against Ranarius."

"There are weapons other than sorcery," said Caina.

But the Defender's doubt was justified. In a straight fight, she could not take Ranarius, and neither could Corvalis. The master magus simply had too much sorcerous strength at his command. Unless they managed to ambush him or catch him off guard...

She heard a groan, leather and chain mail shifting against the floor.

"Ah," said the Defender. "The other one awakes."

"I suppose," said Nicasia, "that we shall have to do the master's bidding."

Caina flinched in alarm.

Corvalis was waking up. He had been trained as an assassin, and when he regained consciousness, the first thing he was going to do was to look around.

And once he saw the golden light in Nicasia's eyes, it would be the last thing he ever did.

"Corvalis," said Caina. "Corvalis!"

She heard him groan in response. Gods, how she wanted to open her eyes and look at him.

"Corvalis!" she said again.

"Marina?" said Corvalis, his voice thick. "What..."

"Don't open your eyes," said Caina.

"Why? What..."

"Listen to me!" said Caina. "Don't open your eyes. The earth elemental is possessing Nicasia. If she looks into your eyes, she'll turn you into a statue. That's how Ranarius has been doing it. He's been using Nicasia."

"No one ever suspects a timid slave girl," said Nicasia. "That's what the master always says."

There was a long pause.

"Where are we?" said Corvalis at last.

"A storeroom in the Palace, I think," said Caina. "Ranarius overpowered us and took us here. Corvalis, the Stone itself is the greater earth elemental."

"It is my liege," rumbled the Defender.

"What the devil was that?" said Corvalis, and she heard him struggling against the ropes.

"The Defender," said Caina, "the earth elemental inside Nicasia."

"Then you turned my sister to stone?" said Corvalis.

"As I was bound to do," said the Defender.

"Can you change her back?" said Corvalis, desperate hope in his voice. "Can you turn her back to living flesh?"

There was a long pause.

"He looks so sad," said Nicasia. "Doesn't he look sad?"

"The effect will wear off in four or five centuries," said the Defender. "But I could restore her. The master explicitly commanded me not to do so, though."

"Then you will not have a master soon," said Corvalis.

"Unlikely," said the Defender, "since you cannot even untie yourself."

"Corvalis," said Caina. "So long as we keep our eyes closed and don't touch Nicasia, the elemental won't harm us. Can you get loose?"

"I'm trying," said Corvalis. "The wall is rough enough that I might be able to saw through the rope. But it will take a while."

"We might not have that kind of time," said Caina. "Ranarius is going to start awakening the greater earth elemental any moment. And if he does, he's going to destroy Cyrioch."

Corvalis grunted. "If I can just get to the dagger in my boot..."

The grating shriek of rusty hinges cut off his words.

Someone had opened the door to the storeroom.

A moment later a rough voice laughed.

Caina stiffened. She knew that voice.

Sicarion.

"Who are you?" said Nicasia. "I don't like you. I think you're a bad man."

Again Sicarion laughed. "You are correct. I am indeed a very bad man. In fact, my dear, I may be the worst man you have ever met."

"The patchwork assassin," said the Defender. "What a curious aura you have. Like a sculpture fashioned from carrion."

"True," said Sicarion. "And you would like to turn me to a sculpture, wouldn't you? But so long as I don't touch you, you won't attack me."

"Maybe I don't like you," said Nicasia. "You are a bad man. And you'll have to open your eyes sooner or later."

"Again, true," said Sicarion. "But there are senses other than the physical, are there not?"

Caina heard him stop a few paces away. It took every bit of

willpower she had not to open her eyes, and she strained against the rope, hoping to scrape through it. But it was no use.

Sicarion would kill both her and Corvalis long before she broke free.

"Mistress," he said. "You seem to be in some trouble."

"Which pleases you to no end, I'm sure," said Corvalis. "I suppose Ranarius gave us to you as a gift."

"As much as it would delight me to cut the tongue from your mouth," said Sicarion, "I have other business. I am here to kill Ranarius."

"He's the reason you came to Cyrioch," said Caina. "The disciple of the Moroaica you came to kill."

"Correct," said Sicarion. "The Moroaica does not tolerate disloyalty in her disciples, and Ranarius has been exceptionally disloyal."

"I'm surprised you didn't side with him," said Caina. "He's going to kill a lot of people."

"Yes," said Sicarion, and Caina could imagine the smile on his face. "But the Moroaica will kill many more, once she is free."

"And that's why the Moroaica sent you to kill him," said Caina. "Because she knew he was going to become a threat to her."

"So why are you here?" said Corvalis. "The Moroaica wants you to kill Ranarius, so go kill him. Or did you decide to kill us first?"

Sicarion said nothing.

Caina started to laugh.

"What," said Sicarion, "is so funny?"

"You don't think you can kill Ranarius on your own," said Caina, "do you?"

"It's your fault," Sicarion said to Corvalis. "I came to Cyrioch to kill Ranarius, not to find you. If you had just let me kill you, I would have disposed of Ranarius in short order. Now he's fortified himself in the Gallery of the Well. If I catch him off-guard, I can kill him...but if I fail, he'll kill me, and rather quickly."

"So you want our help," said Caina.

"Well," said Sicarion. "You were going to fight him anyway."

"Absolutely not," said Corvalis. "I know what you are, Sicarion. You'll try to kill us the moment we turn our backs."

Sicarion sighed. "I do want to kill you. However, I am serious about an alliance. If I wasn't, I would have killed you already, and then would have no need to endure this tedious conversation."

A faint tremor went through the floor.

"Ah," said Sicarion. "Do you feel that? It's beginning."

"My liege stirs in his slumber," said the Defender.

"The spell is long and complex," said Sicarion, "but Ranarius is a skilled magus. It will not take him much longer. Do you want to stop him, or would you rather continue this debate?"

"We can take Ranarius without your help," said Corvalis.

"Perhaps," said Sicarion, "but I doubt you can untie yourselves without my help."

"He has a point," said Caina.

"You can't possibly be considering this" said Corvalis.

"We need his help," said Caina. "We aren't getting out of here on our own." She took a deep breath. "And we can always kill him after we stop Ranarius."

"He'll do the same," said Corvalis.

Sicarion laughed with delight. "Of course! You defeated me in Artifel, and I always repay my debts. And you, mistress...the Moroaica would be better served by a different body. She'll be wroth after I slay you...but she will get over it."

"But not until Ranarius is dead," said Caina.

"He will betray us," said Corvalis.

"Yes," said Caina. "But if he was going to simply kill us, he would have done it already."

"Perhaps you'll understand this, Aberon," said Sicarion. "I want to kill you very badly...but I want to kill Ranarius even more. So I'll use you to kill him, and then I'll kill you. Elegant, no?"

Another faint tremor went through the floor.

"All right," said Corvalis.

"Cut us loose," said Caina.

"As you wish, mistress," said Sicarion.

His boots clicked against the floor, and suddenly she felt his presence looming over her. His smell, a mixture of rotting flesh and half-congealed blood, flooded her nostrils. A brush of cool metal against her wrists, a tug at her ankles, and the ropes fell away.

Caina stood, stretching her sore limbs.

"You next, Aberon," said Sicarion, and Caina heard him cross the room.

"Watch where you're cutting," said Corvalis.

"Oh, I do," said Sicarion. "With great interest. I'm not terribly happy with my current hands. Perhaps I'll replace them with yours."

She heard the jangle of chain mail and weapons as Corvalis climbed to his feet. Caina tensed, wondered if the men would fight, but she heard nothing but heavy breathing. And a faint groaning noise, like overstressed rock beginning to move.

"We haven't much time," said Sicarion. "Come."

"Wait," said Caina.

She stepped towards Nicasia.

"What are you doing?" said Nicasia.

Caina took another step forward, reaching out with her hands. "I'm going to touch you, but I'm not going to harm you. I'm going to take that collar off your neck."

"What do you possibly hope to accomplish?" said the Defender. "Even if you destroy the collar, the master's bracelet will maintain the binding spell."

"We don't have time for this folly," said Sicarion. "Come!"

"As loath as I am to agree with Sicarion," said Corvalis, "he has a point."

Caina ignored them both. "Maybe we'll be victorious and kill Ranarius," she said. Her hand closed around Nicasia's thin shoulder, and neither the slave girl nor the elemental made any response. "Then you'll be free...and I hope you'll turn Corvalis's sister and the others back to flesh. Or maybe Ranarius will kill us, but his bracelet will be damaged in the fighting. Then you can flee before he captures you again. But if you do flee...I hope you'll consider turning the statues back to people once more."

She felt Nicasia's neck, the jade collar cold beneath her fingers. Caina took a deep breath to steady her hands, and slid her ghost-silver dagger from its sheath. Working by touch alone, she hooked the dagger under the collar and started to tug. The weapon grew hot beneath her fingers, and Nicasia gave a sudden cry.

The jade collar shattered, the pieces clinking as they fell to the floor.

"That felt...strange," said Nicasia.

"Did it do anything?" said Caina.

"No," said the Defender. "I am still bound to the master's will. So I suggest you do not open your eyes."

Another shock went through the floor, more violent this time.

"We must go!" said Sicarion.

"Fine," said Caina, sliding her ghostsilver dagger back into its sheath.

"Follow me," said Sicarion.

Caina started towards the of the door, hands held out before her.

"Ghost," said the Defender.

She hesitated.

"I turned your allies to statues," said the Defender. "Were you to open your eyes, I would do the same to you, and feel not the slightest regret." Yet she heard a hint of doubt in the alien voice. "Why would you aid me? Why?"

"I don't like slavers," said Caina.

Neither Nicasia nor the Defender spoke as Caina followed Corvalis and Sicarion from the room.

25

ELEMENTAL

"It should be safe to open your eyes," said Sicarion.

Caina took a deep breath and looked around.

She stood in a corridor in the slaves' quarters, not far from where Marzhod had spoken with Tiria. Corvalis stood nearby, hands on his weapons, his eyes fixed on Sicarion. The scarred man leaned against the wall, his deformed face calm, but his eyes were narrowed.

"Will Nicasia come after us?" said Caina.

"Unlikely," murmured Sicarion. "Bound elementals do exactly as they are told, and no more. Unless Ranarius gave it specific instructions to chase us down, it will stay there until Ranarius fetches it." He sneered at her. "Unless the slave girl decides of her own accord to come after us. Since you were so kind to her."

"We'll need help," said Caina. "The Ghost mercenaries in the Palace will aid us. And if we tell Lord Corbould what happened, we can get assistance from the Imperial Guard."

"We can't," said Sicarion, "since Lord Corbould and Lord Khosrau have abandoned the Palace for a more defensible location in the city, lest the assassins strike again. The slaves have no wish to be murdered in their beds, so they've all fled. The Palace is deserted."

Another jolt went through the floor, dust falling from the ceiling. Caina thought of all that stone balanced above her head and shuddered. "We're on our own. More convenient that way. No witnesses to kill."

"Ranarius will be in the Gallery of the Well," said Caina.

Sicarion waved a hand through the air. "And he's raised some kind of defensive spell around the Gallery." He gave an irritated shake of his head. "I can't tell what is it."

"We'll find out when we get there," said Corvalis. "Let's go."

They ran through the corridors. By unspoken agreement, Caina and Corvalis let Sicarion take the lead. Caina would never turn her back on the scarred assassin. Sicarion flashed a mocking smile over his shoulder at her and kept running.

They left the slaves' quarters behind and ran through the rich corridors of the Palace. Elaborate hangings of Anshani silk covered the walls, while niches held statues in the Nighmarian style or gleaming Istarish weapons. Weapons and statues and silk all trembled as the floor vibrated. The vibrations grew stronger, and Caina wondered if the Palace of Splendors would collapse around them even before Ranarius woke the Stone.

They ran into one of the lesser courtyards ringing the Gallery of the Well itself. A wide reflecting pool filled most of the courtyard to the left, though Caina thought it looked deep enough to serve as a cistern in the event of a siege. A single narrow bridge of stone stretched over the pool. An elaborate garden filled most of the courtyard to the right.

The archway straight ahead led to the Gallery of the Well. Through the archway Caina saw flashes of golden light, and she felt a faint tingle, growing ever stronger, as Ranarius summoned mighty forces.

Sicarion stopped.

"What are you waiting for?" said Corvalis.

"There's a ward here," said Sicarion. "It might blast us to ash if we blunder into it. If I can disarm it..."

The floor heaved, and Caina stumbled. For a terrible moment she thought they were too late, that Ranarius had finished his spell and the great elemental was rising…

Then she heard the grinding noise coming from the marble flagstones.

The floor splintered, a dome of jagging stone rising up. It swelled higher and higher, five feet, ten feet, twenty. As it did, it unfolded into a rough human shape, a crude statue wrought of jagged, broken rock. Twin golden flames flickered in the rough craters of its eyes, and Caina felt the pressure of the strange thing's gaze.

"Oh," said Sicarion, drawing his sword and dagger.

"What is that?" said Corvalis, raising his own weapons.

"A lesser earth elemental," said Sicarion. "Ranarius must have summoned it to act as his guardian.

"Why hasn't it turned us to stone?" said Caina.

"It isn't strong enough," said Sicarion. "But it's a twenty-foot giant made of broken rock. It's going to pound us into bloody paste."

The elemental loosed a rumbling roar and surged forward.

It was like watching an avalanche.

"Move!" said Sicarion, and the scarred man raced left, his cloak flapping out behind him. Caina ran right, hoping to avoid the elemental's attention. Corvalis charged straight at the hulking stone figure. What was he doing? Did he have some clever plan for dealing with the elemental?

The elemental raised a massive stone leg to crush him, and Corvalis darted to the side. His sword and dagger lashed in a vicious stroke, the blades raking across the back of the elemental's leg in a hamstringing blow.

The elemental did not even notice the strike. Its leg hammered down, and Corvalis only just dodged it. He backed away across the courtyard, his blades held out before him.

"Idiot!" Sicarion circled the reflecting pool. "It's made of rock! You can't kill it with a sword!"

"What do you suggest?" said Corvalis. "A hammer and a chisel?"

"This," said Sicarion, raising his hand, and Caina felt the tingle of Sicarion's sorcery. A peculiar blue light flickered around his sword. A heartbeat after that, Corvalis's sword and dagger glimmered with their own blue glow.

Caina drew a dagger and saw the blade glow, her skin tingling with the presence of sorcery. She almost threw the weapon away in revulsion.

"You cannot destroy its physical form!" said Sicarion. The elemental took a lumbering step towards Corvalis. "You can only break the spells binding the spirit. The spell on our weapons will do that. Hit the flames in its eyes – the spell is centered there."

Caina drew her ghostsilver dagger. No blue light glimmered around its blade. Ghostsilver was proof against sorcery. Did that mean it could disrupt the spell binding the elemental, even without Sicarion's aid?

Time to find out.

Sicarion charged the elemental from the right, his sword trailing blue light, while Corvalis came from the left. Caina rushed towards it, hoping to draw the elemental's attention. Yet the hulking shape ignored her, instead turning towards Corvalis, raising fists like massive boulders.

Caina snatched a throwing knife from her belt and flung it, her arm snapping like a cracked whip. The blue-glowing blade shot through the air, struck the elemental's forehead, and bounced away. Her next throw was more accurate, and the blade whirred into the elemental's right eye. The elemental bellowed in rage, and for a moment the golden flames in its eyes flickered and dimmed.

Sicarion had been right. If Caina could get close enough, she suspected a solid stab from her ghostsilver dagger could break the binding spell.

Except, of course, the elemental's eyes were twenty feet off the ground.

Sicarion reached the elemental first, swinging his blade with heavy two-handed strokes. He struck the flat of his sword against the elemental's leg, the weapon clanging with every strike. The blue light caused the elemental pain, or at least annoyance, and the creature flinched from the impacts. Corvalis attacked from the left, hammering at the elemental with the flats of his sword and dagger. The elemental bellowed in fury, swinging its massive fists, and Sicarion and Corvalis danced away. It took a few stumbling steps after them, and for a moment its legs lost cohesion.

But only for a moment, and then the creature pursued Corvalis.

Corvalis retreated, dodging around the creature's hammer-like blows, lashing at its fists whenever they drew close enough. With every hit, the elemental growled in pain. But its rage had fixed upon Corvalis and it pursued him. Sicarion circled around the elemental, striking blow after blow, but the elemental only flinched a little from his hits. Sooner or later the elemental would wear them down, and then the creature would have them.

Unless Caina did something clever.

She sprinted in front of Corvalis and hurled a knife. A flash of blue light, and again the blade drove home in the elemental's left eye. A shudder went through the creature's body of rubble and boulders. The knife fell free and the golden fires of its eyes blazed with new fury.

And again the creature's head turned to face Corvalis.

"Run!" he shouted.

Caina stood motionless.

The elemental was ignoring her. Her throwing knives had caused it more injury than Corvalis's blades, but still the creature lumbered after him. Why?

The realization dawned on Caina.

The elemental couldn't see her. The shadow-cloak hid her from divinatory sorcery and protected her mind from sorcerous intrusion. Could it also hide her from the sight of spirits?

Ridiculous. The Defender had been able to see her...

But the Defender was inside Nicasia's body. It had seen her through Nicasia's eyes of flesh. The lesser earth elemental was only a spirit bound within an ambulatory pile of rubble.

A plan came to Caina.

She ran towards the elemental and threw back the cowl of her shadow-cloak. A ripple went through the creature's body, and its misshapen head swiveled towards her. Caina drew another third throwing knife and flung it. The blade struck the elemental's left eye with a flash of blue light, and the creature loosed an ear-splitting roar of outrage.

It turned towards her, Corvalis forgotten, and Caina grinned in triumph.

Then the elemental raced towards her, faster than it had moved in pursuit of Corvalis.

Faster than she had expected, actually.

Caina sprinted, leading the elemental across the courtyard. The creature thundered after her, every footstep sending another tremor through the earth. She risked a glance over her shoulder, saw the elemental drawing closer, racing after her with the speed of a galloping horse.

That was bad.

"Marina!" shouted Corvalis, and she saw Sicarion grinning. He thought the elemental was going to smash her and free the Moroaica.

Well, in the next few heartbeats, she would find out if he was right or not.

She sprinted onto the narrow bridge over the reflecting pool.

The earth elemental followed her, still bellowing.

And then the sound of shattering stone swallowed the elemental's enraged roar.

The bridge heaved and Caina toppled to her knees, grabbing at the railing for support. She turned to see a quarter of the bridge collapse into the pool, the elemental following it.

At once the clear water grew cloudy as the dust in the elemental's body turned into mud and silt. Golden light flashed and flared in the elemental's eyes, distorted through the murky waters. The elemental took one step forward, and then another.

And then its body fell apart. Chunks of stone settled to the bottom of the reflecting pool. The golden light in its eyes went dark as its head fell apart.

Nothing remained of the creature but a pile of motionless, muddy rock.

Caina let out a long breath and pulled herself back up.

Sicarion and Corvalis stood at the edge of the pool, staring at her.

"How did you do that?" demanded Sicarion.

Caina shrugged. "I didn't do anything. It was an elemental spirit of the earth. It could control earth, rock and stone...but I wagered it couldn't control water."

Corvalis laughed. "Remind me not to bet against you. I don't have the money to spare."

Caina nodded. "Get out of the way."

She sprinted forward and jumped over the broken stub of the bridge. Her boots slapped at the edge of the pool, and Corvalis caught her arm and pulled her the rest of the way over.

"Thanks," said Caina.

Corvalis nodded. "That was...astonishing. I was sure that thing was going to kill us all. And then you tricked it...and that was that."

"It...yes," said Caina. She was aware of his fingers against her arm. It was a ridiculous thing to notice. She had just escaped death from the elemental, and was going to almost certain death at the hands of Ranarius. And yet...

The ground shook beneath them.

"As touching as this scene is," said Sicarion, "Ranarius is about to blow up Cyrioch." He grinned. "Do you think watching all those children die is going to be heartwarming?"

"The little devil is right," said Corvalis. "Let's go."

Caina nodded, retrieved her throwing knives from the courtyard, and headed for the Gallery of the Well, Sicarion and Corvalis following.

26

THE STONE OF CYRIOCH

A flare of golden light illuminated the Gallery of the Well.

Caina felt the crawling tingle of Ranarius's sorcery grow stronger and stronger. The ground vibrated beneath her boots, a low rumbling filling her ears. From time to time the floor heaved, the walls groaning.

The Stone was waking up.

Caina ducked into the shadows of the archway and looked into the Gallery, Sicarion and Corvalis besides her.

Ranarius stood a few feet from the Well, arms thrown back, robes rippling in a wind that rose from the Well itself. Pulse of golden light flickered from the depths of the Well. Ranarius shouted the words to his spell, sorcerous energy charging the air. Caina's stomach clenched with nausea, her skin tingling, but she ignored the discomfort.

"Can you shoot him from here?" murmured Caina.

"Aye," whispered Corvalis. He carried a shortbow beneath his cloak, along with a small quiver of arrows. "From this distance, I can put an arrow in his chest. Unless he's bothered to ward himself against steel."

Sicarion whispered a spell under his breath and traced his hand before him. "He did."

"Damnation," muttered Caina. She had hoped Ranarius would grow overconfident, but one did not survive as a disciple of the Moroaica by taking foolish risks. "Could you dispel the ward?"

"Probably," said Sicarion. "But if I try, he'll sense it. Better for you to sneak up behind him and put that ghostsilver blade of yours into his back."

"Folly," said Corvalis. "He would see her before she got within fifty paces."

"How fast can you take his ward down?" said Caina.

"A few seconds," said Sicarion.

"Could you shoot him the moment Sicarion dispelled the ward?" Caina said, looking at Corvalis.

Corvalis nodded, lifted his shortbow, and set an arrow to the string.

"Do it," said Caina.

"As you command, mistress," said Sicarion, voice heavy with mockery. He took a deep breath, lifted his free hand, and muttered a spell, blue light flaring around his fingertips.

Ranarius lowered his arms and turned, frowning.

His eyes widened in alarm as he saw them.

"Oh, damn it," said Caina. Ranarius began casting a spell, his hands moving in rapid motions. "Sicarion!"

Sicarion pointed, blue light flashing around Ranarius. "Now! Shoot him!"

Corvalis loosed his arrow as Ranarius cast his spell.

A violent gust of wind blew through the Gallery, tugging at Caina's cloak. It caught Corvalis's arrow, throwing it off course.

Apparently Ranarius had learned more than one spell from Andromache.

"Go!" shouted Sicarion. "Fools! Take him before he casts another spell!"

Caina sprinted into the Gallery, ghostsilver dagger in her right hand, throwing knife in her left. Corvalis dashed to her left, while Sicarion ran straight at the master magus. Ranarius flung out his hands, and Caina felt a sharp spike of potent sorcery. Blue light flashed around him, and Caina hurled the knife. It was a long throw, but her aim was true. Yet her blade rebounded from Ranarius's throat as if it had struck a wall of stone.

He had renewed his ward against steel.

Corvalis and Sicarion charged Ranarius, and the master magus gestured at them. Invisible force hammered into the two men and flung them across the gleaming marble. Sicarion rolled a dozen feet and landed upon one knee, while Corvalis pushed himself up with a groan.

Caina readied another throwing knife. Ranarius would not see the knife as a danger, but if she could get close enough to use her ghostsilver dagger...

Ranarius lifted his hands, and Caina prepared to charge.

"Sicarion!" spat Ranarius, his voice full of loathing. "I didn't recognize you. You had a different face when last we met."

"You burned away most of the last one," said Sicarion.

The tingling against Caina's skin grew stronger and sharper.

"The Ghost and the Kindred," said Ranarius, glancing from Caina to Corvalis and back to Sicarion. "I suppose you set them free?"

"They wanted you dead," said Sicarion, "as do I. A certain commonality of purpose makes for a convenient alliance."

"Why don't you kill both of them and join me?" said Ranarius. "Your heart craves murder. Kill me, and when I awaken the elemental within the Stone, you'll help me murder all of Cyrioch."

The tingling grew stronger. Caina looked at the Well, but the pulses of light had not grown any stronger, and as far as she could tell, Ranarius was not casting another spell.

Sicarion laughed. "I have no wish to die myself. You're like a child playing with a loaded crossbow, Ranarius. You're going to shoot yourself in the face." The master magus's eyes narrowed. "You can't control a greater elemental, and it will crush you when it awakes. Not on purpose, probably. Like a man stepping on an ant. It won't even know that you're there." His hideous face stretched in a grin. "So I'll just have to content myself with killing you."

"You could be free, Sicarion," said Ranarius. Caina took a step towards him, and he gave no response. She took another step, and then his cold eyes fell upon her. "The Moroaica is trapped inside her. I can turn the Ghost to stone, and the Moroaica will be sealed away for centuries. You'll be free to as you wish."

"What I wish to is kill," said Sicarion. "And working for the mistress, I can kill far more people than I could on my own." His smile widened. "She'll kill the world."

"What a tedious vision," said Ranarius. "It's just as well that you won't live to realize it."

He thrust out his hand, the tingling redoubling, and Caina realized that the entire conversation had been a ruse. Ranarius had been gathering power for another spell the entire time.

"Corvalis!" she shouted, sprinting for Ranarius. "Watch...

Ranarius raised his hands and blinding white light fell out of the sky.

A lightning bolt.

The blast struck the ground, shattering the marble tiles for a dozen paces in every direction. A wall of hot air slammed into Caina and hurled her to the ground, and she rolled across the broken shards, every hair on her body standing on end.

For a moment she could not move.

At last she sat up, her body aching, and saw Corvalis lying motionless a dozen yards away.

Dead? She couldn't tell.

"Gods," she heard Ranarius say. "Andromache always made that look easy."

Sicarion still stood, surrounded by a faint blue glow.

"Is that the best you can do?" said the scarred man. "A Kyracian stormsinger's trick?"

Ranarius laughed. "Do you really think to challenge me, Sicarion? You're good enough with a blade, but your sorcery is no match for my own." He lifted a palm. "Observe."

Caina got to one knee, her limbs throbbing, and felt the surge of Ranarius's spell. Sicarion stumbled several steps, his blue glow flickering, and thrust his own hand. A dozen shards of broken stone floated into the air and hurtled themselves at Ranarius, moving with the speed of crossbow bolts. Ranarius laughed and made a pushing motion, and the shards shot past him, spinning around him in a blurring orbit.

"Psychokinetic manipulation?" he shouted. "Elementary! Surely you can do better!"

He gestured, sending the shards flying at Sicarion, and a score more rose from the ground. Sicarion cast another spell, and most of the rubble missed him, but some struck him. His wards turned aside most, but Caina saw bloody gashes appear on his forearms and jaw.

The assassin and the master magus reeled in combat, flinging spell after spell at each other. Ranarius gestured, and one of the pillars exploded to send a rain of rocks at the scarred man. Sicarion snapped his fingers, and he vanished in a flash of silver light, only to reappear as a dozen illusory copies of himself. Ranarius swept his right hand, and the rain of rocks widened to fall upon the illusionary images, each one disappearing in a burst of silver light.

But none of Sicarion's spells hindered Ranarius, and the master magus drove the assassin back step by step.

Caina staggered back to her feet.

Every inch of her body ached as if she had been beaten by rods, but she could stand. She considered charging at Ranarius. Sicarion held his full attention, but if she drew too close, he would probably kill her with a single spell. His wards turned steel, but not stone. Could she pick up a stone and throw it at his head? She would get one shot, and if the rock failed to stun him...

She saw Corvalis get to one knee, bow in hand.

"Sicarion!" Caina shouted. "Break his ward! Now!"

Sicarion spat a curse, blood flying from his lips, but blue light flashed around his fingertips.

A heartbeat later the same blue light flashed around Ranarius.

Caina flung her knife, and this time the blade found purchase. It sank into the magus's shoulder, and Ranarius stumbled with a scream of pain. A hissing noise, and one of Corvalis's arrows appeared in his stomach. Caina ran at him, driving her aching legs towards the magus. One blow, one solid blow, and she could end this...

Ranarius screamed again and threw out his hands.

Invisible force exploded from him. The shockwave slammed into Caina, threw her into the air, and sent her spinning over the ground, chunks of broken rock raining around her. She came to a stop, bruised and bleeding and cut, and saw Corvalis collapse motionless to the ground. Sicarion reeled like a drunken man, raising his hands to cast another spell.

Ranarius was faster.

The snarling magus made a hooking gesture, and a slender whirlwind of gray clouds appeared around Sicarion. The whirlwind picked Sicarion up and flung him into the air like a catapult stone. Caina caught a brief glimpse of him soaring over the roof of the Palace, arms and legs flailing, and then the scarred assassin vanished from sight.

"I should have done that years ago," spat Ranarius, voice tight with pain. His enraged eyes fell upon Caina. "As for you..."

He gestured, and Caina floated up, caught in the grip of his psychokinetic power. She struggled, but his will held her fast. She flung a knife, but Ranarius had rebuilt his ward, and the blade bounced away from his skin.

"Damned Ghost," said Ranarius.

She flung another knife. It ricocheted away from him, and he scooped up the weapon.

"Gods, that hurts," said Ranarius, his free hand going to the arrow in his stomach as he walked towards her. "But I know enough of the necromantic sciences to heal myself. Though I'll have to steal life energy for it." He smiled. "A fitting end for Corvalis, isn't it? All those months to save his sister, and in the end his life force will heal the man he hates."

Caina flung her last knife, and it bounced away.

"You can't kill me," she said, trying to put defiance into her voice. "You'll set the Moroaica free."

"You're right," said Ranarius. "Instead, I'm going to stab you in the gut and leave you to bleed out. It should take you a few hours to die. That will give you time to watch me kill Corvalis." He smiled. "And it will let the Moroaica watch as I awaken the great elemental, as I bind its power to my service. I think that is a fitting punishment for all the torment she inflicted upon me, don't you?"

Ranarius stopped before her, gripped her throwing knife in his left hand, and drew back his arm to stab.

He showed no fear of the ghostsilver dagger clutched in her hand. And why should he? His wards had deflected her weapons again and again, and this time Sicarion was not here to dispel his defenses.

So the look of shock on his face was absolute when Caina stabbed him.

She aimed for his heart, but her arm trembled with pain, and the ghostsilver blade dug a bloody furrow across his chest. Ranarius howled and staggered back, arm coming up to block. Caina's next blow caught him on the left wrist, and the blade sank between the bones of his forearm. Ranarius shrieked and tried to pull free, the dagger sawing against the jade bracelet.

The bracelet shivered and shattered into a dozen fragments.

Ranarius pulled free and gestured with his good arm, and the invisible force holding Caina hammered her to the ground. She screamed in pain, the force pressing upon her like a massive weight. He was going to crush the life out of her, use his sorcery to squeeze every drop of blood from her flesh.

"Die!" shouted Ranarius. "Damn you, Ghost!" Every trace of ascetic calm had vanished from his face. "Die, die, die, die..."

At least Caina had freed Nicasia. With any luck, the slave girl was running from the Palace as fast as her legs could carry her. Perhaps Ranarius would bleed to death before he could finish the spell and awaken the Stone.

Before he could kill Corvalis.

The pressure pinning her doubled, and Caina's vision began to turn black...

"Ranarius."

The deep voice rolled over the Gallery of the Well like a thunderclap.

Ranarius turned, his face gone white, and some of the pressure holding Caina faded.

Nicasia stepped from behind a pillar.

She had been watching the entire fight.

"Master, master," said Nicasia, her voice singsong. "You're hurt. Master is hurt, Master is hurt!"

"Go back to your chambers!" said Ranarius. "You cannot disobey me! The damned Ghost shattered the bracelet, but the collar..."

His voice trailed off as he saw Nicasia's unadorned neck, and Caina saw the horror blossom on his face.

"No," he said, voice hoarse.

"Master is bleeding," said Nicasia, walking towards him. "Just as my mother and father bled when you killed them and took me."

"Stay away from me!" said Ranarius, and more of the pressure pinning Caina faded away. He thrust out his hand. Caina felt the surge of sorcery, but Nicasia's fingers moved in a dismissive gesture, and the power of the spell faded away.

"Mortal sorcery?" said the Defender. "Surely you know better, Ranarius. You will need more power to bind me." Nicasia's lips stretched in a smile. "But, ah. You have exhausted your powers fighting."

"You look so tired, master," said Nicasia. "Perhaps it is time for you to rest?"

Ranarius staggered back, clutching his wounded stomach. "I command you to stay away from me!"

"Ranarius," said the Defender. "You cannot command me. What do your philosophers say? Sow the wind and reap the whirlwind?" Pleasure filled the alien voice. "Behold the whirlwind."

Ranarius tried to cast another spell, but it was far too late.

Nicasia surged forward with all the momentum and power of an avalanche. Her right hand caught Ranarius's collar, and she lifted the magus into the air, her thin arm taut with the Defender's strength. He screamed and clawed at her, but to no avail.

"Look at me, master," said Nicasia.

Her free hand reached for her blindfold.

"Look at me," said the Defender as Nicasia tugged the blindfold away. "See what your skill has wrought."

Ranarius closed his eyes, trembling, and Caina got to her feet, her head spinning.

"Look at me!" thundered the Defender.

And Ranarius opened his eyes. He should have known better. Perhaps he couldn't stop himself, could not stop himself from seeing what so many of his victims had seen in their last moments.

Caina looked away as Ranarius screamed, golden light falling over his face.

Then the scream stopped as his mouth and lips turned to stone.

An instant later a statue of a master magus stood before Nicasia. Ranarius's face was frozen forever, his eyes bulging with fear. Nicasia tilted her head to the side, as if examining a work of art.

"He will stay like this for centuries, you know," said Nicasia.

Caina took a quick step to the side, making sure to stay out of Nicasia's line of sight.

"But a few centuries," said the Defender, "is not so long a time, is it? Something more permanent is required."

Nicasia's fist hammered into the chest's statue. Ranarius shattered into thousands of pale white shards, bouncing and rolling across the Gallery like tumbling white bones. One final tremor went through the ground, and the golden glow from the heart of the Well faded away.

The greater elemental had returned to its slumber.

"I thank you, Ghost," said the Defender. "You have secured my freedom."

"Our freedom," said Nicasia.

"Will you return to the netherworld now?" said Caina.

"I...cannot," said the Defender. Nicasia wound the blindfold around her eyes and turned to face Caina. "Not so long as this child lives. I have no wish to see her dead."

"The emotions of a mortal," said Caina.

"Yes," said the Defender. "It is...troubling. Emotions should not afflict one such as I. Still, forty or fifty years is but a blink of an eye. A short enough time to sojourn in mortal flesh."

"You might think differently in fifty years," said Caina. "A lot can happen in that time."

Nicasia smiled, and her own voice came from her lips. "I like you. You are a good woman. Can we do anything for you? You freed us."

"I think so," said Caina. "Wait here."

She crossed the Gallery to where Corvalis lay, hoping he wasn't dead. To have come so far, to have endured so much, only to die at the end...

But his eyelids were fluttering, and he sat up as she approached.

"Marina," he muttered. "We're not dead?"

"No," said Caina.

She helped him to stand, and he leaned on her arm.

"Ranarius?" said Corvalis.

"He looked into Nicasia's eyes," said Caina. "He shouldn't have done that."

Despair crossed his face. "Then the elemental...the Defender returned to the netherworld?"

"Come with me," said Caina.

She ought to report to Theodosia, she knew. With the chaos in the Palace, both Theodosia and Marzhod needed to know what had happened.

But Caina had to do something else first.

~

An hour later they reached Corvalis's apartment below the potter's shop.

"There," said Corvalis, pushing aside the curtain. The muscles in his temples worked. "She's in there."

"I remember her," said Nicasia, gazing at the statue of Claudia. "She was a good woman. I'm sorry the master made us turn her into stone."

"Can you turn her back?" said Caina.

Nicasia grinned at her.

"Yes," said the Defender.

The former slave girl faced the statue, removing her blindfold, and Caina and Corvalis both took a step back. Golden light flared in the gloomy apartment, painting the walls with light, and for an instant it looked as if the statue of white stone had been fashioned from brilliant gold.

And then the light faded...and a young woman in a black robe with a red sash stood in the place of the statue. Nicasia donned her blindfold, and the young woman looked back and forth in astonishment. She was a a few years younger than Corvalis, with the same green eyes and blond hair, though hers was much longer.

"Sister?" said Corvalis, his voice a hoarse rasp.

"Corvalis," whispered the young woman. "I...remember. It's like a dream, but I remember all of it. I remember everything. And you...you..."

Corvalis took a step forward, and Claudia Aberon rushed to him and buried herself in his arms. She wept, and to Caina's astonishment, she saw tears glittering on Corvalis's hard face.

He caught her gaze. "Thank you."

"Well, you did help us against the Kindred," said Caina, and she grinned.

The Ghosts paid their debts.

And so did Caina.

27

NEVER FOR ME

"Perhaps," said Lord Khosrau, "I should have seen it long ago."

He gazed through the open arches between the pillars, over the sprawling houses and mansions and warehouses of Cyrioch. Caina was struck by how much older he looked, how much wearier. Perhaps he had always been so tired, and hidden it beneath his mask of joviality.

She stood behind Theodosia's chair, again dressed and disguised as the maid Marina. Which was just as well, given that bruises covered her arms and legs. The sound of hammering and scraping rose from the arches. The Palace had been badly damaged during Armizid's death and the peculiar earthquakes that followed, and workmen and slaves now labored to repair it.

"It is always difficult to see treachery, my lord," said Theodosia. "Especially from those closest to us."

Khosrau, Corbould, and Theodosia at the table, taking breakfast together. Save for Caina, they were alone. Khosrau, who was no fool, had figured out that Theodosia had high rank in the Ghosts. No doubt he suspected Caina as well.

"He was always so joyless," said Khosrau. "So grim, so serious. I tried to lighten his spirits. A lord has a role to play, like any other man...but that is no reason not to enjoy himself."

"I think," said Theodosia, "that your son loved his own dignity, his own prestige, more than anything else."

"A grave error," said Corbould. "A lord of the Empire must maintain his dignity at all times. But prestige is only a tool to aid in ruling the Empire, not an end to itself."

"Indeed," said Khosrau, and he sighed.

"Then I may tell the Emperor," said Corbould, "that Cyrica will remain loyal?"

"You may, my friend," said Khosrau. "For Cyrica to rebel and declare itself a kingdom would be madness. Cyrica is not strong enough to stand on its own. And the Emperor is a better master than the Shahenshah of Anshan or the Padishah of Istarinmul." He looked at Theodosia. "Certainly the servants of the Shahenshah would not have gone to such lengths to save one fat old man."

"Well," said Theodosia. "You do appreciate opera, after all."

Khosrau barked out a laugh. "Cyrica will remain loyal to the Empire, my lord Corbould. Our farms shall grow the wheat and the cotton that shall feed and clothe the Legions as they drive back the soldiers of Istarinmul."

Corbould smiled. It was one of the few times Caina could recall him ever doing that. "Thank you, my lord Khosrau. That is the best news I have received since Rezir Shahan and Andromache of House Kardamnos were slain."

"Yes, this mysterious Balarigar," said Khosrau. "I had thought him a legend, but it appears I was wrong."

Corbould grunted. "A trick. Some clever Ghost playing on the legend of the Balarigar." He gave Theodosia a look.

Theodosia sniffed. "I'm sure I don't know, my lord."

"Well, keep your secrets, as spies must," said Corbould. "But I will not criticize your methods. The ruse was effective enough, and it drove Armizid to confess the truth. Though I still think this 'Balarigar' is a construction of Ghost trickery."

Caina carefully kept from smiling.

"It won't last, you know," said Khosrau. He waved a thick hand in the direction of the city. "All of this. Cyrica holds too many slaves, and someday they will rise up, and we won't be able to stop them. And too many nobles agreed with Armizid. I shall have a difficult time keeping them in line."

Theodosia grinned. "Concerning that, my lord Khosrau...the Ghosts may be able to offer a little help."

~

LATER THAT DAY Caina disguised herself as a common caravan guard and made her way to the Painted Whore and Marzhod's workroom.

His workroom was busy.

A long table lay covered with books and documents from the Kindred Elder's study. Barius and a few of Marzhod's clerks sat at the table, working through the pages. Barius made notes in a ledger, chuckling to himself every few pages. Saddiq stood against the wall, thick arms folded over his massive chest, and grinned as she approached.

"Nightfighter," he rumbled. "It is good to see you with eyes of flesh instead of stone."

"So you do remember everything that happened while you were stone?" said Caina.

Saddiq shrugged. "It is...like a dream. As if I dreamed that I were wrapped in ice, and nothing seemed to matter. It was not...painful, no. Still, I do not miss it."

"I certainly do not," said Barius. "It is hard to turn a profit will frozen in stone."

"A fine sentiment," said Marzhod from his desk.

Caina stepped towards him. "Theodosia wants to know..."

Marzhod grinned. "What I've found? Oh, enough information to make me rich a second time." He pointed at the Book of Blood and Gold on the center of the clerks' table. "Half the nobility of Cyrica has hired the Kindred to kill the other half at some point. Not to mention the merchants, the magi, even some of the priests...there are secrets enough in that book to send most of the rich men in Cyrioch to the executioner's block."

"And you're going to blackmail them," said Caina.

"Of course," said Marzhod. "Running the Ghost circle of Cyrioch is hardly cheap. I'll merely let these men know that I'm more than happy to keep their secrets...in exchange for a nominal fee. And if they get restive, if they decide Cyrica should become part of Anshan...why, they'll get another little reminder. A man can hardly lead a rebellion if he's gotten himself beheaded for hiring assassins."

Caina nodded and turned to go.

"Nightfighter," said Marzhod.

She stopped.

"You are," he said, "not quite as big a fool as I thought."

Caina thought of Nadirah, of the slaves Marzhod had smuggled out of Cyrica in exchange for their loyalty.

"And you," she said, "are not quite the heartless villain I thought you to be." She paused. "Mostly."

Barius guffawed.

Marzhod glared at him. "A man does have a reputation to maintain."

Caina nodded again and left.

~

THAT NIGHT CAINA lay in her bed and dreamed, and the Moroaica came to her in the swirling gray mists.

"You did well," said Moroaica.

Caina scowled. "Your praise means ever so much to me."

A faint smile flickered over Jadriga's red lips. "I was not sure you would prevail against Ranarius. But you did. You proved the cleverer, and Ranarius was destroyed by the forces he foolishly sought to command."

"Just as you would have been," said Caina, "had you opened that pit below Black Angel Tower."

The Moroaica's smile widened. "But you are triumphant.

Ranarius is defeated, Lord Khosrau is alive, and the Cyricans will remain loyal to your Emperor. Does that not please you?"

Caina shrugged. "It is better than civil war."

"But you...what does your victory mean for you?" said Jadriga. "You are still alone. You are still like me, a creature of death and steel. You have saved the families and happiness of others...but you will never save your own. You shall remain alone..."

"Unless I join with your great work," said Caina. "Yes, I've heard this speech from you before."

Jadriga's smile did not waver. "Together, child of the Ghosts. Together you and I can remake the world. A world with no more pain, no more sorrow, no more death. We shall build a better world than the gods ever did."

"That's mad," said Caina. "As mad as Ranarius thinking he could control the earth elemental."

"It is only madness if I do not have the power to do it," said Jadriga, "and I do. Join with me, and I shall show you."

"No," said Caina. "For the last time, no."

The Moroaica's dark eyes glinted above her red smile. "No matter. I can wait."

"How long?" said Caina.

"Why, for the rest of your life."

The Moroaica waved her hand and the dream vanished.

~

THE NEXT MORNING CAINA ROSE, practiced the unarmed forms for an hour, bathed herself, and dressed.

Then she walked to another suite in the Inn of the Defender and knocked.

"Come in!" came a woman's voice, warm and cheerful.

Caina stepped into a richly furnished sitting room. The first thing she saw was Nicasia. The former slave girl stood before a mirror, her blindfold off, examining herself in a mirror. She had traded her ragged gray slave's tunic for a gown of gold with red trim.

"I do not understand," said the Defender's voice from Nicasia's lips, "this mortal obsession with adorning yourself. Flesh is flesh. Why sheath it in silks or adorn it with jewels?"

"Because," said Nicasia, "it looks so pretty! Doesn't it look pretty?"

"I think," said the woman's voice, "that it looks very pretty."

Claudia Aberon stood by the window, watching Nicasia. She had exchanged her black magus's robe for a green gown that matched her eyes, black embroidery marking the sleeves and bodice. She looked startlingly beautiful. Caina wondered if she intended to marry and raise children.

As Caina never could.

"Ghost," said Claudia, and she smiled. "Come, please, sit with me."

Caina sat on one of the sofas, and Claudia sat next to her.

"I just wanted to thank you," said Claudia. "I would not be here if not for your efforts."

Caina shrugged. "I would not leave anyone trapped like that, sealed in stone for centuries."

They sat in silence for a moment.

"You don't," said Claudia, "like me very much, do you?"

Caina decided to be honest. "No."

"Because I am a magus."

"Yes," said Caina. She frowned. "I...have known many sorcerers. I have yet to meet one that had not been corrupted by their power."

Claudia nodded. "That I can understand. The Magisterium is filled with cruel men and women. But it needn't be so. Sorcery is a tool like any other. It just needs to be used responsibly, to help people, not to rule over them."

"Those are fine-sounding words," said Caina. "Corvalis...Corvalis thinks you are a good woman. Perhaps his eyes are clouded because you are his sister. But he has seen enough cruelty from the Magisterium and your father to know the truth when he sees it. If Corvalis thinks you are a good woman...that is enough for me."

Claudia grinned. "So you won't gut me here and now?"

Caina laughed. "Corvalis went to all that effort to save you. I wouldn't want it to be in vain."

"No," said Claudia. "Corvalis speaks very highly of you."

"Dare I ask what he said?" said Caina.

"He says you are cleverer than anyone he has ever met," said Claudia. "He said the Kindred taught him that the deadliest weapon was not a sword or poison or an arrow, but the mind, and that you have grasped that truth better than anyone."

"That's hardly flattering," said Caina. But it wasn't inaccurate, was it?

She was a killer, like it or not, and her mind was a weapon.

"But he also said you were wise," said Claudia. "That you knew why to fight, not just how. And that you saved his life, again and again." She reached over and grabbed Caina's hand. "Thank you...thank you for saving him. I...could not have borne it, if he had been slain."

"You do love him," said Caina, "don't you?"

"Yes," said Claudia. "He has had a harder life than me. But that does not mean my life has been easy. Our father is a cruel tyrant. When we were children...sometimes Corvalis was all that kept me from going mad. When our father sold him to the Kindred, I was sure he had been killed. When he returned, even after what the Kindred had done to him...it was like a gift from the gods themselves." She squeezed Caina's fingers once more, and then released her hand. "Thank you for saving him."

They sat in silence once more.

"What will you do now?" said Caina at last.

"I shall join the Ghosts," said Claudia. "Theodosia offered it to me, and I accepted. I am a renegade magus, and there is no place else for me to go. I always wanted to use my powers for good, to help people. Corvalis told me about the things you have done. If not for your courage, Ranarius would have destroyed Cyrica and the Empire would have fallen into civil war. You saved so many lives! Perhaps...perhaps I can do as much, someday."

Caina nodded. "Corvalis will go with you, I expect."

Claudia grinned. "Well, I am an outcast magus, and he is a renegade Kindred. Where else shall we go?"

Caina had expected nothing else. Yet she still felt a faint pang at the words. She would have liked...

What, exactly?

She pushed aside the thought and moved on.

"What about Nicasia?" said Caina.

"She will come with me," said Claudia. "She has suffered much. And someone needs to look after her. Why not me?"

"You are a good woman," said Nicasia, her blindfold over her eyes once more.

"I wish to see more of the mortal world," said the Defender. "Your society of spies travels a great deal, and I shall learn more of the mortal realm this way."

Caina nodded. A renegade magus, a renegade Kindred, and a former slave possessed by an earth elemental. Halfdan would put the odd trio to good use, indeed.

"Thank you again," said Claudia.

Caina stood. "I am glad for you." She remembered the Moroaica's words. "And I am happy that I could save the families of others. There has been enough death already."

She left without another word.

~

AS THE SUN SET, Caina sat alone in Theodosia's sitting room, paging through a book.

Theodosia had gone to one of Lord Khosrau's dinners with Lord Corbould, and with the Kindred destroyed and Armizid dead, they would be safe enough. Claudia and Nicasia had gone as well, accompanied by Corvalis, disguised as members of the opera company. Any attacker who escaped Corvalis's blades and avoided Claudia's spells would see the golden fire of Nicasia's eyes.

And that would be the last thing any foes ever saw.

Caina was alone.

Perhaps that was how it should be.

The Moroaica was right about that, at least. Caina's family was dead, and she would never have children of her own. But she could save the families of others, just as she had rescued Tanya and Nicolai from the Moroaica, just as she had reunited Corvalis with his sister.

That was enough for her.

She had seen and endured terrible things. But it had not been in vain. And...

Someone knocked at the sitting room door.

Caina frowned and reached into the sleeve of her dress for a throwing knife. "Who is it?"

"Corvalis."

She blinked. "Come in."

Corvalis entered, and Caina rose.

He dressed as he always did, in chain mail and a cloak, sword and dagger at his belt. She had never seen him without weapons. No doubt he felt undressed without them just as Caina did.

"I thought you would be with Claudia," said Caina, "at Lord Khosrau's dinner."

Corvalis shrugged. "I changed my mind. Claudia enjoys that sort of thing, but I do not. I would worry for her safety, but Ranarius is dead and the Kindred are destroyed. Nicasia will be with her."

"I hope she keeps her blindfold on," said Caina. "It would be unfortunate if she turned half the nobles of Cyrica to stone."

He laughed. "Though it would be amusing to see the looks on their faces."

"So you're not with Claudia," said Caina. "Why did you come here?"

Corvalis took a step closer. "I wanted to thank you myself. For saving my life. For freeing Claudia."

Caina shrugged. "I promised I would, when you helped us against the Kindred. And you kept your word."

"But if you had not helped me, I would have perished. Sicarion would have killed me. Or Ranarius would have killed me, or had Nicasia turn me to stone. Instead Claudia is restored, Nicasia is free, and I am alive." His voice was quiet. "Thank you."

"I was glad to do it," said Caina. She hesitated. "I told you...what happened to me. At least some of it. I could not save my family. So at least we could save your sister."

Corvalis nodded, his eyes on her face.

They stared at each other for a moment.

"Claudia said you're going to join the Ghosts," said Caina at last.

"Aye," said Corvalis. "Where else shall we go? I'm not the sort of man to settle down as a shopkeeper, and I suppose the Ghosts could make good use of our skills. And perhaps I'll get to take a shot at my father one day." He shook his head. "I thought I would kill him or die trying. Now I am not so eager to die."

"You have more to live for," said Caina. "Claudia."

"Aye," said Corvalis.

He took another step towards her. They stood almost face to face now, and Caina had to incline her head to look up at him.

"So you just came here to thank me?" said Caina.

"No," said Corvalis.

"To find out my real name?" said Caina. "I never did tell you, and you kept asking. It's Caina, if you must know. Caina, of House Amalas."

Corvalis blinked. "So you are noble-born? Caina. But I did not come here to ask your real name."

"Then why else?"

He stood so close they were almost touching. She saw the heartbeat pulsing in his temples, felt his breath against her face.

"Because," said Corvalis, "I could not live with myself if I did not do this at least once."

He took her face in his hands, leaned down, and kissed her on the lips. Her hands closed around his arms. It went on and on, and Caina felt her heart hammering against her ribs, a slow warmth spreading through her chest.

After a moment he pulled back, looking down at her.

"Can you live with yourself now?" said Caina, her voice hoarse.

Corvalis nodded.

"Then," said Caina, "I think you had better do that again."

He did.

EPILOGUE

Sicarion could not get his new face to fit properly.

He limped down the busy street, ignoring the pain in his left leg. His new left leg, since the old one had been smashed to pulp when he hit the ground. He had also needed a new right arm, new ribs, and several new teeth.

Fortunately, slaves filled Cyrioch, and no one minded when one went missing.

Or three or four.

Sicarion stopped at the Plaza of Majesty, stretching his new jaw, and looked at the Palace of Splendors. He had been sure that Ranarius would overpower both the Ghost and Corvalis, but his pessimism had been misplaced. The Ghost had triumphed. He should not have underestimated her.

He could see why the mistress wanted her so badly.

Still, part of him thought it a pity Ranarius had not been able to awaken the greater elemental. The thought of death on that scale made Sicarion shiver.

But that was just as well.

For when the Moroaica completed her great work, the entire world would die.

~

MARZHOD SAT at his work table in the Painted Whore, paging through the Kindred Elder's store of letters. A wide smile spread over his face. Marzhod was already wealthy, but before he was done, he was going to be richer than Lord Khosrau himself.

He decided to pay Nadirah a visit later. Seducing her into bed was always a great deal of work, but worth the effort in the end...

A boot tapped against the floorboards.

Marzhod looked up, frowning. He had left the door locked. No one should have been able to get in here.

A man in a hooded gray cloak stood over the table, a rod of peculiar shining metal in his left hand.

Marzhod did not have time to shout, let alone draw a weapon, before darkness claimed him.

"Boss?"

Marzhod blinked.

He sat at his work table, the door to the corridor standing open. Saddiq stepped into the room, hand on his sword hilt.

"What is it?" said Marzhod, his voice thick.

"You wanted to know when Barius returned," said Saddiq.

"Aye," said Marzhod. Had he fallen asleep and left the door unlocked? That was criminally stupid. Still, he had been under a great deal of strain lately.

He would have to take greater care in the future.

~

THE MAN in the gray cloak stepped into the streets, leaving the Painted Whore behind.

The memories in the Ghost circlemaster's mind had told him everything he needed to know. The Moroaica was loose in the world, but trapped in a body she could not control.

The Moroaica would be destroyed.

Along with, perhaps regrettably, the body of her host.

THE END

ABOUT THE AUTHOR

Standing over six feet tall, Jonathan Moeller has the piercing blue eyes of a Conan of Cimmeria, the bronze-colored hair of a Visigothic warrior-king, and the stern visage of a captain of men, none of which are useful in his career as a computer repairman, alas.

He has written the DEMONSOULED series of sword-and-sorcery novels, and continues to write THE GHOSTS sequence about assassin and spy Caina Amalas, the COMPUTER BEGINNER'S GUIDE series of computer books, and numerous other works.

Visit his website at:

http://www.jonathanmoeller.com

Visit his technology blog at:

http://www.computerbeginnersguides.com